C.S. Lewis

TALES OF NARNIA

The Silver Chair

The Last Battle

Illustrated by
Pauline Baynes

WHSMITH
EXCLUSIVE
· BOOKS ·

The Silver Chair
First published 1953 by Geoffrey Bles
First published by William Collins Sons & Co Ltd 1974

The Last Battle
First published 1956 by The Bodley Head
First published by William Collins Sons & Co Ltd 1989

This edition produced exclusively for
W H Smith Ltd by William Collins Sons & Co Ltd 1990

ISBN 0 00 184669-8

Printed and bound in Great Britain by
Mackays of Chatham PLC, Chatham, Kent

TALES OF NARNIA

CONTENTS

The Silver Chair

A MAP OF THE
WILD LANDS
OF THE NORTH
N
W
E
S
LANTERN
WASTE
GREAT RIVER

HARFANG
Ruined city of the Giants
GIANT BRIDGE
ETTINSMOOR
GORGE
R. SHRIBBLE
MARSHES
ARNIA
SEA

To Nicholas Hardie

CONTENTS

CHAPTER ONE

BEHIND THE GYM

It was a dull autumn day and Jill Pole was crying behind the gym.

She was crying because they had been bullying her. This is not going to be a school story, so I shall say as little as possible about Jill's school, which is not a pleasant subject. It was "Co-educational," a school for both boys and girls, what used to be called a "mixed" school; some said it was not nearly so mixed as the minds of the people who ran it. These people had the idea that boys and girls should be allowed to do what they liked. And unfortunately what ten or fifteen of the biggest boys and girls liked best was bullying the others. All sorts of things, horrid things, went on which at an ordinary school would have been found out and stopped in half a term; but at this school they weren't. Or even if they were, the people who did them were not expelled or punished. The Head said they were interesting psychological cases and sent for them and talked to them for hours. And if you knew the right sort of things to say to the Head, the main result was that you became rather a favourite than otherwise.

That was why Jill Pole was crying on that dull autumn day on the damp little path which runs between the back of the gym and the shrubbery. And she hadn't nearly finished her cry when a boy came round the corner of the gym whistling, with his hands in his pockets. He nearly ran into her.

"Can't you look where you're going?" said Jill Pole.

"All *right*," said the boy, "you needn't start –" and then he noticed her face. "I say, Pole," he said, "what's up?"

Jill only made faces; the sort you make when you're

trying to say something but find that if you speak you'll start crying again.

"It's *Them*, I suppose – as usual," said the boy grimly, digging his hands farther into his pockets.

Jill nodded. There was no need for her to say anything, even if she could have said it. They both knew.

"Now, look here," said the boy, "there's no good us all –"

He meant well, but he *did* talk rather like someone beginning a lecture. Jill suddenly flew into a temper (which is quite a likely thing to happen if you have been interrupted in a cry).

"Oh, go away and mind your own business," she said. "Nobody asked you to come barging in, did they? And you're a nice person to start telling us what we all ought to do, aren't you? I suppose you mean we ought to spend all our time sucking up to Them, and currying favour, and dancing attendance on Them like you do."

"Oh, Lor!" said the boy, sitting down on the grassy bank at the edge of the shrubbery and very quickly getting up again because the grass was soaking wet. His name unfortunately was Eustace Scrubb, but he wasn't a bad sort.

"Pole!" he said. "Is that fair? Have I been doing anything of the sort this term? Didn't I stand up to Carter about the rabbit? And didn't I keep the secret about Spivvins – under torture too? And didn't I –"

"I d-don't know and I don't care," sobbed Jill.

Scrubb saw that she wasn't quite herself yet and very sensibly offered her a peppermint. He had one too. Presently Jill began to see things in a clearer light.

"I'm sorry, Scrubb," she said presently. "I wasn't fair. You have done all that – this term."

"Then wash out last term if you can," said Eustace. "I was a different chap then. I was – gosh! what a little tick I was."

"Well, honestly, you were," said Jill.

"You think there has been a change, then?" said Eustace.

"It's not only me," said Jill. "Everyone's been saying so. *They*'ve noticed it. Eleanor Blakiston heard Adela Pennyfather talking about it in our changing room yesterday. She said, 'Someone's got hold of that Scrubb kid. He's quite unmanageable this term. We shall have to attend to *him* next.'"

Eustace gave a shudder. Everyone at Experiment House knew what it was like being "attended to" by *Them*.

Both children were quiet for a moment. The drops dripped off the laurel leaves.

"Why were you so different last term?" said Jill presently.

"A lot of queer things happened to me in the hols," said Eustace mysteriously.

"What sort of things?" asked Jill.

Eustace didn't say anything for quite a long time. Then he said:

"Look here, Pole, you and I hate this place about as much as anybody can hate anything, don't we?"

"I know I do," said Jill.

"Then I really think I can trust you."

"Dam' good of you," said Jill.

"Yes, but this is a really terrific secret. Pole, I say, are you good at believing things? I mean things that everyone here would laugh at?"

"I've never had the chance," said Jill, "but I think I would be."

"Could you believe me if I said I'd been right out of the world – outside this world – last hols?"

"I wouldn't know what you meant."

"Well, don't let's bother about worlds then. Supposing I

told you I'd been in a place where animals can talk and where there are – er – enchantments and dragons – and – well, all the sorts of things you have in fairy-tales." Scrubb felt terribly awkward as he said this and got red in the face.

"How did you get there?" said Jill. She also felt curiously shy.

"The only way you can – by Magic," said Eustace almost in a whisper. "I was with two cousins of mine. We were just – whisked away. They'd been there before."

Now that they were talking in whispers Jill somehow felt it easier to believe. Then suddenly a horrible suspicion came over her and she said (so fiercely that for the moment she looked like a tigress):

"If I find you've been pulling my leg I'll never speak to you again; never, never, never."

"I'm not," said Eustace. "I swear I'm not. I swear by – by everything."

(When I was at school one would have said, "I swear by the Bible." But Bibles were not encouraged at Experiment House.)

"All right," said Jill, "I'll believe you."

"And tell nobody?"

"What do you take me for?"

They were very excited as they said this. But when they had said it and Jill looked round and saw the dull autumn sky and heard the drip off the leaves and thought of all the hopelessness of Experiment House (it was a thirteen-week term and there were still eleven weeks to come) she said:

"But after all, what's the good? We're not there: we're here. And we jolly well can't get *there*. Or can we?"

"That's what I've been wondering," said Eustace. "When we came back from That Place, Someone said that the two Pevensie kids (that's my two cousins) could never go there again. It was their third time, you see. I suppose they've had their share. But he never said I couldn't. Surely he would have said so, unless he meant that I was to get back? And I can't help wondering, can we – could we –?"

"Do you mean, do something to make it happen?"

Eustace nodded.

"You mean we might draw a circle on the ground – and write in queer letters in it – and stand inside it – and recite charms and spells?"

"Well," said Eustace after he had thought hard for a bit. "I believe that was the sort of thing I was thinking of, though I never did it. But now that it comes to the point, I've an idea that all those circles and things are rather rot. I don't think he'd like them. It would look as if we thought we could make him do things. But really, we can only ask him."

"Who is this person you keep on talking about?"

"They call him Aslan in That Place," said Eustace.

"What a curious name!"

"Not half so curious as himself," said Eustace solemnly. "But let's get on. It can't do any harm, just asking. Let's stand side by side, like this. And we'll hold out our arms in front of us with the palms down: like they did in Ramandu's island –"

"Whose island?"

"I'll tell you about that another time. And he might like us to face the east. Let's see, where is the east?"

"I don't know," said Jill.

"It's an extraordinary thing about girls that they never know the points of the compass," said Eustace.

"You don't know either," said Jill indignantly.

"Yes I do, if only you didn't keep on interrupting. I've got it now. That's the east, facing up into the laurels. Now, will you say the words after me?"

"What words?" asked Jill.

"The words I'm going to say, of course," answered Eustace. "Now –"

And he began, "Aslan, Aslan, Aslan!"

"Aslan, Aslan, Aslan," repeated Jill.

"Please let us two go into –"

At that moment a voice from the other side of the gym was heard shouting out, "Pole? Yes. I know where she is. She's blubbing behind the gym. Shall I fetch her out?"

Jill and Eustace gave one glance at each other, dived under the laurels, and began scrambling up the steep, earthy slope of the shrubbery at a speed which did them great credit. (Owing to the curious methods of teaching at Experiment House, one did not learn much French or Maths or Latin or things of that sort; but one did learn a lot about getting away quickly and quietly when They were looking for one.)

After about a minute's scramble they stopped to listen, and knew by the noises they heard that they were being followed.

"If only the door was open again!" said Scrubb as they went on, and Jill nodded. For at the top of the shrubbery was a high stone wall and in that wall a door by which you could get out on to open moor. This door was nearly always locked. But there had been times when people had found it open; or perhaps there had been only one time. But you may imagine how the memory of even one time kept people hoping, and trying the door; for if it should

happen to be unlocked it would be a splendid way of getting outside the school grounds without being seen.

Jill and Eustace, now both very hot and very grubby from going along bent almost double under the laurels, panted up to the wall. And there was the door, shut as usual.

"It's sure to be no good," said Eustace with his hand on the handle; and then, "O-o-oh. By Gum!!" For the handle turned and the door opened.

A moment before, both of them had meant to get through that doorway in double quick time, if by any chance the door was not locked. But when the door actually opened, they both stood stock still. For what they saw was quite different from what they had expected.

They had expected to see the grey, heathery slope of the

moor going up and up to join the dull autumn sky. Instead, a blaze of sunshine met them. It poured through the doorway as the light of a June day pours into a garage when you open the door. It made the drops of water on the grass glitter like beads and showed up the dirtiness of Jill's tear-stained face. And the sunlight was coming from what certainly did look like a different world – what they could see of it. They saw smooth turf, smoother and brighter than Jill had ever seen before, and blue sky, and, darting to and fro, things so bright that they might have been jewels or huge butterflies.

Although she had been longing for something like this, Jill felt frightened. She looked at Scrubb's face and saw that he was frightened too.

"Come on, Pole," he said in a breathless voice.

"Can we get back? Is it safe?" asked Jill.

At that moment a voice shouted from behind, a mean, spiteful little voice. "Now then, Pole," it squeaked. "Everyone knows you're there. Down you come." It was the voice of Edith Jackle, not one of Them herself but one of their hangers-on and tale-bearers.

"Quick!" said Scrubb. "Here. Hold hands. We mustn't get separated." And before she quite knew what was happening, he had grabbed her hand and pulled her through the door, out of the school grounds, out of England, out of our whole world into That Place.

The sound of Edith Jackle's voice stopped as suddenly as the voice on the radio when it is switched off. Instantly there was a quite different sound all about them. It came from those bright things overhead, which now turned out to be birds. They were making a riotous noise, but it was much more like music – rather advanced music which you don't quite take in at the first hearing – than birds' songs ever are in our world. Yet, in spite of the singing, there was a sort of background of immense silence. That silence, combined with the freshness of the air, made Jill

think they must be on the top of a very high mountain.

Scrubb still had her by the hand and they were walking forward, staring about them on every side. Jill saw that huge trees, rather like cedars but bigger, grew in every direction. But as they did not grow close together, and as there was no undergrowth, this did not prevent one from seeing a long way into the forest to left and right. And as far as Jill's eye could reach, it was all the same – level turf, darting birds with yellow, or dragonfly blue, or rainbow plumage, blue shadows, and emptiness. There was not a breath of wind in that cool, bright air. It was a very lonely forest.

Right ahead there were no trees: only blue sky. They went straight on without speaking till suddenly Jill heard Scrubb say, "Look out!" and felt herself jerked back. They were at the very edge of a cliff.

Jill was one of those lucky people who have a good head for heights. She didn't mind in the least standing on the edge of a precipice. She was rather annoyed with Scrubb for pulling her back – "just as if I was a kid", she said – and she wrenched her hand out of his. When she saw how very white he had turned, she despised him.

"What's the matter?" she said. And to show that she was not afraid, she stood very near the edge indeed; in fact, a good deal nearer than even she liked. Then she looked down.

She now realized that Scrubb had some excuse for looking white, for no cliff in our world is to be compared with this. Imagine yourself at the top of the very highest cliff you know. And imagine yourself looking down to the very bottom. And then imagine that the precipice goes on below that, as far again, ten times as far, twenty times as far. And when you've looked down all that distance imagine little white things that might, at first glance, be mistaken for sheep, but presently you realize that they are clouds – not little wreaths of mist but the enormous white, puffy clouds which are themselves as big as most mountains. And at last, in between those clouds, you get your first glimpse of the real bottom, so far away that you can't make out whether it's field or wood, or land or water: farther below those clouds than you are above them.

Jill stared at it. Then she thought that perhaps, after all, she would step back a foot or so from the edge; but she didn't like to for fear of what Scrubb would think. Then

she suddenly decided that she didn't care what he thought, and that she would jolly well get away from that horrible edge and never laugh at anyone for not liking heights again. But when she tried to move, she found she couldn't. Her legs seemed to have turned into putty. Everything was swimming before her eyes.

"What are you doing, Pole? Come back – blithering little idiot!" shouted Scrubb. But his voice seemed to be coming from a long way off. She felt him grabbing at her. But by now she had no control over her own arms and legs. There was a moment's struggling on the cliff edge. Jill was too frightened and dizzy to know quite what she was doing, but two things she remembered as long as she lived (they often came back to her in dreams). One was that she had wrenched herself free of Scrubb's clutches; the other was that, at the same moment, Scrubb himself, with a terrified scream, had lost his balance and gone hurtling to the depths.

Fortunately, she was given no time to think over what she had done. Some huge, brightly coloured animal had rushed to the edge of the cliff. It was lying down, leaning over, and (this was the odd thing) blowing. Not roaring or snorting, but just blowing from its wide-opened mouth; blowing out as steadily as a vacuum cleaner sucks in. Jill was lying so close to the creature that she could feel the breath vibrating steadily through its body. She was lying still because she couldn't get up. She was nearly fainting: indeed, she wished she could really faint, but faints don't come for the asking. At last she saw, far away below her, a tiny black speck floating away from the cliff and slightly upwards. As it rose, it also got farther away. By the time it was nearly on a level with the cliff-top it was so far off that she lost sight of it. It was obviously moving away from them at a great speed. Jill couldn't help thinking that the creature at her side was blowing it away.

So she turned and looked at the creature. It was a lion.

CHAPTER TWO

JILL IS GIVEN A TASK

WITHOUT a glance at Jill the lion rose to its feet and gave one last blow. Then, as if satisfied with its work, it turned and stalked slowly away, back into the forest.

"It must be a dream, it must, it must," said Jill to herself. "I'll wake up in a moment." But it wasn't, and she didn't.

"I do wish we'd never come to this dreadful place," said Jill. "I don't believe Scrubb knew any more about it than I do. Or if he did, he had no business to bring me here without warning me what it was like. It's not my fault he fell over that cliff. If he'd left me alone we should both be all right." Then she remembered again the scream that Scrubb had given when he fell, and burst into tears.

Crying is all right in its way while it lasts. But you have to stop sooner or later, and then you still have to decide what to do. When Jill stopped, she found she was dreadfully thirsty. She had been lying face downward, and now she sat up. The birds had ceased singing and there was perfect silence except for one small, persistent sound, which seemed to come from a good distance away. She listened carefully, and felt almost sure it was the sound of running water.

Jill got up and looked round her very carefully. There was no sign of the lion; but there were so many trees about that it might easily be quite close without her seeing it. For all she knew, there might be several lions. But her thirst was very bad now, and she plucked up her courage to go and look for that running water. She went on tiptoes, stealing cautiously from tree to tree, and stopping to peer round her at every step.

The wood was so still that it was not difficult to decide where the sound was coming from. It grew clearer every moment and, sooner than she expected, she came to an open glade and saw the stream, bright as glass, running across the turf a stone's throw away from her. But although the sight of the water made her feel ten times thirstier than before, she didn't rush forward and drink. She stood as still as if she had been turned into stone, with her mouth wide open. And she had a very good reason; just on this side of the stream lay the lion.

It lay with its head raised and its two fore-paws out in front of it, like the lions in Trafalgar Square. She knew at once that it had seen her, for its eyes looked straight into hers for a moment and then turned away – as if it knew her quite well and didn't think much of her.

"If I run away, it'll be after me in a moment," thought Jill. "And if I go on, I shall run straight into its mouth." Anyway, she couldn't have moved if she had tried, and she couldn't take her eyes off it. How long this lasted, she could not be sure; it seemed like hours. And the thirst became so bad that she almost felt she would not mind being eaten by the lion if only she could be sure of getting a mouthful of water first.

"If you're thirsty, you may drink."

They were the first words she had heard since Scrubb had spoken to her on the edge of the cliff. For a second she stared here and there, wondering who had spoken. Then the voice said again, "If you are thirsty, come and drink," and of course she remembered what Scrubb had said about animals talking in that other world, and realized that it was the lion speaking. Anyway, she had seen its lips move this time, and the voice was not like a man's. It was deeper, wilder, and stronger; a sort of heavy, golden voice. It did not make her any less frightened than she had been before, but it made her frightened in rather a different way.

"Are you not thirsty?" said the Lion.

"I'm *dying* of thirst," said Jill.

"Then drink," said the Lion.

"May I – could I – would you mind going away while I do?" said Jill.

The Lion answered this only by a look and a very low growl. And as Jill gazed at its motionless bulk, she realized that she might as well have asked the whole mountain to move aside for her convenience.

The delicious rippling noise of the stream was driving her nearly frantic.

"Will you promise not to – do anything to me, if I do come?" said Jill.

"I make no promise," said the Lion.

Jill was so thirsty now that, without noticing it, she had come a step nearer.

"*Do* you eat girls?" she said.

"I have swallowed up girls and boys, women and men, kings and emperors, cities and realms," said the Lion. It didn't say this as if it were boasting, nor as if it were sorry, nor as if it were angry. It just said it.

"I daren't come and drink," said Jill.

"Then you will die of thirst," said the Lion.

"Oh dear!" said Jill, coming another step nearer. "I suppose I must go and look for another stream then."

"There is no other stream," said the Lion.

It never occurred to Jill to disbelieve the Lion – no one who had seen his stern face could do that – and her mind suddenly made itself up. It was the worst thing she had ever had to do, but she went forward to the stream, knelt down, and began scooping up water in her hand. It was the coldest, most refreshing water she had ever tasted. You didn't need to drink much of it, for it quenched your thirst at once. Before she tasted it she had been intending to make a dash away from the Lion the moment she had finished. Now, she realized that this would be on the whole the most dangerous thing of all. She got up and stood there with her lips still wet from drinking.

"Come here," said the Lion. And she had to. She was almost between its front paws now, looking straight into its face. But she couldn't stand that for long; she dropped her eyes.

"Human Child," said the Lion. "Where is the Boy?"

"He fell over the cliff," said Jill, and added, "Sir." She didn't know what else to call him, and it sounded cheek to call him nothing.

"How did he come to do that, Human Child?"

"He was trying to stop me from falling, Sir."

"Why were you so near the edge, Human Child?"

"I was showing off, Sir."

"That is a very good answer, Human Child. Do so no more. And now" (here for the first time the Lion's face became a little less stern) "the Boy is safe. I have blown him to Narnia. But your task will be the harder because of what you have done."

"Please, what task, Sir?" said Jill.

"The task for which I called you and him here out of your own world."

This puzzled Jill very much. "It's mistaking me for someone else," she thought. She didn't dare to tell the Lion this, though she felt things would get into a dreadful muddle unless she did.

"Speak your thought, Human Child," said the Lion.

"I was wondering – I mean – could there be some mistake? Because nobody called me and Scrubb, you know. It was we who asked to come here. Scrubb said we were to call to – to Somebody – it was a name I wouldn't know – and perhaps the Somebody would let us in. And we did, and then we found the door open.'

"You would not have called to me unless I had been calling to you," said the Lion.

"Then you are Somebody, Sir?" said Jill.

"I am. And now hear your task. Far from here in the land of Narnia there lives an aged king who is sad because he has no prince of his blood to be king after him. He has no heir because his only son was stolen from him many years ago, and no one in Narnia knows where that prince went or whether he is still alive. But he is. I lay on you this command, that you seek this lost prince until either you have found him and brought him to his father's house, or else died in the attempt, or else gone back into your own world."

"How, please?" said Jill.

"I will tell you, Child," said the Lion. "These are the signs by which I will guide you in your quest. First; as soon as the Boy Eustace sets foot in Narnia, he will meet an old and dear friend. He must greet that friend at once;

if he does, you will both have good help. Second; you must journey out of Narnia to the north till you come to the ruined city of the ancient giants. Third; you shall find a writing on a stone in that ruined city, and you must do what the writing tells you. Fourth; you will know the lost prince (if you find him) by this, that he will be the first person you have met in your travels who will ask you to do something in my name, in the name of Aslan."

As the Lion seemed to have finished, Jill thought she should say something. So she said, "Thank you very much. I see."

"Child," said Aslan, in a gentler voice than he had yet used, "perhaps you do not see quite as well as you think. But the first step is to remember. Repeat to me, in order, the four signs."

Jill tried, and didn't get them quite right. So the Lion corrected her, and made her repeat them again and again till she could say them perfectly. He was very patient over this, so that, when it was done, Jill plucked up courage to ask:

"Please, how am I to get to Narnia?"

"On my breath," said the Lion. "I will blow you into the west of the world as I blew Eustace."

"Shall I catch him in time to tell him the first sign? But I suppose it won't matter. If he sees an old friend, he's sure to go and speak to him, isn't he?"

"You will have no time to spare," said the Lion. "That is why I must send you at once. Come. Walk before me to the edge of the cliff."

Jill remembered very well that if there was no time to spare, that was her own fault. "If I hadn't made such a fool of myself, Scrubb and I would have been going together. And he'd have heard all the instructions as well as me," she thought. So she did as she was told. It was very alarming walking back to the edge of the cliff, especially as the Lion did not walk with her but behind her – making no noise on his soft paws.

But long before she had got anywhere near the edge, the voice behind her said, "Stand still. In a moment I will blow. But, first, remember, remember, remember the signs. Say them to yourself when you wake in the morning and when you lie down at night, and when you wake in the middle of the night. And whatever strange things may happen to you, let nothing turn your mind from following the signs. And secondly, I give you a warning. Here on the mountain I have spoken to you clearly: I will not often do so down in Narnia. Here on the mountain, the air is clear and your mind is clear; as you drop down into Narnia, the air will thicken. Take great care that it does not confuse your mind. And the signs which you have learned here will not look at all as you expect them to look, when you meet them there. That is why it is so important to know them by heart and pay no attention to appearances. Remember the signs and believe the signs. Nothing else matters. And now, daughter of Eve, farewell –"

The voice had been growing softer towards the end of this speech and now it faded away altogether. Jill looked behind her. To her astonishment she saw the cliff already more than a hundred yards behind her, and the Lion himself a speck of bright gold on the edge of it. She had been setting her teeth and clenching her fists for a terrible blast of lion's breath; but the breath had really been so gentle that she had not even noticed the moment at which she left the earth. And now, there was nothing but air for thousands upon thousands of feet below her.

She felt frightened only for a second. For one thing, the world beneath her was so very far away that it seemed to have nothing to do with her. For another, floating on the breath of the Lion was so extremely comfortable. She found she could lie on her back or on her face and twist any way she pleased, just as you can in water (if you've learned to float really well). And because she was moving at the same pace as the breath, there was no wind, and the air seemed beautifuly warm. It was not in the least like being in an aeroplane, because there was no noise and no vibration. If Jill had ever been in a balloon she might have thought it more like that; only better.

When she looked back now she could take in for the first time the real size of the mountain she was leaving. She wondered why a mountain so huge as that was not covered with snow and ice – "but I suppose all that sort of thing is different in this world," thought Jill. Then she looked below her; but she was so high that she couldn't make out whether she was floating over land or sea, nor what speed she was going at.

"By Jove! The signs!" said Jill suddenly. "I'd better repeat them." She was in a panic for a second or two, but she found she could still say them all correctly. "So that's all right," she said, and lay back on the air as if it was a sofa, with a sigh of contentment.

"Well, I do declare," said Jill to herself some hours later, "I've been asleep. Fancy sleeping on air. I wonder if anyone's done it before. I don't suppose they have. Oh bother – Scrubb probably has! On this same journey, a little bit before me. Let's see what it looks like down below."

What it looked like was an enormous, very dark blue plain. There were no hills to be seen, but there were biggish white things moving slowly across it. "Those must be clouds," she thought. "But far bigger than the ones we saw from the cliff. I suppose they're bigger because they're nearer. I must be getting lower. Bother this sun."

The sun which had been high overhead when she began her journey was now getting into her eyes. This meant that it was getting lower, ahead of her. Scrubb was quite right in saying that Jill (I don't know about girls in general) didn't think much about points of the compass. Otherwise she would have known, when the sun began getting in her eyes, that she was travelling pretty nearly due west.

Staring at the blue plain below her, she presently noticed that there were little dots of brighter, paler colour in it here and there. "It's the sea!" thought Jill. "I do believe those are islands." And so they were. She might have felt rather jealous if she had known that some of them were islands which Scrubb had seen from a ship's deck and even landed on; but she didn't know this. Then, later on, she began to see that there were little wrinkles on the blue flatness: little wrinkles which must be quite big ocean waves if you were down among them. And now, all along the horizon there was a thick dark line which grew thicker and darker so quickly that you could see it growing. That was the first sign she had had of the great speed at which she was travelling. And she knew that the thickening line must be land.

Suddenly from her left (for the wind was in the south) a great white cloud came rushing towards her, this time on the same level as herself. And before she knew where she was, she had shot right into the middle of its cold, wet fogginess. That took her breath away, but she was in it only for a moment. She came out blinking in the sunlight and found her clothes wet. (She had on a blazer and sweater and shorts and stockings and pretty thick shoes; it had been a muddy sort of day in England.) She came out lower than she had gone in; and as soon as she did so she noticed something which, I suppose, she ought to have been expecting, but which came as a surprise and a shock. It was Noises. Up till then she had travelled in total silence. Now, for the first time, she heard the noise of waves and the crying of seagulls. And now, too, she smelled the smell of the sea. There was no mistake about her speed now. She saw two waves meet with a smack and a spout of foam go up between them; but she had hardly seen it before it was a hundred yards behind her. The land was getting nearer at a great pace. She could see mountains far inland, and other nearer mountains on her left. She could see bays and headlands, woods and fields, stretches of sandy beach. The sound of waves breaking on the shore was growing louder every second and drowning the other sea noises.

Suddenly the land opened right ahead of her. She was coming to the mouth of a river. She was very low now, only a few feet above the water. A wave-top came against her toe and a great splash of foam spurted up, drenching her nearly to the waist. Now she was losing speed. Instead of being carried up the river she was gliding in to the river bank on her left. There were so many things to notice that she could hardly take them all in; a smooth, green lawn, a ship so brightly coloured that it looked like an enormous piece of jewellery, towers and battlements, banners fluttering in the air, a crowd, gay clothes, armour, gold, swords, a sound of music. But this was all jumbled. The first thing that she knew clearly was that she had alighted and was standing under a thicket of trees close by the river side, and there, only a few feet away from her, was Scrubb.

The first thing she thought was how very grubby and untidy and generally unimpressive he looked. And the second was "How wet I am!"

CHAPTER THREE

THE SAILING OF THE KING

WHAT made Scrubb look so dingy (and Jill too, if she could only have seen herself) was the splendour of their surroundings. I had better describe them at once.

Through a cleft in those mountains which Jill had seen far inland as she approached the land, the sunset light was pouring over a level lawn. On the far side of the lawn, its weather-vanes glittering in the light, rose a many-towered and many-turreted castle; the most beautiful castle Jill had ever seen. On the near side was a quay of white marble and, moored to this, the ship: a tall ship with high forecastle and high poop, gilded and crimson, with a great flag at the mast-head, and many banners waving from the decks, and a row of shields, bright as silver, along the bulwarks. The gang-plank was laid to her, and at the foot of it, just ready to go on board, stood an old, old man. He wore a rich mantle of scarlet which opened in front to show his silver mail shirt. There was a thin circlet of gold on his head. His beard, white as wool, fell nearly to his waist. He stood straight enough, leaning one hand on the shoulder of a richly dressed lord who seemed younger than himself: but you could see he was very old and frail. He looked as if a puff of wind could blow him away, and his eyes were watery.

Immediately in front of the King – who had turned round to speak to his people before going on board the ship – there was a little chair on wheels, and, harnessed to it, a little donkey: not much bigger than a big retriever. In this chair sat a fat little dwarf. He was as richly dressed as the King, but because of his fatness and because he was sitting hunched up among cushions, the effect was quite different: it made him look like a shapeless little bundle of fur and silk and velvet. He was as old as the King, but more hale and hearty, with very keen eyes. His bare head, which was bald and extremely large, shone like a gigantic billiard ball in the sunset light.

Farther back, in a half-circle, stood what Jill at once

knew to be the courtiers. They were well worth looking at for their clothes and armour alone. As far as that went, they looked more like a flower-bed than a crowd. But what really made Jill open her eyes and mouth as wide as they would go, was the people themselves. If "people" was the right word. For only about one in every five was human. The rest were things you never see in our world. Fauns, satyrs, centaurs: Jill could give a name to these, for she had seen pictures of them. Dwarfs too. And there were a lot of animals she knew as well; bears, badgers, moles, leopards, mice, and various birds. But then they were so very different from the animals which one called by the same names in England. Some of them were much bigger – the mice, for instance, stood on their hind legs and were over two feet high. But quite apart from that, they all looked different. You could see by the expression in their faces that they could talk and think just as well as you could.

"Golly!" thought Jill. "So it's true after all." But next moment she added, "I wonder are they friendly?" For she had just noticed, on the outskirts of the crowd, one or two giants and some people whom she couldn't give a name to at all.

At that moment Aslan and the signs rushed back into her mind. She had forgotten all about them for the last half-hour.

"Scrubb!" she whispered, grabbing his arm. "Scrubb, quick! Do you see anyone you know?"

"So *you've* turned up again, have you?" said Scrubb disagreeably (for which he had some reason). "Well, keep quiet, can't you? I want to listen."

"Don't be a fool," said Jill. "There isn't a moment to lose. Don't you see some old friend here? Because you've got to go and speak to him at once."

"What are you talking about?" said Scrubb.

"It's Aslan – the Lion – says you've got to," said Jill despairingly. "I've seen him."

"Oh, you have, have you? What did he say?"

"He said the very first person you saw in Narnia would be an old friend, and you'd got to speak to him at once."

"Well, there's nobody here I've ever seen in my life before; and anyway, I don't know whether this is Narnia."

"Thought you said you'd been here before," said Jill.

"Well, you thought wrong then."

"Well, I like that! You told me –"

"For heaven's sake dry up and let's hear what they're saying."

The King was speaking to the Dwarf, but Jill couldn't

hear what he said. And, as far as she could make out, the Dwarf made no answer, though he nodded and wagged his head a great deal. Then the King raised his voice and addressed the whole court: but his voice was so old and cracked that she could understand very little of his speech – especially since it was all about people and places she had never heard of. When the speech was over, the King stooped down and kissed the Dwarf on both cheeks, straightened himself, raised his right hand as if in blessing, and went, slowly and with feeble steps, up the gangway and on board the ship. The courtiers appeared to be greatly moved by his departure. Handkerchiefs were got out, sounds of sobbing were heard in every direction. The gangway was cast off, trumpets sounded from the poop, and the ship moved away from the quay. (It was being towed by a rowing-boat, but Jill didn't see that.)

"Now –" said Scrubb, but he didn't get any farther, because at that moment a large white object – Jill thought for a second that it was a kite – came gliding through the air and alighted at his feet. It was a white owl, but so big that it stood as high as a good-sized dwarf.

It blinked and peered as if it were short-sighted, and put its head a little on one side, and said in a soft, hooting kind of voice:

"Tu-whoo, tu-whoo! Who are you two?"

"My name's Scrubb, and this is Pole," said Eustace. "Would you mind telling us where we are?"

"In the land of Narnia, at the King's castle of Cair Paravel."

"Is that the King who's just taken ship?"

"Too true, too true," said the Owl sadly, shaking its big head. "But who are you? There's something magic about you two. I saw you arrive: you *flew*. Everyone else was so busy seeing the King off that nobody knew. Except me. I happened to notice you, you flew."

"We were sent here by Aslan," said Eustace in a low voice.

"Tu-whoo, tu-whoo!" said the Owl, ruffling out its feathers. "This is almost too much for me, so early in the evening. I'm not quite myself till the sun's down."

"And we've been sent to find the lost Prince," said Jill, who had been anxiously waiting to get into the conversation.

"It's the first I've heard about it," said Eustace. "What prince?"

"You had better come and speak to the Lord Regent at once," it said. "That's him, over there in the donkey carriage; Trumpkin the Dwarf." The bird turned and began leading the way, muttering to itself, "Whoo! Tu-whoo! What a to-do! I can't think clearly yet. It's too early."

"What is the King's name?" asked Eustace.

"Caspian the Tenth," said the Owl. And Jill wondered why Scrubb had suddenly pulled up short in his walk and turned an extraordinary colour. She thought she had never seen him look so sick about anything. But before she had time to ask any questions they had reached the dwarf, who was just gathering up the reins of his donkey and preparing to drive back to the castle. The crowd of courtiers had broken up and were going in the same direction, by ones and twos and little knots, like people coming away from watching a game or a race.

"Tu-whoo! Ahem! Lord Regent," said the Owl, stooping down a little and holding its beak near the Dwarf's ear.

"Heh? What's that?" said the Dwarf.

"Two strangers, my lord," said the Owl.

"Rangers! What d'ye mean?" said the Dwarf. "I see two uncommonly grubby man-cubs. What do they want?"

"My name's Jill," said Jill, pressing forward. She was very eager to explain the important business on which they had come.

"The girl's called Jill," said the Owl, as loud as it could.

"What's that?" said the Dwarf. "The girls are all killed! I don't believe a word of it. What girls? Who killed 'em?"

"Only one girl, my lord," said the Owl. "Her name is Jill."

"Speak up, speak up," said the Dwarf. "Don't stand there buzzing and twittering in my ear. Who's been killed?"

"Nobody's been killed," hooted the Owl.

"Who?"

"NOBODY."

"All right, all right. You needn't shout. I'm not so deaf as all that. What do you mean by coming here to tell me that nobody's been killed? Why should anyone have been killed?"

"Better tell him I'm Eustace," said Scrubb.

"The boy's Eustace, my lord," hooted the Owl as loud as it could.

"Useless?" said the Dwarf irritably. "I dare say he is. Is that any reason for bringing him to court? Hey?"

"Not useless," said the Owl. "EUSTACE."

"Used to it, is he? I don't know what you're talking about, I'm sure. I tell you what it is, Master Glimfeather; when I was a young Dwarf there used to be *talking* beasts and birds in this country who really could talk. There wasn't all this mumbling and muttering and whispering. It wouldn't have been tolerated for a moment. Not for a moment, Sir. Urnus, my trumpet please –"

A little Faun who had been standing quietly beside the Dwarf's elbow all this time now handed him a silver ear-trumpet. It was made like the musical instrument called a serpent, so that the tube curled right round the Dwarf's neck. While he was getting it settled the Owl, Glimfeather, suddenly said to the children in a whisper:

"My brain's a bit clearer now. Don't say anything about the lost Prince. I'll explain later. It wouldn't do, wouldn't do, Tu-Whoo! Oh *what* a to-do!"

"Now," said the Dwarf, "if you *have* anything sensible to say, Master Glimfeather, try and say it. Take a deep breath and don't attempt to speak too quickly."

With help from the children, and in spite of a fit of coughing on the part of the Dwarf, Glimfeather explained that the strangers had been sent by Aslan to visit the court of Narnia. The Dwarf glanced quickly up at them with a new expression in his eyes.

"Sent by the Lion Himself, hey?" he said. "And from – m'm – from that other Place – beyond the world's end, hey?"

"Yes, my lord," bawled Eustace into the trumpet.

"Son of Adam and Daughter of Eve, hey?" said the Dwarf. But people at Experiment House haven't heard of Adam and Eve, so Jill and Eustace couldn't answer this. But the Dwarf didn't seem to notice.

"Well, my dears," he said, taking first one and then the other by the hand and bowing his head a little. "You are very heartily welcome. If the good King, my poor Master, had not this very hour set sail for Seven Isles, he would have been glad of your coming. It would have brought back his youth to him for a moment – for a moment. And now, it is high time for supper. You shall tell me your business in full council tomorrow morning. Master Glimfeather, see that bedchambers and suitable clothes and all else are provided for these guests in the most honourable fashion. And – Glimfeather – in your ear –"

Here the Dwarf put his mouth close to the Owl's head and, no doubt, intended to whisper: but, like other deaf people, he wasn't a very good judge of his own voice, and both children heard him say, "See that they're properly washed."

After that, the Dwarf touched up his donkey and it set off towards the castle at something between a trot and a waddle (it was a very fat little beast), while the Faun, the Owl, and the children followed at a rather slower pace. The sun had set and the air was growing cool.

They went across the lawn and then through an orchard and so to the North Gate of Cair Paravel, which stood wide open. Inside, they found a grassy courtyard. Lights were already showing from the windows of the great hall on their right and from a more complicated mass of buildings straight ahead. Into these the Owl led them, and there a most delightful person was called to look after Jill. She was not much taller than Jill herself, and a good deal slenderer, but obviously full grown, graceful as a willow, and her hair was willowy too, and there seemed to be moss in it. She brought Jill to a round room in one of the turrets, where there was a little bath sunk in the floor and a fire of sweet-smelling woods burning on the flat hearth and a lamp hanging by a silver chain from the vaulted roof. The window looked west into the strange land of Narnia, and Jill saw the red remains of the sunset still glowing behind distant mountains. It made her long for more adventures and feel sure that this was only the beginning.

When she had had her bath, and brushed her hair, and put on the clothes that had been laid out for her – they were the kind that not only felt nice, but looked nice and smelled nice and made nice sounds when you moved as well – she would have gone back to gaze out of that exciting window, but she was interrupted by a bang on the door.

"Come in," said Jill. And in came Scrubb, also bathed and splendidly dressed in Narnian clothes. But his face didn't look as if he were enjoying it.

"Oh, here you are at last," he said crossly, flinging himself into a chair. "I've been trying to find you for ever so long."

"Well, now you have," said Jill. "I say, Scrubb, isn't it all simply too exciting and scrumptious for words." She had forgotten all about the signs and the lost Prince for the moment.

"Oh! That's what you think, is it?" said Scrubb: and then, after a pause, "I wish to goodness we'd never come."

"Why on earth?"

"I can't bear it," said Scrubb. "Seeing the King – Caspian – a doddering old man like that. It's – it's frightful."

"Why, what harm does it do you?"

"Oh, you don't understand. Now that I come to think of it, you couldn't. I didn't tell you that this world has a different time from ours."

"How do you mean?"

"The time you spend here doesn't take up any of our time. Do you see? I mean, however long we spend here, we shall still get back to Experiment House at the moment we left it –"

"That won't be much fun –"

"Oh, dry up! Don't keep interrupting. And when you're back in England – in our world – you can't tell how time is going here. It might be any number of years in Narnia while we're having one year at home. The Pevensies explained it all to me, but, like a fool, I forgot about it. And now apparently it's been about seventy years – Narnian years – since I was here last. Do you see now? And I come back and find Caspian an old, old man."

"Then the King *was* an old friend of yours!" said Jill. A horrid thought had struck her.

"I should jolly well think he was," said Scrubb miserably. "About as good a friend as a chap could have. And last time he was only a few years older than me. And to see that old man with a white beard, and to remember Caspian as he was the morning we captured the Lone Islands, or in the fight with the Sea Serpent – oh, it's frightful. It's worse than coming back and finding him dead."

"Oh, shut up," said Jill impatiently. "It's far worse than you think. We've muffed the first Sign." Of course Scrubb did not understand this. Then Jill told him about her conversation with Aslan and the four signs and the task of finding the lost prince which had been laid upon them.

"So you see," she wound up, "you did see an old friend, just as Aslan said, and you ought to have gone and spoken to him at once. And now you haven't, and everything is going wrong from the very beginning."

"But how was I to know?" said Scrubb.

"If you'd only listened to me when I tried to tell you, we'd be all right," said Jill.

"Yes, and if you hadn't played the fool on the edge of that cliff and jolly nearly murdered me – all right, I said *murder*, and I'll say it again as often as I like, so keep your hair on – we'd have come together and both known what to do."

"I suppose he *was* the first person you saw?" said Jill. "You must have been here hours before me. Are you sure you didn't see anyone else first?"

"I was only here about a minute before you," said Scrubb. "He must have blown you quicker than me. Making up for lost time: the time *you* lost."

"Don't be a perfect beast, Scrubb," said Jill. "Hallo! What's that?"

It was the castle bell ringing for supper, and thus what looked like turning into a first-rate quarrel was happily cut short. Both had a good appetite by this time.

Supper in the great hall of the castle was the most splendid thing either of them had ever seen; for though Eustace had been in that world before, he had spent his whole visit at sea and knew nothing of the glory and courtesy of the Narnians at home in their own land. The banners hung from the roof, and each course came in with trumpeters and kettledrums. There were soups that would make your mouth water to think of, and the lovely fishes called pavenders, and venison and peacock and pies, and ices and jellies and fruit and nuts, and all manner of wines and fruit drinks. Even Eustace cheered up and admitted that it was "something like". And when all the serious eating and drinking was over, a blind poet came forward and struck up the grand old tale of Prince Cor and Aravis and the horse Bree, which is called *The*

Horse and his Boy and tells of an adventure that happened in Narnia and Calormen and the lands between, in the Golden Age when Peter was High King in Cair Paravel. (I haven't time to tell it now, though it is well worth hearing.)

When they were dragging themselves upstairs to bed, yawning their heads off, Jill said, "I bet we sleep well, tonight"; for it had been a full day. Which just shows how little anyone knows what is going to happen to them next.

CHAPTER FOUR

A PARLIAMENT OF OWLS

It is a very funny thing that the sleepier you are, the longer you take about getting to bed; especially if you are lucky enough to have a fire in your room. Jill felt she couldn't even start undressing unless she sat down in front of the fire for a bit first. And once she had sat down, she didn't want to get up again. She had already said to herself about five times, "I must go to bed", when she was startled by a tap on the window.

She got up, pulled the curtain, and at first saw nothing but darkness. Then she jumped and started backwards, for something very large had dashed itself against the window, giving a sharp tap on the glass as it did so. A very unpleasant idea came into her head – "Suppose they have giant moths in this country! Ugh!" But then the thing came back, and this time she was almost sure she saw a beak, and that the beak had made that tapping noise. "It's some huge bird," thought Jill. "Could it be an eagle?" She didn't very much want a visit even from an eagle, but she opened the window and looked out. Instantly, with a great whirring noise, the creature alighted on the window-sill and stood there filling up the whole window, so that Jill had to step back to make room for it. It was the Owl.

"Hush, hush! Tu-whoo, tu-whoo," said the Owl. "Don't make a noise. Now, are you two really in earnest about what you've got to do?"

"About the lost Prince, you mean?" said Jill. "Yes, we've got to be." For now she remembered the Lion's voice and face, which she had nearly forgotten during the feasting and story-telling in the hall.

"Good!" said the Owl. "Then there's no time to waste.

You must get away from here at once. I'll go and wake the other human. Then I'll come back for you. You'd better change those court clothes and put on something you can travel in. I'll be back in two twos. Tu-whoo!" And without waiting for an answer, he was gone.

If Jill had been more used to adventures, she might have doubted the Owl's word, but this never occurred to her: and in the exciting idea of a midnight escape she forgot her sleepiness. She changed back into sweater and shorts – there was a guide's knife on the belt of the shorts which might come in useful – and added a few of the things that had been left in the room for her by the girl with the willowy hair. She chose a short cloak that came down to her knees and had a hood ("just the thing, if it rains," she thought), a few handkerchiefs and a comb. Then she sat down and waited.

She was getting sleepy again when the Owl returned.

"Now we're ready," it said.

"You'd better lead the way," said Jill. "I don't know all these passages yet."

"Tu-whoo!" said the Owl. "We're not going through the castle. That would never do. You must ride on me. We shall fly."

"Oh!" said Jill, and stood with her mouth open, not much liking the idea. "Shan't I be too heavy for you?"

"Tu-whoo, tu-whoo! Don't you be a fool. I've already carried the other one. Now. But we'll put out that lamp first."

As soon as the lamp was out, the bit of the night which you saw through the window looked less dark – no longer black, but grey. The Owl stood on the window-sill with his back to the room and raised his wings. Jill had to climb on to his short fat body and get her knees under the wings and grip tight. The feathers felt beautifully warm and soft but there was nothing to hold on by. "I wonder how Scrubb liked *his* ride!" thought Jill. And just as she was thinking this, with a horrid plunge they had left the window-sill, and the wings were making a flurry round her ears, and the

night air, rather cool and damp, was flying in her face.

It was much lighter than she expected, and though the sky was overcast, one patch of watery silver showed where the moon was hiding above the clouds. The fields beneath her looked grey, and the trees black. There was a certain amount of wind – a hushing, ruffling sort of wind which meant that rain was coming soon.

The Owl wheeled round so that the castle was now ahead of them. Very few of the windows showed lights. They flew right over it, northwards, crossing the river: the air grew colder, and Jill thought she could see the white reflection of the Owl in the water beneath her. But soon they were on the north bank of the river, flying above wooded country.

The Owl snapped at something which Jill couldn't see.

"Oh, don't, please!" said Jill. "Don't jerk like that. You nearly threw me off."

"I beg your pardon," said the Owl. "I was just nabbing a bat. There's nothing so sustaining, in a small way, as a nice plump little bat. Shall I catch you one?"

"No, thanks," said Jill with a shudder.

He was flying a little lower now and a large, black-looking object was looming up towards them. Jill had just time to see that it was a tower – a partly ruinous tower, with a lot of ivy on it, she thought – when she found herself ducking to avoid the archway of a window, as the Owl squeezed with her through the ivied cobwebby opening, out of the fresh, grey night into a dark place inside the top of the tower. It was rather fusty inside and, the moment she slipped off the Owl's back, she knew (as one usually does somehow) that it was quite crowded. And when voices began saying out of the darkness from every direction "Tu-whoo! Tu-whoo!" she knew it was crowded with owls. She was rather relieved when a very different voice said:

"Is that you, Pole?"

"Is that you, Scrubb?" said Jill.

"Now," said Glimfeather, "I think we're all here. Let us hold a parliament of owls."

"Tu-whoo, tu-whoo. True for you. That's the right thing to do," said several voices.

"Half a moment," said Scrubb's voice. "There's something I want to say first."

"Do, do, do," said the owls; and Jill said, "Fire ahead."

"I suppose all you chaps – owls, I mean," said Scrubb, "I suppose you all know that King Caspian the Tenth, in his young days, sailed to the eastern end of the world. Well, I was with him on that journey: with him and Reepicheep the Mouse, and the Lord Drinian and all of them. I know it sounds hard to believe, but people don't grow older in our world at the same speed as they do in yours. And what I want to say is this, that I'm the King's man; and if this parliament of owls is any sort of plot against the King, I'm having nothing to do with it."

"Tu-whoo, tu-whoo, we're all the King's owls too," said the owls.

"What's it all about then?" said Scrubb.

"It's only this," said Glimfeather. "That if the Lord Regent, the Dwarf Trumpkin, hears you are going to look for the lost Prince, he won't let you start. He'd keep you under lock and key sooner."

"Great Scott!" said Scrubb. "You don't mean that Trumpkin is a traitor? I used to hear a lot about him in the old days, at sea. Caspian – the King, I mean – trusted him absolutely."

"Oh no," said a voice. "Trumpkin's no traitor. But more than thirty champions (knights, centaurs, good giants, and all sorts) have at one time or another set out to look for the lost Prince, and none of them have ever come back. And at last the King said he was not going to have all the bravest Narnians destroyed in the search for his son. And now nobody is allowed to go."

"But surely he'd let *us* go," said Scrubb. "When he knew who I was and who had sent me."

("Sent both of us," put in Jill.)

"Yes," said Glimfeather, "I think, very likely, he would. But the King's away. And Trumpkin will stick to the rules. He's as true as steel, but he's deaf as a post and very peppery. You could never make him see that this might be the time for making an exception to the rule."

"You might think he'd take some notice of *us*, because we're owls and everyone knows how wise owls are," said someone else. "But he's so old now he'd only say, 'You're a mere chick. I remember you when you were an egg. Don't come trying to teach *me*, Sir. Crabs and crumpets!'"

This owl imitated Trumpkin's voice rather well, and there were sounds of owlish laughter all round. The children began to see that the Narnians all felt about Trumpkin as people feel at school about some crusty teacher, whom everyone is a little afraid of and everyone makes fun of and nobody really dislikes.

"How long is the King going to be away?" asked Scrubb.

"If only we knew!" said Glimfeather. "You see, there has been a rumour lately that Aslan himself has been seen in the islands – in Terebinthia, I think it was. And the King said he would make one more attempt before he died to see Aslan face to face again, and ask his advice about who is to be King after him. But we're all afraid that, if he doesn't meet Aslan in Terebinthia, he'll go on east, to Seven Isles and Lone Islands – and on and on. He never talks about it, but we all know he has never forgotten that voyage to the world's end. I'm sure in his heart of hearts he wants to go there again."

"Then there's no good waiting for him to come back?" said Jill.

"No, no good," said the Owl. "Oh, what a to-do! If only you two had known and spoken to him at once! He'd have arranged everything – probably given you an army to go with you in search of the Prince."

Jill kept quiet at this and hoped Scrubb would be sporting enough not to tell all the owls why this hadn't happened. He was, or very nearly. That is, he only muttered under his breath, "Well, it wasn't *my* fault," before saying out loud:

"Very well. We'll have to manage without it. But there's just one thing more I want to know. If this owls' parliament, as you call it, is all fair and above board and means no mischief, why does it have to be so jolly secret – meeting in a ruin in dead of night, and all that?"

"Tu-whoo! Tu-whoo!" hooted several owls. "Where should we meet? When would anyone meet except at night?"

"You see," explained Glimfeather, "most of the creatures in Narnia have such unnatural habits. They do things by day, in broad blazing sunlight (ugh!) when everyone ought to be asleep. And, as a result, at night they're so blind and stupid that you can't get a word out of them. So we owls have got into the habit of meeting at sensible hours, on our own, when we want to talk about things."

"I see," said Scrubb. "Well now, let's get on. Tell us all about the lost Prince." Then an old owl, not Glimfeather, related the story.

About ten years ago, it appeared, when Rilian, the son of Caspian, was a very young knight, he rode with the Queen his mother on a May morning in the north parts of Narnia. They had many squires and ladies with them and all wore garlands of fresh leaves on their heads, and horns at their sides; but they had no hounds with them, for they were maying, not hunting. In the warm part of the day they came to a pleasant glade where a fountain flowed freshly out of the earth, and there they dismounted and ate and drank and were merry. After a time the Queen felt sleepy, and they spread cloaks for her on the grassy bank, and Prince Rilian with the rest of the party went a little way from her, that their tales and laughter might not wake her. And so, presently, a great serpent came out of the thick wood and stung the Queen in her hand. All heard her cry out and rushed towards her, and Rilian was first at her side. He saw the worm gliding away from her and made after it with his sword drawn. It was great, shining, and as green as poison, so that he could see it well: but it glided away into thick bushes and he could not come at it. So he returned to his mother, and found them all busy about her.

But they were busy in vain, for at the first glance of her face Rilian knew that no physic in the world would do her good. As long as the life was in her she seemed to be trying hard to tell him something. But she could not speak clearly and, whatever her message was, she died without delivering it. It was then hardly ten minutes since they had first heard her cry.

They carried the dead Queen back to Cair Paravel, and she was bitterly mourned by Rilian and by the King, and by all Narnia. She had been a great lady, wise and gracious and happy, King Caspian's bride whom he had brought home from the eastern end of the world. And men said that the blood of the stars flowed in her veins. The Prince took his mother's death very hardly, as well he might. After that, he was always riding on the northern marches of Narnia, hunting for that venomous worm, to kill it and be avenged. No one remarked much on this, though the Prince came home from these wanderings looking tired and distraught. But about a month after the Queen's death, some said they could see a change in him. There was a look in his eyes as of a man who has seen visions, and though he would be out all day, his horse did not bear the signs of hard riding. His chief friend among the older courtiers was the Lord Drinian, he who had been his father's captain on that great voyage to the east parts of the earth.

One evening Drinian said to the Prince, "Your Highness must soon give over seeking the worm. There is no true vengeance on a witless brute as there might be on a man. You weary yourself in vain." The Prince answered him, "My Lord, I have almost forgotten the worm this seven days." Drinian asked him why, if that were so, he rode so continually in the northern woods. "My lord," said the Prince, "I have seen there the most beautiful thing that was ever made." "Fair Prince," said Drinian, "of your courtesy let me ride with you tomorrow, that I also may see this fair thing." "With a good will," said Rilian.

Then in good time on the next day they saddled their horses and rode a great gallop into the northern woods and alighted at that same fountain where the Queen got her death. Drinian thought it strange that the Prince should choose that place of all places, to linger in. And there they rested till it came to high noon: and at noon Drinian looked up and saw the most beautiful lady he had ever seen; and she stood at the north side of the fountain and said no word but beckoned to the Prince with her hand as if she bade him come to her. And she was tall and great, shining, and wrapped in a thin garment as green as poison. And the Prince stared at her like a man out of his wits. But suddenly the lady was gone, Drinian knew not where; and they two returned to Cair Paravel. It stuck in Drinian's mind that this shining green woman was evil.

Drinian doubted very much whether he ought not to tell this adventure to the King, but he had little wish to be a blab and a tale-bearer and so he held his tongue. But afterwards he wished he had spoken. For next day Prince Rilian rode out alone. That night he came not back, and from that hour no trace of him was ever found in Narnia nor any neighbouring land, and neither his horse nor his hat nor his cloak nor anything else was ever found. Then Drinian in the bitterness of his heart went to Caspian and said, "Lord King, slay me speedily as a great traitor: for by my silence I have destroyed your son." And he told him the story. Then Caspian caught up a battle-axe and rushed upon the Lord Drinian to kill him, and Drinian stood still as a stock for the death blow. But when the axe was raised, Caspian suddenly threw it away and cried out, "I have lost my queen and my son: shall I lose my friend also?" And he fell upon the Lord Drinian's neck and embraced him and both wept, and their friendship was not broken.

Such was the story of Rilian. And when it was over, Jill said, "I bet that serpent and that woman were the same person."

"True, true, we think the same as you," hooted the owls.

"But we don't think she killed the Prince," said Glimfeather, "because no bones –"

"We know she didn't," said Scrubb. "Aslan told Pole he was still alive somewhere."

"That almost makes it worse," said the oldest owl. "It means she has some use for him, and some deep scheme against Narnia. Long, long ago, at the very beginning, a

White Witch came out of the North and bound our land in snow and ice for a hundred years. And we think this may be some of the same crew."

"Very well, then," said Scrubb. "Pole and I have got to find this Prince. Can you help us?"

"Have you any clue, you two?" asked Glimfeather.

"Yes," said Scrubb. "We know we've got to go north. And we know we've got to reach the ruins of a giant city."

At this there was a greater tu-whooing than ever, and noises of birds shifting their feet and ruffling their feathers, and then all the owls started speaking at once. They all explained how very sorry they were that they themselves could not go with the children on their search for the lost Prince. "You'd want to travel by day, and we'd want to travel by night," they said. "It wouldn't do, wouldn't do." One or two owls added that even here in the ruined tower it wasn't nearly so dark as it had been when they began, and that the parliament had been going on quite long enough. In fact, the mere mention of a journey to the ruined city of giants seemed to have damped the spirits of those birds. But Glimfeather said:

"If they want to go that way – into Ettinsmoor – we must take them to one of the Marsh-wiggles. They're the only people who can help them much."

"True, true. Do," said the owls.

"Come on, then," said Glimfeather. "I'll take one. Who'll take the other? It must be done tonight."

"I will: as far as the Marsh-wiggles," said another owl.

"Are you ready?" said Glimfeather to Jill.

"I think Pole's asleep," said Scrubb.

CHAPTER FIVE

PUDDLEGLUM

Jill was asleep. Ever since the owls' parliament began she had been yawning terribly and now she had dropped off. She was not at all pleased at being waked again, and at finding herself lying on bare boards in a dusty belfry sort of place, completely dark, and almost completely full of owls. She was even less pleased when she heard that they had to set off for somewhere else – and not, apparently, for bed – on the Owl's back.

"Oh, come on, Pole, buck up," said Scrubb's voice. "After all, it *is* an adventure."

"I'm sick of adventures," said Jill crossly.

She did, however, consent to climb on to Glimfeather's back, and was thoroughly waked up (for a while) by the unexpected coldness of the air when he flew out with her into the night. The moon had disappeared and there were no stars. Far behind her she could see a single lighted window well above the ground; doubtless, in one of the towers of Cair Paravel. It made her long to be back in that delightful bedroom, snug in bed, watching the firelight on the walls. She put her hands under her cloak and wrapped it tightly round her. It was uncanny to hear two voices in the dark air a little distance away; Scrubb and his owl were talking to one another. "*He* doesn't sound tired," thought Jill. She did not realize that he had been on great adventures in that world before and that the Narnian air was bringing back to him a strength he had won when he sailed the Eastern Seas with King Caspian.

Jill had to pinch herself to keep awake, for she knew that if she dozed on Glimfeather's back she would probably fall off. When at last the two owls ended their flight, she climbed stiffly off Glimfeather and found herself on flat ground. A chilly wind was blowing and they appeared to be in a place without trees. "Tu-whoo, tu-whoo!" Glimfeather was calling. "Wake up, Puddleglum. Wake up. It is on the Lion's business."

For a long time there was no reply. Then, a long way off, a dim light appeared and began to come nearer. With it came a voice.

"Owls ahoy!" it said. "What is it? Is the King dead? Has an enemy landed in Narnia? Is it a flood? Or dragons?"

When the light reached them, it turned out to be that of a large lantern. She could see very little of the person who held it. He seemed to be all legs and arms. The owls were talking to him, explaining everything, but she was too tired to listen. She tried to wake herself up a bit when she realized that they were saying goodbye to her. But she could never afterwards remember much except that, sooner or later, she and Scrubb were stooping to enter a low doorway and then (oh, thank heavens) were lying down on something soft and warm, and a voice was saying:

"There you are. Best we can do. You'll lie cold and hard. Damp too, I shouldn't wonder. Won't sleep a wink, most likely; even if there isn't a thunderstorm or a flood or the wigwam doesn't fall down on top of us all, as I've known them do. Must make the best of it–" But she was fast asleep before the voice had ended.

When the children woke late next morning they found that they were lying, very dry and warm, on beds of straw in a dark place. A triangular opening let in the daylight.

"Where on earth are we?" asked Jill.

"In the wigwam of a Marsh-wiggle," said Eustace.

"A what?"

"A Marsh-wiggle. Don't ask me what it is. I couldn't see it last night. I'm getting up. Let's go and look for it."

"How beastly one feels after sleeping in one's clothes," said Jill, sitting up.

"I was just thinking how nice it was not to have to dress," said Eustace.

"Or wash either, I suppose," said Jill scornfully. But Scrubb had already got up, yawned, shaken himself, and crawled out of the wigwam. Jill did the same.

What they found outside was quite unlike the bit of

Narnia they had seen on the day before. They were on a great flat plain which was cut into countless little islands by countless channels of water. The islands were covered with coarse grass and bordered with reeds and rushes. Sometimes there were beds of rushes about an acre in extent. Clouds of birds were constantly alighting in them and rising from them again – duck, snipe, bitterns, herons. Many wigwams like that in which they had passed the night could be seen dotted about, but all at a good distance from one another; for Marsh-wiggles are people who like privacy. Except for the fringe of the forest several miles to the south and west of them, there was not a tree in sight. Eastward the flat marsh stretched to low sand-hills on the horizon, and you could tell by the salt tang in the wind which blew from that direction that the sea lay over there. To the North there were low pale-coloured hills, in places bastioned with rock. The rest was all flat marsh. It would have been a depressing place on a wet evening. Seen under a morning sun, with a fresh wind blowing, and the air filled with the crying of birds, there was something fine and fresh and clean about its loneliness. The children felt their spirits rise.

"Where has the thingummy got to, I wonder?" said Jill.

"The Marsh-wiggle," said Scrubb, as if he were rather proud of knowing the word. "I expect – hullo, that must be him." And then they both saw him, sitting with his back to them, fishing, about fifty yards away. He had been hard to see at first because he was nearly the same colour as the marsh and because he sat so still.

"I suppose we'd better go and speak to him," said Jill. Scrubb nodded. They both felt a little nervous.

As they drew nearer, the figure turned its head and showed them a long thin face with rather sunken cheeks, a tightly shut mouth, a sharp nose, and no beard. He was wearing a high, pointed hat like a steeple, with an enormously wide flat brim. The hair, if it could be called hair, which hung over his large ears was greeny-grey, and each lock was flat rather than round, so that they were like tiny reeds. His expression was solemn, his complexion muddy, and you could see at once that he took a serious view of life.

"Good morning, Guests," he said. "Though when I say *good* I don't mean it won't probably turn to rain or it might be snow, or fog, or thunder. You didn't get any sleep, I dare say."

"Yes we did, though," said Jill. "We had a lovely night."

"Ah," said the Marsh-wiggle, shaking his head. "I see you're making the best of a bad job. That's right. You've been well brought up, you have. You've learned to put a good face on things."

"Please, we don't know your name," said Scrubb.

"Puddleglum's my name. But it doesn't matter if you forget it. I can always tell you again."

The children sat down on each side of him. They now saw that he had very long legs and arms, so that although his body was not much bigger than a dwarf's, he would be taller than most men when he stood up. The fingers of his hands were webbed like a frog's, and so were his bare feet which dangled in the muddy water. He was dressed in earth-coloured clothes that hung loose about him.

"I'm trying to catch a few eels to make an eel stew for our dinner," said Puddleglum. "Though I shouldn't wonder if I didn't get any. And you won't like them much if I do."

"Why not?" asked Scrubb.

"Why, it's not in reason that you should like our sort of victuals, though I've no doubt you'll put a bold face on it. All the same, while I am a catching of them, if you two could try to light the fire – no harm trying –! The wood's behind the wigwam. It may be wet. You could light it inside the wigwam, and then we'd get all the smoke in our eyes. Or you could light it outside, and then the rain would come and put it out. Here's my tinder-box. You won't know how to use it, I expect."

But Scrubb had learned that sort of thing on his last adventure. The children ran back together to the wigwam, found the wood (which was perfectly dry) and succeeded in lighting a fire with rather less than the usual difficulty. Then Scrubb sat and took care of it while Jill went and had some sort of wash – not a very nice one – in the nearest channel. After that she saw to the fire and he had a wash. Both felt a good deal fresher, but very hungry.

Presently the Marsh-wiggle joined them. In spite of his expectation of catching no eels, he had a dozen or so, which he had already skinned and cleaned. He put a big pot on, mended the fire, and lit his pipe. Marsh-wiggles smoke a very strange, heavy sort of tobacco (some people say they mix it with mud) and the children noticed the smoke from Puddleglum's pipe hardly rose in the air at all. It trickled out of the bowl and downwards and drifted along the ground like a mist. It was very black and set Scrubb coughing.

"Now," said Puddleglum. "Those eels will take a mortal long time to cook, and either of you might faint with hunger before they're done. I knew a little girl – but I'd better not tell you that story. It might lower your spirits, and that's a thing I never do. So, to keep your minds off your hunger, we may as well talk about our plans."

"Yes, do let's," said Jill. "Can you help us to find Prince Rilian?"

The Marsh-wiggle sucked in his cheeks till they were hollower than you would have thought possible. "Well, I don't know that you'd call it *help*," he said. "I don't know that anyone can exactly *help*. It stands to reason we're not likely to get very far on a journey to the North, not at this time of the year, with the winter coming on soon and all. And an early winter too, by the look of things. But you mustn't let that make you down-hearted. Very likely, what with enemies, and mountains, and rivers to cross, and losing our way, and next to nothing to eat, and sore feet, we'll hardly notice the weather. And if we don't get far enough to do any good, we may get far enough not to get back in a hurry."

Both children noticed that he said "we", not "you", and both exclaimed at the same moment. "Are you coming with us?"

"Oh yes, I'm coming of course. Might as well, you see. I don't suppose we shall ever see the King back in Narnia,

now that he's once set off for foreign parts; and he had a nasty cough when he left. Then there's Trumpkin. He's failing fast. And you'll find there'll have been a bad harvest after this terrible dry summer. And I shouldn't wonder if some enemy attacked us. Mark my words."

"And how shall we start?" said Scrubb.

"Well," said the Marsh-wiggle very slowly, "all the others who ever went looking for Prince Rilian started from that same fountain where the Lord Drinian saw the lady. They went north, mostly. And as none of them ever came back, we can't exactly say how they got on."

"We've got to start by finding a ruined city of giants," said Jill. "Aslan said so."

"Got to start by *finding* it, have we?" answered Puddleglum. "Not allowed to start by *looking* for it, I suppose?"

"That's what I meant, of course," said Jill. "And then, when we've found it–"

"Yes, when!" said Puddleglum very drily.

"Doesn't anyone know where it is?" asked Scrubb.

"I don't know about Anyone," said Puddleglum. "And I won't say I haven't heard of that Ruined City. You wouldn't start from the fountain, though. You'd have to go across Ettinsmoor. That's where the Ruined City is, if it's anywhere. But I've been as far in that direction as most people and I never got to any ruins, so I won't deceive you."

"Where's Ettinsmoor?" said Scrubb.

"Look over there northward," said Puddleglum, pointing with his pipe. "See those hills and bits of cliff? That's the beginning of Ettinsmoor. But there's a river between it and us; the river Shribble. No bridges, of course."

"I suppose we can ford it, though," said Scrubb.

"Well, it *has* been forded," admitted the Marsh-wiggle.

"Perhaps we shall meet people on Ettinsmoor who can tell us the way," said Jill.

"You're right about meeting people," said Puddleglum.

"What sort of people live there?" she asked.

"It's not for me to say they aren't all right in their own way," answered Puddleglum. "If you like their way."

"Yes, but what *are* they?" pressed Jill. "There are so

many queer creatures in this country. I mean, are they animals, or birds, or dwarfs, or what?"

The Marsh-wiggle gave a long whistle. "Phew!" he said. "Don't you know? I thought the owls had told you. They're giants."

Jill winced. She had never liked giants even in books, and she had once met one in a nightmare. Then she saw Scrubb's face, which had turned rather green, and thought to herself, "I bet he's in a worse funk than I am." That made her feel braver.

"The King told me long ago," said Scrubb – "that time when I was with him at sea – that he'd jolly well beaten those giants in war and made them pay him tribute."

"That's true enough," said Puddleglum. "They're at peace with us all right. As long as we stay on our own side of the Shribble, they won't do us any harm. Over on their side, on the Moor – Still, there's always a chance. If we don't get near any of them, and if none of them forget themselves, and if we're not seen, it's just possible we might get a long way."

"Look here!" said Scrubb, suddenly losing his temper, as people so easily do when they have been frightened. "I don't believe the whole thing can be half as bad as you're making out; any more than the beds in the wigwam were hard or the wood was wet. I don't think Aslan would ever have sent us if there was so little chance as all that."

He quite expected the Marsh-wiggle to give him an angry reply, but he only said, "That's the spirit, Scrubb. That's the way to talk. Put a good face on it. But we all need to be very careful about our tempers, seeing all the hard times we shall have to go through together. Won't do to quarrel, you know. At any rate, don't begin it too soon. I know these expeditions usually *end* that way: knifing one another, I shouldn't wonder, before all's done. But the longer we can keep off it –"

"Well, if you feel it's so hopeless," interrupted Scrubb, "I think you'd better stay behind. Pole and I can go on alone, can't we, Pole?"

"Shut up and don't be an ass, Scrubb," said Jill hastily, terrified lest the Marsh-wiggle should take him at his word.

"Don't you lose heart, Pole," said Puddleglum. "I'm coming, sure and certain. I'm not going to lose an opportunity like this. It will do me good. They all say – I mean, the other wiggles all say – that I'm too flighty; don't take life seriously enough. If they've said it once, they've said it a thousand times. 'Puddleglum,' they've said, 'you're altogether too full of bobance and bounce and high spirits. You've got to learn that life isn't all fricasseed frogs and eel pie. You want something to sober you down a bit. We're only saying it for your own good, Puddleglum.' That's what they say. Now a job like this – a journey up north just as winter's beginning, looking for a Prince that probably isn't there, by way of a ruined city that no one has ever seen – will be just the thing. If that doesn't steady a chap, I don't know what will." And he rubbed his big frog-like hands together as if he were talking of going to a party or a pantomime. "And now," he added, "let's see how those eels are getting on."

When the meal came it was delicious and the children had two large helpings each. At first the Marsh-wiggle wouldn't believe that they really liked it, and when they had eaten so much that he had to believe them, he fell back on saying that it would probably disagree with them horribly. "What's food for wiggles may be poison for humans, I shouldn't wonder," he said. After the meal they had tea, in tins (as you've seen men having it who are working on the road), and Puddleglum had a good many sips out of a square black bottle. He offered the children some of it, but they thought it very nasty.

The rest of the day was spent in preparations for an early

start tomorrow morning. Puddleglum, being far the biggest, said he would carry three blankets, with a large bit of bacon rolled up inside them. Jill was to carry the remains of the eels, some biscuit, and the tinder-box. Scrubb was to carry both his own cloak and Jill's when they didn't want to wear them. Scrubb (who had learned some shooting when he sailed to the East under Caspian) had Puddleglum's second-best bow, and Puddleglum had his best one; though he said that what with winds, and damp bowstrings, and bad light, and cold fingers, it was a hundred to one against either of them hitting anything. He and Scrubb both had swords – Scrubb had brought the one which had been left out for him in his room at Cair Paravel, but Jill had to be content with her knife. There would have been a quarrel about this, but as soon as they started sparring the wiggle rubbed his hands and said, "Ah, there you are. I thought as much. That's what usually happens on adventures." This made them both shut up.

All three went to bed early in the wigwam. This time the children really had a rather bad night. That was because Puddleglum, after saying, "You'd better try for some sleep, you two; not that I suppose any of us will close an eye tonight," instantly went off into such a loud, continuous snore that, when Jill at last got to sleep, she dreamed all night about road-drills and waterfalls and being in express trains in tunnels.

CHAPTER SIX

THE WILD WASTE LANDS OF THE NORTH

AT about nine o'clock next morning three lonely figures might have been seen picking their way across the Shribble by the shoals and stepping-stones. It was a shallow, noisy stream, and even Jill was not wet above her knees when they reached the northern bank. About fifty yards ahead, the land rose up to the beginning of the moor, everywhere steeply, and often in cliffs.

"I suppose *that's* our way!" said Scrubb, pointing left and west to where a stream flowed down from the moor through a shallow gorge. But the Marsh-wiggle shook his head.

"The giants mainly live along the side of that gorge," he said. "You might say the gorge was like a street to them. We'll do better straight ahead, even though it's a bit steep."

They found a place where they could scramble up, and in about ten minutes stood panting at the top. They cast a longing look back at the valley-land of Narnia and then turned their faces to the North. The vast, lonely moor stretched on and up as far as they could see. On their left was rockier ground. Jill thought that must be the edge of the giants' gorge and did not much care about looking in that direction. They set out.

It was good, springy ground for walking, and a day of pale winter sunlight. As they got deeper into the moor, the loneliness increased: one could hear peewits and see an occasional hawk. When they halted in the middle of the morning for a rest and a drink in a little hollow by a stream, Jill was beginning to feel that she might enjoy adventures after all, and said so.

"We haven't had any yet," said the Marsh-wiggle.

Walks after the first halt – like school mornings after break or railway journeys after changing trains – never go on as they were before. When they set out again, Jill noticed that the rocky edge of the gorge had drawn nearer. And the rocks were less flat, more upright, than they had been. In fact they were like little towers of rock. And what funny shapes they were!

"I do believe," thought Jill, "that all the stories about giants might have come from those funny rocks. If you were coming along here when it was half dark, you could easily think those piles of rock were giants. Look at that one, now! You could almost imagine that the lump on top was a head. It would be rather too big for the body, but it would do well enough for an ugly giant. And all that bushy stuff – I suppose it's heather and birds' nests, really – would do quite well for hair and beard. And the things sticking out on each side are quite like ears. They'd be horribly big, but then I dare say giants would have big ears, like elephants. And – o-o-o-h! –"

Her blood froze. The thing moved. It was a real giant. There was no mistaking it; she had seen it turn its head. She had caught a glimpse of the great, stupid, puff-cheeked face. All the things were giants, not rocks. There were forty or fifty of them, all in a row; obviously standing with their feet on the bottom of the gorge and their elbows resting on the edge of the gorge, just as men might stand leaning on a wall – lazy men, on a fine morning after breakfast.

"Keep straight on," whispered Puddleglum, who had noticed them too. "Don't look at them. And whatever you do, don't *run*. They'd be after us in a moment."

So they kept on, pretending not to have seen the giants. It was like walking past the gate of a house where there is a fierce dog, only far worse. There were dozens and dozens of these giants. They didn't look angry – or kind – or interested at all. There was no sign that they had seen the travellers.

Then – whizz-whizz-whizz – some heavy object came hurtling through the air, and with a crash a big boulder fell about twenty paces ahead of them. And then – thud! – another fell twenty feet behind.

"Are they aiming at us?" asked Scrubb.

"No," said Puddleglum. "We'd be a good deal safer if they were. They're trying to hit *that* – that cairn over there to the right. They won't hit *it*, you know. *It's* safe enough; they're such very bad shots. They play cock-shies most fine mornings. About the only game they're clever enough to understand."

It was a horrible time. There seemed no end to the line of giants, and they never ceased hurling stones, some of which fell extremely close. Quite apart from the real danger, the very sight and sound of their faces and voices were enough to scare anyone. Jill tried not to look at them.

After about twenty-five minutes the giants apparently had a quarrel. This put an end to the cock-shies, but it is not pleasant to be within a mile of quarrelling giants. They stormed and jeered at one another in long, meaningless words of about twenty syllables each. They foamed and gibbered and jumped in their rage, and each jump shook the earth like a bomb. They lammed each other on the head with great, clumsy stone hammers; but their skulls were so hard that the hammers bounced off again, and then the monster who had given the blow would drop his hammer and howl with pain because it had stung his fingers. But he was so stupid that he would do exactly the same thing a minute later. This was a good thing in the long run, for by the end of an hour all the giants were so hurt that they sat down and began to cry. When they sat down, their heads were below the edge of the gorge, so that you saw them no more; but Jill could hear them howling and blubbering and boo-hooing like great babies even after the place was a mile behind.

That night they bivouacked on the bare moor, and Puddleglum showed the children how to make the best of their blankets by sleeping back to back. (The backs keep each other warm and you can then have both blankets on top.) But it was chilly even so, and the ground was hard and lumpy. The Marsh-wiggle told them they would feel more comfortable if only they thought how very much colder it would be later on and farther north; but this didn't cheer them up at all.

They travelled across Ettinsmoor for many days, saving the bacon and living chiefly on the moor-fowl (they were not, of course, *talking* birds) which Eustace and the wiggle shot. Jill rather envied Eustace for being able to shoot; he had learned it on his voyage with King Caspian. As there were countless streams on the moor, they were never short of water. Jill thought that when, in books, people live on what they shoot, it never tells you what a long, smelly, messy job it is plucking and cleaning dead birds, and how cold it makes your fingers. But the great thing was that they met hardly any giants. One giant saw them, but he only roared with laughter and stumped away about his own business.

About the tenth day, they reached a place where the country changed. They came to the northern edge of the moor and looked down a long, steep slope into a different, and grimmer, land. At the bottom of the slope were cliffs: beyond these, a country of high mountains, dark precipices, stony valleys, ravines so deep and narrow that one could not see far into them, and rivers that poured out of echoing gorges to plunge sullenly into black depths. Needless to say, it was Puddleglum who pointed out a sprinkling of snow on the more distant slopes.

"But there'll be more on the north side of them, I shouldn't wonder," he added.

It took them some time to reach the foot of the slope and, when they did, they looked down from the top of the cliffs at a river running below them from west to east. It was walled in by precipices on the far side as well as on their own, and it was green and sunless, full of rapids and waterfalls. The roar of it shook the earth even where they stood.

"The bright side of it is," said Puddleglum, "that if we break our necks getting down the cliff, then we're safe from being drowned in the river."

"What about *that*?" said Scrubb suddenly, pointing upstream to their left. Then they all looked and saw the last thing they were expecting – a bridge. And what a bridge, too! It was a huge, single arch that spanned the gorge from cliff-top to cliff-top; and the crown of that arch was as high above the cliff-tops as the dome of St Paul's is above the street.

"Why, it must be a giants' bridge!" said Jill.

"Or a sorcerer's, more likely," said Puddleglum. "We've got to look out for enchantments in a place like this. I think it's a trap. I think it'll turn into mist and melt away just when we're out on the middle of it."

"Oh, for goodness' sake, don't be such a wet blanket," said Scrubb. "Why on earth shouldn't it be a proper bridge?"

"Do you think any of the giants we've seen would have sense to build a thing like that?" said Puddleglum.

"But mightn't it have been built by other giants?" said Jill. "I mean, by giants who lived hundreds of years ago, and were far cleverer than the modern kind. It might have been built by the same ones who built the giant city we're looking for. And that would mean we were on the right track – the old bridge leading to the old city!"

"That's a real brain-wave, Pole," said Scrubb. "It must be that. Come on."

So they turned and went to the bridge. And when they reached it, it certainly seemed solid enough. The single stones were as big as those at Stonehenge and must have been squared by good masons once, though now they were cracked and crumbled. The balustrade had apparently been covered with rich carvings, of which some traces remained; mouldering faces and forms of giants, minotaurs, squids, centipedes, and dreadful gods. Puddleglum still didn't trust it, but he consented to cross it with the children.

The climb up to the crown of the arch was long and heavy. In many places the great stones had dropped out, leaving horrible gaps through which you looked down on the river foaming thousands of feet below. They saw an eagle fly through under their feet. And the higher they went, the colder it grew, and the wind blew so that they could hardly keep their footing. It seemed to shake the bridge.

When they reached the top and could look down the

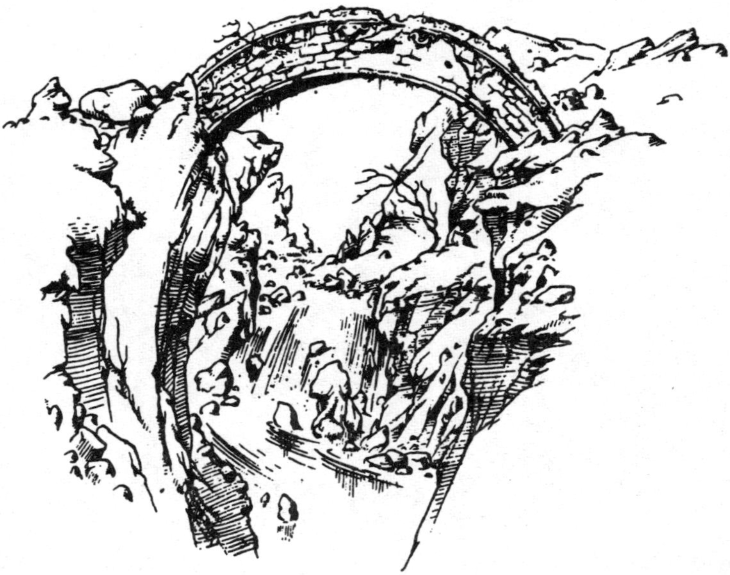

farther slope of the bridge, they saw what looked like the remains of an ancient giant road stretching away before them into the heart of the mountains. Many stones of its pavement were missing and there were wide patches of grass between those that remained. And riding towards them on that ancient road were two people of normal grown-up human size.

"Keep on. Move towards them," said Puddleglum. "Anyone you meet in a place like this is as likely as not to be an enemy, but we mustn't let them think we're afraid."

By the time they had stepped off the end of the bridge on to the grass, the two strangers were quite close. One was a knight in complete armour with his visor down. His armour and his horse were black; there was no device on his shield and no banneret on his spear. The other was a

lady on a white horse, a horse so lovely that you wanted to kiss its nose and give it a lump of sugar at once. But the lady, who rode side-saddle and wore a long, fluttering dress of dazzling green, was lovelier still.

"Good day, t-r-r-avellers," she cried out in a voice as sweet as the sweetest bird's song, trilling her R's delightfully. "Some of you are young pilgrims to walk this rough waste."

"That's as may be, Ma'am," said Puddleglum very stiffly and on his guard.

"We're looking for the ruined city of the giants," said Jill.

"The r-r-ruined city?" said the Lady. "That is a strange place to be seeking. What will you do if you find it?"

"We've got to –" began Jill, but Puddleglum interrupted.

"Begging your pardon, Ma'am. But we don't know you or your friend – a silent chap, isn't he? – and you don't know us. And we'd as soon not talk to strangers about our business, if you don't mind. Shall we have a little rain soon, do you think?"

The Lady laughed: the richest, most musical laugh you can imagine. "Well, children," she said, "you have a wise, solemn old guide with you. I think none the worse of him for keeping his own counsel, but I'll be free with mine. I have often heard the name of the giantish City Ruinous, but never met any who would tell me the way thither. This road leads to the burgh and castle of Harfang, where dwell the gentle giants. They are as mild, civil, prudent, and courteous as those of Ettinsmoor are foolish, fierce, savage, and given to all beastliness. And in Harfang you may or may not hear tidings of the City Ruinous, but certainly you shall find good lodgings and merry hosts. You would be wise to winter there, or, at the least, to tarry certain days for your ease and refreshment. There you shall have steaming baths, soft beds, and bright hearths; and the roast and the baked and the sweet and the strong will be on the table four times in a day."

"I say!" exclaimed Scrubb. "That's something like! Think of sleeping in a bed again."

"Yes, and having a hot bath," said Jill. "Do you think they'll ask us to stay? We don't know them, you see."

"Only tell them," answered the Lady, "that She of the Green Kirtle salutes them by you, and has sent them two fair Southern children for the Autumn Feast."

"Oh, thank you, thank you ever so much," said Jill and Scrubb.

"But have a care," said the Lady. "On whatever day you reach Harfang, that you come not to the door too late. For they shut their gates a few hours after noon, and it is the custom of the castle that they open to none when once they have drawn bolt, how hard so ever he knock."

The children thanked her again, with shining eyes, and the Lady waved to them. The Marsh-wiggle took off his steeple-hat and bowed very stiffly. Then the silent Knight and the Lady started walking their horses up the slope of the bridge with a great clatter of hoofs.

"Well!" said Puddleglum. "I'd give a good deal to know where *she's* coming from and where she's going. Not the sort you expect to meet in the wilds of Giantland, is she? Up to no good, I'll be bound."

"Oh rot!" said Scrubb. "I thought she was simply super. And think of hot meals and warm rooms. I do hope Harfang isn't a long way off."

"Same here," said Jill. "And hadn't she a scrumptious dress. And the horse!"

"All the same," said Puddleglum, "I wish we knew a bit more about her."

"I *was* going to ask her all about herself," said Jill. "But how could I when you wouldn't tell her anything about us?"

"Yes," said Scrubb. "And why were you so stiff and unpleasant. Didn't you like them?"

"Them?" said the wiggle. "Who's *them*? I only saw one."

"Didn't you see the Knight?" asked Jill.

"I saw a suit of armour," said Puddleglum. "Why didn't he speak?"

"I expect he was shy," said Jill. "Or perhaps he just

wants to look at her and listen to her lovely voice. I'm sure I would if I was him."

"I was wondering," remarked Puddleglum, "what you'd really see if you lifted up the visor of that helmet and looked inside."

"Hang it all," said Scrubb. "Think of the shape of the armour! What *could* be inside it except a man?"

"How about a skeleton?" asked the Marsh-wiggle with ghastly cheerfulness. "Or perhaps," he added as an afterthought, "nothing at all. I mean, nothing you could see. Someone invisible."

"Really, Puddleglum," said Jill with a shudder, "you do have the most horrible ideas. How do you think of them all?"

"Oh, bother his ideas!" said Scrubb. "He's always expecting the worst, and he's always wrong. Let's think about those Gentle Giants and get on to Harfang as quickly as we can. I wish I knew how far it is."

And now they nearly had the first of those quarrels which Puddleglum had foretold: not that Jill and Scrubb hadn't been sparring and snapping at each other a good deal before, but this was the first really serious disagreement. Puddleglum didn't want them to go to Harfang at all. He said that he didn't know what a giant's idea of being "gentle" might be, and that, anyway, Aslan's signs had said nothing about staying with giants, gentle or otherwise. The children, on the other hand, who were sick of wind and rain, and skinny fowl roasted over campfires, and hard, cold earth to sleep on, were absolutely dead set to visit the Gentle Giants. In the end, Puddleglum agreed to do so, but only on one condition. The others must give an absolute promise that, unless he gave them leave, they would not tell the Gentle Giants that they came from Narnia or that they were looking for

Prince Rilian. And they gave him this promise, and went on.

After that talk with the Lady things got worse in two different ways. In the first place the country was much harder. The road led through endless, narrow valleys down which a cruel north wind was always blowing in their faces. There was nothing that could be used for firewood, and there were no nice little hollows to camp in, as there had been on the moor. And the ground was all stony, and made your feet sore by day and every bit of you sore by night.

In the second place, whatever the Lady had intended by telling them about Harfang, the actual effect on the children was a bad one. They could think about nothing but beds and baths and hot meals and how lovely it would be to get indoors. They never talked about Aslan, or even about the lost prince, now. And Jill gave up her habit of repeating the signs over to herself every night and morning. She said to herself, at first, that she was too tired, but she soon forgot all about it. And though you might have expected that the idea of having a good time at Harfang would have made them more cheerful, it really made them more sorry for themselves and more grumpy and snappy with each other and with Puddleglum.

At last they came one afternoon to a place where the gorge in which they were travelling widened out and dark fir woods rose on either side. They looked ahead and saw that they had come through the mountains. Before them lay a desolate, rocky plain: beyond it, further mountains capped with snow. But between them and those further mountains rose a low hill with an irregular flattish top.

"Look! Look!" cried Jill, and pointed across the plain; and there, through the gathering dusk, from beyond the flat hill, everyone saw lights. Lights! Not moonlight, nor fires, but a homely cheering row of lighted windows. If you have never been in the wild wilderness, day and night, for weeks, you will hardly understand how they felt.

"Harfang!" cried Scrubb and Jill in glad, excited voices; and "Harfang," repeated Puddleglum in a dull, gloomy voice. But he added, "Hullo! Wild geese!" and had the bow off his shoulder in a second. He brought down a good fat goose. It was far too late to think of reaching Harfang that day. But they had a hot meal and a fire, and started the night warmer than they had been for over a week. After the fire had gone out, the night grew bitterly cold, and when they woke next morning, their blankets were stiff with frost.

"Never mind!" said Jill, stamping her feet. "Hot baths tonight!"

CHAPTER SEVEN

THE HILL OF THE STRANGE TRENCHES

THERE is no denying it was a beast of a day. Overhead was a sunless sky, muffled in clouds that were heavy with snow; underfoot, a black frost; blowing over it, a wind that felt as if it would take your skin off. When they got down into the plain they found that this part of the ancient road was much more ruinous than any they had yet seen. They had to pick their way over great broken stones and between boulders and across rubble: hard going for sore feet. And, however tired they got, it was far too cold for a halt.

At about ten o'clock the first tiny snow flakes came loitering down and settled on Jill's arm. Ten minutes later they were falling quite thickly. In twenty minutes the ground was noticeably white. And by the end of half an hour a good steady snowstorm, which looked as if it meant to last all day, was driving in their faces so that they could hardly see.

In order to understand what followed, you must keep on remembering how little they could see. As they drew near the low hill which separated them from the place where the lighted windows had appeared, they had no general view of it at all. It was a question of seeing the next few paces ahead, and, even for that, you had to screw up your eyes. Needless to say, they were not talking.

When they reached the foot of the hill they caught a glimpse of what might be rocks on each side – squarish rocks, if you looked at them carefully, but no one did. All were more concerned with the ledge right in front of them which barred their way. It was about four feet high. The

Marsh-wiggle, with his long legs, had no difficulty in jumping onto the top of it, and he then helped the others up. It was a nasty wet business for them, though not for him, because the snow now lay quite deep on the ledge. They then had a stiff climb – Jill fell once – up very rough ground for about a hundred yards, and came to a second ledge. There were four of these ledges altogether, at quite irregular intervals.

As they struggled on to the fourth ledge, there was no mistaking the fact that they were now at the top of the

flat hill. Up till now the slope had given them some shelter; here, they got the full fury of the wind. For the hill, oddly enough, was quite as flat on top as it had looked from a distance: a great level tableland which the storm tore across without resistance. In most places the snow was still hardly lying at all, for the wind kept catching it up off the ground in sheets and clouds, and hurling it in their faces. And round their feet little eddies of snow ran about as you sometimes see them doing over ice. And, indeed, in many places, the surface was almost as smooth as ice. But to make matters worse it was crossed and criss-crossed with curious banks or dykes, which sometimes divided it up into squares and oblongs. All these of course had to be climbed; they varied from two to five feet in height and were about a couple of yards thick. On the north side of each bank the snow already lay in deep drifts; and after each climb you came down into a drift and got wet.

Fighting her way forward with hood up and head down and numb hands inside her cloak, Jill had glimpses of other odd things on that horrible tableland – things on her right that looked vaguely like factory chimneys, and, on her left, a huge cliff, straighter than any cliff ought to be. But she wasn't at all interested and didn't give them a thought. The only things she thought about were her cold hands (and nose and chin and ears) and hot baths and beds at Harfang.

Suddenly she skidded, slid about five feet, and found herself to her horror sliding down into a dark, narrow chasm which seemed that moment to have appeared in front of her. Half a second later she had reached the bottom. She appeared to be in a kind of trench or groove, only about three feet wide. And though she was shaken by the fall, almost the first thing she noticed was the relief of being out of the wind; for the walls of the trench rose high above her. The next thing she noticed was, naturally, the anxious faces of Scrubb and Puddleglum looking down at her from the edge.

"Are you hurt, Pole?" shouted Scrubb.

"*Both* legs broken, I shouldn't wonder," shouted Puddleglum.

Jill stood up and explained that she was all right, but they'd have to help her out.

"What is it you've fallen into?" asked Scrubb.

"It's a kind of trench, or it might be a kind of sunken lane or something," said Jill. "It runs quite straight."

"Yes, by Jove," said Scrubb. "And it runs due north! I

wonder is it a sort of road? If it was, we'd be out of this infernal wind down there. Is there a lot of snow at the bottom?"

"Hardly any. It all blows over the top, I suppose."

"What happens farther on?"

"Half a sec. I'll go and see," said Jill. She got up and walked along the trench; but before she had gone far, it turned sharply to the right. She shouted this information back to the others.

"What's round the corner?" asked Scrubb.

Now it happened that Jill had the same feeling about twisty passages and dark places underground, or even nearly underground, that Scrubb had about the edges of cliffs. She had no intention of going round that corner alone; especially when she heard Puddleglum bawling out from behind her:

"Be careful, Pole. It's just the sort of place that might lead to a dragon's cave. And in a giant country, there might be giant earth-worms or giant beetles."

"I don't think it goes anywhere much," said Jill, coming hastily back.

"I'm jolly well going to have a look," said Scrubb. "What do you mean by *anywhere much*, I should like to know?" So he sat down on the edge of the trench (everyone was too wet by now to bother about being a bit wetter) and then dropped in. He pushed past Jill and, though he didn't say anything, she felt sure that he knew she had funked it. So she followed him close, but took care not to get in front of him.

It proved, however, a disappointing exploration. They went round the right-hand turn and straight on for a few paces. Here there was a choice of ways: straight on again, or sharp to the right. "That's no good," said Scrubb, glancing down the right-hand turn, "that would be taking us back – south." He went straight on, but once more, in a few steps, they found a second turn to the right. But this time there was no choice of ways, for the trench they had been following here came to a dead end.

"No good," grunted Scrubb. Jill lost no time in turning and leading the way back. When they returned to the place where Jill had first fallen in, the Marsh-wiggle with his long arms had no difficulty in pulling them out.

But it was dreadful to be out on top again. Down in those narrow slits of trenches, their ears had almost begun to thaw. They had been able to see clearly and breathe easily and hear each other speak without shouting. It was absolute misery to come back into the withering coldness. And it did seem hard when Puddleglum chose that moment for saying:

"Are you still sure of those signs, Pole? What's the one we ought to be after, now?"

"Oh, come *on*! Bother the signs," said Pole. "Something about someone mentioning Aslan's name, I think. But I'm jolly well not going to give a recitation here."

As you see, she had got the order wrong. That was because she had given up saying the signs over every night. She still really knew them, if she troubled to think: but she was no longer so "pat" in her lesson as to be sure of reeling them off in the right order at a moment's notice and without thinking. Puddleglum's question annoyed her because, deep down inside her, she was already annoyed with herself for not knowing the Lion's lesson quite so well as she felt she ought to have known it. This annoyance, added to the misery of being very cold and tired, made her say, "Bother the signs." She didn't perhaps quite mean it.

"Oh, that was next, was it?" said Puddleglum. "Now I wonder, are you right? Got 'em mixed, I shouldn't wonder. It seems to me, this hill, this flat place we're on, is worth stopping to have a look at. Have you noticed –"

"Oh Lor!" said Scrubb, "is this a time for stopping to admire the view? For goodness' sake let's get on."

"Oh, look, look, look," cried Jill and pointed. Everyone turned, and everyone saw. Some way off to the north, and a good deal higher up than the tableland on which they stood, a line of lights had appeared. This time, even more obviously than when the travellers had seen them the night before, they were windows: smaller windows that made one think deliciously of bedrooms, and larger windows that made one think of great halls with fires roaring on the hearth and hot soup or juicy sirloins smoking on the table.

"Harfang!" exclaimed Scrubb.

"That's all very well," said Puddleglum. "But what I was saying was –"

"Oh, shut up," said Jill crossly. "We haven't a moment to lose. Don't you remember what the Lady said about their locking up so early? We must get there in time, we must, we must. We'll *die* if we're shut out on a night like this."

"Well, it isn't exactly a night, not yet," began Puddleglum; but the two children both said, "Come on," and began stumbling forward on the slippery tableland as quickly as their legs would carry them. The Marsh-wiggle followed them: still talking, but now that they were forcing their way into the wind again, they could not have heard him even if they had wanted to. And they didn't want. They were thinking of baths and beds and hot drinks; and the idea of coming to Harfang too late and being shut out was almost unbearable.

In spite of their haste, it took them a long time to cross the flat top of that hill. And even when they had crossed it, there were still several ledges to climb down on the far side. But at last they reached the bottom and could see what Harfang was like.

It stood on a high crag, and in spite of its many towers was more a huge house than a castle. Obviously, the Gentle Giants feared no attack. There were windows in the outside wall quite close to the ground – a thing no one would have in a serious fortress. There were even odd little doors here and there, so that it would be quite easy to get in and out of the castle without going through the courtyard. This raised the spirits of Jill and Scrubb. It made the whole place look more friendly and less forbidding.

At first the height and steepness of the crag frightened them, but presently they noticed that there was an easier way up on the left and that the road wound up towards

it. It was a terrible climb, after the journey they had already had, and Jill nearly gave up. Scrubb and Puddleglum had to help her for the last hundred yards.

But in the end they stood before the castle gate. The portcullis was up and the gate open.

However tired you are, it takes some nerve to walk up to a giant's front door. In spite of all his previous warnings against Harfang, it was Puddleglum who showed most courage.

"Steady pace, now," he said. "Don't look frightened, whatever you do. We've done the silliest thing in the world by coming at all: but now that we *are* here, we'd best put a bold face on it."

With these words he strode forward into the gateway, stood still under the arch where the echo would help his voice, and called out as loud as he could.

"Ho! Porter! Guests who seek lodging."

And while he was waiting for something to happen, he took off his hat and knocked off the heavy mass of snow which had gathered on its wide brim.

"I say," whispered Scrubb to Jill. "He may be a wet blanket, but he has plenty of pluck – and cheek."

A door opened, letting out a delicious glow of firelight, and the Porter appeared. Jill bit her lips for fear she should scream. He was not a perfectly enormous giant; that is to say, he was rather taller than an apple tree but nothing like so tall as a telegraph pole. He had bristly red hair, a leather jerkin with metal plates fastened all over it so as to make a kind of mail shirt, bare knees (very hairy indeed) and things like puttees on his legs. He stooped down and goggled at Puddleglum.

"And what sort of creature do you call yourself," he said.

Jill took her courage in both hands. "Please," she said, shouting up at the giant. "The Lady of the Green Kirtle salutes the King of the Gentle Giants, and has sent us two Southern children and this Marsh-wiggle (his name's

Puddleglum) to your Autumn Feast. – If it's quite convenient, of course," she added.

"O-ho!" said the Porter. "That's quite a different story. Come in, little people, come in. You'd best come into the lodge while I'm sending word to his Majesty." He looked at the children with curiosity. "Blue faces," he said. "I didn't know they were that colour. Don't care about it myself. But I dare say you look quite nice to one another. Beetles fancy other beetles, they do say."

"Our faces are only blue with cold," said Jill. "We're not this colour *really*."

"Then come in and get warm. Come in, little shrimps," said the Porter. They followed him into the lodge. And though it was rather terrible to hear such a big door clang shut behind them, they forgot about it as soon as they saw the thing they had been longing for ever since supper time last night – a fire. And such a fire! It looked as if four or five whole trees were blazing on it, and it was so hot they couldn't go within yards of it. But they all flopped down on the brick floor, as near as they could bear the heat, and heaved great sighs of relief.

"Now, youngster," said the Porter to another giant who had been sitting in the back of the room, staring at the visitors till it looked as if his eyes would start out of his head, "run across with this message to the House." And he repeated what Jill had said to him. The younger giant, after a final stare, and a great guffaw, left the room.

"Now, Froggy," said the Porter to Puddleglum, "you look as if you wanted some cheering up." He produced a black bottle very like Puddleglum's own, but about twenty times larger. "Let me see, let me see," said the Porter. "I can't give you a cup or you'll drown yourself. Let me see. This salt-cellar will be just the thing. You needn't mention it over at the House. The silver *will* keep on getting over here, and it's not my fault."

The salt-cellar was not very like one of ours, being narrower and more upright, and made quite a good cup for Puddleglum, when the giant set it down on the floor beside him. The children expected Puddleglum to refuse it, distrusting the Gentle Giants as he did. But he muttered, "It's rather late to be thinking of precautions now that we're inside and the door shut behind us." Then he sniffed at the liquor. "Smells all right," he said. "But that's nothing to go by. Better make sure," and took a sip. "Tastes all right, too," he said. "But it might do that at the *first* sip. How does it go on?" He took a larger sip. "Ah!" he said. "But is it the same all the way down?" and took another. "There'll be something nasty at the bottom, I shouldn't wonder," he said, and finished the drink. He licked his lips and remarked to the children, "This'll be a test, you see. If I curl up, or burst, or turn into a lizard, or something, then you'll know not to take anything they offer you." But the giant, who was too far up to hear the things Puddleglum had been saying under his breath, roared with laughter and said, "Why, Froggy, you're a man. See him put it away!"

"Not a man . . . Marsh-wiggle," replied Puddleglum in a somewhat indistinct voice. "Not frog either: Marsh-wiggle."

At that moment the door opened behind them and the younger giant came in saying, "They're to go to the throne-room at once."

The children stood up but Puddleglum remained sitting and said, "Marsh-wiggle. Marsh-wiggle. Very respectable Marsh-wiggle. Respectowiggle."

"Show them the way, young 'un," said the giant

Porter. "You'd better carry Froggy. He's had a drop more than's good for him."

"Nothing wrong with me," said Puddleglum. "Not a frog. Nothing frog with me. I'm a respectabiggle."

But the young giant caught him up by the waist and signed to the children to follow. In this undignified way they crossed the courtyard. Puddleglum, held in the giant's fist, and vaguely kicking the air, did certainly look very like a frog. But they had little time to notice this, for they soon entered the great doorway of the main castle – both their hearts beating faster than usual – and, after pattering along several corridors at a trot to keep up with the giant's paces, found themselves blinking in the light of an enormous

room, where lamps glowed and a fire roared on the hearth and both were reflected from the gilding of roof and cornice. More giants than they could count stood on their left and right, all in magnificent robes; and on two thrones at the far end, sat two huge shapes that appeared to be the King and Queen.

About twenty feet from the thrones, they stopped. Scrubb and Jill made an awkward attempt at a bow (girls are not taught how to curtsey at Experiment House) and the young giant carefully put Puddleglum down on the floor, where he collapsed into a sort of sitting position. With his long limbs he looked, to tell the truth, uncommonly like a large spider.

CHAPTER EIGHT

THE HOUSE OF HARFANG

"Go on, Pole, do your stuff," whispered Scrubb.

Jill found that her mouth was so dry that she couldn't speak a word. She nodded savagely at Scrubb.

Thinking to himself that he would never forgive her (or Puddleglum either), Scrubb licked his lips and shouted up to the King giant.

"If you please, Sire, the Lady of the Green Kirtle salutes you by us and said you'd like to have us for your Autumn Feast."

The giant King and Queen looked at each other, nodded to each other, and smiled in a way that Jill didn't exactly like. She liked the King better than the Queen. He had a fine, curled beard and a straight eagle-like nose, and was really rather good-looking as giants go. The Queen was dreadfully fat and had a double chin and a fat, powdered face – which isn't a very nice thing at the best of times, and of course looks much worse when it is ten times too big. Then the King put out his tongue and licked his lips. Anyone might do that: but his tongue was so very large and red, and came out so unexpectedly, that it gave Jill quite a shock.

"Oh, what *good* children!" said the Queen. ("Perhaps she's the nice one after all," thought Jill.)

"Yes indeed," said the King. "Quite excellent children. We welcome you to our court. Give me your hands."

He stretched down his great right hand – very clean and with any number of rings on the fingers, but also with terrible pointed nails. He was much too big to shake the hands which the children, in turn, held up to him; but he shook the arms.

"And what's *that*?" asked the King, pointing to Puddleglum.

"Reshpeckobiggle," said Puddleglum.

"Oh!" screamed the Queen, gathering her skirts close about her ankles. "The horrid thing! It's alive."

"He's quite all right, your Majesty, really, he is," said Scrubb hastily. "You'll like him much better when you get to know him. I'm sure you will."

I hope you won't lose all interest in Jill for the rest of the book if I tell you that at this moment she began to cry. There was a good deal of excuse for her. Her feet and hands and ears and nose were still only just beginning to thaw; melted snow was trickling off her clothes; she had had hardly anything to eat or drink that day; and her legs were aching so that she felt she could not go on standing much longer. Anyway, it did more good at the moment than anything else would have done, for the Queen said:

"Ah, the poor child! My lord, we do wrong to keep our guests standing. Quick, some of you! Take them away. Give them food and wine and baths. Comfort the little girl. Give her lollipops, give her dolls, give her physics, give her all you can think of – possets and comfits and caraways and lullabies and toys. Don't cry, little girl, or you won't be good for anything when the feast comes."

Jill was just as indignant as you and I would have been at the mention of toys and dolls; and, though lollipops and comfits might be all very well in their way, she very much hoped that something more solid would be provided. The Queen's foolish speech, however, produced excellent results, for Puddleglum and Scrubb were at once picked up by gigantic gentlemen-in-waiting, and Jill by a gigantic maid of honour, and carried off to their rooms.

Jill's room was about the size of a church, and would have been rather grim if it had not had a roaring fire on

the hearth and a very thick crimson carpet on the floor. And here delightful things began to happen to her. She was handed over to the Queen's old Nurse, who was, from the giants' point of view, a little old woman almost bent double with age, and, from the human point of view, a giantess small enough to go about an ordinary room without knocking her head on the ceiling. She was very capable, though Jill did wish she wouldn't keep on clicking her tongue and saying things like "Oh la, la! Ups-a-daisy" and "There's a duck" and "Now we'll be all right, my poppet". She filled a giant foot-bath with hot water and helped Jill into it. If you can swim (as Jill could) a giant bath is a lovely thing. And giant towels, though a bit rough and coarse, are lovely too, because there are acres of them. In fact you don't need to dry at all, you just roll about on them in front of the fire and enjoy yourself. And when that was over, clean, fresh, warmed clothes were put on Jill: very splendid clothes and a little too big for her, but clearly made for humans not giantesses. "I suppose if that woman in the green kirtle comes here, they must be used to guests of our size," thought Jill.

She soon saw that she was right about this, for a table and chair of the right height for an ordinary grown-up human were placed for her, and the knives and forks and spoons were the proper size too. It was delightful to sit down, feeling warm and clean at last. Her feet were still bare and it was lovely to tread on the giant carpet. She sank in it well over her ankles and it was just the thing for sore feet. The meal – which I suppose we must call dinner, though it was nearer tea time – was cock-a-leekie soup, and hot roast turkey, and a steamed pudding, and roast chestnuts, and as much fruit as you could eat.

The only annoying thing was that the Nurse kept coming in and out, and every time she came in, she brought a gigantic toy with her – a huge doll, bigger than Jill herself, a wooden horse on wheels, about the size of an elephant, a drum that looked like a young gasometer, and a woolly lamb. They were crude, badly made things, painted in very bright colours, and Jill hated the sight of them. She kept on telling the Nurse she didn't want them, but the Nurse said:

"Tut-tut-tut-tut. You'll want 'em all right when you've had a bit of a rest, I know! Te-he-he! Beddy bye, now. A precious poppet!"

The bed was not a giant bed but only a big four-poster, like what you might see in an old-fashioned hotel; and very small it looked in that enormous room. She was very glad to tumble into it.

"Is it still snowing, Nurse?" she asked sleepily.

"No. Raining now, ducky!" said the giantess. "Rain'll wash away all the nasty snow. Precious poppet will be able to go out and play tomorrow!" And she tucked Jill up and said good night.

I know nothing so disagreeable as being kissed by a

giantess. Jill thought the same, but was asleep in five minutes.

The rain fell steadily all the evening and all the night, dashing against the windows of the castle, and Jill never heard it but slept deeply, past supper time and past midnight. And then came the deadest hour of the night and nothing stirred but mice in the house of the giants. At that hour there came to Jill a dream. It seemed to her that she awoke in the same room and saw the fire, sunk low and red, and in the firelight the great wooden horse. And the horse came of its own will, rolling on its wheels across the carpet, and stood at her head. And now it was no longer a horse, but a lion as big as the horse. And then it was not a toy lion, but a real lion, The Real Lion, just as she had seen him on the mountain beyond the world's end. And a smell of all sweet-smelling things there are filled the room. But there was some trouble in Jill's mind, though she could not think what it was, and the tears streamed down her face and wet the pillow. The Lion told her to repeat the signs, and she found that she had forgotten them all. At that, a great horror came over her. And Aslan took her up in his jaws (she could feel his lips and his breath but not his teeth) and carried her to the window and made her look out. The moon shone bright; and written in great letters across the world or the sky (she did not know which) were the words UNDER ME. After that, the dream faded away, and when she woke, very late next morning, she did not remember that she had dreamed at all.

She was up and dressed and had finished breakfast in front of the fire when the Nurse opened the door and said: "Here's pretty poppet's little friends come to play with her."

In came Scrubb and the Marsh-wiggle.

"Hullo! Good morning," said Jill. "Isn't this fun? I've

slept about fifteen hours, I believe. I do feel better, don't you?"

"*I* do," said Scrubb, "but Puddleglum says he has a headache. Hullo! – your window has a window seat. If we got up on that, we could see out." And at once they all did so: and at the first glance Jill said, "Oh, how perfectly dreadful!"

The sun was shining and, except for a few drifts, the snow had been almost completely washed away by the rain. Down below them, spread out like a map, lay the flat hill-top which they had struggled over yesterday afternoon; seen from the castle, it could not be mistaken for anything but the ruins of a gigantic city. It had been flat, as Jill now saw, because it was still, on the whole, paved, though in places the pavement was broken. The criss-cross banks were what was left of the walls of huge buildings which might once have been giants' palaces and temples. One bit of wall, about five hundred feet high, was still standing; it was that which she had thought was a cliff. The things that had looked like factory chimneys were enormous pillars, broken off at unequal heights; their fragments lay at their bases like felled trees of monstrous stone. The ledges which they had climbed down on the north side of the hill – and also, no doubt the other ledges which they had climbed up on the south side – were the remaining steps of giant stairs. To crown all, in large, dark lettering across the centre of the pavement, ran the words UNDER ME.

The three travellers looked at each other in dismay, and, after a short whistle, Scrubb said what they were all thinking, "The second and third signs muffed." And at that moment Jill's dream rushed back into her mind.

"It's my fault," she said in despairing tones. "I – I'd given up repeating the signs every night. If I'd been thinking about them I could have seen it was the city, even *in* all that snow."

"I'm worse," said Puddleglum. "I *did* see, or nearly. I thought it looked uncommonly like a ruined city."

"You're the only one who isn't to blame," said Scrubb. "You *did* try to make us stop."

"Didn't try hard enough, though," said the Marsh-wiggle. "And I'd no call to be trying. I ought to have done it. As if I couldn't have stopped you two with one hand each!"

"The truth is," said Scrubb, "we were so jolly keen on getting to this place that we weren't bothering about anything else. At least I know I was. Ever since we met that woman with the knight who didn't talk, we've been thinking of nothing else. We'd nearly forgotten about Prince Rilian."

"I shouldn't wonder," said Puddleglum, "if that wasn't exactly what she intended."

"What I don't quite understand," said Jill, "is how we didn't see the lettering? Or could it have come there since last night. Could he – Aslan – have put it there in the night? I had such a queer dream." And she told them all about it.

"Why, you chump!" said Scrubb. "We did see it. We got into the lettering. Don't you see? We got into the letter E in ME. That was your sunk lane. We walked along the bottom stroke of the E, due north – turned to our right along the upright – came to another turn to the right – that's the middle stroke – and then went on to the top left-hand corner, or (if you like) the north-eastern corner of the letter, and came back. Like the bally idiots we are." He kicked the window seat savagely, and went on, "So it's no good, Pole. I know what you were thinking because I was thinking the same. You were thinking how nice it would have been if Aslan hadn't put the instructions on the stones of the ruined city till after we'd passed it. And then it would have been his fault, not ours. So likely, isn't it? No. We must just own up. We've only four signs to go by, and we've muffed the first three."

"You mean I have," said Jill. "It's quite true. I've spoiled everything ever since you brought me here. All the same – I'm frightfully sorry and all that – all the same, what *are* the instructions? UNDER ME doesn't seem to make much sense."

"Yes it does, though," said Puddleglum. "It means we've got to look for the Prince under that city."

"But how can we?" asked Jill.

"That's the question," said Puddleglum, rubbing his big, frog-like hands together. "How can we *now*? No doubt, if we'd had our minds on our job when we were at the Ruinous City, we'd have been shown how – found a little door, or a cave, or a tunnel, met someone to help us. Might have been (you never know) Aslan himself. We'd have got down under those paving-stones somehow or other. Aslan's instructions always work: there are no exceptions. But how to do it *now* – that's another matter."

"Well, we shall just have to go back, I suppose," said Jill.

"Easy, isn't it?" said Puddleglum. "We might try opening that door to begin with." And they all looked at the door and saw that none of them could reach the handle, and that almost certainly no one could turn it if they did.

"Do you think they won't let us out if we ask?" said Jill. And nobody said, but everyone thought, "Supposing they don't."

It was not a pleasant idea. Puddleglum was dead

against any idea of telling the giants their real business and simply asking to be let out; and of course the children couldn't tell without his permission, because they had promised. And all three felt pretty sure that there would be no chance of escaping from the castle by night. Once they were in their rooms with the doors shut, they would be prisoners till morning. They might, of course, ask to have their doors left open, but that would rouse suspicions.

"Our only chance," said Scrubb, "is to try to sneak away by daylight. Mightn't there be an hour in the afternoon when most of the giants are asleep? – and if we could steal down into the kitchen, mightn't there be a back door open?"

"It's hardly what I call a Chance," said the Marsh-wiggle. "But it's all the chance we're likely to get." As a matter of fact, Scrubb's plan was not quite so hopeless as you might think. If you want to get out of a house without being seen, the middle of the afternoon is in some ways a better time to try it than the middle of the night. Doors and windows are more likely to be open; and if you *are* caught, you can always pretend you weren't meaning to go far and had no particular plans. (It is very hard to make either giants or grown-ups believe this if you're found climbing out of a bedroom window at one o'clock in the morning.)

"We must put them off their guard, though," said Scrubb. "We must pretend we love being here and are longing for this Autumn Feast."

"That's tomorrow night," said Puddleglum. "I heard one of them say so."

"I see," said Jill. "We must pretend to be awfully excited about it, and keep on asking questions. They think we're absolute infants anyway, which will make it easier."

"Gay," said Puddleglum with a deep sigh. "That's what we've got to be. Gay. As if we hadn't a care in the world. Frolicsome. You two youngsters haven't always got very high spirits, I've noticed. You must watch me, and do as I do. I'll be gay. Like this" – and he assumed a ghastly grin. "And frolicsome" – here he cut a most mournful caper. "You'll soon get into it, if you keep your eyes on me. They think I'm a funny fellow already, you see. I dare say you two thought I was a trifle tipsy last night, but I do assure you it was – well, most of it was – put on. I had an idea it would come in useful, somehow."

The children, when they talked over their adventures afterwards, could never feel sure whether this last statement was quite strictly true; but they were sure that Puddleglum thought it was true when he made it.

"All right. Gay's the word," said Scrubb. "Now, if we could only get someone to open this door. While we're fooling about and being gay, we've got to find out all we can about this castle."

Luckily, at that very moment the door opened, and the giant Nurse bustled in saying, "Now, my poppets. Like to come and see the King and all the court setting out on the hunting? Such a pretty sight!"

They lost no time in rushing out past her and climbing down the first staircase they came to. The noise of hounds and horns and giant voices guided them, so that in a few minutes they reached the courtyard. The giants were all on foot, for there are no giant horses in that part of the world, and the giants' hunting is done on foot; like beagling in England. The hounds were also of normal size. When Jill saw that there were no horses she was at first dreadfully disappointed, for she felt sure that the great fat Queen would never go after hounds on foot; and it would never do to have her about the house all day. But then she saw the Queen in a kind of litter supported on the shoulders of six young giants. The silly old creature was all got up in green and had a horn at her side.

Twenty or thirty giants, including the King, were assembled, ready for the sport, all talking and laughing fit to deafen you: and down below, nearer Jill's level, there were wagging tails, and barking, and loose, slobbery mouths and noses of dogs thrust into your hand. Puddleglum was just beginning to strike what he thought a gay and gamesome attitude (which might have spoiled everything if it had been noticed) when Jill put on her most attractively childish smile, rushed across to the Queen's litter and shouted up to the Queen.

"Oh, please! You're not going *away*, are you? You will come back?"

"Yes, my dear," said the Queen. "I'll be back tonight."

"Oh, *good*. How lovely!" said Jill. "And we *may* come to the feast tomorrow night, mayn't we? We're so longing for tomorrow night! And we do love being here. And while you're out, we may run over the whole castle and see everything, mayn't we? Do say yes."

The Queen did say yes, but the laughter of all the courtiers nearly drowned her voice.

CHAPTER NINE

HOW THEY DISCOVERED SOMETHING WORTH KNOWING

THE others admitted afterwards that Jill had been wonderful that day. As soon as the King and the rest of the hunting party had set off, she began making a tour of the whole castle and asking questions, but all in such an innocent, babyish way that no one could suspect her of any secret design. Though her tongue was never still, you could hardly say she talked: she *prattled* and giggled. She made love to everyone – the grooms, the porters, the housemaids, the ladies-in-waiting, and the elderly giant lords whose hunting days were past. She submitted to being kissed and pawed about by any number of giantesses, many of whom seemed sorry for her and called her "a poor little thing" though none of them explained why. She made especial friends with the cook and discovered the all-important fact there was a scullery door which let you out through the outer wall, so that you did not have to cross the courtyard or pass the great gatehouse. In the kitchen she pretended to be greedy, and ate all sorts of scraps which the cook and scullions delighted to give her. But upstairs among the ladies she asked questions about how she would be dressed for the great feast, and how long she would be allowed to sit up, and whether she would dance with some very, very small giant. And then (it made her hot all over when she remembered it afterwards) she would put her head on one side in an idiotic fashion which grown-ups, giant and otherwise, thought very fetching, and shake her curls, and fidget, and say, "Oh, I do wish it was tomorrow night, don't you? Do you think the time will go quickly till then?" And all the giantesses said she was a perfect little darling; and some of them dabbed their eyes with enormous handkerchiefs as if they were going to cry.

"They're dear little things at that age," said one giantess to another. "It seems almost a pity . . ."

Scrubb and Puddleglum both did their best, but girls do that kind of thing better than boys. Even boys do it better than Marsh-wiggles.

At lunchtime something happened which made all three of them more anxious than ever to leave the castle of the Gentle Giants. They had lunch in the great hall at a little table of their own, near the fireplace. At a bigger table, about twenty yards away, half a dozen old giants were lunching. Their conversation was so noisy, and so high up in the air, that the children soon took no more notice of it than you would of hooters outside the window or traffic noises in the street. They were eating cold venison, a kind of food which Jill had never tasted before, and she was liking it.

Suddenly Puddleglum turned to them, and his face had gone so pale that you could see the paleness under the natural muddiness of his complexion. He said:

"Don't eat another bite."

"What's wrong?" asked the other two in a whisper.

"Didn't you hear what those giants were saying? 'That's a nice tender haunch of venison,' said one of them. 'Then that stag was a liar,' said another. 'Why?' said the first one. 'Oh,' said the other. 'They say that when he was caught he said, Don't kill me, I'm tough. You won't like me.'" For a moment Jill did not realize the full meaning of this. But she did when Scrubb's eyes opened wide with horror and he said:

"So we've been eating a *Talking* stag."

This discovery didn't have exactly the same effect on all of them. Jill, who was new to that world, was sorry for the poor stag and thought it rotten of the giants to have killed him. Scrubb, who had been in that world before and had at least one Talking beast as his dear friend, felt horrified; as you might feel about a murder. But Puddleglum, who was Narnian born, was sick and faint, and felt as you would feel if you found you had eaten a baby.

"We've brought the anger of Aslan on us," he said. "That's what comes of not attending to the signs. We're under a curse, I expect. If it was allowed, it would be the best thing we could do, to take these knives and drive them into our own hearts."

And gradually even Jill came to see it from his point of view. At any rate, none of them wanted any more lunch. And as soon as they thought it safe they crept quietly out of the hall.

It was now drawing near to that time of the day on which their hopes of escape depended, and all became nervous. They hung about in passages and waited for things to become quiet. The giants in the hall sat on a dreadfully long time after the meal was over. The bald one was telling a story. When that was over, the three travellers dawdled down to the kitchen. But there were still plenty of giants there, or at least in the scullery, washing up and putting things away. It was agonizing, waiting till these finished their jobs and, one by one, wiped their hands and went away. At last only one old giantess was left in the room. She pottered about, and pottered about, and at last the three travellers realized with horror that she did not intend to go away at all.

"Well, dearies," she said to them. "That job's about through. Let's put the kettle there. That'll make a nice cup of tea presently. Now I can have a little bit of a rest. Just look into the scullery, like good poppets, and tell me if the back door is open."

"Yes, it is," said Scrubb.

"That's right. I always leave it open so as Puss can get in and out, the poor thing."

Then she sat down on one chair and put her feet up on another.

"I don't know as I mightn't have forty winks," said the giantess. "If only that blamey hunting party doesn't come back too soon."

All their spirits leaped up when she mentioned forty winks, and flopped down again when she mentioned the return of the hunting party.

"When do they usually come back?" asked Jill.

"You never can tell," said the giantess. "But there; go and be quiet for a bit, my dearies."

They retreated to the far end of the kitchen, and would have slipped out into the scullery there and then if the giantess had not sat up, opened her eyes, and brushed away a fly. "Don't try it till we're sure she's really asleep," whispered Scrubb. "Or it'll spoil everything." So they all huddled at the kitchen end, waiting and watching. The thought that the hunters might come back at any moment was terrible. And the giantess was fidgety. Whenever they thought she had really gone to sleep, she moved.

"I can't bear this," thought Jill. To distract her mind, she began looking about her. Just in front of her was a clean wide table with two clean pie-dishes on it, and an open book. They were giant pie-dishes of course. Jill thought that she could lie down just comfortably in one of them. Then she climbed up on the bench beside the table to look at the book. She read:

MALLARD. This delicious bird can be cooked in a variety of ways.

"It's a cookery book," thought Jill without much interest, and glanced over her shoulder. The giantess's eyes were shut but she didn't look as if she were properly asleep. Jill glanced back at the book. It was arranged alphabetically: and at the very next entry her heart seemed to stop beating; It ran –

> MAN. This elegant little biped has long been valued as a delicacy. It forms a traditional part of the Autumn Feast, and is served between the fish and the joint. Each Man –

but she could not bear to read any more. She turned round. The giantess had wakened up and was having a fit of coughing. Jill nudged the other two and pointed to the book. They also mounted the bench and bent over the huge pages. Scrubb was still reading about how to cook Men when Puddleglum pointed to the next entry below it. It was like this:

> MARSH-WIGGLE. Some authorities reject this animal altogether as unfit for giants' consumption because of its stringy consistency and muddy flavour. The flavour can, however, be greatly reduced if –

Jill touched his feet, and Scrubb's, gently. All three looked back at the giantess. Her mouth was slightly open and from her nose there came a sound which at that moment was more welcome to them than any music; she snored. And now it was a question of tip-toe work, not daring to go too fast, hardly daring to breathe, out through the scullery (giant sculleries smell horrid), out at last into the pale sunlight of a winter afternoon.

They were at the top of a rough little path which ran steeply down. And, thank heavens, on the right side of the castle; the City Ruinous was in sight. In a few minutes they were back on the broad, steep road which led down from the main gate of the castle. They were also in full view from every single window on that side. If it had been one, or two, or five windows there'd be a reasonable chance that no one might be looking out. But there were nearer fifty than five. They now realized, too, that the road on which they were, and indeed all the ground between them and the City Ruinous, didn't offer as much cover as would hide a fox; it was all coarse grass and pebbles and flat stones. To make matters worse, they were now in the clothes that the giants had provided for them last night: except

Puddleglum, whom nothing would fit. Jill wore a vivid green robe, rather too long for her, and over that a scarlet mantle fringed with white fur. Scrubb had scarlet stockings, blue tunic and cloak, a gold-hilted sword, and a feathered bonnet.

"Nice bits of colour, you two are," muttered Puddleglum. "Show up very prettily on a winter day. The worst archer in the world couldn't miss either of you if you were in range. And talking of archers, we'll be sorry not to have our own bows before long, I shouldn't wonder. Bit thin, too, those clothes of yours, are they?"

"Yes, I'm freezing already," said Jill.

A few minutes ago when they had been in the kitchen, she had thought that if only they could once get out of the castle, their escape would be almost complete. She now realized that the most dangerous part of it was still to come.

"Steady, steady," said Puddleglum. "Don't look back. Don't walk too quickly. Whatever you do, don't run. Look as if we were just taking a stroll, and then, if anyone sees us, he might, just possibly, not bother. The moment we look like people running away, we're done."

The distance to the City Ruinous seemed longer than Jill would have believed possible. But bit by bit they were covering it. Then came a noise. The other two gasped. Jill, who didn't know what it was, said, "What's that?"

"Hunting horn," whispered Scrubb.

"But don't run even now," said Puddleglum. "Not until I give the word."

This time Jill couldn't help glancing over her shoulder. There, about half a mile away, was the hunt returning from behind them on the left.

They walked on. Suddenly a great clamour of giant voices arose: then shouts and hollas.

"They've seen us. Run," said Puddleglum.

Jill gathered up her long skirts – horrible things for running in – and ran. There was no mistaking the danger now. She could hear the music of the hounds. She could hear the King's voice roaring out, "After them, after them, or we'll have no man-pies tomorrow."

She was last of the three now, cumbered with her dress, slipping on loose stones, her hair getting in her mouth, running-pains across her chest. The hounds were much nearer. Now she had to run uphill, up the stony slope which led to the lowest step of the giant stairway. She had no idea what they would do when they got there, or how they would be any better off even if they reached the top.

But she didn't think about that. She was like a hunted animal now; as long as the pack was after her, she must run till she dropped.

The Marsh-wiggle was ahead. As he came to the lowest

step he stopped, looked a little to his right, and all of a sudden darted into a little hole or crevice at the bottom of it. His long legs, disappearing into it, looked very like those of a spider. Scrubb hesitated and then vanished after him. Jill, breathless and reeling, came to the place about a minute later. It was an unattractive hole – a crack between the earth and the stone about three feet long and hardly more than a foot high. You had to fling yourself flat on your face and crawl in. You couldn't do it so very quickly either. She felt sure that a dog's teeth would close on her heel before she had got inside.

"Quick, quick. Stones. Fill up the opening," came Puddleglum's voice in the darkness beside her. It was pitch black in there, except for the grey light in the opening by which they had crawled in. The other two were working hard. She could see Scrubb's small hands and the Marsh-wiggle's big, frog-like hands black against the light, working desperately to pile up stones. Then she realized how important this was and began groping for large stones herself, and handing them to the others. Before the dogs were baying and yelping at the cave mouth, they had it pretty well filled; and now, of course, there was no light at all.

"Farther in, quick," said Puddleglum's voice.

"Let's all hold hands," said Jill.

"Good idea," said Scrubb. But it took them quite a long time to find one another's hands in the darkness. The dogs were sniffing at the other side of the barrier now.

"Try if we can stand up," suggested Scrubb. They did and found that they could. Then, Puddleglum holding out a hand behind him to Scrubb, and Scrubb holding a hand out behind him to Jill (who wished very much that she was the middle one of the party and not the last), they began groping with their feet and stumbling forwards into the blackness. It was all loose stones underfoot. Then Puddleglum came up to a wall of rock. They turned a little to their right and went on. There were a good many more twists and turns. Jill had now no sense of direction at all, and no idea where the mouth of the cave lay.

"The question is," came Puddleglum's voice out of the darkness ahead, "whether, taking one thing with another, it wouldn't be better to go back (if we *can*) and give the giants a treat at that feast of theirs, instead of losing our way in the guts of a hill where, ten to one, there's dragons and deep holes and gases and water and – Ow! Let go! Save yourselves. I'm –"

After that all happened quickly. There was a wild cry, a swishing, dusty, gravelly noise, a rattle of stones, and Jill found herself sliding, sliding, hopelessly sliding, and sliding quicker every moment down a slope that grew steeper every moment. It was not a smooth, firm slope, but a slope of small stones and rubbish. Even if you could have stood up, it would have been no use. Any bit of that slope you had put your foot on would have slid away from under you and carried you down with it. But Jill was more lying than standing. And the farther they all slid, the more they disturbed all the stones and earth, so that the general downward rush of everything (including themselves) got faster and louder and dustier and dirtier. From the sharp cries and swearing of the other two, Jill got the idea that many of the stones which she was dislodging were hitting Scrubb and Puddleglum pretty hard. And now she was going at a furious rate and felt sure she would be broken to bits at the bottom.

Yet somehow they weren't. They were a mass of bruises, and the wet sticky stuff on her face appeared to be blood. And such a mass of loose earth, shingle, and larger stones was piled up round her (and partly over her) that she couldn't get up. The darkness was so complete that it made no difference at all whether you had your eyes open or shut. There was no noise. And that was the very worst moment Jill had ever known in her life. Supposing she was alone: supposing the others . . . Then she heard movements around her. And presently all three, in shaken voices, were explaining that none of them seemed to have any broken bones.

"We can never get up that again," said Scrubb's voice.

"And have you noticed how warm it is?" said the voice of Puddleglum. "That means we're a long way down. Might be nearly a mile."

No one said anything. Some time later Puddleglum added:

"My tinder-box has gone."

After another long pause Jill said, "I'm terribly thirsty."

No one suggested doing anything. There was so obviously nothing to be done. For the moment, they did not feel it quite so badly as one might have expected; that was because they were so tired.

Long, long afterwards, without the slightest warning, an utterly strange voice spoke. They knew at once that it was not the one voice in the whole world for which each had secretly been hoping; the voice of Aslan. It was a dark, flat voice – almost, if you know what that means, a pitch-black voice. It said:

"What make you here, creatures of the Overworld?"

CHAPTER TEN

TRAVELS WITHOUT THE SUN

"WHO's there?" shouted the three travellers.

"I am the Warden of the Marches of Underland, and with me stand a hundred Earthmen in arms," came the reply. "Tell me quickly who you are and what is your errand in the Deep Realm?"

"We fell down by accident," said Puddleglum, truthfully enough.

"Many fall down, and few return to the sunlit lands," said the voice. "Make ready now to come with me to the Queen of the Deep Realm."

"What does she want with us?" asked Scrubb cautiously.

"I do not know," said the voice. "Her will is not to be questioned but obeyed."

While he said these words there was a noise like a soft explosion and immediately a cold light, grey with a little blue in it, flooded the cavern. All hope that the speaker had been idly boasting when he spoke of his hundred armed followers died at once. Jill found herself blinking and staring at a dense crowd. They were of all sizes, from little gnomes barely a foot high to stately figures taller than men. All carried three-pronged spears in their hands, and all were dreadfully pale, and all stood as still as statues. Apart from that, they were very different; some had tails and others not, some wore great beards and others had very round, smooth faces, big as pumpkins. There were long, pointed noses, and long, soft noses like small trunks, and great blobby noses. Several had single horns in the middle of their foreheads. But in one respect they were all alike: every face in the whole hundred was as sad as a face could be. They were so sad that, after the first glance, Jill almost forgot to be afraid of them. She felt she would like to cheer them up.

"Well!" said Puddleglum, rubbing his hands. "This is

just what I needed. If these chaps don't teach me to take a serious view of life, I don't know what will. Look at that fellow with the walrus moustache – or that one with the –"

"Get up," said the leader of the Earthmen.

There was nothing else to be done. The three travellers scrambled to their feet and joined hands. One wanted the touch of a friend's hand at a moment like that. And the Earthmen came all round them, padding on large, soft feet, on which some had ten toes, some twelve, and others none.

"March," said the Warden: and march they did.

The cold light came from a large ball on the top of a long pole, and the tallest of the gnomes carried this at the head of the procession. By its cheerless rays they could see that they were in a natural cavern; the walls and roof were knobbed, twisted, and gashed into a thousand fantastic shapes, and the stony floor sloped downward as they proceeded. It was worse for Jill than for the others, because she hated dark, underground places. And when, as they went on, the cave got lower and narrower, and when, at last, the light-bearer stood aside, and the gnomes, one by one, stooped down (all except the very smallest ones) and stepped into a little dark crack and disappeared, she felt she could bear it no longer.

"I can't go in there, I can't! I can't! I won't," she panted. The Earthmen said nothing but they all lowered their spears and pointed them at her.

"Steady, Pole," said Puddleglum. "Those big fellows wouldn't be crawling in there if it didn't get wider later on. And there's one thing about this underground work, we shan't get any rain."

"Oh, you don't understand. I can't," wailed Jill.

"Think how *I* felt on that cliff, Pole," said Scrubb. "You go first, Puddleglum, and I'll come after her."

"That's right," said the Marsh-wiggle, getting down on his hands and knees. "You keep a grip of my heels, Pole, and Scrubb will hold on to yours. Then we'll all be comfortable."

"Comfortable!" said Jill. But she got down and they crawled in on their elbows. It was a nasty place. You had to go flat on your face for what seemed like half an hour, though it may really have been only five minutes. It was hot. Jill felt she was being smothered. But at last a dim light showed ahead, the tunnel grew wider and higher, and they came out, hot, dirty, and shaken, into a cave so large that it scarcely seemed like a cave at all.

It was full of a dim, drowsy radiance, so that here they had no need of the Earthmen's strange lantern. The floor was soft with some kind of moss and out of this grew many strange shapes, branched and tall like trees, but flabby like mushrooms. They stood too far apart to make a forest; it was more like a park. The light (a greenish grey) seemed to come both from them and from the moss, and it was not strong enough to reach the roof of the cave, which must have been a long way overhead. Across the mild, soft, sleepy place they were now made to march. It was very sad, but with a quiet sort of sadness like soft music.

Here they passed dozens of strange animals lying on the turf, either dead or asleep, Jill could not tell which. These were mostly of a dragonish or bat-like sort; Puddleglum did not know what any of them were.

"Do they grow here?" Scrubb asked the Warden. He seemed very surprised at being spoken to, but replied, "No. They are all beasts that have found their way down by chasms and caves, out of Overland into the Deep Realm. Many come down, and few return to the sunlit lands. It is said that they will all wake at the end of the world."

His mouth shut like a box when he had said this, and in the great silence of that cave the children felt that they would not dare to speak again. The bare feet of the gnomes, padding on the deep moss, made no sound. There was no wind, there were no birds, there was no sound of water. There was no sound of breathing from the strange beasts.

When they had walked for several miles, they came to a wall of rock, and in it a low archway leading into another cavern. It was not, however, so bad as the last entrance and Jill could go through it without bending her head. It brought them into a smaller cave, long and narrow, about the shape and size of a cathedral. And here, filling almost the whole length of it, lay an enormous man fast asleep. He was far bigger than any of the giants, and his face was not like a giant's, but noble and beautiful. His breast rose and fell gently under the snowy beard which covered him to the waist. A pure, silver light (no one saw where it came from) rested upon him.

"Who's that?" asked Puddleglum. And it was so long since anyone had spoken, that Jill wondered how he had the nerve.

"That is old Father Time, who once was a King in Overland," said the Warden. "And now he has sunk down into the Deep Realm and lies dreaming of all the things that are done in the upper world. Many sink down, and few return to the sunlit lands. They say he will wake at the end of the world."

And out of that cave they passed into another, and then into another and another, and so on till Jill lost count, but always they were going downhill and each cave was lower than the last, till the very thought of the weight and depth of earth above you was suffocating. At last they came to a place where the Warden commanded his cheerless lantern to be lit again. Then they passed into a cave so wide and dark that they could see nothing of it except that right in front of them a strip of pale sand ran down into still water. And there, beside a little jetty, lay a ship without mast or sail but with many oars. They were made to go on board her and led forward to the bows where there was a clear space in front of the rowers' benches and a seat running round inside the bulwarks.

"One thing I'd like to know," said Puddleglum, "is whether anyone from our world – from up-a-top, I mean – has ever done this trip before?"

"Many have taken ship at the pale beaches," replied the Warden, "and –"

"Yes, I know," interrupted Puddleglum. "*And few return to the sunlit lands*. You needn't say it again. You *are* a chap of one idea, aren't you?"

The children huddled close together on each side of Puddleglum. They had thought him a wet blanket while they were still above ground, but down here he seemed the only comforting thing they had. Then the pale lantern was hung up amidships, the Earthmen sat to the oars, and the ship began to move. The lantern cast its light only a very

short way. Looking ahead, they could see nothing but smooth, dark water, fading into absolute blackness.

"Oh, whatever will become of us?" said Jill despairingly.

"Now don't you let your spirits down, Pole," said the Marsh-wiggle. "There's one thing you've got to remember. We're back on the right lines. We were to go under the Ruined City, and we *are* under it. We're following the instructions again."

Presently they were given food – flat, flabby cakes of some sort which had hardly any taste. And after that, they gradually fell asleep. But when they woke, everything was just the same; the gnomes still rowing, the ship still gliding on, still dead blackness ahead. How often they woke and slept and ate and slept again, none of them could ever remember. And the worst thing about it was that you began to feel as if you had always lived on that ship, in that darkness, and to wonder whether sun and blue skies and wind and birds had not been only a dream.

They had almost given up hoping or being afraid about anything when at last they saw lights ahead: dreary lights, like that of their own lantern. Then, quite suddenly, one of these lights came close and they saw that they were passing another ship. After that they met several ships. Then, staring till their eyes hurt, they saw that some of the lights ahead were shining on what looked like wharfs, walls, towers, and moving crowds. But still there was hardly any noise.

"By Jove," said Scrubb. "A city!" and soon they all saw that he was right.

But it was a queer city. The lights were so few and far apart that they would hardly have done for scattered cottages in our world. But the little bits of the place which you could see by the lights were like glimpses of a great seaport. You could make out in one place a whole crowd of ships loading or unloading; in another, bales of stuff and warehouses; in a third, walls and pillars that suggested great palaces or temples; and always, wherever the light fell, endless crowds – hundreds of Earthmen, jostling one another as they padded softly about their business in narrow streets, broad squares, or up great flights of steps. Their continued movement made a sort of soft, murmuring noise as the ship drew nearer and nearer; but there was not a song or a shout or a bell or the rattle of a wheel anywhere. The City was as quiet, and nearly as dark, as the inside of an ant-hill.

At last their ship was brought alongside a quay and made fast. The three travellers were taken ashore and marched up into the City. Crowds of Earthmen, no two alike, rubbed shoulders with them in the crowded streets, and the sad light fell on many sad and grotesque faces. But no one showed any interest in the strangers. Every gnome seemed to be as busy as it was sad, though Jill never found what they were so busy about. But the endless moving, shoving, hurrying, and the soft pad-pad-pad went on.

At last they came to what appeared to be a great castle, though few of the windows in it were lighted. Here they were taken in and made to cross a courtyard, and to climb many staircases. This brought them in the end to a great murkily lit room. But in one corner of it – oh joy! – there was an archway filled with a quite different sort of light; the honest, yellowish, warm light of such a lamp as humans use. What showed by this light inside the archway was the foot of a staircase which wound upward between walls of stone. The light seemed to come from the top. Two Earthmen stood one on each side of the arch like sentries, or footmen.

The Warden went up to these two, and said, as if it were a password:

"Many sink down to the Underworld."

"And few return to the sunlit lands," they answered, as if it were the countersign. Then all three put their heads together and talked. At last one of the two gnomes-in-waiting said, "I tell you the Queen's grace is gone from hence on her great affair. We had best keep these top dwellers in strait prison till her homecoming. Few return to the sunlit lands."

At that moment the conversation was interrupted by what seemed to Jill the most delightful noise in the world. It came from above, from the top of the staircase; and it was a clear, ringing, perfectly human voice, the voice of a young man.

"What coil are you keeping down there, Mullugutherum?" it shouted. "Overworlders, ha! Bring them up to me, and that presently."

"Please it your Highness to remember," began Mullugutherum, but the voice cut him short.

"It pleases my Highness principally to be obeyed, old mutterer. Bring them up," it called.

Mullugutherum shook his head, motioned to the travellers to follow and began going up the staircase. At every step the light increased. There were rich tapestries hanging on the walls. The lamplight shone golden through thin curtains at the staircase-head. The Earthmen parted the curtains and stood aside. The three passed in. They were in a beautiful room, richly tapestried, with a bright fire on a clean hearth, and red wine and cut glass sparkling on the table. A young man with fair hair rose to greet them. He was handsome and looked both bold and kind, though there was something about his face that didn't seem quite right. He was dressed in black and altogether looked a little bit like Hamlet.

"Welcome, Overworlders," he cried. "But stay a moment! I cry you mercy! I have seen you two fair children, and this, your strange governor, before. Was it not you three that met me by the bridge on the borders of Ettinsmoor when I rode there by my Lady's side?"

"Oh . . . you were the black knight who never spoke?" exclaimed Jill.

"And was that lady the Queen of Underland?" asked Puddleglum, in no very friendly voice. And Scrubb, who was thinking the same, burst out, "Because if it was, I think she was jolly mean to send us off to a castle of giants who intended to eat us. What harm had we ever done her, I should like to know?"

"How?" said the Black Knight with a frown. "If you were not so young a warrior, Boy, you and I must have fought to the death on this quarrel. I can hear no words against my Lady's honour. But of this you may be assured, that whatever she said to you, she said of a good intent. You do not know her. She is a nosegay of all virtues, as truth, mercy, constancy, gentleness, courage, and the rest. I say what I know. Her kindness to me alone, who can in no way reward her, would make an admirable history. But you shall know and love her hereafter. Meanwhile, what is your errand in the Deep Lands?"

And before Puddleglum could stop her, Jill blurted out, "Please we are trying to find Prince Rilian of Narnia." And then she realized what a frightful risk she had taken; these people might be enemies. But the Knight showed no interest.

"Rilian? Narnia?" he said carelessly. "Narnia? What land is that? I have never heard the name. It must be a thousand leagues from those parts of the Overworld that I know. But it was a strange fantasy that brought you seeking this – how do you call him? – Billian? Trillian? in my Lady's realm. Indeed, to my certain knowledge, there is no such man here." He laughed very loudly at this, and Jill thought to herself, "I wonder is *that* what's wrong with his face? Is he a bit silly?"

"We had been told to look for a message on the stones of the City Ruinous," said Scrubb. "And we saw the words UNDER ME."

The Knight laughed even more heartily than before. "You were the more deceived," he said. "Those words meant nothing to your purpose. Had you but asked my Lady, she could have given you better counsel. For those words are all that is left of a longer script, which in ancient times, as she well remembers, expressed this verse:

> Though under Earth and throneless now I be,
> Yet, while I lived, all Earth was under me.

From which it is plain that some great king of the ancient giants, who lies buried there, caused this boast to be cut in the stone over his sepulchre; though the breaking up of some stones, and the carrying away of others for new buildings, and the filling up of the cuts with rubble, has left only two words that can still be read. Is it not the merriest jest in the world that you should have thought they were written to you?"

This was like cold water down the back to Scrubb and

Jill; for it seemed to them very likely that the words had nothing to do with their quest at all, and that they had been taken in by a mere accident.

"Don't you mind him," said Puddleglum. "There *are* no accidents. Our guide is Aslan; and he was there when the giant King caused the letters to be cut, and he knew already all things that would come of them; including *this*."

"This guide of yours must be a long liver, friend," said the Knight with another of his laughs.

Jill began to find them a little irritating.

"And it seems to me, Sir," answered Puddleglum, "that this Lady of yours must be a long liver too, if she remembers the verse as it was when they first cut it."

"Very shrewd, Frog-face," said the Knight, clapping Puddleglum on the shoulder and laughing again. "And you have hit the truth. She is of divine race, and knows neither age nor death. I am the more thankful to her for all her infinite bounty to such a poor mortal wretch as I. For you must know, Sirs, I am a man under most strange afflictions, and none but the Queen's grace would have had patience with me. Patience, said I? But it goes far beyond that. She has promised me a great kingdom in Overland, and, when I am king, her own most gracious hand in marriage. But the tale is too long for you to hear fasting and standing. Hi there, some of you! Bring wine and Updwellers' food for my guests. Please you, be seated, gentlemen. Little maiden, sit in this chair. You shall hear it all."

CHAPTER ELEVEN

IN THE DARK CASTLE

When the meal (which was pigeon pie, cold ham, salad, and cakes) had been brought, and all had drawn their chairs up to the table and begun, the Knight continued:

"You must understand, friends, that I know nothing of who I was and whence I came into this Dark World. I remember no time when I was not dwelling, as now, at the court of this all but heavenly Queen; but my thought is that she saved me from some evil enchantment and brought me hither of her exceeding bounty. (Honest Frog-foot, your cup is empty. Suffer me to refill it.) And this seems to me the likelier because even now I am bound by a spell, from which my Lady alone can free me. Every night there comes an hour when my mind is most horribly changed, and, after my mind, my body. For first I become furious and wild and would rush upon my dearest friends to kill them, if I were not bound. And soon after that, I turn into the likeness of a great serpent, hungry, fierce, and deadly. (Sir, be pleased to take another breast of pigeon, I entreat you.) So they tell me, and they certainly speak truth, for my Lady says the same. I myself know nothing of it, for when my hour is past I awake forgetful of all that vile fit and in my proper shape and sound mind – saving that I am somewhat wearied. (Little lady, eat one of these honey cakes, which are brought for me from some barbarous land in the far south of the world.) Now the Queen's majesty knows by her art that I shall be freed from this enchantment when once she has made me king of a land in the Overworld and set its crown upon my head. The land is already chosen and the very place of our breaking out. Her Earthmen have worked day and night digging a way beneath it, and have now gone so far and so high that they tunnel not a score of feet beneath the very grass on which the Updwellers of that country walk. It will be very soon now that those Uplanders' fate will come upon them. She herself is at the diggings tonight, and I expect a message to go to her. Then the thin roof of earth which still keeps me from my kingdom will be broken through, and with her to guide me and a thousand Earthmen at my back, I shall ride forth in arms, fall suddenly on our enemies, slay their chief men, cast down their strong places, and doubtless be their crowned king within four and twenty hours."

"It's a bit rough luck on *them*, isn't it?" said Scrubb.

"Thou art a lad of a wondrous, quick-working wit!" exclaimed the Knight. "For, on my honour, I had never thought of it so before. I see your meaning." He looked slightly, very slightly troubled for a moment or two; but his face soon cleared and he broke out, with another of his loud laughs, "But fie on gravity! Is it not the most comical and ridiculous thing in the world to think of them all going about their business and never dreaming that under their peaceful fields and floors, only a fathom down, there is a great army ready to break out upon them like a fountain! And they never to have suspected! Why, they themselves, when once the first smart of their defeat is over, can hardly choose but laugh at the thought!"

"I don't think it's funny at all," said Jill. "I think you'll be a wicked tyrant."

"What?" said the Knight, still laughing and patting her head in a quite infuriating fashion. "Is our little maid a deep politician? But never fear, sweetheart. In ruling that land, I shall do all by the counsel of my Lady, who will then be my Queen too. Her word shall be my law, even as my word will be law to the people we have conquered."

"Where I come from," said Jill, who was disliking him more every minute, "they don't think much of men who are bossed about by their wives."

"Shalt think otherwise when thou hast a man of thine own, I warrant you," said the Knight, apparently thinking this very funny. "But with my Lady, it is another matter. I am well content to live by her word, who has already saved me from a thousand dangers. No mother has taken pains more tenderly for her child, than the Queen's grace has for me. Why, look you, amid all her cares and business, she rideth out with me in the Overworld many a time and oft to accustom my eyes to the sunlight. And then I must go fully armed and with visor down, so that no man may see my face, and I must speak to no one. For she has found out by art magical that this would hinder my deliverance from the grievous enchantment I lie under. Is not that a lady worthy of a man's whole worship?"

"Sounds a very nice lady indeed," said Puddleglum in a voice which meant exactly the opposite.

They were thoroughly tired of the Knight's talk before they had finished supper. Puddleglum was thinking, "I wonder what game that witch is really playing with this young fool." Scrubb was thinking, "He's a great baby, really: tied to that woman's apron strings; he's a sap." And Jill was thinking, "He's the silliest, most conceited, selfish pig I've met for a long time." But when the meal was over, the Knight's mood had changed. There was no more laughter about him.

"Friends," he said, "my hour is now very near. I am ashamed that you should see me yet I dread being left alone. They will come in presently and bind me hand and foot to yonder chair. Alas, so it must be: for in my fury, they tell me, I would destroy all that I could reach."

"I say," said Scrubb, "I'm awfully sorry about your

enchantment of course, but what will those fellows do to *us* when they come to bind you? They talked of putting us in prison. And we don't like all those dark places very

much. We'd much rather stay here till you're . . . better . . . if we may."

"It is well thought of," said the Knight. "By custom none but the Queen herself remains with me in my evil hour. Such is her tender care for my honour that she would not willingly suffer any ears but her own to hear the words I utter in that frenzy. But I could not easily persuade my attendant gnomes that you should be left with me. And I think I hear their soft feet even now upon the stairs. Go through yonder door: it leads into my other apartments. And there, either await my coming when they have unbound me; or, if you will, return and sit with me in my ravings."

They followed his directions and passed out of the room by a door which they had not yet seen opened. It brought them, they were pleased to see, not into darkness but into a lighted corridor. They tried various doors and found (what they very badly needed) water for washing and even a looking glass. "He never offered us a wash before supper," said Jill, drying her face. "Selfish, self-centred pig."

"Are we going back to watch the enchantment, or shall we stay here?" said Scrubb.

"Stay here, I vote," said Jill. "I'd much rather not see it." But she felt a little inquisitive all the same.

"No, go back," said Puddleglum. "We may pick up some information, and we need all we can get. I am sure that Queen is a witch and an enemy. And those Earthmen would knock us on the head as soon as look at us. There's a stronger smell of danger and lies and magic and treason about this land than I've ever smelled before. We need to keep our eyes and ears open."

They went back down the corridor and gently pushed the door open. "It's all right," said Scrubb, meaning that there were no Earthmen about. Then they all came back into the room where they had supped.

The main door was now shut, concealing the curtain between which they had first entered. The Knight was seated in a curious silver chair, to which he was bound by his ankles, his knees, his elbows, his wrists, and his waist. There was sweat on his forehead and his face was filled with anguish.

"Come in, friends," he said, glancing quickly up. "The fit is not yet upon me. Make no noise, for I told that prying chamberlain that you were in bed. Now . . . I can feel it coming. Quick! Listen while I am master of myself. When the fit is upon me, it well may be that I shall beg and implore you, with entreaties and threatenings, to loosen my bonds. They say I do. I shall call upon you by all that is most dear and most dreadful. But do not listen to me. Harden your hearts and stop your ears. For while I am bound you are safe. But if once I were up and out of this chair, then first would come my fury, and after that" – he shuddered – "the change into a loathsome serpent."

"There's no fear of our loosing you," said Puddleglum. "We've no wish to meet wild men; or serpents either."

"I should think not," said Scrubb and Jill together.

"All the same," added Puddleglum in a whisper. "Don't let's be too sure. Let's be on our guard. We've muffed everything else, you know. He'll be cunning, I shouldn't wonder, once he gets started. Can we trust one another? Do we all promise that whatever he says we don't touch those cords? *Whatever* he says, mind you?"

"Rather!" said Scrubb.

"There's nothing in the world he can say or do that'll make me change my mind," said Jill.

"Hush! Something's happening," said Puddleglum.

The Knight was moaning. His face was as pale as putty, and he writhed in his bonds. And whether because she was sorry for him, or for some other reason, Jill thought that he looked a nicer sort of man than he had looked before.

"Ah," he groaned. "Enchantments, enchantments . . . the heavy, tangled, cold, clammy web of evil magic. Buried alive. Dragged down under the earth, down into the sooty blackness . . . how many years is it? . . . Have I lived ten years, or a thousand years, in the pit? Maggot-men all around me. Oh, have mercy. Let me out, let me go back. Let me feel the wind and see the sky . . . There used to be a little pool. When you looked down into it you could see all the trees growing upside-down in the water, all green, and below them, deep, very deep, the blue sky."

He had been speaking in a low voice; now he looked up, fixed his eyes upon them, and said loud and clear:

"Quick! I am sane now. Every night I am sane. If only I

could get out of this enchanted chair, it would last. I should be a man again. But every night they bind me, and so every night my chance is gone. But you are not enemies. I am not *your* prisoner. Quick! Cut these cords."

"Stand fast! Steady," said Puddleglum to the two children.

"I beseech you to hear me," said the Knight, forcing himself to speak calmly. "Have they told you that if I am released from this chair I shall kill you and become a serpent? I see by your faces that they have. It is a lie. It is at this hour that I am in my right mind: it is all the rest of the day that I am enchanted. You are not Earthmen nor witches. Why should you be on their side? Of your courtesy, cut my bonds."

"Steady! Steady! Steady!" said the three travellers to one another.

"Oh, you have hearts of stone," said the Knight. "Believe me, you look upon a wretch who has suffered almost more than any mortal can bear. What wrong have I ever done you, that you should side with my enemies to keep me in such miseries? And the minutes are slipping past. *Now* you can save me; when this hour has passed, I shall be witless again – the toy and lap-dog, nay, more likely the pawn and tool, of the most devilish sorceress that ever planned the woe of men. And this night, of all nights, when she is away! You take from me a chance that may never come again."

"This is dreadful. I do wish we'd stayed away till it was over," said Jill.

"Steady!" said Puddleglum.

The prisoner's voice was now rising into a shriek. "Let me go, I say. Give me my sword. My sword! Once I am free I shall take such revenge on Earthmen that Underland will talk of it for a thousand years!"

"Now the frenzy is beginning," said Scrubb. "I hope those knots are all right."

"Yes," said Puddleglum. "He'd have twice his natural strength if he got free now. And I'm not clever with my sword. He'd get us both, I shouldn't wonder; and then Pole on her own would be left to tackle the snake."

The prisoner was now so straining at his bonds that they cut into his wrists and ankles. "Beware," he said. "Beware. One night I *did* break them. But the witch was there that time. You will not have her to help you tonight. Free me now, and I am your friend. I'm your mortal enemy else."

"Cunning, isn't he?" said Puddleglum.

"Once and for all," said the prisoner, "I adjure you to set me free. By all fears and all loves, by the bright skies of Overland, by the great Lion, by Aslan himself, I charge you –"

"Oh!" cried the three travellers as though they had been hurt. "It's the sign," said Puddleglum. "It was the *words* of the sign," said Scrubb more cautiously. "Oh, what *are* we to do?" said Jill.

It was a dreadful question. What had been the use of promising one another that they would not on any account set the Knight free, if they were now to do so the first time he happened to call upon a name they really cared about? On the other hand, what had been the use of learning the signs if they weren't going to obey them? Yet could Aslan have really meant them to unbind anyone – even a lunatic – who asked it in his name? Could it be a mere accident? Or how if the Queen of the Underworld knew all about the signs and had made the Knight learn this name simply in order to entrap them? But then, supposing this was the real sign? . . . They had muffed three already; they daren't muff the fourth.

"Oh, if only we knew!" said Jill.

"I think we do know," said Puddleglum.

"Do you mean you think everything will come right if we do untie him?" said Scrubb.

"I don't know about that," said Puddleglum. "You see, Aslan didn't tell Pole what would happen. He only told her what to do. That fellow will be the death of us once he's up, I shouldn't wonder. But that doesn't let us off following the sign."

They all stood looking at one another with bright eyes. It was a sickening moment. "All right!" said Jill suddenly. "Let's get it over. Good-bye, everyone . . .!" They all shook hands. The Knight was screaming by now; there was foam on his cheeks.

"Come on, Scrubb," said Puddleglum. He and Scrubb drew their swords and went over to the captive.

"In the name of Aslan," they said and began methodically cutting the cords. The instant the prisoner was free, he crossed the room in a single bound, seized his own sword (which had been taken from him and laid on the table), and drew it.

"You first!" he cried and fell upon the silver chair. That must have been a good sword. The silver gave way before its edge like string, and in a moment a few twisted fragments, shining on the floor, were all that was left. But as the chair broke, there came from it a bright flash, a sound like small thunder, and (for one moment) a loathsome smell.

"Lie there, vile engine of sorcery," he said, "lest your mistress should ever use you for another victim." Then he turned and surveyed his rescuers; and the something wrong, whatever it was, had vanished from his face.

"What?" he cried, turning to Puddleglum. "Do I see before me a Marsh-wiggle – a real, live, honest, Narnian Marsh-wiggle?"

"Oh, so you *have* heard of Narnia after all?" said Jill.

"Had I forgotten it when I was under the spell?" asked the Knight. "Well, that and all other bedevilments are now over. You may well believe that I know Narnia, for I am Rilian, Prince of Narnia, and Caspian the great King is my father."

"Your Royal Highness," said Puddleglum, sinking on one knee (and the children did the same), "we have come hither for no other end than to seek you."

"And who are you, my other deliverers?" said the Prince to Scrubb and Jill.

"We were sent by Aslan himself from beyond the world's end to seek your Highness," said Scrubb. "I am Eustace who sailed with him to the island of Ramandu."

"I owe all three of you a greater debt than I can ever pay," said Prince Rilian. "But my father? Is he yet alive?"

"He sailed east again before we left Narnia, my lord," said Puddleglum. "But your Highness must consider that the King is very old. It is ten to one his Majesty must die on the voyage."

"He is old, you say. How long then have I been in the power of the witch?'

"It is more than ten years since your Highness was lost in the woods at the north side of Narnia."

"Ten years!" said the Prince, drawing his hand across his face as if to rub away the past. "Yes, I believe you. For now that I am myself I can remember that enchanted life, though while I was enchanted I could not remember my true self. And now, fair friends – but wait! I hear their feet (does it not sicken a man, that padding woolly tread! faugh!) on the stairs. Lock the door, boy. Or stay. I have a better thought than that. I will fool these Earthmen, if Aslan gives me the wit. Take your cue from me."

He walked resolutely to the door and flung it wide open.

CHAPTER TWELVE

THE QUEEN OF UNDERLAND

Two Earthmen entered, but instead of advancing into the room, they placed themselves one on each side of the door, and bowed deeply. They were followed immediately by the last person whom anyone had expected or wished to see: the Lady of the Green Kirtle, the Queen of Underland. She stood dead still in the doorway, and they could see her eyes moving as she took in the whole situation – the three strangers, the silver chair destroyed, and the Prince free, with his sword in his hand.

She turned very white; but Jill thought it was the sort of whiteness that comes over some people's faces not when they are frightened but when they are angry. For a moment the Witch fixed her eyes on the Prince, and there was murder in them. Then she seemed to change her mind.

"Leave us," she said to the two Earthmen. "And let none disturb us till I call, on pain of death." The gnomes padded away obediently, and the Witch-queen shut and locked the door.

"How now, my lord Prince," she said. "Has your nightly fit not yet come upon you, or is it over so soon? Why stand you here unbound? Who are these aliens? And is it they who have destroyed the chair which was your only safety?"

Prince Rilian shivered as she spoke to him. And no wonder: it is not easy to throw off in half an hour an enchantment which has made one a slave for ten years. Then, speaking with a great effort, he said:

"Madam, there will be no more need of that chair. And you, who have told me a hundred times how deeply you pitied me for the sorceries by which I was bound, will doubtless hear with joy that they are now ended for ever. There was, it seems, some small error in your Ladyship's way of treating them. These, my true friends, have delivered me. I am now in my right mind, and there are two things I will say to you. First – as for your Ladyship's design of putting me at the head of an army of Earthmen so that I may break out into the Overworld and there, by main force, make myself king over some nation that never did me wrong – murdering their natural lords and holding their throne as a bloody and foreign tyrant – now that I know myself, I do utterly abhor and renounce it as plain villainy. And second: I am the King's son of Narnia, Rilian, the only child of Caspian, Tenth of that name, whom some call Caspian the Seafarer. Therefore, Madam, it is my purpose, as it is also my duty, to depart suddenly from your Highness's court into my own country. Please it you to grant me and my friends safe conduct and a guide through your dark realm."

Now the Witch said nothing at all, but moved gently across the room, always keeping her face and eyes very steadily towards the Prince. When she had come to a little ark set in the wall not far from the fireplace, she opened it, and took out first a handful of a green powder. This she threw on the fire. It did not blaze much, but a very sweet and drowsy smell came from it. And all through the conversation which followed, that smell grew stronger, and filled the room, and made it harder to think. Secondly, she took out a musical instrument rather like a mandolin. She began to play it with her fingers – a steady, monotonous thrumming that you didn't notice after a few minutes. But the less you noticed it, the more it got into your brain and your blood. This also made it hard to think. After she had thrummed for a time (and the sweet smell was now strong) she began speaking in a sweet, quiet voice.

"Narnia?" she said. "Narnia? I have often heard your Lordship utter that name in your ravings. Dear Prince, you are very sick. There is no land called Narnia."

"Yes there is, though, Ma'am," said Puddleglum. "You see, I happen to have lived there all my life."

"Indeed," said the Witch. "Tell me, I pray you, where that country is?"

"Up there," said Puddleglum, stoutly, pointing overhead. "I – I don't know exactly where."

"How?" said the Queen, with a kind, soft, musical laugh. "Is there a country up among the stones and mortar of the roof?"

"No," said Puddleglum, struggling a little to get his breath. "It's in Overworld."

"And what, or where, pray is this . . . how do you call it . . . *Overworld*?"

"Oh, don't be so silly," said Scrubb, who was fighting hard against the enchantment of the sweet smell and the thrumming. "As if you didn't know! It's up above, up where you can see the sky and the sun and the stars. Why, you've been there yourself. We met you there."

"I cry you mercy, little brother," laughed the Witch (you couldn't have heard a lovelier laugh). "I have no memory of that meeting. But we often meet our friends in strange places when we dream. And unless all dreamed alike, you must not ask them to remember it."

"Madam," said the Prince sternly, "I have already told your Grace that I am the King's son of Narnia."

"And shalt be, dear friend," said the Witch in a soothing voice, as if she was humouring a child, "shalt be king of many imagined lands in thy fancies."

"We've been there, too," snapped Jill. She was very

angry because she could feel enchantment getting hold of her every moment. But of course the very fact that she could still feel it, showed that it had not yet fully worked.

"And thou art Queen of Narnia too, I doubt not, pretty one," said the Witch in the same coaxing, half-mocking tone.

"I'm nothing of the sort," said Jill, stamping her foot. "*We* come from another world."

"Why, this is a prettier game than the other," said the Witch. "Tell us, little maid, where is this other world? What ships and chariots go between it and ours?"

Of course a lot of things darted into Jill's head at once: Experiment House, Adela Pennyfather, her own home, radio-sets, cinemas, cars, aeroplanes, ration-books, queues. But they seemed dim and far away. (*Thrum – thrum – thrum* – went the strings of the Witch's instrument.) Jill couldn't remember the names of the things in our world. And this time it didn't come into her head that she was being enchanted, for now the magic was in its full strength; and of course, the more enchanted you get, the more certain you feel that you are not enchanted at all. She found herself saying (and at the moment it was a relief to say):

"No. I suppose that other world must be all a dream."

"Yes. It *is* all a dream," said the Witch, always thrumming.

"Yes, all a dream," said Jill.

"There never was such a world," said the Witch.

"No," said Jill and Scrubb, "never was such a world."

"There never was any world but mine," said the Witch.

"There never was any world but yours," said they.

Puddleglum was still fighting hard. "I don't know rightly what you all mean by a world," he said, talking like a man who hasn't enough air. "But you can play that fiddle till your fingers drop off, and still you won't make me forget Narnia; and the whole Overworld too. We'll never see it *again*, I shouldn't wonder. You may have blotted it out and turned it dark like this, for all I know. Nothing more likely. But I know I was there once. I've seen the sky full of stars. I've seen the sun coming up out of the sea of a morning and sinking behind the mountains at night. And I've seen him up in the midday sky when I couldn't look at him for brightness."

Puddleglum's words had a very rousing effect. The other three all breathed again and looked at one another like people newly awaked.

"Why, there it is!" cried the Prince. "Of course! The blessing of Aslan upon this honest Marsh-wiggle. We have all been dreaming, these last few minutes. How could we have forgotten it? Of course we've all seen the sun."

"By Jove, so we have!" said Scrubb. "Good for you, Puddleglum! You're the only one of us with any sense, I do believe."

Then came the Witch's voice, cooing softly like the voice of a wood-pigeon from the high elms in an old garden at three o'clock in the middle of a sleepy, summer afternoon; and it said:

"What is this *sun* that you all speak of? Do you mean anything by the word?"

"Yes, we jolly well do," said Scrubb.

"Can you tell me what it's like?" asked the Witch (*thrum, thrum, thrum*, went the strings).

"Please it your Grace," said the Prince, very coldly and politely. "You see that lamp. It is round and yellow and gives light to the whole room; and hangeth moreover from the roof. Now that thing which we call the sun is

like the lamp, only far greater and brighter. It giveth light to the whole Overworld and hangeth in the sky."

"Hangeth from what, my lord?" asked the Witch; and then, while they were all still thinking how to answer her, she added, with another of her soft, silver laughs: "You see? When you try to think out clearly what this *sun* must be, you cannot tell me. You can only tell me it is like the lamp. Your *sun* is a dream; and there is nothing in that dream that was not copied from the lamp. The lamp is the real thing; the *sun* is but a tale, a children's story."

"Yes, I see now," said Jill in a heavy, hopeless tone. "It must be so." And while she said this, it seemed to her to be very good sense.

Slowly and gravely the Witch repeated, "There is no *sun*." And they all said nothing. She repeated, in a softer and deeper voice. "There is no *sun*." After a pause, and after a struggle in their minds, all four of them said together. "You are right. There is no sun." It was such a relief to give in and say it.

"There never was a *sun*," said the Witch.

"No. There never was a sun," said the Prince, and the Marsh-wiggle, and the children.

For the last few minutes Jill had been feeling that there was something she must remember at all costs. And now she did. But it was dreadfully hard to say it. She felt as if huge weights were laid on her lips. At last, with an effort that seemed to take all the good out of her, she said:

"There's Aslan."

"Aslan?" said the Witch, quickening ever so slightly the pace of her thrumming. "What a pretty name! What does it mean?"

"He is the great Lion who called us out of our own world," said Scrubb, "and sent us into this to find Prince Rilian."

"What is a *lion*?" asked the Witch.

"Oh, hang it all!" said Scrubb. "Don't you know? How can we describe it to her? Have you ever seen a cat?"

"Surely," said the Queen. "I love cats."

"Well, a lion is a little bit – only a little bit, mind you – like a huge cat – with a mane. At least, it's not like a horse's mane, you know, it's more like a judge's wig. And it's yellow. And terrifically strong."

The Witch shook her head. "I see," she said, "that we should do no better with your *lion*, as you call it, than we did with your *sun*. You have seen lamps, and so you imagined a bigger and better lamp and called it the *sun*. You've seen cats, and now you want a bigger and better cat, and it's to be called a *lion*. Well, 'tis a pretty make-believe, though, to say truth, it would suit you all better if you were younger. And look how you can put nothing into your make-believe without copying it from the real world, this world of mine, which is the only world. But even you children are too old for such play. As for you, my lord Prince, that art a man full grown, fie upon you! Are you not ashamed of such toys? Come, all of you. Put away these childish tricks. I have work for you all in the real world. There is no Narnia, no Overworld, no sky, no sun, no Aslan. And now, to bed all. And let us begin a wiser life tomorrow. But, first, to bed; to sleep; deep sleep, soft pillows, sleep without foolish dreams."

The Prince and the two children were standing with their heads hung down, their cheeks flushed, their eyes half closed; the strength all gone from them; the enchantment almost complete. But Puddleglum, desperately gathering all his strength, walked over to the fire. Then he did a very brave thing. He knew it wouldn't hurt him quite as much as it would hurt a human; for his feet (which were bare) were webbed and hard and cold-blooded like a duck's. But he knew it would hurt him badly enough; and so it did. With his bare foot he stamped on the fire, grinding a large part of it into ashes on the flat hearth. And three things happened at once.

First, the sweet heavy smell grew very much less. For though the whole fire had not been put out, a good bit of it had, and what remained smelled very largely of burnt Marsh-wiggle, which is not at all an enchanting smell. This instantly made everyone's brain far clearer. The Prince and the children held up their heads again and opened their eyes.

Secondly, the Witch, in a loud, terrible voice, utterly different from all the sweet tones she had been using up till now, called out, "What are you doing? Dare to touch my fire again, mud-filth, and I'll turn the blood to fire inside your veins."

Thirdly, the pain itself made Puddleglum's head for a moment perfectly clear and he knew exactly what he really thought. There is nothing like a good shock of pain for dissolving certain kinds of magic.

"One word, Ma'am," he said, coming back from the fire; limping, because of the pain. "One word. All you've been saying is quite right, I shouldn't wonder. I'm a chap who always liked to know the worst and then put the best face I can on it. So I won't deny any of what you said. But there's one thing more to be said, even so. Suppose we *have* only dreamed, or made up, all those things – trees and grass and sun and moon and stars and Aslan himself. Suppose we have. Then all I can say is that, in that case, the made-up things seem a good deal more important than the real ones. Suppose this black pit of a kingdom of yours *is* the only world. Well, it strikes me as a pretty poor one. And that's a funny thing, when you come to think of it. We're just babies making up a game, if you're right. But four babies playing a game can make a play-world which licks your real world hollow. That's why I'm going to stand by the play-world. I'm on Aslan's side even if there isn't any Aslan to lead it. I'm going to live as like a Narnian as I can even if there isn't any Narnia. So, thanking you kindly for our supper, if these two gentlemen and the young lady are ready, we're leaving your court at once and setting out in the dark to spend our lives looking for Overland. Not that our lives will be very long, I should think; but that's a small loss if the world's as dull a place as you say."

"Oh, hurrah! Good old Puddleglum!" cried Scrubb and Jill. But the Prince shouted suddenly, "Ware! Look to the Witch."

When they did look their hair nearly stood on end.

The instrument dropped from her hands. Her arms appeared to be fastened to her sides. Her legs were intertwined with each other, and her feet had disappeared. The long green train of her skirt thickened and grew solid, and seemed to be all one piece with the writhing green pillar of her interlocked legs. And that writhing green pillar was curving and swaying as if it had no joints, or else were all joints. Her head was thrown far back and while her nose grew longer and longer, every other part of her face seemed to disappear, except her eyes. Huge flaming eyes they were now, without brows or lashes. All this takes time to write down; it happened so quickly that there was only just time to see it. Long before there was time to do anything, the change was complete, and the great serpent which the Witch had become, green as poison, thick as Jill's waist, had flung two or three coils of its loathsome body round the Prince's legs. Quick as lightning another great loop darted round, intending to pinion his sword-arm to his side. But the Prince was just in time. He raised his arms and got them clear: the living knot closed only round his chest – ready to crack his ribs like firewood when it drew tight.

The Prince caught the creature's neck in his left hand, trying to squeeze it till it choked. This held its face (if you could call it a face) about five inches from his own. The forked tongue flickered horribly in and out, but could not reach him. With his right hand he drew back his sword for the strongest blow he could give. Meanwhile Scrubb and Puddleglum had drawn their weapons and rushed to his aid. All three blows fell at once: Scrubb's (which did not even pierce the scales and did no good) on the body of the snake below the Prince's hand, but the Prince's own blow and Puddleglum's both on its neck. Even that did not quite kill it, though it began to loosen its hold on Rilian's legs and chest. With repeated blows they hacked off its head. The horrible thing went on coiling and moving like a bit of wire long after it had died; and the floor, as you may imagine, was a nasty mess.

The Prince, when he had breath, said, "Gentlemen, I thank you." Then the three conquerors stood staring at one another and panting, without another word, for a long time. Jill had very wisely sat down and was keeping quiet; she was saying to herself, "I do hope I don't faint – or blub – or do anything idiotic."

"My royal mother is avenged," said Rilian presently. "This is undoubtedly the same worm that I pursued in vain by the fountain in the forest of Narnia, so many years ago. All these years I have been the slave of my mother's slayer. Yet I am glad, gentlemen, that the foul Witch took to her serpent form at the last. It would not have suited well either with my heart or with my honour to have slain a woman. But look to the lady." He meant Jill.

"I'm all right, thanks," said she.

"Damsel," said the Prince, bowing to her. "You are of a high courage, and therefore, I doubt not, you come of a noble blood in your own world. But come, friends. Here is some wine left. Let us refresh ourselves and each pledge his fellows. After that, to our plans."

"A jolly good idea, Sir," said Scrubb.

CHAPTER THIRTEEN

UNDERLAND WITHOUT THE QUEEN

ALL felt that they had earned what Scrubb called a "breather". The Witch had locked the door and told the Earthmen not to disturb her, so there was no danger of interruption for the present. Their first business was, of course, Puddleglum's burnt foot. A couple of clean shirts from the Prince's bedroom, torn into strips, and well greased on the inside with butter and salad oil off the supper table, made a fairly good dressing. When this had been applied, they all sat down and had a little refreshment, and discussed plans for escaping from the Underworld.

Rilian explained that there were quite a lot of outlets by which one could get to the surface; he had been taken out through most of them at one time or another. But he had never gone out alone, only with the Witch; and he had always reached these outlets by going in a ship across the Sunless Sea. What the Earthmen would say if he went down to the harbour without the Witch, and with four strangers, and simply ordered a ship, no one could guess. But most likely they would ask awkward questions. On the other hand the new outlet, the one for the invasion of Overworld, was on this side of the sea, and only a few miles away. The Prince knew that it was nearly finished; only a few feet of earth divided the diggings from the outer air. It was even possible that it had now been quite finished. Perhaps the Witch had come back to tell him this and to start the attack. Even if it was not, they could probably dig themselves out by that route in a few hours – if they could only get there without being stopped, and if only they found the diggings unguarded. But those were the difficulties.

"If you ask me –" began Puddleglum, when Scrubb interrupted.

"I say," he asked, "what's that noise?"

"I've been wondering that for some time!" said Jill.

They had all, in fact, been hearing the noise but it had begun and increased so gradually that they did not know when they had first noticed it. For a time it had been only a vague disquiet like gentle winds, or traffic very far away. Then it swelled to a murmur like the sea. Then came rumblings and rushings. Now there seemed to be voices as well and also a steady roaring that was not voices.

"By the Lion," said Prince Rilian, "it seems this silent land has found a tongue at last." He rose, walked to the window, and drew aside the curtains. The others crowded round him to look out.

The very first thing they noticed was a great red glow. Its reflection made a red patch on the roof of the Underworld thousands of feet above them, so that they could see a rocky ceiling which had perhaps been hidden in darkness ever since the world was made. The glow itself came from the far side of the city so that many buildings, grim and great, stood up blackly against it. But it also cast its light down many streets that ran from it towards the castle. And in those streets something very strange was going on. The closely-packed, silent crowds of Earthmen had vanished. Instead, there were figures darting about by ones, or twos, or threes. They behaved like people who do not want to be seen: lurking in shadow behind buttresses or in doorways, and then moving quickly across the open into fresh places of hiding. But the strangest thing of all, to anyone who knew the gnomes, was the noise. Shouts and cries came from all directions. But from the harbour there came a low, rumbling roar which grew steadily louder and was already shaking the whole city.

"What's happened to the Earthmen?" said Scrubb. "Is it *them* shouting?"

"'Tis hardly possible," said the Prince. "I never heard one of the rascals so much as speak with a loud voice in all the weary years of my bondage. Some new devilry, I don't doubt."

"And what is that red light over there?" asked Jill. "Is something on fire?"

"If you ask me," said Puddleglum, "I should say that was the central fires of the Earth breaking out to make a new volcano. We'll be in the middle of it, I shouldn't wonder."

"Look at that ship!" said Scrubb. "Why's it coming on so quickly? No one's rowing it."

"Look, look!" said the Prince. "The ship is already far this side of the harbour – it is in the street. Look! All the ships are driving into the city! By my head, the sea's rising. The flood is upon us. Aslan be praised, this castle stands on high ground. But the water comes on grimly fast."

"Oh, what *can* be happening?" cried Jill. "Fire and water and all those people dodging about the streets."

"I'll tell you what it is," said Puddleglum. "That Witch has laid a train of magic spells so that whenever she was killed, at that same moment her whole kingdom would fall to pieces. She's the sort that wouldn't so much mind dying herself if she knew that the chap who killed her was going to be burned, or buried, or drowned five minutes later."

"Hast hit it, friend wiggle," said the Prince. "When our swords hacked off the Witch's head, that stroke ended all her magic works, and now the Deep Lands are falling to pieces. We are looking on the end of Underworld."

"That's it, Sir," said Puddleglum. "Unless it should happen to be the end of the whole world."

"But are we just going to stay here and – wait?" gasped Jill.

"Not by my counsel," said the Prince. "I would save my horse, Coalblack, and the Witch's Snowflake (a noble beast and worthy of a better mistress) which are both stabled in the courtyard. After that, let us make shift to get out to high ground and pray that we shall find an outlet. The horses can carry two each at need, and if we put them to it they may outstrip the flood."

"Will your Highness not put on armour?" asked Puddleglum. "I don't like the look of *those*" – and he pointed down to the street. Everyone looked down. Dozens of creatures (and now that they were close, they obviously were Earthmen) were coming up from the direction of the harbour. But they were not moving like an aimless crowd. They behaved like modern soldiers in an attack, making rushes and taking cover, anxious not to be seen from the castle windows.

"I dare not see the inside of that armour again," said the Prince. "I rode in it as in a movable dungeon, and it stinks of magic and slavery. But I will take the shield."

He left the room and returned with a strange light in his eyes a moment later.

"Look, friends," he said, holding out the shield towards them. "An hour ago it was black and without device; and now, this." The shield had turned bright as silver, and on it, redder than blood or cherries, was the figure of the Lion.

"Doubtless," said the Prince, "this signifies that Aslan

will be our good lord, whether he means us to live or die. And all's one, for that. Now, by my counsel, we shall all kneel and kiss his likeness, and then all shake hands one with another, as true friends that may shortly be parted. And then, let us descend into the city and take the adventure that is sent us."

And they all did as the Prince had said. But when Scrubb shook hands with Jill, he said, "So long, Jill. Sorry I've been a funk and so ratty. I hope you get safe home," and Jill said, "So long, Eustace. And I'm sorry I've been such a pig." And this was the first time they had ever used Christian names, because one didn't do it at school.

The Prince unlocked the door and they all went down the stairs: three of them with drawn swords, and Jill with drawn knife. The attendants had vanished and the great room at the foot of the Prince's stairs was empty. The grey, doleful lamps were still burning and by their light they had no difficulty in passing gallery after gallery and descending stairway after stairway. The noises from outside the castle were not so easily heard here as they had been in the room above. Inside the house all was still as death, and deserted. It was as they turned a corner into the great hall on the ground floor that they met their first Earthman – a fat, whitish creature with a very pig-like face who was gobbling up all the remains of food on the tables. It squealed (the squeal also was very like a pig's) and darted under a bench, whisking its long tail out of Puddleglum's reach in the nick of time. Then it rushed away through the far door too quickly to be followed.

From the hall they came out into the courtyard. Jill, who went to a riding school in the holidays, had just noticed the smell of a stable (a very nice, honest, homely smell it is to meet in a place like Underland) when Eustace said, "Great Scott! Look at that!" A magnificent rocket had risen from somewhere beyond the castle walls and broken into green stars.

"Fireworks!" said Jill in a puzzled voice.

"Yes," said Eustace, "but you can't imagine those Earth people letting them off for fun! It must be a signal."

"And means no good to us, I'll be bound," said Puddleglum.

"Friends," said the Prince, "when once a man is launched on such an adventure as this, he must bid farewell to hopes and fears, otherwise death or deliverance will both come too late to save his honour and his reason. Ho, my beauties" (he was now opening the stable door). "Hey cousins! Steady, Coalblack! Softly now, Snowflake! You are not forgotten."

The horses were both frightened by the strange lights and the noises. Jill, who had been so cowardly about going through a black hole betweeen one cave and another, went in without fear between the stamping and snorting beasts, and she and the Prince had them saddled and bridled in a few minutes. Very fine they looked as they came out into the courtyard, tossing their heads. Jill mounted Snowflake, and Puddleglum got up behind her. Eustace got up behind the Prince on Coalblack. Then with a great echo of hoofs, they rode out of the main gateway into the street.

"Not much danger of being burnt. That's the bright side of it," observed Puddleglum, pointing to their right. There, hardly a hundred yards away, lapping against the walls of the houses, was water.

"Courage!" said the Prince. "The road there goes down steeply. That water has climbed only half up the greatest hill in the city. It might come so near in the first half-hour and come no nearer in the next two. My fear is more of that –" and he pointed with his sword to a great tall Earthman with boar's tusks, followed by six others of assorted shapes and sizes who had just dashed out of a side street and stepped into the shadow of the houses where no one could see them.

The Prince led them, aiming always in the direction of the glowing red light but a little to the left of it. His plan was to get round the fire (if it was a fire) on to high ground, in hope that they might find their way to the new diggings. Unlike the other three, he seemed to be almost enjoying himself. He whistled as he rode, and sang snatches of an old song about Corin Thunder-fist of Archenland. The truth is, he was so glad at being free from his long enchantment that all dangers seemed a game in comparison. But the rest found it an eerie journey.

Behind them was the sound of clashing and entangled ships, and the rumble of collapsing buildings. Overhead was the great patch of lurid light on the roof of the Underworld. Ahead was the mysterious glow, which did not seem to grow any bigger. From the same direction came a continual hubbub of shouts, screams, cat-calls, laughter, squeals, and bellowings; and fireworks of all sorts rose in the dark air. No one could guess what they meant. Nearer to them, the city was partly lit up by the red glow, and partly by the very different light of the dreary Gnome lamps. But there were many places where neither of these lights fell, and those places were jet-black. And in and out of those places the shapes of Earthmen were darting and slipping all the time, always with their eyes fixed on the travellers, always trying to keep out of sight themselves. There were big faces and little faces, huge eyes like fishes' eyes and little eyes like bears'. There were feathers and bristles, horns and tusks, noses like

whipcord, and chins so long that they looked like beards. Every now and then a group of them would get too big or come too near. Then the Prince would brandish his sword and make a show of charging them. And the creatures, with all manner of hootings, squeakings, and cluckings, would dive away into the darkness.

But when they had climbed many steep streets and were far away from the flood, and almost out of the town on the inland side, it began to be more serious. They were now close to the red glow and nearly on a level with it, though they still could not see what it really was. But by its light they could see their enemies more clearly. Hundreds – perhaps a few thousands – of gnomes were all moving towards it. But they were doing so in short rushes, and whenever they stopped, they turned and faced the travellers.

"If your Highness asked me," said Puddleglum, "I'd say those fellows were meaning to cut us off in front."

"That was my thought too, Puddleglum," said the Prince. "And we can never fight our way through so many. Hark you! Let us ride forth close by the edge of yonder house. And even as we reach it, do you slip off into its shadow. The Lady and I will go forward a few paces. Some of these devils will follow us, I doubt not; they are thick behind us. Do you, who have long arms, take one alive if you may, as it passes your ambush. We may get a true tale of it or learn what is their quarrel against us."

"But won't the others all come rushing at us to rescue the one we catch," said Jill in a voice not so steady as she tried to make it.

"Then, Madam," said the Prince, "you shall see us die fighting around you, and you must commend yourself to the Lion. Now, good Puddleglum."

The Marsh-wiggle slipped off into the shadow as quickly as a cat. The others, for a sickening minute or so, went forward at a walk. Then suddenly from behind them there broke out a series of blood-curdling screams, mixed with the familiar voice of Puddleglum, saying, "Now then! Don't cry out before you're hurt, or you *will* be hurt, see? Anyone would think it was a pig being killed."

"That was good hunting," exclaimed the Prince, immediately turning Coalblack and coming back to the corner of the house. "Eustace," he said, "of your courtesy, take Coalblack's head." Then he dismounted, and all three gazed in silence while Puddleglum pulled his catch out into the light. It was a most miserable little gnome, only about three feet long. It had a sort of ridge, like a cock's comb (only hard), on the top of its head, little pink eyes, and a mouth and chin so large and round that its face looked like that of a pigmy hippopotamus. If they had not been in such a tight place, they would have burst into laughter at the sight of it.

"Now, Earthman," said the Prince, standing over it and holding his sword point very near the prisoner's neck, "speak, up, like an honest gnome, and you shall go free. Play the knave with us, and you are but a dead Earthman. Good Puddleglum, how can it speak while you hold its mouth tight shut?"

"No, and it can't bite either," said Puddleglum. "If I had the silly soft hands that you humans have (saving your Highness's reverence) I'd have been all over blood by now. Yet even a Marsh-wiggle gets tired of being chewed.'

"Sirrah," said the Prince to the gnome, "one bite and you die. Let its mouth open, Puddleglum."

"Oo-ee-ee," squealed the Earthman, "let me go, let me go. It isn't me. I didn't do it."

"Didn't do what?" asked Puddleglum.

"Whatever your Honours say I *did* do," answered the creature.

"Tell me your name," said the Prince, "and what you Earthmen are all about today."

"Oh please, your Honours, please, kind gentlemen," whimpered the gnome. "Promise you will not tell the Queen's grace anything I say."

"The Queen's grace, as you call her," said the Prince sternly, "is dead. I killed her myself."

"What!" cried the gnome, opening its ridiculous mouth wider and wider in astonishment. "Dead? The Witch dead? And by your Honour's hand?" It gave a huge sigh of relief and added, "Why then your Honour is a friend!"

The Prince withdrew his sword an inch or so. Puddleglum let the creature sit up. It looked round on the four travellers with its twinkling, red eyes, chuckled once or twice, and began.

CHAPTER FOURTEEN

THE BOTTOM OF THE WORLD

"MY name is Golg," said the gnome. "And I'll tell your Honours all I know. About an hour ago we were all going about our work – *her* work, I should say – sad and silent, same as we've done any other day for years and years. Then there came a great crash and bang. As soon as they heard it, everyone says to himself, I haven't had a song or a dance or let off a squib for a long time; why's that? And everyone thinks to himself, Why, I must have been enchanted. And then everyone says to himself, I'm blessed if I know why I'm carrying this load, and I'm not going to carry it any farther: that's that. And down we all throw our sacks and bundles and tools. Then everyone turns and sees the great red glow over yonder. And everyone says to himself, What's that? and everyone answers himself and says, There's a crack or chasm split open and a nice warm glow coming up through it from the Really Deep Land, a thousand fathom under us."

"Great Scott," exclaimed Eustace, "are there other lands still lower down?"

"Oh yes, your Honour," said Golg. "Lovely places; what we call the Land of Bism. This country where we are now, the Witch's country, is what *we* call the Shallow Lands. It's a good deal too near the surface to suit us. Ugh! You might almost as well be living outside, on the surface itself. You see, we're all poor gnomes from Bism whom the Witch has called up here by magic to work for her. But we'd forgotten all about it till that crash came and the spell broke. We didn't know who we were or where we belonged. We couldn't do anything, or think anything, except what she put into our heads. And it was glum and gloomy things she put there all those years. I've nearly forgotten how to make a joke or dance a jig. But the moment the bang came and the chasm opened and the sea began rising, it all came back. And of course we all set off as quick as we could to get down the crack and home to our own place. And you can see them over there all letting off rockets and standing on their heads for joy. And I'll be very obliged to your Honours if you'll soon let me go and join in."

"I think this is simply splendid," said Jill. "I'm so glad we freed the gnomes as well as ourselves when we cut off the Witch's head! And I'm so glad they aren't really horrid and gloomy any more than the Prince really was – well, what he seemed like."

"That's all very well, Pole," said Puddleglum cautiously. "But those gnomes didn't look to me like chaps who were just running away. It looked more like military formations, if you ask me. Do you look me in the face, Mr Golg, and tell me you weren't preparing for battle?"

"Of course we were, your Honour," said Golg. "You see, we didn't know the Witch was dead. We thought she'd be watching from the castle. We were trying to slip away without being seen. And then when you four came out with swords and horses, of course everyone says to himself, Here it comes: not knowing that his Honour wasn't on the Witch's side. And we were determined to fight like anything rather than give up the hope of going back to Bism."

"I'll be sworn 'tis an honest gnome," said the Prince. "Let go of it, friend Puddleglum. As for me, good Golg, I have been enchanted like you and your fellows, and have but newly remembered myself. And now, one question more. Do you know the way to those new diggings, by which the sorceress meant to lead out an army against Overland?"

"Ee-ee-ee!" squeaked Golg. "Yes, I know that terrible road. I will show you where it begins. But it is no manner of use your Honour asking me to go with you on it. I'll die rather."

"Why?" asked Eustace anxiously. "What's so dreadful about it?"

"Too near the top, the outside," said Golg, shuddering. "That was the worst thing the Witch did to us. We were going to be led out into the open – on to the outside of the world. They say there's no roof at all there; only a horrible great emptiness called the sky. And the diggings have gone so far that a few strokes of the pick would bring you out to it. I wouldn't dare go near them."

"Hurrah! Now you're talking!" cried Eustace, and Jill said, "But it's not horrid at all up there. We like it. We live there."

"I know you Overlanders live there," said Golg. "But I thought it was because you couldn't find your way down inside. You can't really *like* it – crawling about like flies on the top of the world!"

"What about showing us the road at once?" said Puddleglum.

"In a good hour," cried the Prince. The whole party set out. The Prince remounted his charger, Puddleglum climbed up behind Jill, and Golg led the way. As he went, he kept shouting out the good news that the Witch was dead and that the four Overlanders were not dangerous. And those who heard him shouted it on to others, so that in a few minutes the whole of Underland was ringing with shouts and cheers, and gnomes by hundreds and thousands, leaping, turning cart-wheels, standing on their heads, playing leap-frog, and letting off huge crackers, came pressing round Coalblack and Snowflake. And the Prince had to tell the story of his own enchantment and deliverance at least ten times.

In this way they came to the edge of the chasm. It was

about a thousand feet long and perhaps two hundred wide. They dismounted from their horses and came to the edge, and looked down into it. A strong heat smote up into their faces, mixed with a smell which was quite unlike any they had ever smelled. It was rich, sharp, exciting, and made you sneeze. The depth of the chasm was so bright that at first it dazzled their eyes and they could see nothing. When they got used to it they thought they could make out a river of fire, and, on the banks of that river, what seemed to be fields and groves of an unbearable, hot brilliance – though they were dim compared with the river. There were blues, reds, greens, and whites all jumbled together: a very good stained-glass window with the tropical sun staring straight through it at midday might have something the same effect. Down the rugged sides of the chasm, looking black like flies against all that fiery light, hundreds of Earthmen were climbing.

"Your honours," said Golg (and when they turned to look at him they could see nothing but blackness for a few minutes, their eyes were so dazzled). "Your honours, why don't you come down to Bism? You'd be happier there than in that cold, unprotected, naked country out on top. Or at least come down for a short visit."

Jill took it for granted that none of the others would listen to such an idea for a moment. To her horror she heard the Prince saying:

"Truly, friend Golg, I have half a mind to come down with you. For this is a marvellous adventure, and it may be no mortal man has ever looked into Bism before or will ever have the chance again. And I know not how, as the years pass, I shall bear to remember that it was once in my power to have probed the uttermost pit of Earth and that I forbore. But could a man live there? You do not swim in the fire-river itself?"

"Oh no, your Honour. Not we. It's only salamanders live in the fire itself."

"What kind of beast is your salamander?" asked the Prince.

"It is hard to tell their kind, your Honour," said Golg. "For they are too white-hot to look at. But they are most like small dragons. They speak to us out of the fire. They are wonderfully clever with their tongues: very witty and eloquent."

Jill glanced hastily at Eustace. She had felt sure that he would like the idea of sliding down that chasm even less than she did. Her heart sank as she saw that his face was quite changed. He looked much more like the Prince than like the old Scrubb at Experiment House. For all his adventures, and the days when he had sailed with King Caspian, were coming back to him.

"Your Highness," he said. "If my old friend Reepicheep the Mouse were here, he would say we could not now refuse the adventures of Bism without a great impeachment to our honour."

"Down there," said Golg, "I could show you real gold, real silver, real diamonds."

"Bosh!" said Jill rudely. "As if we didn't know that we're below the deepest mines even here."

"Yes," said Golg. "I have heard of those little scratches in the crust that you Topdwellers call mines. But that's where you get dead gold, dead silver, dead gems. Down in Bism we have them alive and growing. There I'll pick you bunches of rubies that you can eat and squeeze you a cup full of diamond-juice. You won't care much about fingering the cold, dead treasures of your shallow mines after you have tasted the live ones of Bism."

"My father went to the world's end," said Rilian thoughtfully. "It would be a marvellous thing if his son went to the bottom of the world."

"If your Highness wants to see your father while he's still alive, which I think he'd prefer," said Puddleglum, "it's about time we were getting on to that road to the diggings."

"And I won't go down that hole, whatever anyone says," added Jill.

"Why, if your Honours are really set to go back to Overworld," said Golg, "there *is* one bit of the road that's rather lower than this. And perhaps, if that flood's still rising –"

"Oh, do, do, do come *on*!" begged Jill.

"I fear it must be so," said the Prince with a deep sigh. "But I have left half of my heart in the land of Bism."

"Please!" begged Jill.

"Where is the road?" asked Puddleglum.

"There are lamps all the way," said Golg. "Your

Honour can see the beginning of the road on the far side of the chasm."

"How long will the lamps burn for?" asked Puddleglum.

At that moment a hissing, scorching voice like the voice of Fire itself (they wondered afterwards if it could have been a salamander's) came whistling up out of the very depths of Bism.

"Quick! Quick! Quick! To the cliffs, to the cliffs, to the cliffs!" it said. "The rift closes. It closes. It closes. Quick! Quick!" And at the same time, with ear-shattering cracks and creaks, the rocks moved. Already, while they looked, the chasm was narrower. From every side belated gnomes were rushing into it. They would not wait to climb down the rocks. They flung themselves headlong and, either

because so strong a blast of hot air was beating up from the bottom, or for some other reason, they could be seen floating downwards like leaves. Thicker and thicker they floated, till their blackness almost blotted out the fiery river and the groves of live gems. "Good-bye to your

Honours. I'm off," shouted Golg, and dived. Only a few were left to follow him. The chasm was now no broader than a stream. Now it was narrow as the slit in a pillar-box. Now it was only an intensely bright thread. Then, with a shock like a thousand goods trains crashing into a thousand pairs of buffers, the lips of rock closed. The hot, maddening smell vanished. The travellers were alone in an Underworld which now looked far blacker than before. Pale, dim, and dreary, the lamps marked the direction of the road.

"Now," said Puddleglum, "it's ten to one we've already stayed too long, but we may as well make a try. Those lamps will give out in five minutes, I shouldn't wonder."

They urged the horses to a canter and thundered along the dusky road in fine style. But almost at once it began going downhill. They would have thought Golg had sent them the wrong way if they had not seen, on the other side of the valley, the lamps going on and upwards as far as the eye could reach. But at the bottom of the valley the lamps shone on moving water.

"Haste," cried the Prince. They galloped down the slope. It would have been nasty enough at the bottom even five minutes later for the tide was running up the valley like a mill-race, and if it had come to swimming, the horses could hardly have won over. But it was still only a foot or two deep, and though it swished terribly round the horses' legs, they reached the far side in safety.

Then began the slow, weary march uphill with nothing ahead to look at but the pale lamps which went up and up as far as the eye could reach. When they looked back they could see the water spreading. All the hills of Underland were now islands, and it was only on those islands that the lamps remained. Every moment some distant light vanished. Soon there would be total darkness everywhere except on the road they were following; and even on the lower part of it behind them, though no lamps had yet gone out, the lamplight shone on water.

Although they had good reason for hurrying, the horses could not go on for ever without a rest. They halted: and in silence they could hear the lapping of water.

"I wonder is what's his name – Father Time – flooded out now," said Jill. "And all those queer sleeping animals."

"I don't think we're as high as that," said Eustace. "Don't you remember how we had to go downhill to reach the sunless sea? I shouldn't think the water has reached Father Time's cave yet."

"That's as may be," said Puddleglum. "I'm more interested in the lamps on this road. Look a bit sickly, don't they?"

"They always did," said Jill.

"Ah," said Puddleglum. "But they're greener now."

"You don't mean to say you think they're going out?" cried Eustace.

"Well, however they work, you can't expect them to last for ever, you know," replied the Marsh-wiggle. "But don't let your spirits down, Scrubb. I've got my eye on the water too, and I don't think it's rising so fast as it did."

"Small comfort, friend," said the Prince. "If we cannot find our way out. I cry you mercy, all. I am to blame for my pride and fantasy which delayed us by the mouth of the land of Bism. Now, let us ride on."

During the hour or so that followed Jill sometimes thought that Puddleglum was right about the lamps, and sometimes thought it was only her imagination. Meanwhile the land was changing. The roof of Underland was so near that even by that dull light they could now see it quite distinctly. And the great, rugged walls of

Underland could be seen drawing closer on each side. The road, in fact, was leading them up into a steep tunnel. They began to pass picks and shovels and barrows and other signs that the diggers had recently been at work. If only one could be sure of getting out, all this was very cheering. But the thought of going on into a hole that would get narrower and narrower, and harder to turn back in, was very unpleasant.

At last the roof was so low that Puddleglum and the Prince knocked their heads against it. The party dismounted and led the horses. The road was uneven here and one had to pick one's steps with some care. That was how Jill noticed the growing darkness. There was no doubt about it now. The faces of the others looked strange and ghastly in the green glow. Then all at once (she couldn't help it) Jill gave a little scream. One light, the next one ahead, went out altogether. The one behind them did the same. Then they were in absolute darkness.

"Courage, friends," came Prince Rilian's voice. "Whether we live or die Aslan will be our good lord."

"That's right, Sir," said Puddleglum's voice. "And you must always remember there's one good thing about being trapped down here: it'll save funeral expenses."

Jill held her tongue. (If you don't want other people to know how frightened you are, this is always a wise thing to do; it's your voice that gives you away.)

"We might as well go on as stand here," said Eustace; and when she heard the tremble in *his* voice, Jill knew how wise she'd been not to trust her own.

Puddleglum and Eustace went first with their arms stretched out in front of them, for fear of blundering into anything; Jill and the Prince followed, leading the horses.

"I say," came Eustace's voice much later, "are my eyes going queer or is there a patch of light up there?"

Before anyone could answer him, Puddleglum called out: "Stop. I'm up against a dead end. And it's earth, not rock. What were you saying, Scrubb?"

"By the Lion," said the Prince, "Eustace is right. There is a sort of –"

"But it's not daylight," said Jill. "It's only a cold blue sort of light."

"Better than nothing, though," said Eustace. "Can we get up to it?"

"It's not right overhead," said Puddleglum. "It's above us, but it's in this wall that I've run into. How would it be, Pole, if you got on my shoulders and saw whether you could get up to it?"

CHAPTER FIFTEEN

THE DISAPPEARANCE OF JILL

THE patch of light did not show up anything down in the darkness where they were standing. The others could only hear, not see, Jill's efforts to get on to the Marsh-wiggle's back. That is, they heard him saying, "You needn't put your finger in my eye," and, "Nor your foot in my mouth either," and, "That's more like it," and, "Now, I'll hold on to your legs. That'll leave your arms free to steady yourself against the earth."

Then they looked up and soon they saw the black shape of Jill's head against the patch of light.

"Well?" they all shouted up anxiously.

"It's a hole," called Jill's voice. "I could get through it if I was a little bit higher."

"What do you see through it?" asked Eustace.

"Nothing much yet," said Jill. "I say, Puddleglum, let go my legs so that I can stand on your shoulders instead of sitting on them. I can steady myself all right against the edge."

They could hear her moving and then much more of her came into sight against the greyness of the opening; in fact all of her down to the waist.

"I say –" began Jill, but suddenly broke off with a cry: not a sharp cry. It sounded more as if her mouth had been muffled up or had something pushed into it. After that she found her voice and seemed to be shouting out as loud as she could, but they couldn't hear the words. Two things then happened at the same moment. The patch of light was completely blocked up for a second or so; and they heard both a scuffling, struggling sound and the voice of the Marsh-wiggle gasping: "Quick! Help! Hold on to her legs.

Someone's pulling her. There! No, here. Too late!"

The opening, and the cold light which filled it, were now perfectly clear again. Jill had vanished.

"Jill! Jill!" they shouted frantically, but there was no answer.

"Why the dickens couldn't you have held her feet?" said Eustace.

"I don't know, Scrubb," groaned Puddleglum. "Born to be a misfit, I shouldn't wonder. Fated. Fated to be Pole's death, just as I was fated to eat Talking Stag at Harfang. Not that it isn't my own fault as well, of course."

"This is the greatest shame and sorrow that could have fallen on us," said the Prince. "We have sent a brave lady into the hands of enemies and stayed behind in safety."

"Don't paint it *too* black, Sir," said Puddleglum. "We're not very safe except for death by starvation in this hole."

"I wonder am *I* small enough to get through where Jill did?" said Eustace.

What had really happened to Jill was this. As soon as she got her head out of the hole she found that she was looking down as if from an upstairs window, not up as if through a trap-door. She had been so long in the dark that her eyes couldn't at first take in what they were seeing: except that she was not looking at the daylit, sunny world which she so wanted to see. The air seemed to be deadly cold, and the light was pale and blue. There was also a good deal of noise going on and a lot of white objects flying about in the air. It was at that moment that she had shouted down to Puddleglum to let her stand up on his shoulders.

When she had done this, she could see and hear a good deal better. The noises she had been hearing turned out to be of two kinds: the rhythmical thump of several feet, and the music of four fiddles, three flutes, and a drum. She also got her own position clear. She was looking out of a hole in a steep bank which sloped down and reached the level about fourteen feet below her. Everything was very white. A lot of people were moving about. Then she gasped! The people were trim little Fauns, and Dryads with leaf-crowned hair floating behind them. For a second they looked as if they were moving anyhow; then she saw that they were really doing a dance – a dance with so many complicated steps and figures that it took you some time to understand it. Then it came over her like a thunderclap that the pale, blue light was really moonlight, and the white stuff on the ground was really snow. And of course! There were the stars staring in a black frosty sky overhead. And the tall black things behind the dancers were trees. They had not only got out into the upper world at last, but had come out in the heart of Narnia. Jill felt she could have fainted with delight; and the music – the wild music, intensely sweet and yet just the least bit eerie too, and full of good magic as the Witch's thrumming had been full of bad magic – made her feel it all the more.

All this takes a long time to tell, but of course it took a very short time to see. Jill turned almost at once to shout down to the others, "I say! It's all right. We're out, and we're home." But the reason she never got further than "I say" was this. Circling round and round the dancers was a ring of Dwarfs, all dressed in their finest clothes; mostly scarlet with fur-lined hoods and golden tassels and big furry top-boots. As they circled round they were all diligently throwing snowballs. (Those were the white things that Jill had seen flying through the air.) They weren't throwing them *at* the dancers as silly boys might have been doing in England. They were throwing them through the dance in such perfect time with the music and with such perfect aim that if all the dancers were in exactly the right places at exactly the right moments, no one would be hit. This is called the Great Snow Dance and it is done every year in Narnia on the first moonlit night when there is snow on the ground. Of course it is a kind of game as well as a dance, because every now and then some dancer will be the least little bit wrong and get a snowball in the face, and then everyone laughs. But a good team of dancers, Dwarfs, and musicians will keep it up for hours without a single hit. On fine nights when the cold and the drum-taps, and the hooting of the owls, and the moonlight, have got into their wild, woodland blood and made it even wilder, they will dance till daybreak. I wish you could see it for yourselves.

What had stopped Jill when she got as far as the *say* of "I say" was of course simply a fine big snowball that came sailing through the dance from a Dwarf on the far side and got her fair and square in the mouth. She didn't in the least mind; twenty snowballs would not have damped her spirits at that moment. But however happy you are feeling, you can't talk with your mouth full of snow. And when, after considerable spluttering, she could speak again, she quite forgot in her excitement that the others, down in the dark, behind her, still didn't know the good news. She simply leaned as far out of the hole as she could, and yelled to the dancers.

"Help! Help! We're buried in the hill. Come and dig us out."

The Narnians, who had not even noticed the little hole in the hillside, were of course very surprised, and looked about in several wrong directions before they found out where the voice was coming from. But when they caught sight of Jill they all came running towards her, and as many as could scrambled up the bank, and a dozen or more hands were stretched up to help her. And Jill caught hold of them and thus got out of the hole and came slithering down the bank head first, and then picked herself up and said:

"Oh, do go and dig the others out. There are three others, besides the horses. And one of them is Prince Rilian."

She was already in the middle of a crowd when she said this, for besides the dancers all sorts of people who had been watching the dance, and whom she had not seen at first, came running up. Squirrels came out of the trees in showers, and so did Owls. Hedgehogs came waddling as fast as their short legs would carry them. Bears and Badgers followed at a slower pace. A great Panther, twitching its tail in excitement, was the last to join the party.

But as soon as they understood what Jill was saying, they all became active. "Pick and shovel, boys, pick and shovel. Off for our tools!" said the Dwarfs, and dashed away into the woods at top speed. "Wake up some Moles, they're the chaps for digging. They're quite as good as Dwarfs," said a voice. "What was that she said about Prince Rilian?" said another. "Hush!" said the Panther. "The poor child's crazed, and no wonder after being lost inside the hill. She doesn't know what she's saying." "That's right," said an old Bear. "Why, she said Prince Rilian was a horse!" – "No, she didn't," said a Squirrel, very pert. "Yes, she did," said another Squirrel, even perter.

"It's quite t-t-t-true. D-d-don't be so silly," said Jill. She spoke like that because her teeth were now chattering with the cold.

Immediately one of the Dryads flung round her a furry cloak which some Dwarf had dropped when he rushed to fetch his mining tools, and an obliging Faun trotted off among the trees to a place where Jill could see firelight in the mouth of a cave, to get her a hot drink. But before it came, all the Dwarfs reappeared with spades and pick-axes and charged at the hillside. Then Jill heard cries of "Hi! What are you doing? Put that sword down," and "Now, young 'un: none of that," and, "He's a vicious one, now, isn't he?" Jill hurried to the spot and didn't know whether to laugh or cry when she saw Eustace's face, very pale and dirty, projecting from the blackness of the hole, and Eustace's right hand brandishing a sword with which he made lunges at anyone who came near him.

For of course Eustace had been having a very different time from Jill during the last few minutes. He had heard Jill cry out and seen her disappear into the unknown. Like the Prince and Puddleglum, he thought that some enemies had caught her. And from down below he didn't see that the pale, blueish light was moonlight. He thought the hole would lead only into some other cave, lit by some ghostly phosphorescence and filled with goodness-knows-what evil creatures of the Underworld. So that when he had persuaded Puddleglum to give him a back, and drawn his sword, and poked out his head, he had really been doing a very brave thing. The others would have done it first if they could, but the hole was too small for them to climb through. Eustace was a little bigger, and a lot clumsier, than Jill, so that when he looked out he bumped his head against the top of the hole and brought a small avalanche of snow down on his face. And so, when he could see again, and saw dozens of figures coming at him as hard as they could run, it is not surprising that he tried to ward them off.

"Stop, Eustace, stop," cried Jill. "They're all friends. Can't you see? We've come up in Narnia. Everything's all right."

Then Eustace did see, and apologized to the Dwarfs (and the Dwarfs said not to mention it), and dozens of thick, hairy, dwarfish hands helped him out just as they had helped Jill out a few minutes before. Then Jill scrambled up the bank and put her head in at the dark opening and shouted the good news in to the prisoners. As she turned away she heard Puddleglum mutter. "Ah, poor Pole. It's been too much for her, this last bit. Turned her head, I shouldn't wonder. She's beginning to see things."

Jill rejoined Eustace and they shook one another by both hands and took in great deep breaths of the free midnight air. And a warm cloak was brought for Eustace and hot drinks, for both. While they were sipping it, the Dwarfs had already got all the snow and all the sods off a large strip of the hillside round the original hole, and the pickaxes and spades were now going as merrily as the feet of Fauns and Dryads had been going in the dance ten minutes before. Only ten minutes! Yet already it felt to Jill and Eustace as if all their dangers in the dark and heat and general smotheriness of the earth must have been only a dream. Out here, in the cold, with the moon and the huge stars overhead (Narnian stars are nearer than stars in our world) and with kind, merry faces all round them, one couldn't quite believe in Underland.

Before they had finished their hot drinks, a dozen or so Moles, newly waked and still very sleepy, and not well pleased, had arrived. But as soon as they understood what it was all about, they joined in with a will. Even the Fauns made themselves useful by carting away the earth in little barrows, and the Squirrels danced and leaped to and fro in great excitement, though Jill never found out exactly what they thought they were doing. The Bears and Owls contented themselves with giving advice, and kept on asking the children if they wouldn't like to come into the cave (that was where Jill had seen the firelight) and get warm and have supper. But the children couldn't bear to go without seeing their friends set free.

No one in our world can work at a job of that sort as Dwarfs and Talking Moles work in Narnia; but then, of course, Moles and Dwarfs don't look on it as work. They like digging. It was therefore not really long before they had opened a great black chasm in the hillside. And out from the blackness into the moonlight – this would have been rather dreadful if one hadn't known who they were – came, first, the long, leggy, steeple-hatted figure of the Marsh-wiggle, and then, leading two great horses, Rilian the Prince himself.

As Puddleglum appeared shouts broke out on every side: "Why, it's a Wiggle – why, it's old Puddleglum – old Puddleglum from the Eastern Marshes – what ever have you been doing, Puddleglum? – there've been search-parties out for you – the Lord Trumpkin has been putting up notices – there's a reward offered!" But all this died away, all in one moment, into dead silence, as quickly as the noise dies away in a rowdy dormitory if the Headmaster opens the door. For now they saw the Prince.

No one doubted for a moment who he was. There were plenty of Beasts and Dryads and Dwarfs and Fauns who remembered him from the days before his enchanting. There were some old ones who could just remember how his father, King Caspian, had looked when he was a young man, and saw the likeness. But I think they would have known him anyway. Pale though he was from long imprisonment in the Deep Lands, dressed in black, dusty, dishevelled, and weary, there was something in his face and air which no one could mistake. That look is in the face of all true kings of Narnia, who rule by the will of Aslan and sit at Cair Paravel on the throne of Peter the High King.

Instantly every head was bared and every knee was bent; a moment later such cheering and shouting, such jumps and reels of joy, such hand-shakings and kissings and embracings of everybody by everybody else broke out that the tears came into Jill's eyes. Their quest had been worth all the pains it cost.

"Please it your Highness," said the oldest of the Dwarfs, "there is some attempt at a supper in the cave yonder, prepared against the ending of the snow-dance –"

"With a good will, Father," said the Prince. "For never had any Prince, Knight, Gentleman, or Bear so good a stomach to his victuals as we four wanderers have tonight."

The whole crowd began to move away through the trees towards the cave. Jill heard Puddleglum saying to those who pressed round him. "No, no, my story can wait.

Nothing worth talking about has happened to me. I want to hear the news. Don't try breaking it to me gently, for I'd rather have it all at once. Has the King been shipwrecked? Any forest fires? No wars on the Calormen border? Or a few dragons, I shouldn't wonder?" And all the creatures laughed aloud and said, "Isn't that just like a Marsh-wiggle?"

The two children were nearly dropping with tiredness and hunger, but the warmth of the cave, and the very sight of it, with the firelight dancing on the walls and dressers and cups and saucers and plates and on the smooth stone floor, just as it does in a farmhouse kitchen, revived them a little. All the same they went fast asleep while supper was being got ready. And while they slept Prince Rilian was talking over the whole adventure with the older and wiser Beasts and Dwarfs. And now they all saw what it meant; how a wicked Witch (doubtless the same kind as that White Witch who had brought the Great Winter on Narnia long ago) had contrived the whole thing, first killing Rilian's mother and enchanting Rilian himself. And they saw how she had dug right under Narnia and was going to break out and rule it through Rilian: and how he had never dreamed that the country of which she would make him king (king in name, but really her slave) was his own country. And from the children's part of the story they saw how she was in league and friendship with the dangerous giants of Harfang. "And the lesson of it all is, your Highness," said the oldest Dwarf, "that those Northern Witches always mean the same thing, but in every age they have a different plan for getting it."

CHAPTER SIXTEEN

THE HEALING OF HARMS

WHEN Jill woke next morning and found herself in a cave, she thought for one horrid moment that she was back in the Underworld. But when she noticed that she was lying on a bed of heather with a furry mantle over her, and saw a cheery fire crackling (as if newly lit) on a stone hearth and, farther off, morning sunlight coming in through the cave's mouth, she remembered all the happy truth. They had had a delightful supper, all crowded into that cave, in spite of being so sleepy before it was properly over. She had a vague impression of Dwarfs crowding round the fire with frying-pans rather bigger than themselves, and the hissing, and delicious smell of sausages, and more, and more, and more sausages. And not wretched sausages half full of bread and soya bean either, but real meaty, spicy ones, fat and piping hot and burst and just the tiniest bit burnt. And great mugs of frothy chocolate, and roast potatoes and roast chestnuts, and baked apples with raisins stuck in where the cores had been, and then ices just to freshen you up after all the hot things.

Jill sat up and looked around. Puddleglum and Eustace were lying not far away, both fast asleep.

"Hi, you two!" shouted Jill in a loud voice. "Aren't you ever going to get up?"

"Shoo, shoo!" said a sleepy voice somewhere above her. "Time to be settling down. Have a good snooze, do, do. Don't make a to-do. Tu-whoo!"

"Why, I do believe," said Jill, glancing up at a white bundle of fluffy feathers which was perched on top of a grandfather clock in one corner of the cave, "I do believe it's Glimfeather!"

"True, true," whirred the Owl, lifting its head out from under its wing and opening one eye. "I came up with a message for the Prince at about two. The squirrels brought us the good news. Message for the Prince. He's gone. You're to follow too. Good-day –" and the head disappeared again.

As there seemed no further hope of getting any information from the Owl, Jill got up and began looking round for any chance of a wash and some breakfast. But almost at once a little Faun came trotting into the cave with a sharp click-clack of his goaty hoofs on the stone floor.

"Ah! You've woken up at last, Daughter of Eve," he said. "Perhaps you'd better wake the Son of Adam. You've got to be off in a few minutes and two Centaurs have very kindly offered to let you ride on their backs down to Cair Paravel." He added in a lower voice. "Of course, you realize it is a most special and unheard-of honour to be allowed to ride a Centaur. I don't know that I ever heard of anyone doing it before. It wouldn't do to keep them waiting."

"Where's the Prince?" was the first question of Eustace and Puddleglum as soon as they had been wakened.

"He's gone down to meet the King, his father, at Cair Paravel," answered the Faun, whose name was Orruns. "His Majesty's ship is expected in harbour any moment. It seems that the King met Aslan – I don't know whether it was in a vision or face to face – before he had sailed far, and Aslan turned him back and told him he would find his long-lost son awaiting him when he reached Narnia."

Eustace was now up and he and Jill set about helping Orruns to get the breakfast. Puddleglum was told to stay in bed. A Centaur called Cloudbirth, a famous healer, or (as Orruns called it) a 'leech', was coming to see to his burnt foot.

"Ah!" said Puddleglum in a tone almost of contentment, "he'll want to have the leg off at the knee, I shouldn't wonder. You see if he doesn't." But he was quite glad to stay in bed.

Breakfast was scrambled eggs and toast and Eustace tackled it just as if he had not had a very large supper in the middle of the night.

"I say, Son of Adam," said the Faun, looking with a certain awe at Eustace's mouthfuls. "There's no need to hurry *quite* so dreadfully as that. I don't think the Centaurs have quite finished *their* breakfasts yet."

"Then they must have got up very late," said Eustace. "I bet it's after ten o'clock."

"Oh no," said Orruns. "They got up before it was light."

"Then they must have waited the dickens of a time for breakfast," said Eustace.

"No, they didn't," said Orruns. "They began eating the minute they awoke."

"Golly!" said Eustace. "Do they eat a very big breakfast?"

"Why, Son of Adam, don't you understand? A Centaur has a man-stomach and a horse-stomach. And of course both want breakfast. So first of all he has porridge and pavenders and kidneys and bacon and omelette and cold ham and toast and marmalade and coffee and beer. And after that he attends to the horse part of himself by grazing for an hour or so and finishing up with a hot mash, some oats, and a bag of sugar. That's why it's such a serious thing to ask a Centaur to stay for the week-end. A very serious thing indeed."

At that moment there was a sound of horse-hoofs tapping on rock from the mouth of the cave, and the children looked up. The two Centaurs, one with a black and one with a golden beard flowing over their magnificent bare chests, stood waiting for them, bending their heads a little so as to look into the cave. Then the children became very polite and finished their breakfast very quickly. No one thinks a Centaur funny when he sees it. They are solemn, majestic people, full of ancient wisdom which they learn from the stars, not easily made either merry or angry; but their anger is terrible as a tidal wave when it comes.

"Good-bye, dear Puddleglum," said Jill, going over to the Marsh-wiggle's bed. "I'm sorry we called you a wet blanket."

"So'm I," said Eustace. "You've been the best friend in the world."

"And I do hope we'll meet again," added Jill.

"Not much chance of that, I should say," replied Puddleglum. "I don't reckon I'm very likely to see my old wigwam again either. And that Prince – he's a nice chap – but do you think he's very strong? Constitution ruined with living underground, I shouldn't wonder. Looks the sort that might go off any day."

"Puddleglum!" said Jill. "You're a regular old humbug. You sound as doleful as a funeral and I believe you're perfectly happy. And you talk as if you were afraid of everything, when you're really as brave as – as a lion."

"Now, speaking of funerals," began Puddleglum, but Jill, who heard the Centaurs tapping with their hoofs behind her, surprised him very much by flinging her arms round his thin neck and kissing his muddy-looking face, while Eustace wrung his hand. Then they both rushed away to the Centaurs, and the Marsh-wiggle, sinking back on his bed, remarked to himself, "Well, I wouldn't have dreamt of her doing that. Even though I *am* a good-looking chap."

To ride on a Centaur is, no doubt, a great honour (and

except Jill and Eustace there is probably no one alive in the world today who has had it) but it is very uncomfortable. For no one who valued his life would suggest putting a saddle on a Centaur, and riding bare-back is no fun; especially if, like Eustace, you have never learned to ride at all. The Centaurs were very polite in a grave, gracious, grown-up kind of way, and as they cantered through the Narnian woods they spoke, without turning their heads, telling the children about the properties of herbs and roots, the influences of the planets, the nine names of Aslan with their meanings, and things of that sort. But however sore and jolted the two humans were, they would now give anything to have that journey over again: to see those glades and slopes sparkling with last night's snow, to be met by rabbits and squirrels and birds that wished you good morning, to breathe again the air of Narnia and hear the voices of the Narnian trees.

They came down to the river, flowing bright and blue in winter sunshine, far below the last bridge (which is at the snug, red-roofed little town of Beruna) and were ferried across in a flat barge by the ferryman; or rather, by the ferry-wiggle, for it is Marsh-wiggles who do most of the watery and fishy kinds of work in Narnia. And when they had crossed they rode along the south bank of the river and presently came to Cair Paravel itself. And at the very moment of their arrival they saw that same bright ship which they had seen when they first set foot in Narnia, gliding up the river like a huge bird. All the court were once more assembled on the green between the castle and the quay to welcome King Caspian home again. Rilian, who had changed his black clothes and was now dressed in a scarlet cloak over silver mail, stood close to the water's edge, bare-headed, to receive his father; and the Dwarf Trumpkin sat beside him in his little donkey-chair. The children saw there would be no chance of reaching the Prince through all that crowd, and, anyway, they now felt rather shy. So they asked the Centaurs if they might go on sitting on their backs a little longer and thus see everything over the heads of the courtiers. And the Centaurs said they might.

A flourish of silver trumpets came over the water from the ship's deck: the sailors threw a rope; rats (Talking Rats, of course) and Marsh-wiggles made it fast ashore; and the ship was warped in. Musicians, hidden somewhere in the crowd, began to play solemn, triumphal music. And soon the King's galleon was alongside and the Rats ran the gangway on board her.

Jill expected to see the old King come down it. But there appeared to be some hitch. A Lord with a pale face came ashore and knelt to the Prince and to Trumpkin. The three were talking with their heads close together for a few minutes, but no one could hear what they said. The music played on, but you could feel that everyone was becoming uneasy. Then four Knights, carrying something and going very slowly, appeared on deck. When they started to come down the gangway you could see what they were carrying: it was the old King on a bed, very pale and still. They set him down. The Prince knelt beside him and embraced him. They could see King Caspian raising his hand to bless his son. And everyone cheered, but it was a half-hearted cheer, for they all felt that something was going wrong. Then suddenly the King's head fell back upon his pillows, the musicians stopped and there was a dead silence. The Prince, kneeling by the King's bed, laid down his head upon it and wept.

There were whisperings and goings to and fro. Then Jill noticed that all who wore hats, bonnets, helmets, or hoods were taking them off – Eustace included. Then she heard a rustling and flapping noise up above the castle; when she looked she saw that the great banner with the golden Lion on it was being brought down to half-mast. And after that, slowly, mercilessly, with wailing strings and disconsolate blowing of horns, the music began again: this time, a tune to break your heart.

They both slipped off their Centaurs (who took no notice of them).

"I wish I was at home," said Jill.

Eustace nodded, saying nothing, and bit his lip.

"I have come," said a deep voice behind them. They turned and saw the Lion himself, so bright and real and strong that everything else began at once to look pale and shadowy compared with him. And in less time than it takes to breathe Jill forgot about the dead King of Narnia and remembered only how she had made Eustace fall over the cliff, and how she had helped to muff nearly all the signs, and about all the snappings and quarrellings. And she wanted to say "I'm sorry" but she could not speak. Then the Lion drew them towards him with his eyes, and bent down and touched their pale faces with his tongue, and said:

"Think of that no more. I will not always be scolding. You have done the work for which I sent you into Narnia."

"Please, Aslan," said Jill, "may we go home now?"

"Yes. I have come to bring you Home," said Aslan. Then he opened his mouth wide and blew. But this time they had no sense of flying through the air: instead, it seemed that they remained still, and the wild breath of Aslan blew away the ship and the dead King and the castle and the snow and the winter sky. For all these things floated off into the air like wreaths of smoke, and suddenly they were standing in a great brightness of mid-summer sunshine, on smooth turf, among mighty trees, and beside a fair, fresh stream.

Then they saw that they were once more on the Mountain of Aslan, high up above and beyond the end of that world in which Narnia lies. But the strange thing was that the funeral music for King Caspian still went on, though no one could tell where it came from. They were walking beside the stream and the Lion went before them: and he became so beautiful, and the music so despairing, that Jill did not know which of them it was that filled her eyes with tears.

Then Aslan stopped, and the children looked into the stream. And there, on the golden gravel of the bed of the stream, lay King Caspian, dead, with the water flowing over him like liquid glass. His long white beard swayed in it like water-weed. And all three stood and wept. Even the Lion wept: great Lion-tears, each tear more precious than the Earth would be if it was a single solid diamond. And Jill noticed that Eustace looked neither like a child crying, nor like a boy crying and wanting to hide it, but like a grown-up crying. At least, that is the nearest she could get to it; but really, as she said, people don't seem to have any particular ages on that mountain.

"Son of Adam," said Aslan, "go into that thicket and pluck the thorn that you will find there, and bring it to me."

Eustace obeyed. The thorn was a foot long and sharp as a rapier.

"Drive it into my paw, Son of Adam," said Aslan, holding up his right fore-paw and spreading out the great pad towards Eustace.

"Must I?" said Eustace.

"Yes," said Aslan.

Then Eustace set his teeth and drove the thorn into the Lion's pad. And there came out a great drop of blood, redder than all redness that you have ever seen or imagined.

And it splashed into the stream over the dead body of the King. At the same moment the doleful music stopped. And the dead King began to be changed. His white beard turned to grey, and from grey to yellow, and got shorter and vanished altogether; and his sunken cheeks grew round and fresh, and the wrinkles were smoothed, and his eyes opened, and his eyes and lips both laughed, and suddenly he leaped up and stood before them – a very young man, or a boy. (But Jill couldn't say which, because of people having no particular ages in Aslan's country. Even in this world, of course, it is the stupidest children who are most childish and the stupidest grown-ups who are most grown-up.) And he rushed to Aslan and flung his arms as far as they would go round the huge neck; and he gave Aslan the strong kisses of a King, and Aslan gave him the wild kisses of a Lion.

At last Caspian turned to the others. He gave a great laugh of astonished joy.

"Why! Eustace!" he said. "Eustace! So you did reach the end of the world after all. What about my second-best sword that you broke on the sea-serpent?"

Eustace made a step towards him with both hands held out, but then drew back with a somewhat startled expression.

"Look here! I say," he stammered. "It's all very well. But aren't you? – I mean didn't you –?"

"Oh, don't be such an ass," said Caspian.

"But," said Eustace, looking at Aslan. "Hasn't he – er – died?"

"Yes," said the Lion in a very quiet voice, almost (Jill thought) as if he were laughing. "He has died. Most people have, you know. Even I have. There are very few who haven't."

"Oh," said Caspian. "I see what's bothering you. You

think I'm a ghost, or some nonsense. But don't you see? I would be that if I appeared in Narnia now: because I don't belong there any more. But one can't be a ghost in one's own country. I might be a ghost if I got into your world. I don't know. But I suppose it isn't yours either, now you're here."

A great hope rose in the children's hearts. But Aslan shook his shaggy head. "No, my dears," he said. "When you meet me here again, you will have come to stay. But not now. You must go back to your own world for a while."

"Sir," said Caspian, "I've always wanted to have just one glimpse of *their* world. Is that wrong?"

"You cannot want wrong things any more, now that you have died, my son," said Aslan. "And you shall see their world – for five minutes of *their* time. It will take no longer for you to set things right there." Then Aslan explained to Caspian what Jill and Eustace were going back to and all about Experiment House: he seemed to know it quite as well as they did.

"Daughter," said Aslan to Jill, "pluck a switch off that bush." She did; and as soon as it was in her hand it turned into a fine new riding crop.

"Now, Sons of Adam, draw your swords," said Aslan. "But use only the flat, for it is cowards and children, not warriors, against whom I send you."

"Are you coming with us, Aslan?" said Jill.

"They shall see only my back," said Aslan.

He led them rapidly through the wood, and before they had gone many paces, the wall of Experiment House appeared before them. Then Aslan roared so that the sun shook in the sky and thirty feet of the wall fell down before them. They looked through the gap, down into the school shrubbery and on to the roof of the gym, all under the same dull autumn sky which they had seen before their adventures began. Aslan turned to Jill and Eustace and breathed upon them and touched their foreheads with his tongue. Then he lay down amid the gap he had made in the wall and turned his golden back to England, and his lordly face towards his own lands. At the same moment Jill saw figures whom she knew only too well running up through the laurels towards them. Most of the gang were there – Adela Pennyfather and Cholmondely Major, Edith Winterblott, 'Spotty' Sorner, big Bannister, and the two loathsome Garrett twins. But suddenly they stopped. Their faces changed, and all the meanness, conceit, cruelty, and sneakishness almost disappeared in one single expression of terror. For they saw the wall fallen down, and a lion as large as a young elephant lying in the gap, and three figures in glittering clothes with weapons in their hands rushing down upon them. For, with the strength of Aslan in them, Jill plied her crop on the girls and Caspian and Eustace plied the flats of their swords on the boys so well that in two minutes all the bullies were running like mad, crying out, 'Murder! Fascists! Lions! It isn't *fair*.' And then the Head (who was, by the way, a woman) came running out to see what was happening. And when she saw the lion and the broken wall and Caspian and Jill and Eustace (whom she quite failed to recognize) she had hysterics and went back to the house and began ringing up the police with stories about a lion escaped from a circus, and escaped convicts who broke down walls and carried drawn swords. In the midst of all this fuss Jill and Eustace slipped quietly indoors and changed out of their bright clothes into ordinary things, and Caspian went back into his own world. And the wall, at Aslan's word, was made whole again. When the police arrived and found no lion, no broken wall, and no convicts, and the Head behaving like a lunatic, there was an inquiry into the whole thing. And in the inquiry all sorts of things about Experiment House came out, and about ten people got expelled. After that, the Head's friends saw that the Head was no use as a Head, so they got her made an Inspector to interfere with other Heads. And when they found she wasn't much good even at that, they got her into Parliament where she lived happily ever after.

Eustace buried his fine clothes secretly one night in the school grounds, but Jill smuggled hers home and wore them at a fancy-dress ball next holidays. And from that day forth things changed for the better at Experiment House, and it became quite a good school. And Jill and Eustace were always friends.

But far off in Narnia, King Rilian buried his father, Caspian the Navigator, Tenth of that name, and mourned for him. He himself ruled Narnia well and the land was happy in his days, though Puddleglum (whose foot was as good as new in three weeks) often pointed out that bright mornings brought on wet afternoons, and that you couldn't expect good times to last. The opening into the hillside was left open, and often in hot summer days the Narnians go in there with ships and lanterns and down to the water and sail to and fro, singing, on the cool, dark underground sea, telling each other stories of the cities that lie fathoms deep below. If ever you have the luck to go to Narnia yourself, do not forget to have a look at those caves.

The Last Battle

CONTENTS

CHAPTER ONE

BY CALDRON POOL

IN the last days of Narnia, far up to the west beyond Lantern Waste and close beside the great waterfall, there lived an Ape. He was so old that no one could remember when he had first come to live in those parts, and he was the cleverest, ugliest, most wrinkled Ape you can imagine. He had a little house, built of wood and thatched with leaves, up in the fork of a great tree, and his name was Shift. There were very few Talking Beasts or Men or Dwarfs, or people of any sort, in that part of the wood, but Shift had one friend and neighbour who was a donkey called Puzzle. At least they both said they were friends, but from the way things went on you might have thought Puzzle was more like Shift's servant than his friend. He did all the work. When they went together to the river, Shift filled the big skin bottles with water but it was Puzzle who carried them back. When they wanted anything from the towns further down the river it was Puzzle who went down with empty panniers on his back and came back with the panniers full and heavy. And all the nicest things that Puzzle brought back were eaten by Shift; for as Shift said, "You see, Puzzle, I can't eat grass and thistles like you, so it's only fair I should make it up in other ways." And Puzzle always said, "Of course, Shift, of course. I see that." Puzzle never complained, because he knew that Shift was far cleverer than himself and he thought it was very kind of Shift to be friends with him at all. And if ever Puzzle did try to argue about anything, Shift would always say, "Now, Puzzle, I understand what needs to be done better than you. You know you're not clever, Puzzle." And Puzzle always said, "No, Shift. It's quite true. I'm *not* clever." Then he would sigh and do whatever Shift had said.

One morning early in the year the pair of them were out walking along the shore of Caldron Pool. Caldron Pool is the big pool right under the cliffs at the western end of Narnia. The great waterfall pours down into it with a noise like everlasting thunder, and the River of Narnia flows out on the other side. The waterfall keeps the Pool always dancing and bubbling and churning round and round as if it were on the boil, and that of course is how it got its name of Caldron Pool. It is liveliest in the early spring when the waterfall is swollen with all the snow that has melted off the mountains from up beyond Narnia in the Western Wild from which the river comes. And as they looked at Caldron Pool Shift suddenly pointed with his dark, skinny finger and said,

"Look! What's that?"

"What's what?" said Puzzle.

"That yellow thing that's just come down the waterfall. Look! There it is again, it's floating. We must find out what it is."

"Must we?" said Puzzle.

"Of course we must," said Shift. "It may be something useful. Just hop into the Pool like a good fellow and fish it out. Then we can have a proper look at it."

"Hop into the Pool?" said Puzzle, twitching his long ears.

"Well how are we to get it if you don't?" said the Ape.

"But – but," said Puzzle, "wouldn't it be better if *you* went in? Because, you see, it's you who wants to know what it is, and I don't much. And you've got hands, you see. You're as good as a Man or a Dwarf when it comes to catching hold of things. I've only got hoofs."

"Really, Puzzle," said Shift, "I didn't think you'd ever say a thing like that. I didn't think it of you, really."

"Why, what have I said wrong?" said the Ass, speaking in rather a humble voice, for he saw that Shift was very deeply offended. "All I meant was –"

"Wanting *me* to go into the water," said the Ape. "As if you didn't know perfectly well what weak chests Apes always have and how easily they catch cold! Very well. I *will* go in. I'm feeling cold enough already in this cruel wind. But I'll go in. I shall probably die. Then you'll be sorry." And Shift's voice sounded as if he was just going to burst into tears.

"Please don't, please don't, please don't," said Puzzle, half braying, and half talking. "I never meant anything of the sort, Shift, really I didn't. You know how stupid I am and how I can't think of more than one thing at a time. I'd forgotten about your weak chest. Of course I'll go in. You mustn't think of doing it yourself. Promise me you won't, Shift."

So Shift promised, and Puzzle went cloppety-clop on his four hoofs round the rocky edge of the Pool to find a place where he could get in. Quite apart from the cold it was no joke getting into that quivering and foaming water, and Puzzle had to stand and shiver for a whole minute before he made up his mind to do it. But then Shift called out from behind him and said: "Perhaps I'd better do it after all, Puzzle." And when Puzzle heard that he said, "No, no. You promised. I'm in now," and in he went.

A great mass of foam got him in the face and filled his mouth with water and blinded him. Then he went under altogether for a few seconds, and when he came up again he was in quite another part of the Pool. Then the swirl caught him and carried him round and round and faster and faster till it took him right under the waterfall itself, and the force of the water plunged him down, deep down, so that he thought he would never be able to hold his breath till he came up again. And when he had come up and when at last he got somewhere near the thing he was trying to catch, it sailed away from him till it too got under the fall and was forced down to the bottom. When it came up again it was further from him than ever. But at last, when he was almost tired to death, and bruised all over and numb with cold, he succeeded in gripping the thing with his teeth. And out he came carrying it in front of him and getting his front hoofs tangled up in it, for it was as big as a large hearthrug, and it was very heavy and cold and slimy.

He flung it down in front of Shift and stood dripping and shivering and trying to get his breath back. But the Ape never looked at him or asked him how he felt. The Ape was too busy going round and round the Thing and spreading it out and patting it and smelling it. Then a wicked gleam came into his eye and he said:

"It is a lion's skin."

"Ee – auh – auh – oh, is it?" gasped Puzzle.

"Now I wonder . . . I wonder . . . I wonder," said Shift to himself, for he was thinking very hard.

"I wonder who killed the poor lion," said Puzzle presently. "It ought to be buried. We must have a funeral."

"Oh, it wasn't a Talking Lion," said Shift. "You needn't bother about *that*. There are no Talking Beasts up beyond the Falls, up in the Western Wild. This skin must have belonged to a dumb, wild lion."

This, by the way, was true. A Hunter, a Man, had killed and skinned this lion somewhere up in the Western Wild several months before. But that doesn't come into this story.

"All the same, Shift," said Puzzle, "even if the skin only belonged to a dumb, wild lion, oughtn't we to give it a decent burial? I mean, aren't all lions rather – well, rather solemn? Because of you know Who. Don't you see?"

"Don't you start getting ideas into your head, Puzzle," said Shift. "Because, you know, thinking isn't your strong point. We'll make this skin into a fine warm winter coat for you."

"Oh, I don't think I'd like that," said the Donkey. "It

would look – I mean, the other Beasts might think – that is to say, I shouldn't feel –"

"What are you talking about?" said Shift, scratching himself the wrong way up as Apes do.

"I don't think it would be respectful to the Great Lion, to Aslan himself, if an ass like me went about dressed up in a lion-skin," said Puzzle.

"Now don't stand arguing, please," said Shift. "What does an ass like you know about things of that sort? You know you're no good at thinking, Puzzle, so why don't you let me do your thinking for you? Why don't you treat me as I treat you? I don't think I can do everything. I know you're better at some things than I am. That's why I let you go into the Pool; I knew you'd do it better than me. But why can't I have my turn when it comes to something I *can* do and you can't? Am I never to be allowed to do anything? Do be fair. Turn and turn about."

"Oh, well, of course, if you put it that way," said Puzzle.

"I tell you what," said Shift. "You'd better take a good brisk trot down river as far as Chippingford and see if they have any oranges or bananas."

"But I'm so tired, Shift," pleaded Puzzle.

"Yes, but you are very cold and wet," said the Ape. "You want something to warm you up. A brisk trot would be just the thing. Besides, it's market day at Chippingford today." And then of course Puzzle said he would go.

As soon as he was alone Shift went shambling along, sometimes on two paws and sometimes on four, till he reached his own tree. Then he swung himself up from branch to branch, chattering and grinning all the time, and went into his little house. He found needle and thread and a big pair of scissors there; for he was a clever Ape and the

Dwarfs had taught him how to sew. He put the ball of thread (it was very thick stuff, more like cord than thread) into his mouth so that his cheek bulged out as if he were sucking a big bit of toffee. He held the needle between his lips and took the scissors in his left paw. Then he came down the tree and shambled across to the lion-skin. He squatted down and got to work.

He saw at once that the body of the lion-skin would be too long for Puzzle and its neck too short. So he cut a good piece out of the body and used it to make a long collar for Puzzle's long neck. Then he cut off the head and sewed the collar in between the head and the shoulders. He put threads on both sides of the skin so that it would tie up under Puzzle's chest and stomach. Every now and then a bird would pass overhead and Shift would stop his work, looking anxiously up. He did not want anyone to see what he was doing. But none of the birds he saw were Talking Birds, so it didn't matter.

Late in the afternoon Puzzle came back. He was not trotting but only plodding patiently along, the way donkeys do.

"There weren't any oranges," he said, "and there weren't any bananas. And I'm very tired." He lay down.

"Come and try on your beautiful new lion-skin coat," said Shift.

"Oh bother that old skin," said Puzzle. "I'll try it on in the morning. I'm too tired tonight."

"You *are* unkind, Puzzle," said Shift. "If *you're* tired what do you think I am? All day long, while you've been having a lovely refreshing walk down the valley, I've been working hard to make you a coat. My paws are so tired I can hardly hold these scissors. And you won't say thank

you – and you won't even look at the coat – and you don't care – and – and –"

"My dear Shift," said Puzzle getting up at once, "I am so sorry. I've been horrid. Of course I'd love to try it on. And it looks simply splendid. Do try it on me at once. Please do."

"Well, stand still then," said the Ape. The skin was very heavy for him to lift, but in the end, with a lot of pulling and pushing and puffing and blowing, he got it on to the donkey. He tied it underneath Puzzle's body and he tied the legs to Puzzle's legs and the tail to Puzzle's tail. A good deal of Puzzle's grey nose and face could be seen through the open mouth of the lion's head. No one who had ever seen a real lion would have been taken in for a moment. But if someone who had never seen a lion looked at Puzzle in his lion-skin he just might mistake him for a lion, if he didn't come too close, and if the light was not too good, and if Puzzle didn't let out a bray and didn't make any noise with his hoofs.

"You look wonderful, wonderful," said the Ape. "If anyone saw you now, they'd think you were Aslan, the Great Lion, himself."

"That would be dreadful," said Puzzle.

"No it wouldn't," said Shift. "Everyone would do whatever you told them."

"But I don't want to tell them anything."

"But you think of the good we could do!" said Shift. "You'd have me to advise you, you know. I'd think of sensible orders for you to give. And everyone would have to obey us, even the King himself. We would set everything right in Narnia."

"But isn't everything right already?" said Puzzle.

"What!" cried Shift. "Everything right? – when there are no oranges or bananas?"

"Well, you know," said Puzzle, "there aren't many people – in fact, I don't think there's anyone but yourself – who wants those sort of things."

"There's sugar too," said Shift.

"H'm yes," said the Ass. "It would be nice if there was more sugar."

"Well then, that's settled," said the Ape. "You will pretend to be Aslan, and I'll tell you what to say."

"No, no, no," said Puzzle. "Don't say such dreadful things. It would be wrong, Shift. I may be not very clever but I know that much. What would become of us if the real Aslan turned up?"

"I expect he'd be very pleased," said Shift. "Probably he sent us the lion-skin on purpose, so that we could set things to right. Anyway, he never *does* turn up, you know. Not nowadays."

At that moment there came a great thunderclap right overhead and the gound trembled with a small earthquake. Both the animals lost their balance and were flung on their faces.

"There!" gasped Puzzle, as soon as he had breath to speak. "It's a sign, a warning. I knew we were doing something dreadfully wicked. Take this wretched skin off me at once."

"No, no," said the Ape (whose mind worked very quickly). "It's a sign the other way. I was just going to say that if the real Aslan, as you call him, meant us to go on with this, he would send us a thunderclap and an earth-tremor. It was just on the tip of my tongue, only the sign itself came before I could get the words out. You've *got* to do it now, Puzzle. And please don't let us have any more arguing. You know you don't understand these things. What could a donkey know about signs?"

CHAPTER TWO

THE RASHNESS OF THE KING

About three weeks later the last of the Kings of Narnia sat under the great oak which grew beside the door of his little hunting lodge, where he often stayed for ten days or so in the pleasant spring weather. It was a low, thatched building not far from the Eastern end of Lantern Waste and some way above the meeting of the two rivers. He loved to live there simply and at ease, away from the state and pomp of Cair Paravel, the royal city. His name was King Tirian, and he was between twenty and twenty-five years old; his shoulders were already broad and strong and his limbs full of hard muscle, but his beard was still scanty. He had blue eyes and a fearless, honest face.

There was no one with him that spring morning except his dearest friend, Jewel the Unicorn. They loved each other like brothers and each had saved the other's life in the wars. The lordly beast stood close beside the King's chair, with its neck bent round polishing its blue horn against the creamy whiteness of its flank.

"I cannot set myself to any work or sport today, Jewel," said the King. "I can think of nothing but this wonderful news. Think you we shall hear any more of it today?"

"They are the most wonderful tidings ever heard in our days or our fathers' or our grandfathers' days, Sire," said Jewel, "if they are true."

"How can they choose but be true?" said the King. "It is more than a week ago that the first birds came flying over us saying, Aslan is here, Aslan has come to Narnia again. And after that it was the squirrels. They had not seen him, but they said it was certain he was in the woods. Then came the Stag. He said he had seen him with his own eyes, a great way off, by moonlight, in Lantern Waste. Then came that dark Man with the beard, the merchant from Calormen. The Calormenes care nothing for Aslan as we do; but the man spoke of it as a thing beyond doubt. And there was the Badger last night; he too had seen Aslan."

"Indeed, Sire," answered Jewel, "I believe it all. If I seem not to, it is only that my joy is too great to let my belief settle itself. It is almost too beautiful to believe."

"Yes," said the King with a great sigh, almost a shiver, of delight. "It is beyond all that I ever hoped for in all my life."

"Listen!" said Jewel, putting his head on one side and cocking his ears forward.

"What is it?" asked the King.

"Hoofs, Sire," said Jewel. "A galloping horse. A very heavy horse. It must be one of the Centaurs. And look, there he is."

A great, golden bearded Centaur, with man's sweat on his forehead and horse's sweat on his chestnut flanks, dashed up to the King, stopped, and bowed low. "Hail, King," it cried in a voice as deep as a bull's.

"Ho, there!" said the King, looking over his shoulder towards the door of the hunting lodge. "A bowl of wine for the noble Centaur. Welcome, Roonwit. When you have found your breath you shall tell us your errand."

A page came out of the house carrying a great wooden bowl, curiously carved, and handed it to the Centaur. The Centaur raised the bowl and said,

"I drink first to Aslan and truth, Sire, and secondly to your Majesty."

He finished the wine (enough for six strong men) at one draught and handed the empty bowl back to the page.

"Now, Roonwit," said the King. "Do you bring us more news of Aslan?"

Roonwit looked very grave, frowning a little.

"Sire," he said. "You know how long I have lived and studied the stars; for we Centaurs live longer than you Men, and even longer than your kind, Unicorn. Never in

all my days have I seen such terrible things written in the skies as there have been nightly since this year began. The stars say nothing of the coming of Aslan, nor of peace, nor of joy. I know by my art that there have not been such disastrous conjunctions of the planets for five hundred years. It was already in my mind to come and warn your Majesty that some great evil hangs over Narnia. But last night the rumour reached me that Aslan is abroad in Narnia. Sire, do not believe this tale. It cannot be. The stars never lie, but Men and Beasts do. If Aslan were really coming to Narnia the sky would have foretold it. If he were really come, all the most gracious stars would be assembled in his honour. It is all a lie."

"A lie!" said the King fiercely. "What creature in Narnia or all the world would dare to lie on such a matter?" And, without knowing it, he laid his hand on his sword hilt.

"That I know not, Lord King," said the Centaur. "But I know there are liars on earth; there are none among the stars."

"I wonder," said Jewel, "whether Aslan might not come though all the stars foretold otherwise. He is not the slave of the stars but their Maker. Is it not said in all the old stories that He is not a tame lion."

"Well said, well said, Jewel," cried the King. "Those are the very words: *not a tame lion*. It comes in many tales."

Roonwit had just raised his hand and was leaning forward to say something very earnestly to the King when all three of them turned their heads to listen to a wailing sound that was quickly drawing nearer. The wood was so thick to the West of them that they could not see the newcomer yet. But they could soon hear the words.

"Woe, woe, woe!" called the voice. "Woe for my brothers and sisters! Woe for the holy trees! The woods are laid waste. The axe is loosed against us. We are being felled. Great trees are falling, falling, falling."

With the last "falling" the speaker came in sight. She was like a woman but so tall that her head was on a level with the Centaur's yet she was like a tree too. It is hard to explain if you have never seen a Dryad but quite unmistakable once you have – something different in the colour, the voice, and the hair. King Tirian and the two Beasts knew at once that she was the nymph of a beech tree.

"Justice, Lord King!" she cried. "Come to our aid. Protect your people. They are felling us in Lantern Waste.

Forty great trunks of my brothers and sisters are already on the ground."

"What, Lady! Felling Lantern Waste? Murdering the talking trees?" cried the King, leaping to his feet and drawing his sword. "How dare they? And who dares it? Now by the Mane of Aslan –"

"A-a-a-h," gasped the Dryad shuddering as if in pain – shuddering time after time as if under repeated blows. Then all at once she fell sideways as suddenly as if both her feet had been cut from under her. For a second they saw her lying dead on the grass and then she vanished. They knew what had happened. Her tree, miles away, had been cut down.

For a moment the King's grief and anger were so great that he could not speak. Then he said:

"Come, friends. We must go up river and find the villains who have done this, with all the speed we may. I will leave not one of them alive."

"Sire, with a good will," said Jewel.

But Roonwit said, "Sire, be wary in your just wrath. There are strange doings on foot. If there should be rebels in arms further up the valley, we three are too few to meet them. If it would please you to wait while –"

"I will not wait the tenth part of a second," said the King. "But while Jewel and I go forward, do you gallop as hard as you may to Cair Paravel. Here is my ring for your token. Get me a score of men-at-arms, all well mounted, and a score of Talking Dogs, and ten Dwarfs (let them all be fell archers), and a Leopard or so, and Stonefoot the Giant. Bring all these after us as quickly as may be."

"With a good will, Sire," said Roonwit. And at once he turned and galloped Eastward down the valley.

The King strode on at a great pace, sometimes muttering to himself and sometimes clenching his fists. Jewel walked beside him, saying nothing; so there was no sound between them but the faint jingle of a rich gold chain that hung round the Unicorn's neck and the noise of two feet and four hoofs.

They soon reached the River and turned up it where there was a grassy road: they had the water on their left and the forest on their right. Soon after that they came to the place where the ground grew rougher and thick wood came down to the water's edge. The road, what there was of it, now ran on the Southern bank and they had to ford the River to reach it. It was up to Tirian's arm-pits, but Jewel (who had four legs and was therefore steadier) kept on his right so as to break the force of the current, and Tirian put his strong arm round the Unicorn's strong neck and they both got safely over. The King was still so angry that he hardly noticed the cold of the water. But of course he dried his sword very carefully on the shoulder of his cloak, which was the only dry part of him, as soon as they came to shore.

They were now going Westward with the River on their right and Lantern Waste straight ahead of them. They had not gone more than a mile when they both stopped and both spoke at the same moment. The King said "What have we here?" and Jewel said "Look!"

"It is a raft," said King Tirian.

And so it was. Half a dozen splendid tree-trunks, all newly cut and newly lopped of their branches, had been lashed together to make a raft, and were gliding swiftly down the river. On the front of the raft there was a water rat with a pole to steer it.

"Hey! Water-Rat! What are you about?" cried the King.

"Taking logs down to sell to the Calormenes, Sire," said the Rat, touching his ear as he might have touched his cap if he had had one.

"Calormenes!" thundered Tirian. "What do you mean? Who gave order for these trees to be felled?"

The River flows so swiftly at that time of the year that the raft had already glided past the King and Jewel. But the Water-Rat looked back over its shoulder and shouted out:

"The Lion's orders, Sire. Aslan himself." He added something more but they couldn't hear it.

The King and the Unicorn stared at one another and both looked more frightened than they had ever been in any battle.

"Aslan," said the King at last, in a very low voice. "Aslan. Could it be true? *Could* he be felling the holy trees and murdering the Dryads?"

"Unless the Dryads have all done something dreadfully wrong –" murmured Jewel.

"But selling them to Calormenes!" said the King. "Is it possible?"

"I don't know," said Jewel miserably. "He's not a *tame* lion."

"Well," said the King at last, "we must go on and take the adventure that comes to us."

"It is the only thing left for us to do, Sire," said the Unicorn. He did not see at the moment how foolish it was for two of them to go on alone; nor did the King. They were too angry to think clearly. But much evil came of their rashness in the end.

Suddenly the King leaned hard on his friend's neck and bowed his head.

"Jewel," he said, "what lies before us? Horrible thoughts arise in my heart. If we had died before today we should have been happy."

"Yes," said Jewel. "We have lived too long. The worst thing in the world has come upon us." They stood like that for a minute or two and then went on.

Before long they could hear the hack-hack-hack of axes falling on timber, though they could see nothing yet because there was a rise of the ground in front of them. When they had reached the top of it they could see right into Lantern Waste itself. And the King's face turned white when he saw it.

Right through the middle of that ancient forest – that forest where the trees of gold and of silver had once grown and where a child from our world had once planted the Tree of Protection – a broad lane had already been opened. It was a hideous lane like a raw gash in the land, full of muddy ruts where felled trees had been dragged down to the river. There was a great crowd of people at work, and a cracking of whips, and horses tugging and straining as they dragged at the logs. The first thing that struck the King and the Unicorn was that about half the people in the crowd were not Talking Beasts but Men. The next thing was that these men were not the fair-haired men of Narnia: they were dark, bearded men from Calormen, that great and cruel country that lies beyond Archenland across the desert to the south. There was no reason, of course, why one should not meet a Calormene or two in Narnia – a merchant or an ambassador – for there was peace between Narnia and Calormen in those days. But Tirian could not understand why there were so many of them: nor why they were cutting down a Narnian forest. He grasped his sword tighter and rolled his cloak round his left arm. They came quickly down among the men.

Two Calormenes were driving a horse which was harnessed to a log. Just as the King reached them the log had got stuck in a bad muddy place.

"Get on, son of sloth! Pull, you lazy pig!" cried the Calormenes, cracking their whips. The horse was already straining himself as hard as he could; his eyes were red and he was covered with foam.

"Work, lazy brute," shouted one of the Calormenes: and as he spoke he struck the horse savagely with his whip. It was then that the really dreadful thing happened.

Up till now Tirian had taken it for granted that the horses which the Calormenes were driving were their own horses; dumb, witless animals like the horses of our own world. And though he hated to see even a dumb horse overdriven, he was of course thinking more about the murder of the Trees. It had never crossed his mind that anyone would dare to harness one of the free Talking Horses of Narnia, much less to use a whip on it. But as that savage blow fell the horse reared up and said, half screaming:

"Fool and tyrant! Do you not see I am doing all I can?"

When Tirian knew that the Horse was one of his own Narnians, there came over him and over Jewel such a rage that they did not know what they were doing. The King's sword went up, the Unicorn's horn went down. They rushed forward together. Next moment both the Calormenes lay dead, the one beheaded by Tirian's sword and the other gored through the heart by Jewel's horn.

CHAPTER THREE

THE APE IN ITS GLORY

"MASTER Horse, Master Horse," said Tirian as he hastily cut its traces, "how came these aliens to enslave you? Is Narnia conquered? Has there been a battle?"

"No, Sire," panted the horse, "Aslan is here. It is all by his orders. He has commanded –"

"'Ware danger, King," said Jewel. Tirian looked up and saw that Calormenes (mixed with a few Talking Beasts) were beginning to run towards them from every direction. The two dead men had died without a cry and so it had taken a moment before the rest of the crowd knew what had happened. But now they did. Most of them had naked scimitars in their hands.

"Quick. On my back," said Jewel.

The King flung himself astride of his old friend who turned and galloped away. He changed direction twice or thrice as soon as they were out of sight of their enemies, crossed a stream, and shouted without slackening his pace, "Whither away, Sire? To Cair Paravel?"

"Hold hard, friend," said Tirian. "Let me off." He slid off the Unicorn's back and faced him.

"Jewel," said the King. "We have done a dreadful deed."

"We were sorely provoked," said Jewel.

"But to leap on them unawares – without defying them – while they were unarmed – faugh! We are two murderers, Jewel. I am dishonoured forever."

Jewel drooped his head. He too was ashamed.

"And then," said the King, "the Horse said it was by Aslan's orders. The Rat said the same. They all say Aslan is here. How if it were true?"

"But, Sire, how *could* Aslan be commanding such dreadful things?"

"He is not a *tame* lion," said Tirian. "How should we know what he would do? We, who are murderers. Jewel, I will go back. I will give up my sword and put myself in the hands of these Calormenes and ask that they bring me before Aslan. Let him do justice on me."

"You will go to your death, then," said Jewel.

"Do you think I care if Aslan dooms me to death?" said the King. "That would be nothing, nothing at all. Would it not be better to be dead than to have this horrible fear that Aslan has come and is not like the Aslan we have believed in and longed for? It is as if the sun rose one day and were a black sun."

"I know," said Jewel. "Or as if you drank water and it were *dry* water. You are in the right, Sire. This is the end of all things. Let us go and give ourselves up."

"There is no need for both of us to go."

"If ever we loved one another, let me go with you now," said the Unicorn. "If you are dead and if Aslan is not Aslan, what life is left for me?"

They turned and walked back together, shedding bitter tears.

As soon as they came to the place where the work was going on the Calormenes raised a cry and came towards them with their weapons in hand. But the King held out his sword with the hilt towards them and said:

"I who was King of Narnia and am now a dishonoured knight give myself up to the justice of Aslan. Bring me before him."

"And I give myself up too," said Jewel.

Then the dark men came round them in a thick crowd, smelling of garlic and onions, their white eyes flashing dreadfully in their brown faces. They put a rope halter round Jewel's neck. They took the King's sword away and tied his hands behind his back. One of the Calormenes, who had a helmet instead of a turban and seemed to be in command, snatched the gold circlet off Tirian's head and hastily put it away somewhere among his clothes. They led the two prisoners uphill to a place where there was a big clearing. And this was what the prisoners saw.

At the centre of the clearing, which was also the highest point of the hill, there was a little hut like a stable, with a thatched roof. Its door was shut. On the grass in front of the door there sat an Ape. Tirian and Jewel, who had been expecting to see Aslan and had heard nothing about an Ape yet, were very bewildered when they saw it. The Ape was of course Shift himself, but he looked ten times uglier than when he lived by Caldron Pool, for he was now dressed up. He was wearing a scarlet jacket which did not fit him very well, having been made for a dwarf. He had jewelled slippers on his hind paws which would not stay on properly because, as you know, the hind paws of an Ape are really like hands. He wore what seemed to be a paper crown on his head. There was a great pile of nuts beside him and he kept cracking nuts with his jaws and spitting out the shells. And he also kept on pulling up the scarlet jacket to scratch himself. A great number of Talking Beasts stood facing him, and nearly every face in that crowd looked miserably worried and bewildered. When they saw who the prisoners were they all groaned and whimpered.

"O Lord Shift, mouthpiece of Aslan," said the chief Calormene. "We bring you prisoners. By our skill and courage and by the permission of the great god Tash we have taken alive these two desperate murderers."

"Give me that man's sword," said the Ape. So they took

the King's sword and handed it, with the sword-belt and all, to the monkey. And he hung it round his own neck: and it made him look sillier than ever.

"We'll see about those two later," said the Ape, spitting out a shell in the direction of the two prisoners. "I got some other business first. They can wait. Now listen to me, everyone. The first thing I want to say is about nuts. Where's that Head Squirrel got to?"

"Here, Sir," said a red squirrel, coming forward and making a nervous little bow.

"Oh you are, are you?" said the Ape with a nasty look. "Now attend to me. I want – I mean, Aslan wants – some more nuts. These you've brought aren't anything like enough. You must bring some more, do you hear? Twice as many. And they've got to be here by sunset tomorrow, and there mustn't be any bad ones or any small ones among them."

A murmur of dismay ran through the other squirrels, and the Head Squirrel plucked up courage to say:

"Please, would Aslan himself speak to us about it? If we might be allowed to see him –"

"Well you won't," said the Ape. "He may be very kind (though it's a lot more than most of you deserve) and come out for a few minutes tonight. Then you can all have a look at him. But he will *not* have you all crowding round him and pestering him with questions. Anything you want to say to him will be passed on through me: if I think it's worth bothering him about. In the meantime all you squirrels had better go and see about the nuts. And make sure they are here by tomorrow evening or, my word! you'll catch it."

The poor squirrels all scampered away as if a dog were after them. This new order was terrible news for them. The nuts they had carefully hoarded for the winter had nearly all been eaten by now; and of the few that were left they had already given the Ape far more than they could spare.

Then a deep voice – it belonged to a great tusked and shaggy Boar – spoke from another part of the crowd.

"But *why* can't we see Aslan properly and talk to him?" it said. "When he used to appear in Narnia in the old days everyone could talk to him face to face."

"Don't you believe it," said the Ape. "And even if it was true, times have changed. Aslan says he's been far too soft with you before, do you see? Well, he isn't going to be soft any more. He's going to lick you into shape this time. He'll teach you to think he's a tame lion!"

A low moaning and whimpering was heard among the Beasts; and, after that, a dead silence which was more miserable still.

"And now there's another thing you got to learn," said the Ape. "I hear some of you are saying I'm an Ape. Well, I'm not. I'm a Man. If I look like an Ape, that's because I'm so very old: hundreds and hundreds of years old. And it's because I'm so old that I'm so wise. And it's because I'm so wise that I'm the only one Aslan is ever going to speak to. He can't be bothered talking to a lot of stupid animals. He'll tell me what you've got to do, and I'll tell the rest of you. And take my advice, and see you do it in double quick time, for he doesn't mean to stand any nonsense."

There was a dead silence except for the noise of a very young badger crying and its mother trying to make it keep quiet.

"And now here's another thing," the Ape went on, fitting a fresh nut into its cheek, "I hear some of the horses are saying, Let's hurry up and get this job of carting timber over as quickly as we can, and then we'll be free again. Well, you can get that idea out of your heads at once. And not only the Horses either. Everybody who can work is going to be made to work in future. Aslan has it all settled with the King of Calormen – The Tisroc, as our dark faced friends the Calormenes call him. All you Horses and Bulls and Donkeys are to be sent down into Calormen to work for your living – pulling and carrying the way horses and such-like do in other countries. And all you digging animals like Moles and Rabbits and Dwarfs are going down to work in The Tisroc's mines. And –"

"No, no, no," howled the Beasts. "It can't be true. Aslan would never sell us into slavery to the King of Calormen."

"None of that! Hold your noise!" said the Ape with a snarl. "Who said anything about slavery? You won't be slaves. You'll be paid – very good wages too. That is to say, your pay will be paid into Aslan's treasury and he will use it all for everybody's good." Then he glanced, and almost winked, at the chief Calormene. The Calormene bowed and replied, in the pompous Calormene way:

"Most sapient Mouthpiece of Aslan, The Tisroc (may-he-live-forever) is wholly of one mind with your lordship in this judicious plan."

"There! You see!" said the Ape. "It's all arranged. And all for your own good. We'll be able, with the money you earn, to make Narnia a country worth living in. There'll be oranges and bananas pouring in – and roads and big cities and schools and offices and whips and muzzles and saddles and cages and kennels and prisons – Oh, everything."

"But we don't want all those things," said an old Bear. "We want to be free. And we want to hear Aslan speak himself."

"Now don't you start arguing," said the Ape, "for it's a thing I won't stand. I'm a Man: you're only a fat, stupid old Bear. What do you know about freedom? You think freedom means doing what you like. Well, you're wrong. That isn't true freedom. True freedom means doing what I tell you."

"H-n-n-h," grunted the Bear and scratched its head; it found this sort of thing hard to understand.

"Please, please," said the high voice of a woolly lamb, who was so young that everyone was surprised he dared to speak at all.

"What is it now?" said the Ape. "Be quick."

"Please," said the Lamb, "I can't understand. What have we to do with the Calormenes? We belong to Aslan. They belong to Tash. They have a god called Tash. They say he has four arms and the head of a vulture. They kill Men on his altar. I don't believe there's any such person as Tash. But if there was, how could Aslan be friends with him?"

All the animals cocked their heads sideways and all their bright eyes flashed towards the Ape. They knew it was the best question anyone had asked yet.

The Ape jumped up and spat at the Lamb.

"Baby!" he hissed. "Silly little bleater! Go home to your mother and drink milk. What do you understand of such things? But the others, listen. Tash is only another name for Aslan. All that old idea of us being right and the Calormenes wrong is silly. We know better now. The Calormenes use different words but we all mean the same thing. Tash and Aslan are only two different names for you know Who. That's why there can never be any quarrel between them. Get that into your heads, you stupid brutes. Tash is Aslan: Aslan is Tash."

You know how sad your own dog's face can look sometimes. Think of that and then think of all the faces of those Talking Beasts – all those honest, humble, bewildered Birds, Bears, Badgers, Rabbits, Moles, and Mice – all far sadder than that. Every tail was down, every whisker drooped. It would have broken your heart with very pity to see their faces. There was only one who did not look at all unhappy.

It was a ginger Cat – a great big Tom in the prime of life – who sat bolt upright with his tail curled round his toes, in the very front row of all the Beasts. He had been staring hard at the Ape and the Calormene captain all the time and had never once blinked his eyes.

"Excuse me," said the Cat very politely, "but this interests me. Does your friend from Calormen say the same?"

"Assuredly," said the Calormene. "The enlightened Ape – Man, I mean – is in the right. *Aslan* means neither less nor more than *Tash*."

"Especially, Aslan means *no more* than Tash?" suggested the Cat.

"No more at all," said the Calormene, looking the Cat straight in the face.

"Is that good enough for you, Ginger?" said the Ape.

"Oh certainly," said Ginger coolly. "Thank you very much. I only wanted to be quite clear. I think I am beginning to understand."

Up till now the King and Jewel had said nothing: they were waiting until the Ape should bid them speak, for they thought it was no use interrupting. But now, as Tirian looked round on the miserable faces of the Narnians, and saw how they would all believe that Aslan and Tash were one and the same, he could bear it no longer.

"Ape," he cried with a great voice, "you lie damnably. You lie like a Calormene. You lie like an Ape."

He meant to go on and ask how the terrible god Tash who fed on the blood of his people could possibly be the same as the good Lion by whose blood all Narnia was saved. If he had been allowed to speak, the rule of the Ape might have ended that day; the Beasts might have seen the truth and thrown the Ape down. But before he could say another word two Calormenes struck him in the mouth with all their force, and a third, from behind, kicked his feet from under him. And as he fell, the Ape squealed in rage and terror.

"Take him away. Take him away. Take him where he cannot hear us, nor we hear him. There tie him to a tree. I will – I mean, Aslan will – do justice on him later."

CHAPTER FOUR

WHAT HAPPENED THAT NIGHT

THE King was so dizzy from being knocked down that he hardly knew what was happening until the Calormenes untied his wrists and put his arms straight down by his sides and set him with his back against an ash tree. Then they bound ropes round his ankles and his knees and his waist and his chest and left him there. What worried him worst at the moment – for it is often little things that are hardest to stand – was that his lip was bleeding where they had hit him and he couldn't wipe the little trickle of blood away although it tickled him.

From where he was he could still see the little stable on the top of the hill and the Ape sitting in front of it. He could just hear the Ape's voice still going on and, every now and then, some answer from the crowd, but he could not make out the words.

"I wonder what they've done to Jewel," thought the King.

Presently the crowd of beasts broke up and began going away in different directions. Some passed close to Tirian. They looked at him as if they were both frightened and sorry to see him tied up but none of them spoke. Soon they had all gone and there was silence in the wood. Then hours and hours went past and Tirian became first very thirsty and then very hungry; and as the afternoon dragged on and turned into evening, he became cold too. His back was very sore. The sun went down and it began to be twilight.

When it was almost dark Tirian heard a light pitter-patter of feet and saw some small creatures coming towards him. The three on the left were Mice, and there

was a Rabbit in the middle: on the right were two Moles. Both these were carrying little bags on their backs which gave them a curious look in the dark so that at first he wondered what kind of beasts they were. Then, in a moment, they were all standing up on their hind legs, laying their cool paws on his knees and giving his knees snuffly animal kisses. (They could reach his knees because Narnian Talking Beasts of that sort are bigger than the dumb beasts of the same kind in England.)

"Lord King! dear Lord King," said their shrill voices, "we are so sorry for you. We daren't untie you because Aslan might be angry with us. But we've brought you your supper."

At once the first Mouse climbed nimbly up till he was

perched on the rope that bound Tirian's chest and was wrinkling his blunt nose in front of Tirian's face. Then the second Mouse climbed up and hung on just below the first Mouse. The other beasts stood on the ground and began handing things up.

"Drink, Sire, and then you'll find you are able to eat," said the topmost Mouse, and Tirian found that a little wooden cup was being held to his lips. It was only the size of an egg cup so that he had hardly tasted the wine in it before it was empty. But then the Mouse passed it down and the others re-filled it and it was passed up again and Tirian emptied it a second time. In this way they went on till he had quite a good drink, which was all the better for coming in little doses, for that is more thirst-quenching than one long draught.

"Here is cheese, Sire," said the first Mouse, "but not very much, for fear it would make you too thirsty." And after the cheese they fed him with oat-cakes and fresh butter, and then with some more wine.

"Now hand up the water," said the first Mouse, "and I'll wash the King's face. There is blood on it."

Then Tirian felt something like a tiny sponge dabbing his face, and it was most refreshing.

"Little friends," said Tirian, "how can I thank you for all this?"

"You needn't, you needn't," said the little voices. "What else could we do? *We* don't want any other King. We're your people. If it was only the Ape and the Calormenes who were against you we would have fought till we were cut into pieces before we'd let them tie you up. We would, we would indeed. But we can't go against Aslan."

"Do you think it really is Aslan?" asked the King.

"Oh yes, yes," said the Rabbit. "He came out of the stable last night. We all saw him."

"What was he like?" said the King.

"Like a terrible, great Lion, to be sure," said one of the Mice.

"And you think it is really Aslan who is killing the Wood-Nymphs and making you all slaves to the King of Calormen?"

"Ah, that's bad, isn't it?" said the second Mouse. "It would have been better if we'd died before all this began. But there's no doubt about it. Everyone says it is Aslan's orders. And we've seen him. We didn't think Aslan would be like that. Why, we – we *wanted* him to come back to Narnia."

"He seems to have come back very angry this time," said the first Mouse. "We must all have done something dreadfully wrong without knowing it. He must be punishing us for something. But I do think we might be told what it was!"

"I suppose what we're doing now may be wrong," said the Rabbit.

"I don't care if it is," said one of the Moles. "I'd do it again."

But the others said, "Oh hush," and "Do be careful," and then they all said, "We're sorry, dear King, but we must go back now. It would never do for us to be caught here."

"Leave me at once, dear Beasts," said Tirian. "I would not for all Narnia bring any of you into danger."

"Goodnight, goodnight," said the Beasts, rubbing their noses against his knees. "We will come back – if we can." Then they all pattered away and the wood seemed darker and colder and lonelier than it had been before they came.

The stars came out and time went slowly on – imagine how slowly – while that last King of Narnia stood stiff and sore and upright against the tree in his bonds. But at last something happened.

Far away there appeared a red light. Then it disappeared for a moment and came back again, bigger and stronger. Then he could see dark shapes going to and fro on this side of the light and carrying bundles and throwing them down. He knew now what he was looking at. It was a bonfire, newly lit, and people were throwing bundles of brushwood on to it. Presently it blazed up and Tirian could see that it was on the very top of the hill. He could see quite clearly the stable behind it, all lit up in the red glow, and a great crowd of Beasts and Men between the fire and himself. A small figure, hunched up beside the fire, must be the Ape. It was saying something to the crowd, but he could not hear what. Then it went and bowed three times to the ground in front of the door of the stable. Then it got up and opened the door. And something on four legs – something that walked rather stiffly – came out of the stable and stood facing the crowd.

A great wailing or howling went up, so loud that Tirian could hear some of the words.

"Aslan! Aslan! Aslan!" cried the Beasts. "Speak to us. Comfort us. Be angry with us no more."

From where Tirian was he could not make out very clearly what the thing was; but he could see that it was yellow and hairy. He had never seen the Great Lion. He had never seen a common lion. He couldn't be sure that what he saw was not the real Aslan. He had not expected Aslan to look like that stiff thing which stood and said nothing. But how could one be sure? For a moment horrible thoughts went through his mind: then he remembered

the nonsense about Tash and Aslan being the same and knew that the whole thing must be a cheat.

The Ape put his head close up to the yellow thing's head as if he were listening to something it was whispering to him. Then he turned and spoke to the crowd, and the crowd wailed again. Then the yellow thing turned clumsily round and walked – you might almost say, waddled – back into the stable and the Ape shut the door behind it. After that the fire must have been put out for the light vanished quite suddenly, and Tirian was once more alone with the cold and the darkness.

He thought of other Kings who had lived and died in Narnia in old times and it seemed to him that none of them had ever been so unlucky as himself. He thought of his great-grandfather's great-grandfather King Rilian who had been stolen away by a Witch when he was only a young prince and kept hidden for years in the dark caves beneath the land of the Northern Giants. But then it had all come right in the end, for two mysterious children had suddenly appeared from the land beyond the world's end and had rescued him so that he came home to Narnia and had a long and prosperous reign. "It's not like that with me," said Tirian to himself. Then he went further back and thought about Rilian's father, Caspian the Seafarer, whose wicked uncle King Miraz had tried to murder him and how Caspian had fled away into the woods and lived among the Dwarfs. But that story too had all come right in the end: for Caspian also had been helped by children – only there were four of them that time – who came from somewhere beyond the world and fought a great battle and set him on his father's throne. "But it was all long ago," said Tirian to himself. "That sort of thing doesn't happen now." And then he remembered (for he had always been good at history when he was a boy) how those same four children who had helped Caspian had been in Narnia over a thousand years before; and it was then that they had done the most remarkable thing of all. For then they had defeated the terrible White Witch and ended the Hundred Years of Winter, and after that they had reigned (all four of them together) at Cair Paravel, till they were no longer children but great Kings and lovely Queens, and their reign had been the golden age of Narnia. And Aslan had come into that story a lot. He had come into all the other stories too, as Tirian now remembered. "Aslan – and children from another world," thought Tirian. "They have always come in when things were at their worst. Oh, if only they could now."

And he called out "Aslan! Aslan! Aslan! Come and help us now."

But the darkness and the cold and the quietness went on just the same.

"Let *me* be killed," cried the King. "I ask nothing for myself. But come and save all Narnia."

And still there was no change in the night or the wood, but there began to be a kind of change inside Tirian. Without knowing why, he began to feel a faint hope. And he felt somehow stronger. "Oh Aslan, Aslan," he whispered. "If you will not come yourself, at least send me the helpers from beyond the world. Or let me call them. Let my voice carry beyond the world." Then, hardly knowing that he was doing it, he suddenly cried out in a great voice:

"Children! Children! Friends of Narnia! Quick. Come to me. Across the worlds I call you; I Tirian, King of Narnia, Lord of Cair Paravel, and Emperor of the Lone Islands!"

And immediately he was plunged into a dream (if it was a dream) more vivid than any he had had in his life.

He seemed to be standing in a lighted room where seven people sat round a table. It looked as if they had just finished their meal. Two of those people were very old, an old man with a white beard and an old woman with wise, merry, twinkling eyes. He who sat at the right hand of the old man was hardly full grown, certainly younger than Tirian himself, but his face had already the look of a king and a warrior. And you could almost say the same of the other youth who sat at the right hand of the old woman. Facing Tirian across the table sat a fair-haired girl younger than either of these, and on either side of her a boy and girl who were younger still. They were all dressed in what seemed to Tirian the oddest kind of clothes.

But he had no time to think about details like that, for instantly the younger boy and both the girls started to their feet, and one of them gave a little scream. The old woman started and drew in her breath sharply. The old man must have made some sudden movement too for the wine glass which stood at his right hand was swept off the table: Tirian could hear the tinkling noise as it broke on the floor.

Then Tirian realized that these people could see him; they were staring at him as if they saw a ghost. But he noticed that the king-like one who sat at the old man's right never moved (though he turned pale) except that he clenched his hand very tight. Then he said:

"Speak, if you're not a phantom or a dream. You have a Narnian look about you and we are the seven friends of Narnia."

Tirian was longing to speak, and he tried to cry out aloud that he was Tirian of Narnia, in great need of help. But he found (as I have sometimes found in dreams too) that his voice made no noise at all.

The one who had already spoken to him rose to his feet. "Shadow or spirit or whatever you are," he said, fixing his eyes full upon Tirian. "If you are from Narnia, I charge you in the name of Aslan, speak to me. I am Peter the High King."

The room began to swim before Tirian's eyes. He heard the voices of those seven people all speaking at once, and all getting fainter every second, and they were saying things like, "Look! It's fading." "It's melting away." "It's vanishing." Next moment he was wide awake, still tied to the tree, colder and stiffer than ever. The wood was full of the pale, dreary light that comes before sunrise, and he was soaking wet with dew; it was nearly morning.

That waking was about the worst moment he had ever had in his life.

CHAPTER FIVE

HOW HELP CAME TO THE KING

But his misery did not last long. Almost at once there came a bump, and then a second bump, and two children were standing before him. The wood in front of him had been quite empty a second before and he knew they had not come from behind his tree, for he would have heard them. They had in fact simply appeared from nowhere. He saw at a glance that they were wearing the same queer, dingy sort of clothes as the people in his dream; and he saw, at a second glance, that they were the youngest boy and girl out of that party of seven.

"Gosh!" said the boy, "that took one's breath away! I thought –"

"Hurry up and get him untied," said the girl. "We can talk, afterwards." Then she added, turning to Tirian, "I'm sorry we've been so long. We came the moment we could."

While she was speaking the Boy produced a knife from his pocket and was quickly cutting the King's bonds: too quickly, in fact, for the King was so stiff and numb that when the last cord was cut he fell forward on his hands and knees. He couldn't get up again till he had brought some life back into his legs by a good rubbing.

"I say," said the girl. "It was you, wasn't it, who appeared to us that night when we were all at supper? Nearly a week ago."

"A week, fair maid?" said Tirian. "My dream led me into your world scarce ten minutes since."

"It's the usual muddle about times, Pole," said the Boy.

"I remember now," said Tirian. "That too comes in all the old tales. The time of your strange land is different from ours. But if we speak of Time, 'tis time to be gone from here: for my enemies are close at hand. Will you come with me?"

"Of course," said the girl. "It's you we've come to help."

Tirian got to his feet and led them rapidly down hill, Southward and away from the stable. He knew where he meant to go but his first aim was to get to rocky places where they would leave no trail, and his second to cross some water so that they would leave no scent. This took them about an hour's scrambling and wading and while that was going on nobody had any breath to talk. But even so, Tirian kept on stealing glances at his companions. The wonder of walking beside the creatures from another world made him feel a little dizzy: but it also made all the old stories seem far more real than they had ever seemed before . . . anything might happen now.

"Now," said Tirian as they came to the head of a little valley which ran down before them among young birch trees, "we are out of danger of those villains for a space and may walk more easily." The sun had risen, dew-drops were twinkling on every branch, and birds were singing.

"What about some grub? – I mean for you, Sir, we two have had our breakfast," said the Boy.

Tirian wondered very much what he meant by "grub", but when the Boy opened a bulgy satchel which he was carrying and pulled out a rather greasy and squashy packet, he understood. He was ravenously hungry, though he hadn't thought about it till that moment. There were two hard-boiled egg sandwiches, and two cheese sandwiches, and two with some kind of paste in them. If he hadn't been so hungry he wouldn't have thought much of the paste, for that is a sort of food nobody eats in Narnia. By the time he had eaten all six sandwiches they had come

to the bottom of the valley and there they found a mossy cliff with a little fountain bubbling out of it. All three stopped and drank and splashed their hot faces.

"And now," said the girl as she tossed her wet hair back from her forehead, "aren't you going to tell us who you are and why you were tied up and what it's all about?"

"With a good will, damsel," said Tirian. "But we must keep on the march." So while they went on walking he told them who he was and all the things that had happened to him. "And now," he said at the end, "I am going to a certain tower, one of three that were built in my grandsire's time to guard Lantern Waste against certain perilous outlaws who dwelled there in his day. By Aslan's good will I was not robbed of my keys. In that tower we shall find stores of weapons and mail and some victuals also, though no better than dry biscuit. There also we can lie safe while we make our plans. And now, prithee, tell me who you two are and all your story."

"I'm Eustace Scrubb and this is Jill Pole," said the Boy. "And we were here once before, ages and ages ago, more than a year ago by our time, and there was a chap called Prince Rilian, and they were keeping this chap underground, and Puddleglum put his foot in –"

"Ha!" cried Tirian, "are you then that Eustace and that Jill who rescued King Rilian from his long enchantment?"

"Yes, that's us," said Jill. "So he's *King* Rilian now, is he? Oh of course he would be. I forgot –"

"Nay," said Tirian, "I am the seventh in descent from him. He has been dead over two hundred years."

Jill made a face. "Ugh!" she said. "That's the horrid part about coming back to Narnia." But Eustace went on.

"Well now you know who we are, Sire," he said. "And it was like this. The Professor and Aunt Polly had got all us friends of Narnia together –"

"I know not these names, Eustace," said Tirian.

"They're the two who came into Narnia at the very beginning, the day all the animals learned to talk."

"By the Lion's Mane," cried Tirian. "Those two! The Lord Digory and the Lady Polly! From the dawn of the world! And still in your place? The wonder and the glory of it! But tell me, tell me."

"She isn't really our aunt, you know," said Eustace. "She's Miss Plummer, but we call her Aunt Polly. Well those two got us all together partly just for fun, so that we could all have a good jaw about Narnia (for of course there's no one else we can ever talk to about things like that) but partly because the Professor had a feeling that we were somehow wanted over here. Well then you came in like a ghost or goodness-knows-what and nearly frightened the lives out of us and vanished without saying a word. After that, we knew for certain there was something up.

The next question was how to get here. You can't go just by wanting to. So we talked and talked and at last the Professor said the only way would be by the Magic Rings. It was by those Rings that he and Aunt Polly got here long, long ago when they were only kids, years before we younger ones were born. But the Rings had all been buried in the garden of a house in London (that's our big town, Sire) and the house had been sold. So then the problem was how to get at them. You'll never guess what we did in the end! Peter and Edmund – that's the High King Peter, the one who spoke to you – went up to London to get into the garden from the back, early in the morning before people were up. They were dressed like workmen so that if anyone did see them it would look as if they'd come to do something about the drains. I wish I'd been with them: it must have been glorious fun. And they must have succeeded for next day Peter sent us a wire – that's a sort of message, Sire, I'll explain about it some other time – to say he'd got the Rings. And the day after that was the day Pole and I had to go back to school – we're the only two who are still at school and we're at the same one. So Peter and Edmund were to meet us at a place on the way down to school and hand over the Rings. It had to be us two who were to go to Narnia, you see, because the older ones couldn't come again. So we got into the train – that's a kind of thing people travel in in our world: a lot of wagons chained together – and the Professor and Aunt Polly and Lucy came with us. We wanted to keep together as long as we could. Well there we were in the train. And we were just getting to the station where the others were to meet us, and I was looking out of the window to see if I could see them when suddenly there came a most frightful jerk and a noise: and there we

were in Narnia and there was your Majesty tied up to the tree."

"So you never used the Rings?" said Tirian.

"No," said Eustace. "Never even saw them. Aslan did it all for us in his own way without any Rings."

"But the High King Peter has them," said Tirian.

"Yes," said Jill. "But we don't think he can use them. When the two other Pevensies – King Edmund and Queen Lucy – were last here, Aslan said they would never come to Narnia again. And he said something of the same sort to the High King, only longer ago. You may be sure he'll come like a shot if he's allowed."

"Gosh!" said Eustace. "It's getting hot in this sun. Are we nearly there, Sire?"

"Look," said Tirian and pointed. Not many yards away grey battlements rose above the tree-tops, and after a minute's more walking they came out in an open grassy space. A stream ran across it and on the far side of the stream stood a squat, square tower with very few and narrow windows and one heavy-looking door in the wall that faced them.

Tirian looked sharply this way and that to make sure that no enemies were in sight. Then he walked up to the tower and stood still for a moment fishing up his bunch of keys which he wore inside his hunting-dress on a narrow silver chain that went round his neck. It was a nice bunch of keys that he brought out, for two were golden and many were richly ornamented: you could see at once that they were keys made for opening solemn and secret rooms in palaces, or chests and caskets of sweet-smelling wood that contained royal treasures. But the key which he now put into the lock of the door was big and plain and more rudely made. The lock was stiff and for a moment Tirian began to be afraid that he would not be able to turn it: but at last he did and the door swung open with a sullen creak.

"Welcome friends," said Tirian. "I fear this is the best palace that the King of Narnia can now offer to his guests."

Tirian was pleased to see that the two strangers had been well brought up. They both said not to mention it and that they were sure it would be very nice.

As a matter of fact it was not particularly nice. It was rather dark and smelled very damp. There was only one room in it and this room went right up to the stone roof: a wooden staircase in one corner led up to a trap door by which you could get out on the battlements. There were a few rude bunks to sleep in, and a great many lockers and bundles. There was also a hearth which looked as if nobody had lit a fire in it for a great many years.

"We'd better go out and gather some firewood first thing, hadn't we?" said Jill.

"Not yet, comrade," said Tirian. He was determined that they should not be caught unarmed, and began searching the lockers, thankfully remembering that he had always been careful to have these garrison towers inspected once a year and to make sure that they were stocked with all things needful. The bow strings were there in their coverings of oiled silk, the swords and spears were greased against rust, and the armour was kept bright in its wrappings. But there was something even better. "Look you!" said Tirian as he drew out a long mail shirt of a curious pattern and flashed it before the children's eyes.

"That's funny-looking mail, Sire," said Eustace.

"Aye, lad," said Tirian. "No Narnian Dwarf smithied that. 'Tis mail of Calormen, outlandish gear. I have ever kept a few suits of it in readiness, for I never knew when I or my friends might have reason to walk unseen in The Tisroc's land. And look on this stone bottle. In this there is a juice which, when we have rubbed it on our hands and faces, will make us brown as Calormenes."

"Oh hurrah!" said Jill. "Disguise! I love disguises."

Tirian showed them how to pour out a little of the juice into the palms of their hands and then rub it well over their faces and necks, right down to the shoulders, and then on their hands, right up to the elbows. He did the same himself.

"After this has hardened on us," he said, "we may wash in water and it will not change. Nothing but oil and ashes will make us white Narnians again. And now, sweet Jill, let us go see how this mail shirt becomes you. 'Tis something too long, yet not so much as I feared. Doubtless it belonged to a page in the train of one of their Tarkaans."

After the mail shirts they put on Calormene helmets, which are little round ones fitting tight to the head and having a spike on top. Then Tirian took long rolls of some white stuff out of the locker and wound them over the helmets till they became turbans: but the little steel spike still stuck up in the middle. He and Eustace took curved Calormene swords and little round shields. There was no sword light enough for Jill, but he gave her a long, straight hunting knife which might do for a sword at a pinch.

"Hast any skill with the bow, maiden?" said Tirian.

"Nothing worth talking of," said Jill, blushing. "Scrubb's not bad."

"Don't you believe her, Sire," said Eustace. "We've both been practising archery ever since we got back from Narnia last time, and she's about as good as me now. Not that either of us is much."

Then Tirian gave Jill a bow and a quiver full of arrows. The next business was to light a fire, for inside that tower it still felt more like a cave than like anything indoors and set one shivering. But they got warm gathering wood – the sun was now at its highest – and once the blaze was roaring up the chimney the place began to look cheerful. Dinner was, however, a dull meal, for the best they could do was to pound up some of the hard biscuit which they found in a locker and pour it into boiling water, with salt, so as to make a kind of porridge. And of course there was nothing to drink but water.

"I wish we'd brought a packet of tea," said Jill.

"Or a tin of cocoa," said Eustace.

"A firkin or so of good wine in each of these towers would not have been amiss," said Tirian.

CHAPTER SIX

A GOOD NIGHT'S WORK

About four hours later Tirian flung himself into one of the bunks to snatch a little sleep. The two children were already snoring: he had made them go to bed before he did because they would have to be up most of the night and he knew that at their age they couldn't do without sleep. Also, he had tired them out. First he had given Jill some practice in archery and found that, though not up to Narnian standards, she was really not too bad. Indeed she had succeeded in shooting a rabbit (not a *Talking* rabbit, of course: there are lots of the ordinary kind about in Western Narnia) and it was already skinned, cleaned, and hanging up. He had found that both the children knew all about this chilly and smelly job; they had learned that kind of thing on their great journey through Giant-Land in the days of Prince Rilian. Then he had tried to teach Eustace how to use his sword and shield. Eustace had learned quite a lot about sword fighting on his earlier adventures but that had been all with a straight Narnian sword. He had never handled a curved Calormene scimitar and that made it hard, for many of the strokes are quite different and some of the habits he had learned with the long sword had now to be unlearned again. But Tirian found that he had a good eye and was very quick on his feet. He was surprised at the strength of both children: in fact they both seemed to be already much stronger and bigger and more grown-up than they had been when he first met them a few hours ago. It is one of the effects which Narnian air often has on visitors from our world.

All three of them agreed that the very first thing they

must do was to go back to Stable Hill and try to rescue Jewel the Unicorn. After that, if they succeeded, they would try to get away Eastward and meet the little army which Roonwit the Centaur would be bringing from Cair Paravel.

An experienced warrior and huntsman like Tirian can always wake up at the time he wants. So he gave himself till nine o'clock that night and then put all worries out of his head and fell asleep at once. It seemed only a moment later when he woke but he knew by the light and the very feel of things that he had timed his sleep exactly. He got up, put on his helmet-and-turban (he had slept in his mail shirt), and then shook the other two till they woke up. They looked, to tell the truth, very grey and dismal as they climbed out of their bunks and there was a good deal of yawning.

"Now," said Tirian, "we go due North from here – by good fortune 'tis a starry night – and it will be much shorter than our journey this morning, for then we went round-about but now we shall go straight. If we are challenged, then do you two hold your peace and I will do my best to talk like a curst, cruel, proud lord of Calormen. If I draw my sword then thou, Eustace, must do likewise and let Jill leap behind us and stand with an arrow on the string. But if I cry 'Home', then fly for the Tower both of you. And let none try to fight on – not even one stroke – after I have given the retreat: such false valour has spoiled many notable plans in the wars. And now, friends, in the name of Aslan let us go forward."

Out they went into the cold night. All the great Northern stars were burning above the tree-tops. The North-Star of that world is called the Spear-Head: it is brighter than our Pole Star.

For a time they could go straight towards the Spear-Head but presently they came to a dense thicket so that they had to go out of their course to get round it. And after that – for they were still overshadowed by branches – it was hard to pick up their bearings. It was Jill who set them right again: she had been an excellent Guide in England. And of course she knew her Narnian stars perfectly, having travelled so much in the wild Northern Lands, and could work out the direction from other stars even when the Spear-Head was hidden. As soon as Tirian saw that she was the best pathfinder of the three of them he put her in front. And then he was astonished to find how silently and almost invisibly she glided on before them.

"By the Mane!" he whispered to Eustace. "This girl is a wondrous wood-maid. If she had Dryad's blood in her she could scarce do it better."

"She's so small, that's what helps," whispered Eustace. But Jill from in front said: "S-s-s-h, less noise."

All round them the wood was very quiet. Indeed it was far too quiet. On an ordinary Narnia night there ought to have been noises – an occasional cheery "Goodnight" from a Hedgehog, the cry of an Owl overhead, perhaps a flute in the distance to tell of Fauns dancing, or some throbbing, hammering noises from Dwarfs underground. All that was silenced: gloom and fear reigned over Narnia.

After a time they began to go steeply uphill and the trees grew further apart. Tirian could dimly make out the well-known hill-top and the stable. Jill was now going with more and more caution: she kept on making signs to the others with her hand to do the same. Then she stopped dead still and Tirian saw her gradually sink down into the grass and disappear without a sound. A moment later she rose again, put her mouth close to Tirian's ear, and said in the lowest possible whisper, "Get down. *Thee* better." She said *thee* for *see* not because she had a lisp but because she knew the hissing letter S is the part of a whisper most likely to be overheard. Tirian at once lay down, almost as silently as Jill, but not quite, for he was heavier and older. And once they were down, he saw how from that position you could see the edge of the hill sharp against the star-strewn sky. Two black shapes rose against it: one was the stable, and the other, a few feet in front of it, was a Calormene sentry. He was keeping very ill watch: not walking or even standing but sitting with his spear over his shoulder and his chin on his chest. "Well done," said Tirian to Jill. She had shown him exactly what he needed to know.

They got up and Tirian now took the lead. Very slowly, hardly daring to breathe, they made their way up to a little clump of trees which was not more than forty feet away from the sentinel.

"Wait here till I come again," he whispered to the other two. "If I miscarry, fly." Then he sauntered out boldly in full view of the enemy. The man started when he saw him

and was just going to jump to his feet: he was afraid Tirian might be one of his own officers and that he would get into trouble for sitting down. But before he could get up Tirian had dropped on one knee beside him, saying:

"Art thou a warrior of the Tisroc's, may he live for ever? It cheers my heart to meet thee among all these beasts and devils of Narnians. Give me thy hand, friend."

Before he well knew what was happening the Calormene sentry found his right hand seized in a mighty grip. Next instant someone was kneeling on his legs and a dagger was pressed against his neck.

"One noise and thou art dead," said Tirian in his ear. "Tell me where the Unicorn is and thou shalt live."

"B – behind the stable, O My Master," stammered the unfortunate man.

"Good. Rise up and lead me to him."

As the man got up the point of the dagger never left his neck. It only travelled round (cold and rather ticklish) as Tirian got behind him and settled it at a convenient place under his ear. Trembling he went round to the back of the stable.

Though it was dark Tirian could see the white shape of Jewel at once.

"Hush!" he said. "No, do not neigh. Yes, Jewel, it is I. How have they tied thee?"

"Hobbled by all four legs and tied with a bridle to a ring in the stable wall," came Jewel's voice.

"Stand here, sentry, with your back to the wall. So. Now, Jewel: set the point of your horn against this Calormene's breast."

"With a good will, Sire," said Jewel.

"If he moves, rive him to the heart." Then in a few seconds Tirian cut the ropes. With the remains of them he bound the sentry hand and foot. Finally he made him open his mouth, stuffed it full of grass and tied him up from scalp to chin so that he could make no noise, lowered the man into a sitting position and set him against the wall.

"I have done thee some discourtesy, soldier," said Tirian. "But such was my need. If we meet again I may happen to do thee a better turn. Now, Jewel, let us go softly."

He put his left arm round the beast's neck and bent and kissed its nose and both had great joy. They went back as quietly as possible to the place where he had left the children. It was darker in there under the trees and he nearly ran into Eustace before he saw him.

"All's well," whispered Tirian. "A good night's work. Now for home."

They turned and had gone a few paces when Eustace said, "Where are you, Pole?" There was no answer. "Is Jill on the other side of you, Sire?" he asked.

"What?" said Tirian. "Is she not on the other side of you?"

It was a terrible moment. They dared not shout but they whispered her name in the loudest whisper they could manage. There was no reply.

"Did she go from you while I was away?" asked Tirian.

"I didn't see or hear her go," said Eustace. "But she could have gone without my knowing. She can be as quiet as a cat; you've seen for yourself."

At that moment a far off drum beat was heard. Jewel moved his ears forward. "Dwarfs," he said.

"And treacherous Dwarfs, enemies, as likely as not," muttered Tirian.

"And here comes something on hoofs, much nearer," said Jewel.

The two humans and the Unicorn stood dead still. There were now so many different things to worry about that they didn't know what to do. The noise of hoofs came steadily nearer. And then, quite close to them, a voice whispered:

"Hallo! Are you all there?"

Thank heaven, it was Jill's.

"Where the *devil* have you been to?" said Eustace in a furious whisper, for he had been very frightened.

"In the stable," gasped Jill, but it was the sort of gasp you give when you're struggling with suppressed laughter.

"Oh," growled Eustace, "you think it funny, do you? Well all I can say is –"

"Have you got Jewel, Sire?" asked Jill.

"Yes. Here he is. What is that beast with you?"

"That's *him*," said Jill. "But let's be off home before anyone wakes up." And again there came little explosions of laughter.

The others obeyed at once for they had already lingered long enough in that dangerous place and the Dwarf drums seemed to have come a little nearer. It was only after they had been walking Southward for several minutes that Eustace said:

"Got *him*? What do you mean?"

"The false Aslan," said Jill.

"What?" said Tirian. "Where have you been? What have you done?"

"Well, Sire," said Jill. "As soon as I saw that you'd got the sentry out of the way I thought hadn't I better have a look inside the stable and see what really *is* there? So I crawled along. It was as easy as anything to draw the bolt.

Of course it was pitch black inside and smelled like any other stable. Then I struck a light and – would you believe it? – there was nothing at all there but this old donkey with a bundle of lion-skin tied on to his back. So I drew my knife and told him he'd have to come along with me. As a matter of fact I needn't have threatened him with the knife at all. He was very fed up with the stable and quite ready to come – weren't you, Puzzle dear?"

"Great Scott!" said Eustace. "Well I'm – jiggered. I was jolly angry with you a moment ago, and I still think it was mean of you to sneak off without the rest of us: but I must admit – well, I mean to say – well it was a perfectly gorgeous thing to do. If she was a boy she'd have to be knighted, wouldn't she, Sire?"

"If she was a boy," said Tirian, "she'd be whipped for disobeying orders." And in the dark no one could see whether he said this with a frown or a smile. Next minute there was a sound of rasping metal.

"What are you doing, Sire?" asked Jewel sharply.

"Drawing my sword to smite off the head of the accursed Ass," said Tirian in a terrible voice. "Stand clear, girl."

"Oh don't, please don't," said Jill. "Really, you mustn't. It wasn't his fault. It was all the Ape. He didn't know any better. And he's very sorry. And he's a nice Donkey. His name's Puzzle. And I've got my arms round his neck."

"Jill," said Tirian, "you are the bravest and most woodwise of all my subjects, but also the most malapert and disobedient. Well: let the Ass live. What have you to say for yourself, Ass?"

"Me, Sire?" came the Donkey's voice. "I'm sure I'm very sorry if I've done wrong. The Ape said Aslan *wanted* me to dress up like that. And I thought he'd know. I'm not clever like him. I only did what I was told. It wasn't any fun for me living in that stable. I don't even know what's been going on outside. He never let me out except for a minute or two at night. Some days they forgot to give me any water too."

"Sire," said Jewel. "Those Dwarfs are coming nearer and nearer. Do we want to meet them?"

Tirian thought for a moment and then suddenly gave a great laugh out loud. Then he spoke, not this time in a whisper. "By the Lion," he said, "I am growing slow witted! Meet them? Certainly we will meet them. We will meet anyone now. We have this Ass to show them. Let them see the thing they have feared and bowed to. We can show them the truth of the Ape's vile plot. His secret's out. The tide's turned. Tomorrow we shall hang that Ape on the highest tree in Narnia. No more whispering and skulking and disguises. Where are these honest Dwarfs? We have good news for them."

When you have been whispering for hours the mere sound of anyone talking out loud has a wonderfully stirring effect. The whole party began talking and laughing: even Puzzle lifted up his head and gave a grand Haw-hee-haw-hee-hee; a thing the Ape hadn't allowed him

to do for days. Then they set off in the direction of the drumming. It grew steadily louder and soon they could see torchlight as well. They came out on one of those rough roads (we should hardly call them roads at all in England) which ran through Lantern Waste. And there, marching sturdily along, were about thirty Dwarfs, all with their little spades and mattocks over their shoulders. Two armed Calormenes led the column and two more brought up the rear.

"Stay!" thundered Tirian as he stepped out on the road. "Stay, soldiers. Whither do you lead these Narnian Dwarfs and by whose orders?"

CHAPTER SEVEN

MAINLY ABOUT DWARFS

THE two Calormene soldiers at the head of the column, seeing what they took for a Tarkaan or great lord with two armed pages, came to a halt and raised their spears in salute.

"O My Master," said one of them, "we lead these manikins to Calormen to work in the mines of The Tisroc, may-he-live-forever."

"By the great god Tash, they are very obedient," said Tirian. Then suddenly he turned to the Dwarfs themselves. About one in six of them carried a torch and by that flickering light he could see their bearded faces all looking at him with grim and dogged expressions. "Has The Tisroc fought a great battle, Dwarfs, and conquered your land?" he asked, "that thus you go patiently to die in the salt-pits of Pugrahan?"

The two soldiers glared at him in surprise but the Dwarfs all answered, "Aslan's orders, Aslan's orders. He's sold us. What can we do against *him*?"

"Tisroc indeed!" added one and spat. "I'd like to see him try it!"

"Silence, dogs!" said the chief soldier.

"Look!" said Tirian, pulling Puzzle forward into the light. "It has all been a lie. Aslan has not come to Narnia at all. You have been cheated by the Ape. This is the thing he brought out of the stable to show you. Look at it."

What the Dwarfs saw, now that they could see it close, was certainly enough to make them wonder how they had ever been taken in. The lion-skin had got pretty untidy already during Puzzle's imprisonment in the stable and it had been knocked crooked during his journey through the dark wood. Most of it was in a big lump on one shoulder. The head, besides being pushed sideways, had somehow got very far back so that anyone could now see his silly, gentle, donkeyish face gazing out of it. Some grass stuck out of one corner of his mouth, for he'd been doing a little

quiet nibbling as they brought him along. And he was muttering, "It wasn't my fault, I'm not clever. I never said I *was*."

For one second all the Dwarfs were staring at Puzzle with wide open mouths and then one of the soldiers said sharply, "Are you mad, My Master? What are you doing to the slaves?" and the other said, "And who are you?" Neither of their spears was at the salute now – both were down and ready for action.

"Give the password," said the chief soldier.

"This is my password," said the King as he drew his sword. "*The light is dawning, the lie broken.* Now guard thee, miscreant, for I am Tirian of Narnia."

He flew upon the chief soldier like lightning. Eustace, who had drawn his sword when he saw the King draw his, rushed at the other one: his face was deadly pale, but I wouldn't blame him for that. And he had the luck that beginners sometimes do have. He forgot all that Tirian had tried to teach him that afternoon, slashed wildly (indeed I'm not sure his eyes weren't shut) and suddenly found, to his own great surprise, that the Calormene lay dead at his feet. And though that was a great relief, it was, at the moment, rather frightening. The King's fight lasted a second or two longer: then he too had killed his man and shouted to Eustace, "'Ware the other two."

But the Dwarfs had settled the two remaining Calormenes. There was no enemy left.

"Well struck, Eustace!" cried Tirian, clapping him on the back. "Now, Dwarfs, you are free. Tomorrow I will lead you to free all Narnia. Three cheers for Aslan!"

But the result which followed was simply wretched. There was a feeble attempt from a few Dwarfs (about five) which died away all at once: from several others there were sulky growls. Many said nothing at all.

"Don't they understand?" said Jill impatiently. "What's wrong with all you Dwarfs? Don't you hear what the King says? It's all over. The Ape isn't going to rule Narnia any longer. Everyone can go back to ordinary life. You can have fun again. Aren't you glad?"

After a pause of nearly a minute a not-very-nice-looking Dwarf with hair and beard as black as soot said: "And who might you be, Missie?"

"I'm Jill," she said. "The same Jill who rescued King

Rilian from the enchantment – and this is Eustace who did it too – and we've come back from another world after hundreds of years. Aslan sent us."

The Dwarfs all looked at one another with grins; sneering grins, not merry ones.

"Well," said the Black Dwarf (whose name was Griffle), "I don't know how all you chaps feel, but I feel I've heard as much about Aslan as I want to for the rest of my life."

"That's right, that's right," growled the other Dwarfs. "It's all a plant, all a blooming plant."

"What do you mean?" said Tirian. He had not been pale when he was fighting but he was pale now. He had thought this was going to be a beautiful moment, but it was turning out more like a bad dream.

"You must think we're blooming soft in the head, that you must," said Griffle. "We've been taken in once and now you expect us to be taken in again the next minute. We've no more use for stories about Aslan, see! Look at him! An old moke with long ears!"

"By heaven, you make me mad," said Tirian. "Which of us said *that* was Aslan? That is the Ape's imitation of the real Aslan. Can't you understand?"

"And you've got a better imitation, I suppose!" said Griffle. "No thanks. We've been fooled once and we're not going to be fooled again."

"I have not," said Tirian angrily, "I serve the real Aslan."

"Where's he? Who's he? Show him to us!" said several Dwarfs.

"Do you think I keep him in my wallet, fools?" said Tirian. "Who am I that I could make Aslan appear at my bidding? He's not a tame lion."

The moment those words were out of his mouth he realized that he had made a false move. The Dwarfs at once began repeating "not a tame lion, not a tame lion," in a jeering sing-song. "That's what the other lot kept on telling us," said one.

"Do you mean you don't believe in the real Aslan?" said Jill. "But I've seen him. And he has sent us two here out of a different world."

"Ah," said Griffle with a broad smile. "So *you* say. They've taught you your stuff all right. Saying your lessons, ain't you?"

"Churl," cried Tirian, "will you give a lady the lie to her very face?"

"You keep a civil tongue in your head, Mister," replied the Dwarf. "I don't think we want any more Kings – if you *are* Tirian, which you don't look like him – no more than we want any Aslans. We're going to look after ourselves from now on and touch our caps to nobody. See?"

"That's right," said the other Dwarfs. "We're on our own now. No more Aslan, no more Kings, no more silly stories about other worlds. The Dwarfs are for the Dwarfs." And they began to fall into their places and to get ready for marching back to wherever they had come from.

"Little beasts!" said Eustace. "Aren't you even going to say *thank you* for being saved from the salt-mines?"

"Oh, we know all about that," said Griffle over his shoulder. "You wanted to make use of us, that's why you rescued us. You're playing some game of your own. Come on you chaps."

And the Dwarfs struck up the queer little marching song which goes with the drum-beat, and off they tramped into the darkness.

Tirian and his friends stared after them. Then he said the single word "Come," and they continued their journey.

They were a silent party. Puzzle felt himself to be still in disgrace, and also he didn't really quite understand what had happened. Jill, besides being disgusted with the Dwarfs, was very impressed with Eustace's victory over the Calormene and felt almost shy. As for Eustace, his heart was still beating rather quickly. Tirian and Jewel walked sadly together in the rear. The King had his arm on the Unicorn's shoulder and sometimes the Unicorn nuzzled the King's cheek with his soft nose. They did not try to comfort one another with words. It wasn't very easy to think of anything to say that would be comforting. Tirian had never dreamed that one of the results of an Ape's setting up as a false Aslan would be to stop people from believing in the real one. He had felt quite sure that the Dwarfs would rally to his side the moment he showed them how they had been deceived. And then next night he would have led them to Stable Hill and shown Puzzle to all the creatures and everyone would have turned against the Ape and, perhaps after a scuffle with the Calormenes, the whole thing would have been over. But now, it seemed, he could count on nothing. How many other Narnians might turn the same way as the Dwarfs?

"Somebody's coming after us, I think," said Puzzle suddenly.

They stopped and listened. Sure enough, there was a thump-thump of small feet behind them.

"Who goes there!" shouted the King.

"Only me, Sire," came a voice. "Me, Poggin the Dwarf. I've only just managed to get away from the others. I'm on your side, Sire: and on Aslan's. If you can put a Dwarfish sword in my fist, I'd gladly strike a blow on the right side before all's done."

Everyone crowded round him and welcomed him and praised him and slapped him on the back. Of course one single Dwarf could not make a very great difference, but it was somehow very cheering to have even one. The whole party brightened up. But Jill and Eustace didn't stay bright for very long, for they were now yawning their heads off and too tired to think about anything but bed.

It was at the coldest hour of the night, just before dawn, that they got back to the Tower. If there had been a meal ready for them they would have been glad enough to eat, but the bother and delay of getting one was not to be thought of. They drank from a stream, splashed their faces with water, and tumbled into their bunks, except for Puzzle and Jewel who said they'd be more comfortable outside. This perhaps was just as well, for a Unicorn and a fat, full-grown Donkey indoors always make a room feel rather crowded.

Narnian Dwarfs, though less than four feet high, are for their size about the toughest and strongest creatures there are, so that Poggin, in spite of a heavy day and a late night, woke fully refreshed before any of the others. He at once took Jill's bow, went out and shot a couple of wood pigeons. Then he sat plucking them on the doorstep and chatting to Jewel and Puzzle. Puzzle looked and felt a good deal better this morning. Jewel, being a Unicorn and therefore one of the noblest and delicatest of beasts, had been very kind to him, talking to him about things of the sort they could both understand like grass and sugar and the care of one's hoofs. When Jill and Eustace came out of the Tower yawning and rubbing their eyes at almost half past ten, the Dwarf showed them where they could gather plenty of a Narnian weed called Wild Fresney, which looks rather like our wood-sorrel but tastes a good deal nicer when cooked. (It needs a little butter and pepper to make it perfect, but they hadn't got these.) So that what with one thing and another, they had the makings of a capital stew for their breakfast or dinner, whichever you choose to call it. Tirian went a little further off into the wood with an axe and brought back some branches for fuel. While the meal was cooking – which seemed a very long time, especially as it smelled nicer and nicer the nearer it came to being done – the King found a complete Dwarfish outfit for Poggin: mail shirt, helmet, shield, sword, belt, and dagger. Then he inspected Eustace's sword and found that Eustace had put it back in the sheath all messy from killing the Calormene. He was scolded for that and made to clean and polish it.

All this while Jill went to and fro, sometimes stirring the pot and sometimes looking out enviously at the Donkey and the Unicorn who were contentedly grazing. How many times that morning she wished she could eat grass!

But when the meal came everyone felt it had been worth waiting for, and there were second helpings all round. When everyone had eaten as much as he could, the three humans and the Dwarf came and sat on the doorstep, the four-footed ones lay down facing them, the Dwarf (with permission both from Jill and from Tirian) lit his pipe, and the King said:

"Now, friend Poggin, you have more news of the enemy, belike, than we. Tell us all you know. And first, what tale do they tell of my escape?"

"As cunning a tale, Sire, as ever was devised," said Poggin. "It was the Cat, Ginger, who told it, and most likely made it up too. This Ginger, Sire – oh, he's a sly-boots if ever a cat was – said he was walking past the tree to which those villains bound your Majesty. And he said (saving your reverence) that you were howling and swearing and cursing Aslan: 'language I wouldn't like to repeat' were the words he used, looking ever so prim and proper – you know the way a Cat can when it pleases. And then, says Ginger, Aslan himself suddenly appeared in a flash of lightning and swallowed your Majesty up at one mouthful. All the Beasts trembled at this story and some fainted right away. And of course the Ape followed it up. There, he says, see what Aslan does to those who don't respect him. Let that be a warning to you all. And the poor creatures wailed and whined and said, it will, it will. So that in the upshot your Majesty's escape has not set them thinking whether you still have loyal friends to aid you, but only made them more afraid and more obedient to the Ape."

"What devilish policy!" said Tirian. "This Ginger, then, is close in the Ape's counsels."

"It's more a question by now, Sire, if the Ape is in *his* counsels," replied the Dwarf. "The Ape has taken to drinking, you see. My belief is that the plot is now mostly carried on by Ginger or Rishda – that's the Calormene captain. And I think some words that Ginger has scattered among the Dwarfs are chiefly to blame for the scurvy return they made you. And I'll tell you why. One of those dreadful midnight meetings had just broken up the night before last and I'd gone a bit of the way home when I found I'd left my pipe behind. It was a real good 'un, an old favourite, so I went back to look for it. But before I got to the place where I'd been sitting (it was black as pitch there) I heard a cat's voice say *Mew* and a Calormene voice say 'here . . . speak softly,' so I just stood as still as if I was frozen. And these two were Ginger and Rishda Tarkaan as they call him. 'Noble Tarkaan,' said the Cat in that silky voice of his, 'I just wanted to know exactly what we both meant today about Aslan meaning *no more* than Tash.' 'Doubtless, most sagacious of cats,' says the other, 'you have perceived my meaning.' 'You mean,' says Ginger, 'that there's no such person as either.' 'All who are enlightened know that,' said the Tarkaan. 'Then we can understand one another,' purrs the Cat. 'Do you, like me, grow a little weary of the Ape?' 'A stupid, greedy brute,' says the other, 'but we must use him for the present. Thou and I must provide for all things in secret and make the Ape do our will.' 'And it would be better, wouldn't it,' said Ginger, 'to let some of the more enlightened Narnians into our counsels: one by one as we find them apt. For the Beasts who really believe in Aslan may turn at any moment: and will, if the Ape's folly betrays his secret. But those who care neither for Tash nor Aslan but have only an eye to their own profit and such reward as The Tisroc may give them when Narnia is a Calormene province, will be firm.' 'Excellent Cat,' said the Captain. 'But choose which ones carefully.'"

While the Dwarf had been speaking the day seemed to have changed. It had been sunny when they sat down. Now Puzzle shivered. Jewel shifted his head uneasily. Jill looked up.

"It's clouding over," she said.

"And it's so cold," said Puzzle.

"Cold enough, by the Lion!" said Tirian, blowing on his hands. "And faugh! What foul smell is this?"

"Phew!" gasped Eustace. "It's like something dead. Is there a dead bird somewhere about? And why didn't we notice it before?"

With a great upheaval Jewel scrambled to his feet and pointed with his horn.

"Look!" he cried. "Look at it! Look, look!"

Then all six of them saw; and over all their faces there came an expression of uttermost dismay.

CHAPTER EIGHT

WHAT NEWS THE EAGLE BROUGHT

In the shadow of the trees on the far side of the clearing something was moving. It was gliding very slowly Northward. At a first glance you might have mistaken it for smoke, for it was grey and you could see things through it. But the deathly smell was not the smell of smoke. Also, this thing kept its shape instead of billowing and curling as smoke would have done. It was roughly the shape of a man but it had the head of a bird; some bird of prey with a cruel, curved beak. It had four arms which it held high above its head, stretching them out Northward as if it wanted to snatch all Narnia in its grip; and its fingers – all twenty of them – were curved like its beak and had long, pointed, bird-like claws instead of nails. It floated on the grass instead of walking, and the grass seemed to wither beneath it.

After one look at it Puzzle gave a screaming bray and darted into the Tower. And Jill (who was no coward, as you know) hid her face in her hands to shut out the sight of it. The others watched it for perhaps a minute, until it streamed away into the thicker trees on their right and disappeared. Then the sun came out again, and the birds once more began to sing.

Everyone started breathing properly again and moved. They had all been still as statues while it was in sight.

"What was it?" said Eustace in a whisper.

"I have seen it once before," said Tirian. "But that time it was carved in stone and overlaid with gold and had solid diamonds for eyes. It was when I was no older than thou, and had gone as a guest to The Tisroc's court in Tashbaan.

He took me into the great temple of Tash. There I saw it, carved above the altar."

"Then that – that thing – was Tash?" said Eustace.

But instead of answering him Tirian slipped his arm behind Jill's shoulders and said, "How is it with you, Lady?"

"A-all right," said Jill, taking her hands away from her pale face and trying to smile. "I'm all right. It only made me feel a little sick for a moment."

"It seems, then," said the Unicorn, "that there is a real Tash, after all."

"Yes," said the Dwarf. "And this fool of an Ape, who didn't believe in Tash, will get more than he bargained for! He called for Tash: Tash has come."

"Where has it – he – the Thing – gone to?" said Jill.

"North into the heart of Narnia," said Tirian. "It has

come to dwell among us. They have called it and it has come."

"Ho, ho, ho!" chuckled the Dwarf, rubbing his hairy hands together. "It will be a surprise for the Ape. People shouldn't call for demons unless they really mean what they say."

"Who knows if Tash will be visible to the Ape?" said Jewel.

"Where has Puzzle got to?" said Eustace.

They all shouted out Puzzle's name and Jill went round to the other side of the Tower to see if he had gone there.

They were quite tired of looking for him when at last his large grey head peered cautiously out of the doorway and he said, "Has it gone away?" And when at last they got him to come out, he was shivering the way a dog shivers before a thunderstorm.

"I see now," said Puzzle, "that I really have been a very bad donkey. I ought never to have listened to Shift. I never thought things like this would begin to happen."

"If you'd spent less time saying you weren't clever and more time trying to be as clever as you could –" began Eustace but Jill interrupted him.

"Oh leave poor old Puzzle alone," she said. "It was all a mistake; wasn't it, Puzzle dear?" And she kissed him on the nose.

Though rather shaken by what they had seen, the whole party now sat down again and went on with their talk.

Jewel had little to tell them. While he was a prisoner he had spent nearly all his time tied up at the back of the stable, and had of course heard none of the enemies' plans. He had been kicked (he'd done some kicking back too) and beaten and threatened with death unless he would say that he believed it was Aslan who was brought out and shown to them by firelight every night. In fact he was going to be executed this very morning if he had not been rescued. He didn't know what had happened to the Lamb.

The question they had to decide was whether they would go to Stable Hill again that night, show Puzzle to the Narnians and try to make them see how they had been tricked, or whether they should steal away Eastward to meet the help which Roonwit the Centaur was bringing up from Cair Paravel and return against the Ape and his Calormenes in force. Tirian would very much like to have followed the first plan: he hated the idea of leaving the Ape to bully his people one moment longer than need be. On the other hand, the way the Dwarfs had behaved last night was a warning. Apparently one couldn't be sure how people would take it even if he showed them Puzzle. And there were the Calormene soldiers to be reckoned with. Poggin thought there were about thirty of them. Tirian felt sure that if the Narnians all rallied to his side, he and Jewel and the children and Poggin (Puzzle didn't count for much) would have a good chance of beating them. But how if half the Narnians – including all the Dwarfs – just sat and looked on? or even fought against him? The risk was too great. And there was, too, the cloudy shape of Tash. What might it do?

And then, as Poggin pointed out, there was no harm in leaving the Ape to deal with his own difficulties for a day or two. He would have no Puzzle to bring out and show now. It wasn't easy to see what story he – or Ginger – could make up to explain that. If the Beasts asked night after night to see Aslan, and no Aslan was brought out, surely even the simplest of them would get suspicious.

In the end they all agreed that the best thing was to go off and try to meet Roonwit.

As soon as they had decided this, it was wonderful how much more cheerful everyone became. I don't honestly think that this was because any of them was afraid of a fight (except perhaps Jill and Eustace). But I daresay that each of them, deep down inside, was very glad not to go any nearer – or not yet – to that horrible bird-headed thing which, visible or invisible, was now probably haunting Stable Hill. Anyway, one always feels better when one has made up one's mind.

Tirian said they had better remove their disguises, as they didn't want to be mistaken for Calormenes and perhaps attacked by any loyal Narnians they might meet. The Dwarf made up a horrid-looking mess of ashes from the hearth and grease out of the jar of grease which was kept for rubbing on swords and spear-heads. Then they took off their Calormene armour and went down to the stream. The nasty mixture made a lather just like soft soap: it was a pleasant, homely sight to see Tirian and the two children kneeling beside the water and scrubbing the backs of their necks or puffing and blowing as they splashed the lather off. Then they went back to the Tower with red, shiny faces, like people who have been given an extra good wash before a party. They re-armed themselves in true Narnian style, with straight swords and three-cornered shields. "Body of me," said Tirian. "That is better. I feel a true man again."

Puzzle begged very hard to have the lion-skin taken off him. He said it was too hot and the way it was rucked up on his back was uncomfortable: also, it made him look so silly. But they told him he would have to wear it a bit longer, for they still wanted to show him in that get-up to the other Beasts, even though they were now going to meet Roonwit first.

What was left of the pigeon-meat and rabbit-meat was not worth bringing away but they took some biscuits. Then Tirian locked the door of the Tower and that was the end of their stay there.

It was a little after two in the afternoon when they set out, and it was the first really warm day of that spring. The young leaves seemed to be much further out than yesterday: the snow-drops were over, but they saw several primroses. The sunlight slanted through the trees, birds sang, and always (though usually out of sight) there was the noise of running water. It was hard to think of horrible things like Tash. The children felt, "This is really Narnia at last." Even Tirian's heart grew lighter as he walked ahead of them, humming an old Narnian marching song which had the refrain:

> Ho, rumble, rumble, rumble,
> Rumble drum belaboured.

After the King came Eustace and Poggin the Dwarf. Poggin was telling Eustace the names of all the Narnian trees, birds, and plants which he didn't know already. Sometimes Eustace would tell him about English ones.

After them came Puzzle, and after him Jill and Jewel walking very close together. Jill had, as you might say, quite fallen in love with the Unicorn. She thought – and she wasn't far wrong – that he was the shiningest, delicatest, most graceful animal she had ever met: and he was so gentle and soft of speech that, if you hadn't known, you would hardly have believed how fierce and terrible he could be in battle.

"Oh, this *is* nice!" said Jill. "Just walking along like this. I wish there could be more of *this* sort of adventure. It's a pity there's always so much happening in Narnia."

But the Unicorn explained to her that she was quite mistaken. He said that the Sons and Daughters of Adam and Eve were brought out of their own strange world into Narnia only at times when Narnia was stirred and upset, but she mustn't think it was always like that. In between their visits there were hundreds and thousands of years when peaceful King followed peaceful King till you could hardly remember their names or count their numbers, and there was really hardly anything to put into the History Books. And he went on to talk of old Queens and heroes whom she had never heard of. He spoke of Swanwhite the Queen who had lived before the days of the White Witch and the Great Winter, who was so beautiful that when she looked into any forest pool the reflection of her face shone out of the water like a star by night for a year and a day afterwards. He spoke of Moonwood the Hare who had such ears that he could sit by Caldron Pool under the thunder of the great waterfall and hear what men spoke in whispers at Cair Paravel. He told how King Gale, who was ninth in descent from Frank the first of all Kings, had sailed far away into the Eastern seas and delivered the Lone Islanders from a dragon and how, in return, they had given him the Lone Islands to be part of the royal lands of Narnia for ever. He talked of whole centuries in which all Narnia was so happy that notable dances and feasts, or at most tournaments, were the only things that could be remembered, and every day and week had been better than the last. And as he went on, the picture of all those happy years, all the thousands of them, piled up in Jill's mind till it was rather like looking down from a high hill on to a rich, lovely plain full of woods and waters and cornfields, which spread away and away till it got thin and misty from distance. And she said:

"Oh, I do hope we can soon settle the Ape and get back to those good, ordinary times. And then I hope they'll go on for ever and ever and ever. *Our* world is going to have an end some day. Perhaps this one won't. Oh Jewel – wouldn't it be lovely if Narnia just went on and on – like what you said it has been?"

"Nay, sister," answered Jewel, "all worlds draw to an end, except Aslan's own country."

"Well, at least," said Jill, "I hope the end of this one is millions of millions of millions of years away – hallo! what are we stopping for?"

The King and Eustace and the Dwarf were all staring up at the sky. Jill shuddered, remembering what horrors they had seen already. But it was nothing of that sort this time. It was small, and looked black against the blue.

"I dare swear," said the Unicorn, "from its flight, that it is a Talking bird."

"So think I," said the King. "But is it a friend, or a spy of the Ape's?"

"To me, Sire," said the Dwarf, "it has a look of Far-sight the Eagle."

"Ought we to hide under the trees?" said Eustace.

"Nay," said Tirian, "best stand still as rocks. He would see us for certain if we moved."

"Look! He wheels, he has seen us already," said Jewel. "He is coming down in wide circles."

"Arrow on string, Lady," said Tirian to Jill. "But by no means shoot till I bid you. He may be a friend."

If one had known what was going to happen next it would have been a treat to watch the grace and ease with which the huge bird glided down. He alighted on a rocky crag a few feet from Tirian, bowed his crested head, and said in his strange eagle's-voice, "Hail, King."

"Hail, Farsight," said Tirian. "And since you call me King, I may well believe you are not a follower of the Ape and his false Aslan. I am right glad of your coming."

"Sire," said the Eagle, "when you have heard my news you will be sorrier of my coming than of the greatest woe that ever befell you."

Tirian's heart seemed to stop beating at these words, but he set his teeth and said, "Tell on."

"Two sights have I seen," said Farsight. "One was Cair Paravel filled with dead Narnians and living Calormenes: The Tisroc's banner advanced upon your royal battlements: and your subjects flying from the city – this way and that, into the woods. Cair Paravel was taken from the sea. Twenty great ships of Calormen put in there in the dark of the night before last night."

No one could speak.

"And the other sight, five leagues nearer than Cair Paravel, was Roonwit the Centaur lying dead with a Calormene arrow in his side. I was with him in his last hour and he gave me this message to your Majesty: to remember that all worlds draw to an end and that noble death is a treasure which no one is too poor to buy."

"So," said the King, after a long silence, "Narnia is no more."

CHAPTER NINE

THE GREAT MEETING ON STABLE HILL

For a long time they could not speak nor even shed a tear. Then the Unicorn stamped the ground with his hoof, and shook his mane, and spoke.

"Sire," he said, "there is now no need of counsel. We see that the Ape's plans were laid deeper than we dreamed of. Doubtless he has been long in secret traffic with The Tisroc, and as soon as he had found the lion-skin he sent him word to make ready his navy for the taking of Cair Paravel and all Narnia. Nothing now remains for us seven but to go back to Stable Hill, proclaim the truth, and take the adventure that Aslan sends us. And if, by a great marvel, we defeat those thirty Calormenes who are with the Ape, then to turn again and die in battle with the far greater host of them that will soon march from Cair Paravel."

Tirian nodded. But he turned to the children and said: "Now, friends, it is time for you to go hence into your own world. Doubtless you have done all that you were sent to do."

"B – but we've done nothing," said Jill who was shivering, not with fear exactly but because everything was so horrible.

"Nay," said the King, "you loosed me from the tree: you glided before me like a snake last night in the wood and took Puzzle: and you, Eustace, killed your man. But you are too young to share in such a bloody end as we others must meet tonight or, it may be, three days hence. I entreat you – nay, I command you – to return to your own place. I should be put to shame if I let such young warriors fall in battle on my side."

"No, no, no," said Jill (very white when she began speaking and then suddenly very red and then white again.) "We won't, I don't care what you say. We're going to stick to you whatever happens, aren't we, Eustace?"

"Yes, but there's no need to get so worked up about it," said Eustace who had stuck his hands in his pockets (forgetting how very odd that looks when you are wearing a mail shirt). "Because, you see, we haven't any choice. What's the good of talking about our going back! How? We've got no magic for doing it!"

This was very good sense but, at the moment, Jill hated Eustace for saying it. He was fond of being dreadfully matter-of-fact when other people got excited.

When Tirian realized that the two strangers could not get home (unless Aslan suddenly whisked them away), he next wanted them to go across the Southern mountains into Archenland where they might possibly be safe. But they didn't know their way and there was no one to send with them. Also, as Poggin said, once the Calormenes had Narnia they would certainly take Archenland in the next week or so: The Tisroc had always wanted to have these Northern countries for his own. In the end Eustace and Jill begged so hard that Tirian said they could come with him and take their chance – or, as he much more sensibly called it, "the adventure that Aslan would send them".

The King's first idea was that they should not go back to Stable Hill – they were sick of the very name of it by now – till after dark. But the Dwarf told them that if they arrived there by daylight they would probably find the place deserted, except perhaps for a Calormene sentry. The Beasts were far too frightened by what the Ape (and Ginger) had told them about this new angry Aslan – or Tashlan – to go near it except when they were called together for these horrible midnight meetings. And Calormenes are never good woodsmen. Poggin thought that even by daylight they could easily get round to somewhere behind the stable without being seen. This would be much harder to do when the night had come and the Ape might be calling the Beasts together and all the Calormenes were on duty. And when the meeting did begin they could leave Puzzle at the back of the stable, completely out of sight, till the moment at which they wanted to produce him. This was obviously a good thing: for their only chance was to give the Narnians a sudden surprise.

Everyone agreed and the whole party set off on a new line – North-West – towards the hated Hill. The Eagle sometimes flew to and fro above them, sometimes he sat perched on Puzzle's back. No one – not even the King himself except in some great need – would dream of *riding* on a Unicorn.

This time Jill and Eustace walked together. They had been feeling very brave when they were begging to be allowed to come with the others, but now they didn't feel brave at all.

"Pole," said Eustace in a whisper. "I may as well tell you I've got the wind up."

"Oh *you're* all right, Scrubb," said Jill. "You can fight. But I – I'm just shaking, if you want to know the truth."

"Oh shaking's nothing," said Eustace. "I'm feeling I'm going to be sick."

"Don't talk about *that*, for goodness' sake," said Jill.

They went on in silence for a minute or two.

"Pole," said Eustace presently.

"What?" said she.

"What'll happen if we get killed here?"

"Well we'll be dead, I suppose."

"But I mean, what will happen in our own world? Shall we wake up and find ourselves back in that train? Or shall we just vanish and never be heard of any more? Or shall we be dead in England?"

"Gosh. I never thought of that."

"It'll be rum for Peter and the others if they saw me waving out of the window and then when the train comes in we're nowhere to be found! Or if they found two – I mean, if we're dead over there in England."

"Ugh!" said Jill. "What a horrid idea."

"It wouldn't be horrid for *us*," said Eustace. "We shouldn't be there."

"I almost wish – no I don't, though," said Jill.

"What were you going to say?"

"I *was* going to say I wished we'd never come. But I don't, I don't, I don't. Even if we *are* killed. I'd rather be killed fighting for Narnia than grow old and stupid at home and perhaps go about in a bath-chair and then die in the end just the same."

"Or be smashed up by British Railways!"

"Why d'you say that?"

"Well when that awful jerk came – the one that seemed to throw us into Narnia – I thought it *was* the beginning of a railway accident. So I was jolly glad to find ourselves here instead."

While Jill and Eustace were talking about this, the others were discussing their plans and becoming less miserable. That was because they were now thinking of what was to be done this very night and the thought of what had happened to Narnia – the thought that all her glories and joys were over – was pushed away into the back part of their minds. The moment they stopped talking it would come out and make them wretched again: but they kept on talking. Poggin was really quite cheerful about the night's work they had to do. He was sure that the Boar and the Bear, and probably all the Dogs would come over to their side at once. And he couldn't believe that all the other Dwarfs would stick to Griffle. And fighting by firelight and in and out among trees would be an advantage to the weaker side. And then, if they could win tonight, need they really throw their lives away by meeting the main Calormene army a few days later?

Why not hide in the woods, or even up in the Western Waste beyond the great waterfall and live like outlaws? And then they might gradually get stronger and stronger, for Talking Beasts and Archenlanders would be joining them every day. And at last they'd come out of hiding and sweep the Calormenes (who would have got careless by then) out of the country and Narnia would be revived. After all, something very like that had happened in the time of King Miraz!

And Tirian heard all this and thought "But what about Tash?" and felt in his bones that none of it was going to happen. But he didn't say so.

When they got nearer to Stable Hill of course everyone became quiet. Then the real wood-work began. From the moment at which they first saw the Hill to the moment at which they all arrived at the back of the stable, it took them over two hours. It's the sort of thing one couldn't describe properly unless one wrote pages and pages about it. The journey from each bit of cover to the next was a separate adventure, and there were very long waits in between, and several false alarms. If you are a good Scout or a good Guide you will know already what it must have been like. By about sunset they were all safe in a clump of holly trees about fifteen yards

behind the stable. They all munched some biscuit and lay down.

Then came the worst part, the waiting. Luckily for the children they slept for a couple of hours, but of course they woke up when the night grew cold, and what was worse, woke up very thirsty and with no chance of getting a drink. Puzzle just stood, shivering a little with nervousness, and said nothing. But Tirian, with his head against Jewel's flank, slept as soundly as if he were in his royal bed at Cair Paravel, till the sound of a gong beating awoke him and he sat up and saw that there was firelight on the far side of the stable and knew that the hour had come.

"Kiss me, Jewel," he said. "For certainly this is our last night on earth. And if ever I offended against you in any matter great or small, forgive me now."

"Dear King," said the Unicorn, "I could almost wish you had, so that I might forgive it. Farewell. We have known great joys together. If Aslan gave me my choice I would choose no other life than the life I have had and no other death than the one we go to."

Then they woke up Farsight, who was asleep with his head under his wing (it made him look as if he had no head at all), and crept forward to the stable. They left Puzzle (not without a kind word, for no one was angry with him now) just behind it, telling him not to move till someone came to fetch him, and took up their position at one end of the stable.

The bonfire had not been lit for long and was just beginning to blaze up. It was only a few feet away from them, and the great crowd of Narnian creatures were on the other side of it, so that Tirian could not at first see them very well, though of course he saw dozens of eyes shining with the reflection of the fire, as you've seen a rabbit's or cat's eyes in the headlights of a car. And just as Tirian took his place, the gong stopped beating and from somewhere on his left three figures appeared. One was Rishda Tarkaan the Calormene Captain. The second was the Ape. He was holding on to the Tarkaan's hand with one paw and kept whimpering and muttering, "Not so fast, don't go so fast, I'm not *at all* well. Oh my poor head! These midnight meetings are getting too much for me. Apes aren't meant to be up at night: It's not as if I was a rat or a bat – oh my poor head." On the other side of the Ape, walking very soft and stately, with his tail straight up in the air, came Ginger the Cat. They were heading for the bonfire and were so close to Tirian that they would have seen him at once if they had looked in the right direction. Fortunately they did not. But Tirian heard Rishda say to Ginger in a low voice:

"Now, Cat, to thy post. See thou play thy part well."

"Miaow, miaow. Count on me!" said Ginger. Then he stepped away beyond the bonfire and sat down in the front

row of the assembled Beasts: in the audience, as you might say.

For really, as it happened, the whole thing was rather like a theatre. The crowd of Narnians were like the people in the seats; the little grassy place just in front of the stable, where the bonfire burned and the Ape and the Captain stood to talk to the crowd, was like the stage; the stable itself was like the scenery at the back of the stage; and Tirian and his friends were like people peering round from behind the scenery. It was a splendid position. If any of them stepped forward into the full firelight, all eyes would be fixed on him at once: on the other hand, so long as they stood still in the shadow of the end-wall of the stable, it was a hundred to one against their being noticed.

Rishda Tarkaan dragged the Ape up close to the fire. The pair of them turned to face the crowd, and this of course meant that their backs were towards Tirian and his friends.

"Now, Monkey," said Rishda Tarkaan in a low voice. "Say the words that wiser heads have put into thy mouth. And hold up thy head." As he spoke he gave the Ape a little prod or kick from behind with the point of his toe.

"Do leave me alone," muttered Shift. But he sat up straighter and began, in a louder voice – "Now listen, all of you. A terrible thing has happened. A wicked thing. The wickedest thing that ever was done in Narnia. And Aslan –"

"Tashlan, fool," whispered Rishda Tarkaan.

"Tashlan I mean, of course," said the Ape, "is very angry about it."

There was a terrible silence while the Beasts waited to hear what new trouble was in store for them. The little party by the end-wall of the stable also held their breath. What on earth was coming now?

"Yes," said the Ape. "At this very moment, when the Terrible One himself is among us – there in the stable just behind me – one wicked Beast has chosen to do what you'd think no one would dare to do even if *He* were a thousand miles away. It has dressed itself up in a lion-skin and is wandering about in these very woods pretending to be Aslan."

Jill wondered for a moment if the Ape had gone mad. Was he going to tell the whole truth? A roar of horror and rage went up from the Beasts. "Grrr!" came the growls. "Who is he? Where is he? Just let me get my teeth into him!"

"It was seen last night," screamed the Ape, "but it got away. It's a Donkey! A common, miserable Ass! If any of you see that Ass –"

"Grrr!" growled the Beasts. "We will, we will. He'd better keep out of *our* way."

Jill looked at the King: his mouth was open and his face was full of horror. And then she understood the devilish cunning of the enemies' plan. By mixing a little truth with it they had made their lie far stronger. What was the good, now, of telling the Beasts that an ass had been dressed up as a lion to deceive them? The Ape would only say, "That's just what I've said." What was the good of showing them Puzzle in his lion-skin? They would only tear him in pieces. "That's taken the wind out of our sails," whispered Eustace. "The ground is taken from under our feet," said Tirian. "Cursed, cursed cleverness!" said Poggin. "I'll be sworn that this new lie is of Ginger's making."

CHAPTER TEN

WHO WILL GO INTO THE STABLE?

JILL felt something tickling her ear. It was Jewel the Unicorn, whispering to her with the wide whisper of a horse's mouth. As soon as she heard what he was saying she nodded and tip-toed back to where Puzzle was standing. Quickly and quietly she cut the last cords that bound the lion-skin to him. It wouldn't do for him to be caught with *that* on, after what the Ape had said! She would like to have hidden the skin somewhere very far away, but it was too heavy. The best she could do was to kick it in among the thickest bushes. Then she made signs to Puzzle to follow her and they both joined the others.

The Ape was speaking again.

"And after a horrid thing like that, Aslan – Tashlan – is angrier than ever. He says he's been a great deal too good to you, coming out every night to be looked at, see! Well, he's not coming out any more."

Howls and mewings and squeals and grunts were the Animals' answer to this, but suddenly a quite different voice broke in with a loud laugh.

"Hark what the monkey says," it shouted. "We know why he isn't going to bring his precious Aslan out. I'll tell you why: because he hasn't got him. He never had anything except an old donkey with a lion-skin on its back. Now he's lost *that* and he doesn't know what to do."

Tirian could not see the faces on the other side of the fire very well but he guessed this was Griffle the Chief Dwarf. And he was quite certain of it when, a second later, all the Dwarfs' voices joined in, singing: "Don't know what to do! Don't know what to do! Don't know what to do-o-o!"

"Silence!" thundered Rishda Tarkaan. "Silence, children of mud! Listen to me, you other Narnians, lest I give command to my warriors to fall upon you with the edge of the sword. The Lord Shift has already told you of that wicked Ass. Do you think, because of him that there is no *real* Tashlan in the stable! Do you? Beware, beware."

"No, no," shouted most of the crowd. But the Dwarfs said, "That's right, Darkie, you've got it. Come on, Monkey, show us what's in the stable, seeing is believing."

When next there was a moment's quiet the Ape said: "You Dwarfs think you're very clever, don't you? But not so fast. I never said you couldn't see Tashlan. Anyone who likes can see him."

The whole assembly became silent. Then, after nearly a minute, the Bear began in a slow, puzzled voice:

"I don't quite understand all this," it grumbled, "I thought you said –"

"*You* thought!" repeated the Ape. "As if anyone could call what goes on in your head *thinking*. Listen, you others. Anyone can see Tashlan. But he's not coming out. You have to go in and see *him*."

"Oh, thank you, thank you, thank you," said dozens of voices. "That's what we wanted! We can go in and see him face to face. And now he'll be kind and it will all be as it used to be." And the Birds chattered, and the Dogs barked excitedly. Then suddenly, there was a great stirring and a noise of creatures rising to their feet, and in a second the whole lot of them would have been rushing forward and trying to crowd into the stable door all together. But the Ape shouted:

"Get back! Quiet! Not so fast."

The Beasts stopped, many of them with one paw in the air, many with tails wagging, and all of them with heads on one side.

"I thought you said," began the Bear, but Shift interrupted.

"Anyone can go in," he said. "But, one at a time. Who'll go first? He didn't *say* he was feeling very kind. He's been licking his lips a lot since he swallowed up the wicked King the other night. He's been growling a good deal this morning. I wouldn't much like to go into that stable myself tonight. But just as you please. Who'd like to go in first? Don't blame me if he swallows you whole or blasts you into a cinder with the mere terror of his eyes. That's your affair. Now then! Who's first? What about one of you Dwarfs?"

"Dilly, dilly, come and be killed!" sneered Griffle. "How do we know what you've got in there?"

"Ho-ho!" cried the Ape. "So you're beginning to think there's *something* there, eh? Well, all you Beasts were making noise enough a minute ago. What's struck you all dumb? Who's going in first?"

But the Beasts all stood looking at one another and began backing away from the stable. Very few tails were wagging now. The Ape waddled to and fro jeering at them. "Ho-ho-ho!" he chuckled. "I thought you were all so eager to see Tashlan face to face! Changed your mind, eh?"

Tirian bent his head to hear something that Jill was trying to whisper in his ear. "What do you think is really inside the stable?" she said. "Who knows?" said Tirian. "Two Calormenes with drawn swords, as likely as not, one

on each side of the door." "You don't think," said Jill, "it might be . . . you know . . . that horrid thing we saw?" "Tash himself?" whispered Tirian. "There's no knowing. But courage, child: we are all between the paws of the true Aslan."

Then a most surprising thing happened. Ginger the Cat said in a cool, clear voice, not at all as if he was excited, "I'll go in, if you like."

Every creature turned and fixed its eyes on the Cat. "Mark their subtleties, Sire," said Poggin to the King. "This cursed cat is in the plot, in the very centre of it. Whatever is in the stable will not hurt him, I'll be bound. Then Ginger will come out again and say that he has seen some wonder."

But Tirian had no time to answer him. The Ape was calling the Cat to come forward. "Ho-ho!" said the Ape. "So you, a pert Puss, would look upon him face to face. Come on, then! I'll open the door for you. Don't blame me if he scares the whiskers off your face. That's your affair."

And the Cat got up and came out of its place in the crowd, walking primly and daintily, with its tail in the air, not one hair on its sleek coat out of place. It came on till it had passed the fire and was so close that Tirian, from where he stood with his shoulder against the end-wall of the stable, could look right into its face. Its big green eyes never blinked. ("Cool as a cucumber," muttered Eustace. "*It* knows it has nothing to fear.") The Ape, chuckling and making faces, shuffled across beside the Cat: put up his paw: drew the bolt and opened the door. Tirian thought he could hear the Cat purring as it walked into the dark doorway.

"Aii-aii-aouwee! –" The most horrible caterwaul you ever heard made everyone jump. You have been wakened yourself by cats quarrelling or making love on the roof in the middle of the night: you know the sound.

This was worse. The Ape was knocked head over heels by Ginger coming back out of the stable at top speed. If you had not known he was a cat, you might have thought he was a ginger-coloured streak of lightning. He shot across the open grass, back into the crowd. No one wants to meet a cat in that state. You could see animals getting out of his way to left and right. He dashed up a tree, whisked around, and hung head downwards. His tail was bristled out till it was nearly as thick as his whole body: his eyes were like saucers of green fire: along his back every single hair stood on end.

"I'd give my beard," whispered Poggin, "to know whether that brute is only acting or whether it has really found something in there that frightened it!"

"Peace, friend," said Tirian, for the Captain and the Ape were also whispering and he wanted to hear what they said. He did not succeed, except that he heard the Ape once more whimpering "My head, my head," but he got the idea that those two were almost as puzzled by the cat's behaviour as himself.

"Now, Ginger," said the Captain. "Enough of that noise. Tell them what thou hast seen."

"Aii – Aii – Aaow – Awah," screamed the Cat.

"Art thou not called a *Talking* Beast?" said the Captain. "Then hold thy devilish noise and talk."

What followed was rather horrible. Tirian felt quite certain (and so did the others) that the Cat was trying to

say something: but nothing came out of his mouth except the ordinary, ugly cat-noises you might hear from any angry or frightened old Tom in a backyard in England. And the longer he caterwauled the less like a Talking Beast he looked. Uneasy whimperings and little sharp squeals broke out from among the other Animals.

"Look, look!" said the voice of the Bear. "It can't talk. It has forgotten how to talk! It has gone back to being a dumb beast. Look at its face." Everyone saw that it was true. And then the greatest terror of all fell upon those Narnians. For every one of them had been taught – when it was only a chick or a puppy or a cub – how Aslan at the beginning of the world had turned the beasts of Narnia into Talking Beasts and warned them that if they weren't good they might one day be turned back again and be like the poor witless animals one meets in other countries. "And now it is coming upon us," they moaned.

"Mercy! Mercy!" wailed the Beasts. "Spare us, Lord Shift, stand between us and Aslan, you must always go in and speak to him for us. We daren't, we daren't."

Ginger disappeared further up into the tree. No one ever saw him again.

Tirian stood with his hand on his sword-hilt and his head bowed. He was dazed with the horrors of that night. Sometimes he thought it would be best to draw his sword at once and rush upon the Calormenes: then next moment he thought it would be better to wait and see what new turn affairs might take. And now a new turn came.

"My Father," came a clear, ringing voice from the left of the crowd. Tirian knew at once that it was one of the Calormenes speaking, for in The Tisroc's army the common soldiers call the officers "My Master" but the officers call their senior officers "My Father". Jill and Eustace didn't know this but, after looking this way and that, they saw the speaker, for of course people at the sides of the crowd were easier to see than people in the middle where the glare of the fire made all beyond it look rather black. He was young and tall and slender, and even rather beautiful in the dark, haughty, Calormene way.

"My Father," he said to the Captain, "I also desire to go in."

"Peace, Emeth," said the Captain, "Who called thee to counsel? Does it become a boy to speak?"

"My Father," said Emeth. "Truly I am younger than thou, yet I also am of the blood of the Tarkaans even as thou art, and I also am the servant of Tash. Therefore . . ."

"Silence," said Rishda Tarkaan. "Am not I thy Captain? Thou hast nothing to do with this stable. It is for the Narnians."

"Nay, my Father," answered Emeth. "Thou hast said that their Aslan and our Tash are all one. And if that is the truth, then Tash himself is in yonder. And how then sayest thou that I have nothing to do with him? For gladly would I die a thousand deaths if I might look once on the face of Tash."

"Thou art a fool and understandest nothing," said Rishda Tarkaan. "These be high matters."

Emeth's face grew sterner. "Is it then not true that Tash and Aslan are all one?" he asked. "Has the Ape lied to us?"

"Of course they're all one," said the Ape.

"Swear it, Ape," said Emeth.

"Oh dear!" whimpered Shift, "I wish you'd all stop bothering me. My head does ache. Yes, yes, I swear it."

"Then, my Father," said Emeth, "I am utterly determined to go in."

"Fool," began Rishda Tarkaan, but at once the Dwarfs began shouting: "Come along, Darkie. Why don't you let him in? Why do you let Narnians in and keep your own people out? What have you got in there that you don't want your own men to meet?"

Tirian and his friends could only see the back of Rishda Tarkaan, so they never knew what his face looked like as he shrugged his shoulders and said, "Bear witness all that I am guiltless of this young fool's blood. Get thee in, rash boy, and make haste."

Then, just as Ginger had done, Emeth came walking forward into the open strip of grass between the bonfire and the stable. His eyes were shining, his face very solemn, his hand was on his sword-hilt, and he carried his head high. Jill felt like crying when she looked at his face. And Jewel whispered in the King's ear, "By the Lion's Mane, I almost love this young warrior, Calormene though he be. He is worthy of a better god than Tash."

"I do wish we knew what is really inside there," said Eustace.

Emeth opened the door and went in, into the black mouth of the stable. He closed the door behind him. Only a few moments passed – but it seemed longer – before the door opened again. A figure in Calormene armour reeled out, fell on its back, and lay still: the door closed behind it. The Captain leaped towards it and bent down to stare at its face. He gave a start of surprise. Then he recovered himself and turned to the crowd, crying out:

"The rash boy has had his will. He has looked on Tash and is dead. Take warning, all of you."

"We will, we will," said the poor Beasts. But Tirian and his friends stared at the dead Calormene and then at one another. For they, being so close, could see what the crowd, being further off and beyond the fire, could not see: this dead man was not Emeth. He was quite different: an older man, thicker and not so tall, with a big beard.

"Ho-ho-ho," chuckled the Ape. "Any more? Anyone

else want to go in? Well, as you're all shy, I'll choose the next. You, you Boar! On you come. Drive him up, Calormenes. He *shall* see Tashlan face to face."

"O-o-mph," grunted the Boar, rising heavily to his feet. "Come on, then. Try my tusks."

When Tirian saw that brave Beast getting ready to fight for its life – and Calormene soldiers beginning to close in on it with their drawn scimitars – and no one going to its help – something seemed to burst inside him. He no longer cared if this was the best moment to interfere or not.

"Swords out," he whispered to the others. "Arrow on string. Follow."

Next moment the astonished Narnians saw seven figures leap forth in front of the stable, four of them in shining mail. The King's sword flashed in the firelight as he waved it above his head and cried in a great voice:

"Here stand I, Tirian of Narnia, in Aslan's name, to prove with my body that Tash is a foul fiend, the Ape a manifold traitor, and these Calormenes worthy of death. To my side, all true Narnians. Would you wait till your new masters have killed you all one by one?"

CHAPTER ELEVEN

THE PACE QUICKENS

QUICK as lightning, Rishda Tarkaan leaped back out of reach of the King's sword. He was no coward, and would have fought single-handed against Tirian and the Dwarf if need were. But he could not take on the Eagle and the Unicorn as well. He knew how Eagles can fly into your face and peck at your eyes and blind you with their wings. And he had heard from his father (who had met Narnians in battle) that no man, except with arrows, or a long spear, can match a Unicorn, for it rears on its hind legs as it falls upon you and then you have its hoofs and its horn and its teeth to deal with all at once. So he rushed into the crowd and stood calling out:

"To me, to me, warriors of The Tisroc, may-he-live-forever. To me, all loyal Narnians, lest the wrath of Tashlan fall upon you!"

While this was happening two other things happened as well. The Ape had not realized his danger as quickly as the Tarkaan. For a second or so he remained squatting beside the fire staring at the newcomers. Then Tirian rushed upon the wretched creature, picked it up by the scruff of the neck, and dashed back to the stable shouting, "Open the door!" Poggin opened it. "Go and drink your own medicine, Shift!" said Tirian and hurled the Ape through into the darkness. But as the Dwarf banged the door shut again, a blinding greenish-blue light shone out from the inside of the stable, the earth shook, and there was a strange noise – a clucking and screaming as if it was the hoarse voice of some monstrous bird. The Beasts moaned and howled and called out "Tashlan! Hide us from him!" and many fell down, and many hid their faces in their wings or paws. No one except Farsight the Eagle, who has the best eyes of all living things, noticed the face of Rishda Tarkaan at that moment. And from what Farsight saw there he knew at once that Rishda was just as surprised, and nearly frightened, as everyone else. "There goes one," thought Farsight, "who has called on gods he does not believe in. How will it be with him if they have really come?"

The third thing – which also happened at the same moment – was the only really beautiful thing that night. Every single Talking Dog in the whole meeting (there were fifteen of them) came bounding and barking joyously to the King's side. They were mostly great big dogs with thick shoulders and heavy jaws. Their coming was like the breaking of a great wave on the sea-beach: it nearly knocked you down. For though they were Talking Dogs they were just as doggy as they could be: and they all stood up and put their front paws on the shoulders of the humans and licked their faces, all saying at once: "Welcome! Welcome! We'll help, we'll help, help, help. Show us how to help, show us how, how. How-how-how?"

It was so lovely that it made you want to cry. This,

at last, was the sort of thing they had been hoping for. And when, a moment later, several little animals (mice and moles and a squirrel or so) came pattering up, squealing with joy, and saying "See, see. We're here," and when, after that, the Bear and the Boar came too, Eustace began to feel that perhaps, after all, everything might be going to come right. But Tirian gazed round and saw how very few of the animals had moved.

"To me! to me!" he called. "Have you all turned cowards since I was your King?"

"We daren't," whimpered dozens of voices. "Tashlan would be angry. Shield us from Tashlan."

"Where are all the Talking Horses?" said Tirian to the Boar.

"We've seen, we've seen," squealed the Mice. "The Ape has made them work. They're all tied – down at the bottom of the hill."

"Then all you little ones," said Tirian, "you nibblers and gnawers and nutcrackers, away with you as fast as you can scamper and see if the Horses are on our side. And if they are, get your teeth into the ropes and gnaw till the Horses are free and bring them hither."

"With a good will, Sire," came the small voices, and with a whisk of tails those sharp-eyed and sharp-toothed folk were off. Tirian smiled for mere love as he saw them go. But it was already time to be thinking of other things. Rishda Tarkaan was giving his orders.

"Forward," he said. "Take all of them alive if you can and hurl them into the stable or drive them into it. When they are all in we will put fire to it and make them an offering to the great god Tash."

"Ha!" said Farsight to himself. "So that is how he hopes to win Tash's pardon for his unbelief."

The enemy line – about half of Rishda's force – was now moving forward, and Tirian had barely time to give his orders.

"Out on the left, Jill, and try to shoot all you may before they reach us. Boar and Bear next to her. Poggin on my left, Eustace on my right. Hold the right wing, Jewel. Stand by him, Puzzle, and use your hoofs. Hover and strike, Farsight. You Dogs, just behind us. Go in among them after the sword-play has begun. Aslan to our aid!"

Eustace stood with his heart beating terribly, hoping and hoping that he would be brave. He had never seen anything (though he had seen both a dragon and a sea-serpent) that made his blood run so cold as that line of dark-faced bright-eyed men. There were fifteen Calormenes, a Talking Bull of Narnia, Slinkey the Fox, and Wraggle the Satyr. Then he heard twang-and-zipp on his left and one Calormene fell: then twang-and-zipp again and the Satyr was down. "Oh, well done, daughter!" came Tirian's voice; and then the enemy were upon them.

Eustace could never remember what happened in the next two minutes. It was all like a dream (the sort you have when your temperature is over 100) until he heard Rishda Tarkaan's voice calling out from the distance:

"Retire. Back hither and re-form."

Then Eustace came to his senses and saw the Calormenes scampering back to their friends. But not all of them. Two lay dead, pierced by Jewel's horn, one by Tirian's sword. The Fox lay dead at his own feet, and he wondered if it was he who had killed it. The Bull also was down, shot through the eye by an arrow from Jill and gashed in his side by the Boar's tusk. But our side had its losses too. Three dogs were killed and a fourth was hobbling behind the line on three legs and whimpering. The Bear lay on the ground, moving feebly. Then it mumbled in its throaty voice, bewildered to the last, "I – I don't – understand," laid its big head down on the grass as quietly as a child going to sleep, and never moved again.

In fact, the first attack had failed. Eustace didn't seem able to be glad about it: he was so terribly thirsty and his arm ached so.

As the defeated Calormenes went back to their commander, the Dwarfs began jeering at them.

"Had enough, Darkies?" they yelled. "Don't you like it? Why doesn't your great Tarkaan go and fight himself instead of sending you to be killed? Poor Darkies!"

"Dwarfs," cried Tirian. "Come here and use your swords, not your tongues. There is still time. Dwarfs of Narnia! You can fight well, I know. Come back to your allegiance."

"Yah!" sneered the Dwarfs. "Not likely. You're just as

big humbugs as the other lot. We don't want any Kings. The Dwarfs are for the Dwarfs. Boo!"

Then the Drum began: not a Dwarf drum this time, but a big bull's hide Calormene drum. The children from the very first hated the sound. *Boom – boom – ba-ba-boom* it went. But they would have hated it far worse if they had known what it meant. Tirian did. It meant that there were other Calormene troops somewhere near and that Rishda Tarkaan was calling them to his aid. Tirian and Jewel looked at one another sadly. They had just begun to hope that they might win that night: but it would be all over with them if new enemies appeared.

Tirian gazed despairingly round. Several Narnians were standing with the Calormenes, whether through treachery or in honest fear of "Tashlan". Others were sitting still, staring, not likely to join either side. But there were fewer animals now: the crowd was much smaller. Clearly, several of them had just crept quietly away during the fighting.

Boom – boom – ba-ba-boom went the horrible drum. Then another sound began to mix with it. "Listen!" said Jewel: and then "Look!" said Farsight. A moment later there was no doubt what it was. With a thunder of hoofs, with tossing heads, widened nostrils, and waving manes, over a score of Talking Horses of Narnia came charging up the hill. The gnawers and nibblers had done their work.

Poggin the Dwarf and the children opened their mouths to cheer but that cheer never came. Suddenly the air was full of the sound of twanging bow-strings and hissing arrows. It was the Dwarfs who were shooting and – for a moment Jill could hardly believe her eyes – they were shooting the Horses. Dwarfs are deadly archers. Horse

after Horse rolled over. Not one of those noble Beasts ever reached the King.

"Little *Swine*," shrieked Eustace, dancing in his rage. "Dirty, filthy, treacherous little brutes." Even Jewel said, "Shall I run after those Dwarfs, Sire, and spit ten of them on my horn at each plunge?" But Tirian with his face as stern as stone, said, "Stand fast, Jewel. If you must weep, sweetheart (this was to Jill), turn your face aside and see you wet not your bow-string. And peace, Eustace. Do not scold, like a kitchen-girl. No warrior scolds. Courteous words or else hard knocks are his only language."

But the Dwarfs jeered back at Eustace. "That was a surprise for you, little boy, eh? Thought we were on *your* side, did you? No fear. We don't want any Talking Horses. We don't want you to win any more than the other gang. You can't take *us* in. The Dwarfs are for the Dwarfs."

Rishda Tarkaan was still talking to his men, doubtless making arrangements for the next attack and probably wishing he had sent his whole force into the first. The drum boomed on. Then, to their horror, Tirian and his friends heard, far fainter as if from a long way off, an answering drum. Another body of Calormenes had heard Rishda's signal and were coming to support him. You would not have known from Tirian's face that he had now given up all hope.

"Listen," he whispered in a matter-of-fact voice, "we must attack now, before yonder miscreants are strengthened by their friends."

"Bethink you, Sire," said Poggin, "that here we have the good wooden wall of the stable at our backs. If we advance, shall we not be encircled and get sword-points between our shoulders?"

"I would say as you do, Dwarf," said Tirian. "Were it not their very plan to force us into the stable? The further we are from its deadly door, the better."

"The King is right," said Farsight. "Away from this accursed stable, and whatever goblin lives inside it, at all costs."

"Yes, do let's," said Eustace. "I'm coming to hate the very sight of it."

"Good," said Tirian. "Now look yonder to our left. You see a great rock that gleams white like marble in the firelight. First we will fall upon those Calormenes. You, maiden, shall move out on our left and shoot as fast as ever you may into their ranks: and you, Eagle, fly at their faces from the right. Meanwhile we others will be charging them. When we are so close, Jill, that you can no longer shoot at them for fear of striking us, go back to the white rock and wait. You others, keep your ears wide even in the fighting. We must put them to flight in a few minutes or else not at all, for we are fewer than they. As soon as I call *Back*, then rush to join Jill at the white rock, where we shall have protection behind us and can breathe awhile. Now, be off, Jill."

Feeling terribly alone, Jill ran out about twenty feet, put her right leg back and her left leg forward, and set an arrow to her string. She wished her hands were not shaking so. "That's a rotten shot!" she said as her first arrow sped towards the enemy and flew over their heads. But she had another on the string next moment: she knew that speed was what mattered. She saw something big and black darting into the faces of the Calormenes. That was Farsight. First one man, and then another, dropped his sword and put up both his hands to defend his eyes. Then one of her own arrows hit a man, and another hit a Narnian wolf, who had, it seemed, joined the enemy. But she had been shooting only for a few seconds when she had to stop. With a flash of swords and of the Boar's tusks and Jewel's horn, and with deep baying from the dogs, Tirian and his party were rushing on their enemies, like men in a hundred yards' race. Jill was astonished to see how unprepared the Calormenes seemed to be. She did not realize that this was the result of her work and the Eagle's. Very few troops can keep on looking steadily to the front if they are getting arrows in their faces from one side and being pecked by an eagle on the other.

"Oh well done. *Well* done!" shouted Jill. The King's party were cutting their way right into the enemy. The Unicorn was tossing men as you'd toss hay on a fork. Even Eustace seemed to Jill (who after all didn't know very much about swordsmanship) to be fighting brilliantly. The Dogs were at the Calormenes' throats. It was going to work! It was victory at last – With a horrible, cold shock Jill noticed a strange thing. Though Calormenes were falling at each Narnian sword-stroke, they never seemed to get any fewer. In fact, there were actually more of them now than when the fight began. There were more every second. They were running up from every side. They were new Calormenes. These new ones had spears. There was such a crowd of them that she could hardly see her own friends. Then she heard Tirian's voice crying:

"Back! To the rock!"

The enemy had been reinforced. The drum had done its work.

CHAPTER TWELVE

THROUGH THE STABLE DOOR

JILL ought to have been back at the white rock already but she had quite forgotten that part of her orders in the excitement of watching the fight. Now she remembered. She turned at once and ran to it, and arrived there barely a second before the others. It thus happened that all of them, for a moment, had their backs to the enemy. They all wheeled round the moment they had reached it. A terrible sight met their eyes.

A Calormene was running towards the stable door carrying something that kicked and struggled. As he came between them and the fire they could see clearly both the shape of the man and the shape of what he carried. It was Eustace.

Tirian and the Unicorn rushed out to rescue him. But the Calormene was now far nearer to the door then they. Before they had covered half the distance he had flung Eustace in and shut the door on him. Half a dozen more Calormenes had run up behind him. They formed a line on the open space before the stable. There was no getting at it now.

Even then Jill remembered to keep her face turned aside, well away from her bow. "Even if I can't stop blubbing, I *won't* get my string wet," she said.

"'Ware arrows," said Poggin suddenly.

Everyone ducked and pulled his helmet well over his nose. The Dogs crouched behind. But though a few arrows came their way it soon became clear that they were not being shot at. Griffle and his Dwarfs were at their archery again. This time they were coolly shooting at the Calormenes.

"Keep it up, boys!" came Griffle's voice. "All together. Carefully. We don't want Darkies any more than we want Monkeys – or Lions – or Kings. The Dwarfs are for the Dwarfs."

Whatever else you may say about Dwarfs, no one can say they aren't brave. They could easily have got away to some safe place. They preferred to stay and kill as many of both sides as they could, except when both sides were kind enough to save them trouble by killing one another. They wanted Narnia for their own.

What perhaps they had not taken into account was that the Calormenes were mail-clad and the Horses had had no protection. Also the Calormenes had a leader. Rishda Tarkaan's voice cried out:

"Thirty of you keep watch on those fools by the white rock. The rest, after me, that we may teach these sons of earth a lesson."

Tirian and his friends, still panting from their fight and thankful for a few minutes' rest, stood and looked on while the Tarkaan led his men against the Dwarfs. It was a strange scene by now. The fire had sunk lower: the light it gave was now less and of a darker red. As far as one could see, the whole place of assembly was now empty except for the Dwarf and the Calormenes. In that light one couldn't make out much of what was happening. It sounded as if the Dwarfs were putting up a good fight. Tirian could hear Griffle using dreadful language, and every now and then the Tarkaan calling, "Take all you can alive! Take them alive!"

Whatever that fight may have been like, it did not last long. The noise of it died away. Then Jill saw the Tarkaan coming back to the stable: eleven men followed him, dragging eleven bound Dwarfs. (Whether the others had all been killed, or whether some of them had got away, was never known.)

"Throw them into the shrine of Tash," said Rishda Tarkaan.

And when the eleven Dwarfs, one after the other, had been flung or kicked into that dark doorway and the door had been shut again, he bowed low to the stable and said:

"These also are for thy burnt offering, Lord Tash."

And all the Calormenes banged the flats of their swords on their shields and shouted, "Tash! Tash! The great god Tash! Inexorable Tash!" (There was no nonsense about "Tashlan" now.)

The little party by the white rock watched these doings and whispered to one another. They had found a trickle of water coming down the rock and all had drunk eagerly – Jill and Poggin and the King in their hands, while the four-footed ones lapped from the little pool which it had made at the foot of the stone. Such was their thirst that it seemed the most delicious drink they had ever had in their lives, and while they were drinking they were perfectly happy and could not think of anything else.

"I feel in my bones," said Poggin, "that we shall all, one by one, pass through that dark door before morning. I can think of a hundred deaths I would rather have died."

"It is indeed a grim door," said Tirian. "It is more like a mouth."

"Oh, can't we do *anything* to stop it?" said Jill in a shaken voice.

"Nay, fair friend," said Jewel, nosing her gently. "It

may be for us the door to Aslan's country and we shall sup at his table tonight."

Rishda Tarkaan turned his back on the stable and walked slowly to a place in front of the white rock.

"Hearken," he said. "If the Boar and the Dogs and the Unicorn will come over to me and put themselves in my mercy, their lives shall be spared. The Boar shall go to a cage in The Tisroc's garden, the Dogs to The Tisroc's kennels, and the Unicorn, when I have sawn his horn off, shall draw a cart. But the Eagle, the children, and he who was the King shall be offered to Tash this night."

The only answer was growls.

"Get on, warriors," said the Tarkaan. "Kill the beasts, but take the two-legged ones alive."

And then the last battle of the last King of Narnia began.

What made it hopeless, even apart from the numbers of the enemy, was the spears. The Calormenes who had been with the Ape almost from the beginning had had no spears: that was because they had come into Narnia by ones and twos, pretending to be peaceful merchants, and of course they had carried no spears for a spear is not a thing you can hide. The new ones must have come in later, after the Ape was already strong and they could march openly. The spears made all the difference. With a long spear you can kill a boar before you are in reach of his tusks and a unicorn before you are in reach of his horn; if you are very quick and keep your head. And now the levelled spears were closing in on Tirian and his last friends. Next minute they were all fighting for their lives.

In a way it wasn't quite so bad as you might think.

When you are using every muscle to the full – ducking under a spear-point here, leaping over it there, lunging forward, drawing back, wheeling round – you haven't much time to feel either frightened or sad. Tirian knew he could do nothing for the others now; they were all doomed together. He vaguely saw the Boar go down on one side of him, and Jewel fighting furiously on the other. Out of the corner of one eye he saw, but only just saw, a big Calormene pulling Jill away somewhere by her hair. But he hardly thought about any of these things. His only thought now was to sell his life as dearly as he could. The worst of it was that he couldn't keep to the position in which he had started, under the white rock. A man who is fighting a dozen enemies at once must take his chances wherever he can; must dart in wherever he sees an enemy's breast or neck unguarded. In a very few strokes this may get you quite a distance from the spot where you began. Tirian soon found that he was getting further and further to the right, nearer to the stable. He had a vague idea in his mind that there was some good reason for keeping away from it. But he couldn't now remember what the reason was. And anyway, he couldn't help it.

All at once everything came quite clear. He found he was fighting the Tarkaan himself. The bonfire (what was left of it) was straight in front. He was in fact fighting in the very doorway of the stable, for it had been opened and two Calormenes were holding the door, ready to slam it shut the moment he was inside. He remembered everything now, and he realized that the enemy had been edging him to the stable on purpose ever since the fight began. And while he was thinking this he was still fighting the Tarkaan as hard as he could.

A new idea came into Tirian's head. He dropped his sword, darted forward, in under the sweep of the Tarkaan's scimitar, seized his enemy by the belt with both hands, and jumped back into the stable, shouting:

"Come in and meet Tash yourself!"

There was a deafening noise. As when the Ape had been flung in, the earth shook and there was a blinding light.

The Calormene soldiers outside screamed. "Tash, Tash!" and banged the door. If Tash wanted their own Captain, Tash must have him. They, at any rate, did not want to meet Tash.

For a moment or two Tirian did not know where he was or even who he was. Then he steadied himself, blinked, and looked around. It was not dark inside the stable, as he had expected. He was in strong light: that was why he was blinking.

He turned to look at Rishda Tarkaan, but Rishda was not looking at him. Rishda gave a great wail and pointed; then he put his hands before his face and fell flat, face downwards, on the ground. Tirian looked in the direction where the Tarkaan had pointed. And then he understood.

A terrible figure was coming towards them. It was far smaller than the shape they had seen from the Tower, though still much bigger than a man, and it was the same. It had a vulture's head and four arms. Its beak was open and its eyes blazed. A croaking voice came from its beak.

"Thou hast called me into Narnia, Rishda Tarkaan. Here I am. What hast thou to say?"

But the Tarkaan neither lifted his face from the ground nor said a word. He was shaking like a man with a bad

hiccup. He was brave enough in battle: but half his courage had left him earlier that night when he first began to suspect that there might be a real Tash. The rest of it had left him now.

With a sudden jerk – like a hen stooping to pick up a worm – Tash pounced on the miserable Rishda and tucked him under the upper of his two right arms. Then Tash turned his head sidewise to fix Tirian with one of his terrible eyes: for of course, having a bird's head, he couldn't look at you straight.

But immediately, from behind Tash, strong and calm as the summer sea, a voice said:

"Begone, Monster, and take your lawful prey to your own place: in the name of Aslan and Aslan's great Father the Emperor-over-the-Sea."

The hideous creature vanished, with the Tarkaan still under its arm. And Tirian turned to see who had spoken.

And what he saw then set his heart beating as it had never beaten in any fight.

Seven Kings and Queens stood before him, all with crowns on their heads and all in glittering clothes, but the Kings wore fine mail as well and had their swords drawn in their hands. Tirian bowed courteously and was about to speak when the youngest of the Queens laughed. He stared hard at her face, and then gasped with amazement, for he knew her. It was Jill: but not Jill as he had last seen her, with her face all dirt and tears and an old drill dress half slipping off one shoulder. Now she looked cool and fresh, as fresh as if she had just come from bathing. And at first he thought she looked older, but then didn't, and he could never make up his mind on that point. And then he saw that the youngest of the Kings was Eustace: but he also was changed as Jill was changed.

Tirian suddenly felt awkward about coming among these people with the blood and dust and sweat of a battle still on him. Next moment he realized that he was not in that state at all. He was fresh and cool and clean, and dressed in such clothes as he would have worn for a great feast at Cair Paravel. (But in Narnia your good clothes were never your uncomfortable ones. They knew how to make things that felt beautiful as well as looking beautiful in Narnia: and there was no such thing as starch or flannel or elastic to be found from one end of the country to the other.)

"Sire," said Jill coming forward and making a beautiful curtsey, "let me make you known to Peter the High King over all Kings in Narnia."

Tirian had no need to ask which was the High King, for he remembered his face (though here it was far nobler) from his dream. He stepped forward, sank on one knee and kissed Peter's hand.

"High King," he said. "You are welcome to me."

And the High King raised him and kissed him on both cheeks as a High King should. Then he led him to the eldest of the Queens – but even she was not old, and there

were no grey hairs on her head and no wrinkles on her cheek – and said, "Sir, this is that Lady Polly who came into Narnia on the First Day, when Aslan made the trees grow and the Beasts talk." He brought him next to a man whose golden beard flowed over his breast and whose face was full of wisdom. "And this," he said, "is the Lord Digory who was with her on that day. And this is my brother, King Edmund: and this my sister, the Queen Lucy."

"Sir," said Tirian, when he had greeted all these. "If I have read the chronicle aright, there should be another. Has not your Majesty two sisters? Where is Queen Susan?"

"My sister Susan," answered Peter shortly and gravely,

"is no longer a friend of Narnia."

"Yes," said Eustace, "and whenever you've tried to get her to come and talk about Narnia or do anything about Narnia, she says, 'What wonderful memories you have! Fancy your still thinking about all those funny games we used to play when we were children.'"

"Oh Susan!" said Jill. "She's interested in nothing nowadays except nylons and lipstick and invitations. She always was a jolly sight too keen on being grown-up."

"Grown-up, indeed," said the Lady Polly. "I wish she *would* grow up. She wasted all her school time wanting to be the age she is now, and she'll waste all the rest of her life trying to stay that age. Her whole idea is to race on to the silliest time of one's life as quick as she can and then stop there as long as she can."

"Well, don't let's talk about that now," said Peter. "Look! Here are lovely fruit-trees. Let us taste them."

And then, for the first time, Tirian looked about him and realized how very queer this adventure was.

CHAPTER THIRTEEN

HOW THE DWARFS REFUSED TO BE TAKEN IN

TIRIAN had thought – or he would have thought if he had time to think at all – that they were inside a little thatched stable, about twelve feet long and six feet wide. In reality they stood on grass, the deep blue sky was overhead, and the air which blew gently on their faces was that of a day in early summer. Not far away from them rose a grove of trees, thickly leaved, but under every leaf there peeped out the gold or faint yellow or purple or glowing red of fruits such as no one has seen in our world. The fruit made Tirian feel that it must be autumn but there was something in the feel of the air that told him it could not be later than June. They all moved towards the trees.

Everyone raised his hand to pick the fruit he best liked the look of, and then everyone paused for a second. This fruit was so beautiful that each felt "It can't be meant for me . . . surely we're not allowed to pluck it."

"It's all right," said Peter. "I know what we're all thinking. But I'm sure, quite sure, we needn't. I've a feeling we've got to the country where everything is allowed."

"Here goes, then!" said Eustace. And they all began to eat.

What was the fruit like? Unfortunately no one can describe a taste. All I can say is that, compared with those fruits, the freshest grapefruit you've ever eaten was dull, and the juiciest orange was dry, and the most melting pear was hard and woody, and the sweetest wild strawberry was sour. And there were no seeds or stones, and no wasps. If you had once eaten that fruit, all the nicest things in this world would taste like medicines after it. But I can't describe it. You can't find out what it is like unless you can get to that country and taste it for yourself.

When they had eaten enough, Eustace said to King Peter, "You haven't yet told us how you got here. You were just going to, when King Tirian turned up."

"There's not much to tell," said Peter. "Edmund and I were standing on the platform and we saw your train coming in. I remember thinking it was taking the bend far too fast. And I remember thinking how funny it was that our people were probably in the same train though Lucy didn't know about it –"

"Your people, High King?" said Tirian.

"I mean my Father and Mother – Edmund's and Lucy's and mine."

"Why were they?" asked Jill. "You don't mean to say *they* know about Narnia?"

"Oh no, it had nothing to do with Narnia. They were on their way to Bristol. I'd only heard they were going that morning. But Edmund said they'd be bound to be going by that train." (Edmund was the sort of person who knows about railways.)

"And what happened then?" said Jill.

"Well, it's not very easy to describe, is it, Edmund?" said the High King.

"Not very," said Edmund. "It wasn't at all like that other time when we were pulled out of our own world by Magic. There was a frightful roar and something hit me with a bang, but it didn't hurt. And I felt not so much scared as – well, excited. Oh – and this is one queer thing.

I'd had a rather sore knee, from a hack at rugger. I noticed it had suddenly gone. And I felt very light. And then – here we were."

"It was much the same for us in the railway carriage," said the Lord Digory, wiping the last traces of the fruit from his golden beard. "Only I think you and I, Polly, chiefly felt that we'd been unstiffened. You youngsters won't understand. But we stopped feeling old."

"Youngsters, indeed!" said Jill. "I don't believe you two really are much older than we are here."

"Well if we aren't, we have been," said the Lady Polly.

"And what has been happening since you got here?" asked Eustace.

"Well," said Peter, "for a long time (at least I suppose it was a long time) nothing happened. Then the door opened –"

"The door?" said Tirian.

"Yes," said Peter. "The door you came in – or came out – by. Have you forgotten?"

"But where is it?"

"Look," said Peter and pointed.

Tirian looked and saw the queerest and most ridiculous thing you can imagine. Only a few yards away, clear to be seen in the sunlight, there stood up a rough wooden door and, round it, the framework of the doorway: nothing else, no walls, no roof. He walked towards it, bewildered, and the others followed, watching to see what he would do. He walked round to the other side of the door. But it looked just the same from the other side: he was still in the open air, on a summer morning. The door was simply standing up by itself as if it had grown there like a tree.

"Fair Sir," said Tirian to the High King, "this is a great marvel."

"It is the door you came through with that Calormene five minutes ago," said Peter smiling.

"But did I not come in out of the wood into the stable? Whereas this seems to be a door leading from nowhere to nowhere."

"It looks like that if you walk *round* it," said Peter. "But put your eye to that place where there is a crack between two of the planks and look *through*."

Tirian put his eye to the hole. At first he could see nothing but blackness. Then, at his eyes grew used to it, he saw the dull red glow of a bonfire that was nearly going out, and above that, in a black sky, stars. Then he could see dark figures moving about or standing between him and the fire: he could hear them talking and their voices were like those of Calormenes. So he knew that he was looking out through the stable door into the darkness of Lantern Waste where he had fought his last battle. The men were discussing whether to go in and look for Rishda Tarkaan (but none of them wanted to do that) or to set fire to the stable.

He looked round again and could hardly believe his eyes. There was the blue sky overhead, and grassy country spreading as far as he could see in every direction, and his new friends all round him laughing.

"It seems, then," said Tirian, smiling himself, "that the stable seen from within and the stable seen from without are two different places."

"Yes," said the Lord Digory. "Its inside is bigger than its outside."

"Yes," said Queen Lucy. "In our world too, a stable once had something inside it that was bigger than our whole world." It was the first time she had spoken, and from the thrill in her voice, Tirian now knew why. She was drinking everything in even more deeply than the others. She had been too happy to speak. He wanted to hear her speak again, so he said:

"Of your courtesy, Madam, tell on. Tell me your whole adventure."

"After the shock and the noise," said Lucy, "we found

ourselves here. And we wondered at the door, as you did. Then the door opened for the first time (we saw darkness through the doorway when it did) and there came through a big man with a naked sword. We saw by his arms that he was a Calormene. He took his stand beside the door with his sword raised, resting on his shoulder, ready to cut down anyone who came through. We went to him and spoke to him, but we thought he could neither see nor hear us. And he never looked round on the sky and the sunlight and the grass: I think he couldn't see them either. So then we waited a long time. Then we heard the bolt being drawn on the other side of the door. But the man didn't get ready to strike with his sword till he could see who was coming in. So we supposed he had been told to strike some and spare others. But at the very moment when the door opened, all of a sudden Tash was there, on this side of the door; none of us saw where he came from. And through the door there came a big Cat. It gave one look at Tash and ran for its life: just in time, for he pounced at it and the door hit his beak as it was shut. The man could see Tash. He turned very pale and bowed down before the Monster: but it vanished away.

"Then we waited a long time again. At last the door opened for the third time and there came in a young Calormene. I liked him. The sentinel at the door started, and looked very surprised, when he saw him. I think he'd been expecting someone quite different –"

"I see it all now," said Eustace (he had the bad habit of interrupting stories). "The Cat was to go in first and the sentry had orders to do him no harm. Then the Cat was to come out and say he'd seen their beastly Tashlan and *pretend* to be frightened so as to scare the other Animals. But what Shift never guessed was that the real Tash would turn up; so Ginger came out really frightened. And after that, Shift would send in anyone he wanted to get rid of and the sentry would kill them.

And –"

"Friend," said Tirian softly, "you hinder the lady in her tale."

"Well," said Lucy, "the sentry was surprised. That gave the other man just time to get on guard. They had a fight. He killed the sentry and flung him outside the door. Then he came walking slowly forward to where we were. He could see us, and everything else. We tried to talk to him but he was rather like a man in a trance. He kept on saying Tash, Tash, where is Tash? I go to Tash. So we gave it up and he went away somewhere – over there. I liked him. And after that . . . ugh!" Lucy made a face.

"After that," said Edmund, "someone flung a monkey through the door. And Tash was there again. My sister is so tender-hearted she doesn't like to tell you that Tash made one peck and the Monkey was gone!"

"Serve him right!" said Eustace. "All the same, I hope he'll disagree with Tash too."

"And after that," said Edmund, "came about a dozen Dwarfs: and then Jill, and Eustace, and last of all yourself."

"I hope Tash ate the Dwarfs too," said Eustace. "Little swine."

"No, he didn't," said Lucy. "And don't be horrid. Thery're still here. In fact you can see them from here. And I've tried and tried to make friends with them but it's no use."

"*Friends* with them!" cried Eustace. "If you knew how those Dwarfs have been behaving!"

"Oh stop it, Eustace," said Lucy. "Do come and see them. King Tirian, perhaps *you* could do something with them."

"I can feel no great love for Dwarfs today," said Tirian. "Yet at your asking, Lady, I would do a greater thing than this."

Lucy led the way and soon they could all see the Dwarfs. They had a very odd look. They weren't strolling about or enjoying themselves (although the cords with which they had been tied seemed to have vanished) nor were they lying down and having a rest. They were sitting very close together in a little circle facing one another. They never looked round or took any notice of the humans till Lucy and Tirian were almost near enough to touch them. Then the Dwarfs all cocked their heads as if they couldn't see anyone but were listening hard and trying to guess by the sound what was happening.

"Look out!" said one of them in a surly voice. "Mind where you're going. Don't walk into our faces!"

"All right!" said Eustace indignantly. "We're not blind. We've got eyes in our heads."

"They must be darn good ones if you can see in here," said the same Dwarf whose name was Diggle.

"In where?" asked Edmund.

"Why you bone-head, in *here* of course," said Diggle. "In this pitch-black, poky, smelly little hole of a stable."

"Are you blind?" said Tirian.

"Ain't we all blind in the dark!" said Diggle.

"But it isn't dark, you poor stupid Dwarfs," said Lucy. "Can't you see? Look up! Look round! Can't you see the sky and the trees and the flowers? Can't you see *me*?"

"How in the name of all Humbug can I see what ain't there? And how can I see you any more than you can see me in this pitch darkness?"

"But I *can* see you," said Lucy. "I'll prove I can see you. You've got a pipe in your mouth."

"Anyone that knows the smell of baccy could tell that," said Diggle.

"Oh the poor things! This is dreadful," said Lucy. Then she had an idea. She stopped and picked some wild violets. "Listen, Dwarf," she said. "Even if your eyes are wrong, perhaps your nose is all right: can you smell *that*?" She leaned across and held the fresh, damp flowers to Diggle's ugly nose. But she had to jump back quickly in order to avoid a blow from his hard little fist.

"None of that!" he shouted. "How dare you! What do you mean by shoving a lot of filthy stable-litter in my

face? There was a thistle in it too. It's like your sauce! And who are you anyway?"

"Earth-man," said Tirian, "she is the Queen Lucy, sent hither by Aslan out of the deep past. And it is for her sake alone that I, Tirian your lawful King, do not cut all your heads from your shoulders, proved and twice-proved traitors that you are."

"Well if that doesn't beat everything!" exclaimed Diggle. "How *can* you go on talking all that rot? Your wonderful Lion didn't come and help you, did he? Thought not. And now – even now – when you've been beaten and shoved into this black hole, just the same as the rest of us, you're still at your old game. Starting a new lie! Trying to make us believe we're none of us shut up, and it ain't dark, and heaven knows what."

"There *is* no black hole, save in your own fancy, fool," cried Tirian. "Come *out* of it." And, leaning forward, he caught Diggle by the belt and the hood and swung him right out of the circle of Dwarfs. But the moment Tirian put him down, Diggle darted back to his place among the others, rubbing his nose and howling:

"Ow! Ow! What d'you do that for! Banging my face against the wall. You've nearly broken my nose."

"Oh dear!" said Lucy, "What *are* we to do for them?"

"Let 'em alone," said Eustace: but as he spoke the earth trembled. The sweet air grew suddenly sweeter. A brightness flashed behind them. All turned. Tirian turned last because he was afraid. There stood his heart's desire, huge and real, the golden Lion, Aslan himself, and already the others were kneeling in a circle round his forepaws and burying their hands and faces in his mane as he stooped his great head to touch them with his tongue. Then he fixed his eyes upon Tirian, and Tirian came near, trembling, and flung himself at the Lion's feet, and the Lion kissed him and said, "Well done, last of the Kings of Narnia who stood firm at the darkest hour."

"Aslan," said Lucy through her tears, "could you – will you – do something for these poor Dwarfs?"

"Dearest," said Aslan, "I will show you both what I can, and what I cannot, do." He came close to the Dwarfs and gave a low growl: low, but it set all the air shaking. But the Dwarfs said to one another, "Hear that? That's the gang at the other end of the stable. Trying to frighten us. They do it with a machine of some kind. Don't take any notice. They won't take *us* in again!"

Aslan raised his head and shook his mane. Instantly a glorious feast appeared on the Dwarfs' knees: pies and tongues and pigeons and trifles and ices, and each Dwarf had a goblet of good wine in his right hand. But it wasn't much use. They began eating and drinking greedily enough, but it was clear that they couldn't taste it properly. They thought they were eating and drinking only the sort of things you might find in a stable. One said he was trying to eat hay and another said he had a bit of an old turnip and a third said he'd found a raw cabbage leaf. And they raised golden goblets of rich red wine to their lips and said "Ugh! Fancy drinking dirty water out of a trough that a donkey's been at! Never thought we'd come to this." But very soon every Dwarf began suspecting that every other Dwarf had found something nicer than he had, and they started grabbing and snatching, and went on to quarrelling, till in a few minutes there was a free fight and all the good food was smeared on their faces and clothes or trodden under foot. But when at last they sat down to nurse their black eyes and their bleeding noses, they all said:

"Well, at any rate there's no Humbug here. We haven't let anyone take us in. The Dwarfs are for the Dwarfs."

"You see, " said Aslan. "They will not let us help them. They have chosen cunning instead of belief. Their prison is only in their own minds, yet they are in that prison; and so afraid of being taken in that they cannot be taken out. But come, children. I have other work to do."

He went to the Door and they all followed him. He raised his head and roared, "Now it is time!" then louder, "Time!"; then so loud that it could have shaken the stars, "TIME." The Door flew open.

CHAPTER FOURTEEN

NIGHT FALLS ON NARNIA

THEY all stood beside Aslan, on his right side, and looked through the open doorway.

The bonfire had gone out. On the earth all was blackness: in fact you could not have told that you were looking into a wood if you had not seen where the dark shapes of the trees ended and the stars began. But when Aslan had roared yet again, out on their left they saw another black shape. That is, they saw another patch where there were no stars: and the patch rose up higher and higher and became the shape of a man, the hugest of all giants. They all knew Narnia well enough to work out where he must be standing. He must be on the high moorlands that stretch away to the North beyond the River Shribble. Then Jill and Eustace remembered how once long ago, in the deep caves beneath those moors, they had seen a great giant asleep and been told that his name was Father Time, and that he would wake on the day the world ended.

"Yes," said Aslan, though they had not spoken. "While he lay dreaming his name was Time. Now that he is awake he will have a new one."

Then the great giant raised a horn to his mouth. They could see this by the change of the black shape he made against the stars. After that – quite a bit later, because sound travels so slowly – they heard the sound of the horn: high and terrible, yet of a strange, deadly beauty.

Immediately the sky became full of shooting stars. Even one shooting star is a fine thing to see; but these were dozens, and then scores, and then hundreds, till it was like silver rain: and it went on and on. And when it had gone on for some while, one or two of them began to think that there was another dark shape against the sky as well as the giant's. It was in a different place, right overhead, up in the very roof of the sky as you might call it. "Perhaps it is a cloud," thought Edmund. At any rate, there were no stars there: just blackness. But all around, the downpour of stars went on. And then the starless patch began to grow, spreading further and further out from the centre of the sky. And presently a quarter of the whole sky was black, and then a half, and at last the rain of shooting stars was going on only low down near the horizon.

With a thrill of wonder (and there was some terror in it too) they all suddenly realized what was happening. The spreading blackness was not a cloud at all: it was simply emptiness. The black part of the sky was the part in which there were no stars left. All the stars were falling: Aslan had called them home.

The last few seconds before the rain of stars had quite ended were very exciting. Stars began falling all round them. But stars in that world are not the great flaming globes they are in ours. They are people (Edmund and Lucy had once met one). So now they found showers of glittering people, all with long hair like burning silver and spears like white-hot metal, rushing down to them out of the black air, swifter than falling stones. They made a hissing noise as they landed and burnt the grass. And all these stars glided past them and stood somewhere behind, a little to the right.

This was a great advantage, because otherwise, now that there were no stars in the sky, everything would have been completely dark and you could have seen nothing. As it was, the crowd of stars behind them cast a fierce, white light over their shoulders. They could see mile upon mile of Narnian woods spread out before them, looking as if they were floodlit. Every bush and almost every blade of grass had its black shadow behind it. The edge of every leaf stood out so sharp that you'd think you could cut your finger on it.

On the grass before them lay their own shadows. But the great thing was Aslan's shadow. It streamed away to their left, enormous and very terrible. And all this was under a sky that would now be starless forever.

The light from behind them (and a little to their right) was so strong that it lit up even the slopes of the Northern Moors. Something was moving there. Enormous animals were crawling and sliding down into Narnia: great dragons and giant lizards and featherless birds with wings like bats' wings. They disappeared into the woods and for a few minutes there was silence. Then there came – at first from very far off – sounds of wailing and then, from every direction, a rustling and a pattering and a sound of wings. It came nearer and nearer. Soon one could distinguish the scamper of little feet from the padding of big paws, and the clack-clack of light little hoofs from the thunder of great ones. And then one could see thousands of pairs of eyes gleaming. And at last, out of the shadow of the trees, racing up the hill for dear life, by thousands and by millions, came all kinds of creatures – Talking Beasts, Dwarfs, Satyrs, Fauns, Giants, Calormenes, men from Archenland, Monopods, and strange unearthly things from the remote islands of the unknown Western lands. And all these ran up to the doorway where Aslan stood.

This part of the adventure was the only one which seemed rather like a dream at the time and rather hard to remember properly afterwards. Especially, one couldn't say how long it had taken. Sometimes it seemed to have lasted only a few minutes, but at others it felt as if it might have gone on for years. Obviously, unless either the Door had grown very much larger or the creatures had suddenly grown as small as gnats, a crowd like that couldn't ever have tried to get through it. But no one thought about that sort of thing at the time.

The creatures came rushing on, their eyes brighter and brighter as they drew nearer and nearer to the standing Stars. But as they came right up to Aslan one or other of two things happened to each of them. They all looked straight in his face, I don't think they had any choice about that. And when some looked, the expression of their faces changed terribly – it was fear and hatred: except that, on the faces of Talking Bears, the fear and hatred lasted only for a fraction of a second. You could see that they suddenly ceased to the *Talking* Beasts. They were just ordinary animals. And all the creatures who looked at Aslan in that way swerved to their right, his left, and disappeared into his huge black shadow, which (as you have heard) streamed away to the left of the doorway. The children never saw them again. I don't know what became of them. But the others looked in the face of Aslan and loved him, though some of them were very frightened at the same time. And all these came in at the Door, in on Aslan's right. There were some queer specimens among them. Eustace even recognized one of those very Dwarfs who had helped to shoot the Horses. But he had no time to wonder about that sort of thing (and anyway it was no business of his) for a great joy put

everything else out of his head. Among the happy creatures who now came crowding round Tirian and his friends were all those whom they had thought dead. There was Roonwit the Centaur and Jewel the Unicorn and the good Boar and the good Bear, and Farsight the Eagle, and the dear Dogs and the Horses, and Poggin the Dwarf.

"Further in and higher up!" cried Roonwit and thundered away in a gallop to the West. And though they did not understand him, the words somehow set them tingling all over. The Boar grunted at them cheerfully. The Bear was just going to mutter that he still didn't understand, when he caught sight of the fruit-trees behind them. He waddled to those trees as fast as he could and there, no doubt, found something he understood very well. But the Dogs remained, wagging their tails, and Poggin remained, shaking hands with everyone and grinning all over his honest face. And Jewel leaned his snowy white head over the King's shoulder and the King whispered in Jewel's ear. Then everyone turned his attention again to what could be seen through the Doorway.

The Dragons and Giant Lizards now had Narnia to themselves. They went to and fro tearing up the trees by the roots and crunching them up as if they were sticks of rhubarb. Minute by minute the forests disappeared. The whole country became bare and you could see all sorts of things about its shape – all the little humps and hollows – which you had never noticed before. The grass died. Soon Tirian found that he was looking at a world of bare rock and earth. You could hardly believe that anything had ever lived there. The monsters themselves grew old and lay down and died. Their flesh shrivelled up and the bones appeared: soon they were only huge skeletons that lay here and there on the dead rock, looking as if they had died thousands of years ago. For a long time everything was still.

At last something white – a long, level line of whiteness that gleamed in the light of the standing stars – came moving towards them from the Eastern end of the world.

A widespread noise broke the silence: first a murmur then a rumble, then a roar. And now they could see what it was that was coming, and how fast it came. It was a foaming wall of water. The sea was rising. In that tree-less world you could see it very well. You could see all the rivers getting wider and the lakes getting larger, and separate lakes joining into one, and valleys turning into new lakes, and hills turning into islands, and then those islands vanishing. And the high moors to their left and the higher mountains to their right crumbled and slipped down with a roar and a splash into the mounting water; and the water came swirling up to the very threshold of the Doorway (but never passed it) so that the foam splashed about Aslan's forefeet. All now was level water from where they stood to where the waters met the sky.

And out there it began to grow light. A streak of dreary and disastrous dawn spread along the horizon, and widened and grew brighter, till in the end they hardly noticed the light of the stars who stood behind them. At last the sun came up. When it did, the Lord Digory and the Lady Polly looked at one another and gave a little nod: those two, in a different world, had once seen a dying sun, and so they knew at once that this sun also was dying. It was three times – twenty times – as big as it ought to be, and very dark red. As its rays fell upon the great Time-giant, he turned red too: and in the reflection of that sun the whole waste of shoreless waters looked like blood.

Then the Moon came up, quite in her wrong position, very close to the sun, and she also looked red. And at the sight of her the sun began shooting out great flames, like whiskers or snakes of crimson fire, towards her. It is as if he were an octopus trying to draw her to himself in his tentacles. And perhaps he did draw her. At any rate she came to him, slowly at first, but then more and more quickly, till at last his long flames licked round her and the two ran together and became one huge ball like a burning coal. Great lumps of fire came dropping out of it into the sea and clouds of steam rose up.

Then Aslan said, "Now make an end."

The giant threw his horn into the sea. Then he stretched out one arm – very black it looked, and thousands of miles long – across the sky till his hand reached the Sun. He took the Sun and squeezed it in his hand as you would squeeze an orange. And instantly there was total darkness.

Everyone except Aslan jumped back from the ice-cold air which now blew through the Doorway. Its edges were already covered with icicles.

"Peter, High King of Narnia," said Aslan. "Shut the Door."

Peter, shivering with cold, leaned out into the darkness and pulled the Door to. It scraped over ice as he pulled it. Then, rather clumsily (for even in that moment his hands had gone numb and blue) he took out a golden key and locked it.

They had seen strange things enough through that Doorway. But it was stranger than any of them to look round and find themselves in warm daylight, the blue sky above them, flowers at their feet, and laughter in Aslan's eyes.

He turned swiftly round, crouched lower, lashed himself with his tail and shot away like a golden arrow.

"Come further in! Come further up!" he shouted over his shoulder. But who could keep up with him at that pace? They set out walking Westward to follow him.

"So," said Peter, "night falls on Narnia. What, Lucy! You're not *crying*? With Aslan ahead, and all of us here?"

"Don't try to stop me, Peter," said Lucy, "I am sure Aslan would not. I am sure it is not wrong to mourn for Narnia. Think of all that lies dead and frozen behind that door."

"Yes and I *did* hope," said Jill, "that it might go on for ever. I knew *our* world couldn't. I did think Narnia might."

"I saw it begin," said the Lord Digory. "I did not think I would live to see it die."

"Sirs," said Tirian. "The ladies do well to weep. See, I do so myself. I have seen my mother's death. What world but Narnia have I ever known? It were no virtue, but great discourtesy, if we did not mourn."

They walked away from the Door and away from the Dwarfs who still sat crowded together in their imaginary stable. And as they went they talked to one another about old wars and old peace and ancient Kings and all the glories of Narnia.

The Dogs were still with them. They joined in the conversation but not much because they were too busy racing on ahead and racing back and rushing off to sniff at smells in the grass till they made themselves sneeze. Suddenly they picked up a scent which seemed to excite them very much. They all started arguing about it – "Yes it is – No it isn't – That's just what I said – anyone can smell what *that* is – Take your great nose out of the way and let someone else smell."

"What is it, cousins?" said Peter.

"A Calormene, Sire," said several Dogs at once.

"Lead on to him, then," said Peter. "Whether he meets us in peace or war, he shall be welcome."

The Dogs darted on ahead and came back a moment later, running as if their lives depended on it, and barking loudly to say that it really was a Calormene. (Talking Dogs, just like the common ones, behave as if they thought whatever they are doing at the moment immensely important.)

The others followed where the Dogs led them and found a young Calormene sitting under a chestnut tree beside a clear stream of water. It was Emeth. He rose at once and bowed gravely.

"Sir," he said to Peter, "I know not whether you are my friend or my foe, but I should count it my honour to have you for either. Has not one of the poets said that a

noble friend is the best gift and a noble enemy the next best?"

"Sir," said Peter, "I do not know that there need be any war between you and us."

"Do tell us who you are and what's happened to you," said Jill.

"If there's going to be a story, let's all have a drink and sit down," barked the Dogs. "We're quite blown."

"Well of course you will be if you keep tearing about the way you have done," said Eustace.

So the humans sat down on the grass. And when the Dogs had all had a very noisy drink out of the stream they all sat down, bolt upright, panting, with their tongues hanging out of their heads a little on one side to hear the story. But Jewel remained standing, polishing his horn against his side.

CHAPTER FIFTEEN

FURTHER UP AND FURTHER IN

"KNOW, O Warlike Kings," said Emeth, "and you, O ladies whose beauty illuminates the universe, that I am Emeth the seventh son of Harpha Tarkaan of the city of Tehishbaan, Westward beyond the desert. I came lately into Narnia with nine and twenty others under the command of Rishda Rarkaan. Now when I first heard that we should march upon Narnia I rejoiced; for I had heard many things of your Land and desired greatly to meet you in battle. But when I found that we were to go in disguised as merchants (which is a shameful dress for a warrior and the son of a Tarkaan) and to work by lies and trickery, then my joy departed from me. And most of all when I found we must wait upon a Monkey, and when it began to be said that Tash and Aslan were one, then the world became dark in my eyes. For always since I was a boy I have served Tash and my great desire was to know more of him, if it might be, to look upon his face. But the name of Aslan was hateful to me.

"And, as you have seen, we were called together outside the straw-roofed hovel, night after night, and the fire was kindled, and the Ape brought forth out of the hovel something upon four legs that I could not well see. And the people and the Beasts bowed down and did honour to it. But I thought, the Tarkaan is deceived by the Ape: for this thing that comes out of the stable is neither Tash nor any other god. But when I watched the Tarkaan's face, and marked every word that he said to the Monkey, then I changed my mind: for I saw that the Tarkaan did not believe in it himself. And then I understood that he did not believe in Tash at all: for if he had, how could he dare to mock him?

"When I understood this, a great rage fell upon me and I wondered that the true Tash did not strike down both the Monkey and the Tarkaan with fire from heaven. Nevertheless I hid my anger and held my tongue and waited to see how it would end. But last night, as some of you know, the Monkey brought not forth the yellow thing but said that all who desired to look upon Tashlan – for so they mixed the two words to pretend that they were all one – must pass one by one into the hovel. And I said to myself, Doubtless this is some other deception. But when the Cat had followed in and had come out again in a madness of terror, then I said to myself, Surely the true Tash, whom they called on without knowledge or belief, has now come among us, and will avenge himself. And though my heart was turned into water inside me because of the greatness and terror of Tash, yet my desire was stronger than my fear, and I put force upon my knees to stay them from trembling, and on my teeth that they should not chatter, and resolved to look upon the face of Tash though he should slay me. So I offered myself to go into the hovel; and the Tarkaan, though unwillingly, let me go.

"As soon as I had gone in at the door, the first wonder was that I found myself in this great sunlight (as we all are now) though the inside of the hovel had looked dark from outside. But I had no time to marvel at this, for immediately I was forced to fight for my head against one of our own men. As soon as I saw him I understood that the Monkey and the Tarkaan had set him there to slay any who came in if he were not in their secrets: so that this man also was a liar and a mocker and no true servant of Tash. I had the better will to fight him; and having slain the villain, I cast him out behind me through the door.

"Then I looked about me and saw the sky and the wide lands, and smelled the sweetness. And I said, By the Gods, this is a pleasant place: it may be that I am come into the country of Tash. And I began to journey into the strange country and to seek him.

"So I went over much grass and many flowers and among all kinds of wholesome and delectable trees till lo! in a narrow place between two rocks there came to meet me a great Lion. The speed of him was like the ostrich, and his size was an elephant's; his hair was like pure gold and the brightness of his eyes like gold that is liquid in the furnace. He was more terrible than the Flaming Mountain of Lagour, and in beauty he surpassed all that is in the world even as the rose in bloom surpasses the dust of the desert. Then I fell at his feet and thought, Surely this is the hour of death, for the Lion (who is worthy of all honour) will know that I have served Tash all my days and not him. Nevertheless, it is better to see the Lion and die than to be Tisroc of the world and live and not to have seen him. But the Glorious One bent down his golden head and touched my forehead with his tongue and said, Son, thou art welcome. But I said, Alas, Lord, I am no son of thine but the servant of Tash. He answered, Child, all the service thou hast done to Tash, I account as service done to me. Then by reasons of my great desire for wisdom and understanding, I overcame my fear and questioned the Glorious One and said, Lord, is it then true, as the Ape said, that thou and Tash are one? The Lion growled so that the earth shook (but his wrath was not against me) and said, It is false. Not because he and I are one, but because we are opposites, I take to me the services which thou hast done to him. For I and he are of such different kinds that no service which is vile can be done to me, and none which is not vile can be done to him. Therefore if any man swear by Tash and keep his oath for the oath's sake, it is by me that he has truly sworn, though he know it not, and it is I who reward him. And if any man do a cruelty in my name, then, though he says the name Aslan, it is Tash whom he serves and by Tash his deed is accepted. Dost thou understand, Child? I said, Lord, thou knowest how much I understand. But I said also (for the truth constrained me), Yet I have been seeking Tash all my days. Beloved, said the Glorious One, unless thy desire had been for me thou wouldst not have sought so long and so truly. For all find what they truly seek.

"Then he breathed upon me and took away the trembling from my limbs and caused me to stand upon my feet. And after that, he said not much, but that we should meet again, and I must go further up and further in. Then he turned him about in a storm and flurry of gold and was gone suddenly.

"And since then, O Kings and Ladies, I have been wandering to find him and my happiness is so great that it even weakens me like a wound. And this is the marvel of marvels, that he called me Beloved, me who am but as a dog –"

"Eh? What's that?" said one of the Dogs.

"Sir," said Emeth. "It is but a fashion of speech which we have in Calormen."

"Well, I can't say it's one I like very much," said the Dog.

"He doesn't mean any harm," said an older Dog.

"After all, *we* call our puppies *Boys* when they don't behave properly."

"So we do," said the first Dog. "Or *girls*."

"S-s-sh!" said the Old Dog. "That's not a nice word to use. Remember where you are."

"Look!" said Jill suddenly. Someone was coming, rather timidly, to meet them; a graceful creature on four feet, all silvery-grey. And they stared at him for a whole ten seconds before five or six voices said all at once, "Why, it's old Puzzle!" They had never seen him by daylight with the lion-skin off, and it made an extraordinary difference. He was himself now: a beautiful donkey with such a soft, grey coat and such a gentle, honest face that if you had seen him you would have done just what Jill and Lucy did – rushed forward and put your arms round his neck and kissed his nose and stroked his ears.

When they asked him where he had been he said he had

come in at the door along with all the other creatures but he had – well, to tell the truth, he had been keeping out of their way as much as he could; and out of Aslan's way. For the sight of the real Lion had made him so ashamed of all that nonsense about dressing up in a lion-skin that he did not know how to look anyone in the face. But when he saw that all his friends were going away Westward, and after he had had a mouthful of grass ("And I've never tasted such good grass in my life," said Puzzle), he plucked up his courage and followed. "But what I'll do if I really have to meet Aslan, I'm sure I don't know," he added.

"You'll find it will be all right when you really do," said Queen Lucy.

Then they went forward together, always Westward, for that seemed to be the direction Aslan had meant when he cried out, "Further up and futher in." Many other creatures were slowly moving the same way, but that grassy country was very wide and there was no crowding.

It still seemed to be early, and the morning freshness was in the air. They kept on stopping to look round and to look behind them, partly because it was so beautiful but partly also because there was something about it which they could not understand.

"Peter," said Lucy, "where is this, do you suppose?"

"I don't know," said the High King. "It reminds me of somewhere but I can't give it a name. Could it be somewhere we once stayed for a holiday when we were very, very small?"

"It would have to have been a jolly good holiday," said Eustace. "I bet there isn't a country like this anywhere in *our* world. Look at the colours! You couldn't get a blue like the blue on those mountains in our world."

"Is it not Aslan's country?" said Tirian.

"Not like Aslan's country on top of that mountain beyond the Eastern end of the world," said Jill. "I've been there."

"If you ask me," said Edmund, "it's like somewhere in the Narnian world. Look at those mountains ahead – and the big ice-mountains beyond them. Surely they're rather like the mountains we used to see from Narnia, the ones up Westward beyond the Waterfall?"

"Yes, so they are," said Peter. "Only these are bigger."

"I don't think *those* ones are so very like anything in Narnia," said Lucy. "But look there." She pointed Southward to their left, and everyone stopped and turned to look. "Those hills," said Lucy, "the nice woody ones and the blue ones behind – aren't they very like the Southern border of Narnia?"

"Like!" cried Edmund after a moment's silence. "Why, they're exactly like. Look, there's Mount Pire with his forked head, and there's the pass into Archenland and everything!"

"And yet they're not like," said Lucy. "They're different. They have more colours on them and they look further away than I remembered and they're more . . . more . . . oh, I don't know . . ."

"More like the real thing," said the Lord Digory softly.

Suddenly Farsight the Eagle spread his wings, soared

thirty or forty feet up into the air, circled round and then alighted on the ground.

"Kings and Queens," he cried, "we have all been blind. We are only beginning to see where we are. From up there I have seen it all – Ettinsmuir, Beaversdam, the Great River, and Cair Paravel still shining on the edge of the Eastern Sea. Narnia is not dead. This is Narnia."

"But how can it be?" said Peter. "For Aslan told us older ones that we should never return to Narnia, and here we are."

"Yes," said Eustace. "And we saw it all destroyed and the sun put out."

"And it's all so different," said Lucy.

"The Eagle is right," said the Lord Digory. "Listen, Peter. When Aslan said you could never go back to Narnia, he meant the Narnia you were thinking of. But that was not the real Narnia. That had a beginning and an end. It was only a shadow or a copy of the real Narnia which has always been here and always will be here: just as our world, England and all, is only a shadow or copy of something in Aslan's real world. You need not mourn over Narnia, Lucy. All of the old Narnia that mattered, all the dear creatures, have been drawn into the real Narnia through the Door. And of course it is different;

as different as a real thing is from a shadow or as waking life is from a dream." His voice stirred everyone like a trumpet as he spoke these words: but when he added under his breath "It's all in Plato, all in Plato: bless me, what *do* they teach them at these schools!" the older ones laughed. It was so exactly like the sort of thing they had heard him say long ago in that other world where his beard was grey instead of golden. He knew why they were laughing and joined in the laugh himself. But very quickly they all became grave again: for, as you know, there is a kind of happiness and wonder that makes you serious. It is too good to waste on jokes.

It is as hard to explain how this sunlit land was different from the old Narnia as it would be to tell you how the fruits of that country taste. Perhaps you will get some idea of it if you think like this. You may have been in a room in which there was a window that looked out on a lovely bay of the sea or a green valley that wound away among mountains. And in the wall of that room opposite to the window there may have been a looking-glass. And as you turned away from the window you suddenly caught sight of that sea or that valley, all over again, in the looking glass. And the sea in the mirror, or the valley in the mirror, were in one sense just the same as the real ones: yet at the same time they were somehow different – deeper, more wonderful, more like places in a story: in a story you have never heard but very much want to know. The difference between the old Narnia and the new Narnia was like that. The new one was a deeper country: every rock and flower and blade of grass looked as if it meant more. I can't describe it any better than that: if ever you get there you will know what I mean.

It was the Unicorn who summed up what everyone was feeling. He stamped his right fore-hoof on the ground and neighed, and then cried:

"I have come home at last! This is my real country! I belong here. This is the land I have been looking for all my life, though I never knew it till now. The reason why we loved the old Narnia is that it sometimes looked a little like this. Bree-hee-hee! Come further up, come further in!"

He shook his mane and sprang forward into a great gallop – a Unicorn's gallop, which, in our world, would have carried him out of sight in a few moments. But now a most strange thing happened. Everyone else began to run, and they found, to their astonishment, that they could keep up with him: not only the Dogs and the humans but even fat little Puzzle and short-legged Poggin the Dwarf. The air flew in their faces as if they were driving fast in a car without a windscreen. The country flew past as if they were seeing it from the windows of an express train. Faster and faster they raced, but no one got hot or tired or out of breath.

CHAPTER SIXTEEN

FAREWELL TO SHADOWLANDS

If one could run without getting tired, I don't think one would often want to do anything else. But there might be special reasons for stopping, and it was a special reason which made Eustace presently shout:

"I say! Steady! Look what we're coming to!"

And well he might. For now they saw before them Caldron Pool and beyond the Pool the high unclimbable cliffs and, pouring down the cliffs, thousands of tons of water every second, flashing like diamonds in some places and dark, glassy green in others, the Great Waterfall; and already the thunder of it was in their ears.

"Don't stop! Further up and further in," called Farsight, tilting his flight a little upwards.

"It's all very well for *him*," said Eustace, but Jewel also cried out:

"Don't stop. Further up and further in! Take it in your stride."

His voice could only just be heard above the roar of the water but next moment everyone saw that he had plunged into the Pool. And helter-skelter behind him, with splash after splash, all the others did the same. The water was not biting cold as all of them (and especially Puzzle) expected, but of a delicious foamy coolness. They all found they were swimming straight for the Waterfall itself.

"This is absolutely crazy," said Eustace to Edmund.

"I know. And yet –" said Edmund.

"Isn't it wonderful?" said Lucy. "Have you noticed one can't feel afraid, even if one wants to? Try it."

"By Jove, neither one can," said Eustace after he had tried.

Jewel reached the foot of the Waterfall first, but Tirian was only just behind him. Jill was last, so she could see the whole thing better than the others. She saw something white moving steadily up the face of the Waterfall. That white thing was the Unicorn. You couldn't tell whether he was swimming or climbing, but he moved on, higher and higher. The point of his horn divided the water just above his head, and it cascaded out in two rainbow-coloured streams all round his shoulders. Just behind him came King Tirian. He moved his legs and arms as if he were swimming but he moved straight upwards: as if one could swim up the wall of a house.

What looked funniest was the Dogs. During the gallop they had not been at all out of breath, but now, as they swarmed and wriggled upwards, there was plenty of spluttering and sneezing among them; that was because they would keep on barking, and every time they barked they got their mouths and noses full of water. But before Jill had time to notice all these things fully, she was going up the Waterfall herself. It was the sort of thing that would have been quite impossible in our world. Even if you hadn't been drowned, you would have been smashed to pieces by the terrible weight of water against the countless jags of rock. But in that world you could do it. You went on, up and up, with all kinds of reflected lights flashing at you from the water and all manner of coloured stones flashing through it, till it seemed as if you were climbing up light itself – and always higher and higher till the sense of height would have terrified you if you could be terrified, but later it was only gloriously exciting. And then at last one came to the lovely, smooth green curve in which the water poured over the top and found that one was out on the level river above the Waterfall. The current was racing away behind you, but you were such a wonderful swimmer that you could make headway against it. Soon they were all on the bank, dripping but happy.

A long valley opened ahead and great snow-mountains, now much nearer, stood up against the sky.

"Further up and further in," cried Jewel and instantly they were off again.

They were out of Narnia now and up into the Western Wild which neither Tirian nor Peter nor even the Eagle had ever seen before. But the Lord Digory and the Lady Polly had. "Do you remember? Do you remember?" they said – and said it in steady voices too, without panting, though the whole party was now running faster than an arrow flies.

"What, Lord?" said Tirian. "Is it then true, as stories tell, that you two journeyed here on the very day the world was made?"

"Yes," said Digory, "and it seems to me as if it were only yesterday."

"And on a flying horse?" asked Tirian. "Is that part true?"

"Certainly," said Digory. But the Dogs barked, "Faster, faster!"

So they ran faster and faster till it was more like flying than running, and even the Eagle overhead was going no faster than they. And they went through winding valley after winding valley and up the steep sides of hills and, faster than ever, down the other side, following the river and sometimes crossing it and skimming across mountain-lakes as if they were living speed-boats, till at last at the far end of one long lake which looked as blue as a turquoise, they saw a smooth green hill. Its sides were as steep as the sides of a pyramid and round the very top of it ran a green wall: but above the wall rose the branches of trees whose leaves looked like silver and their fruit like gold.

"Further up and further in!" roared the Unicorn, and no one held back. They charged straight at the foot of the hill and then found themselves running up it almost as water from a broken wave runs up a rock out at the point of some bay. Though the slope was nearly as steep as the roof of a house and the grass was smooth as a bowling green, no one slipped. Only when they had reached the very top did they slow up; that was because they found themselves facing great golden gates. And for a moment none of them was bold enough to try if the gates would open. They all felt just as they had felt about the fruit – "Dare we? Is it right? Can it be meant for *us*?"

But while they were standing thus a great horn, wonderfully loud and sweet, blew from somewhere inside that walled garden and the gates swung open.

Tirian stood holding his breath and wondering who would come out. And what came was the last thing he had expected: a little, sleek, bright-eyed Talking Mouse with a red feather stuck in a circlet on its head and its left paw resting on a long sword. It bowed, a most beautiful bow, and said in its shrill voice:

"Welcome, in the Lion's name. Come further up and further in."

Then Tirian saw King Peter and King Edmund and Queen Lucy rush forward to kneel down and greet the Mouse and they all cried out "Reepicheep!" And Tirian breathed fast with the sheer wonder of it, for now he

knew that he was looking at one of the great heroes of Narnia, Reepicheep the Mouse who had fought at the great Battle of Beruna and afterwards sailed to the World's end with King Caspian the Seafarer. But before he had had much time to think of this he felt two strong arms thrown about him and felt a bearded kiss on his cheeks and heard a well remembered voice saying:

"What, lad? Art thicker and taller since I last touched thee!"

It was his own father, the good King Erlian: but not as Tirian had seen him last when they brought him home pale and wounded from his fight with the giant, nor even as Tirian remembered him in his later years when he was a grey-headed warrior. This was his father, young and merry, as he could just remember him from very early days when he himself had been a little boy playing games with his father in the castle garden at Cair Paravel, just before bedtime on summer evenings. The very smell of the bread-and-milk he used to have for supper came back to him.

Jewel thought to himself, "I will leave them to talk for a little and then I will go and greet the good King Erlian. Many a bright apple has he given me when I was but a colt." But next moment he had something else to think of, for out of the gateway there came a horse so mighty and noble that even a Unicorn might feel shy in its presence: a great winged horse. It looked a moment at the Lord Digory and the Lady Polly and neighed out "What, cousins!" and they both shouted "Fledge! Good old Fledge!" and rushed to kiss it.

But by now the Mouse was again urging them to come in. So all of them passed in through the golden gates, into the delicious smell that blew towards them out of that garden and into the cool mixture of sunlight and shadow under the trees, walking on springy turf that was all dotted with white flowers. The very first thing which struck everyone was that the place was far larger than it had seemed from outside. But no one had time to think about that for people were coming up to meet the new-comers from every direction.

Everyone you had ever heard of (if you knew the history of these countries) seemed to be there. There was Glimfeather the Owl and Puddleglum the Marshwiggle, and King Rilian the Disenchanted, and his mother the Star's daughter and his great father Caspian himself. And close beside him were the Lord Drinian and the Lord Berne and Trumpkin the Dwarf and Truffle-hunter the good Badger with Glenstorm the Centaur and a hundred other heroes of the great War of Deliverance. And then from another side came Cor the King of Archenland with King Lune his father and his wife Queen Aravis and the brave prince Corin Thunder-Fist, his brother, and Bree the Horse and Hwin the Mare. And then – which was a wonder beyond all wonders to Tirian – there came from further away in the past, the two good Beavers and Tumnus the Faun. And there was greeting and kissing and hand-shaking and old jokes revived, (you've no idea how good an old joke sounds when you take it out again after a rest of five or six hundred years) and the whole company moved forward to the centre of the orchard where the Phoenix sat in a tree and looked down upon them all, and at the foot of that tree were two thrones and in those two thrones a King and Queen so great and beautiful that everyone bowed down before them. And well they might, for these two were King Frank and Queen Helen from whom all the most ancient Kings of Narnia and Archenland are descended. And Tirian felt as you would feel if you were brought before Adam and Eve in all their glory.

About half an hour later – or it might have been half a hundred years later, for time there is not like time here – Lucy stood with her dear friend, her oldest Narnian friend, the Faun Tumnus, looking down over the wall of that garden, and seeing all Narnia spread out below. But when you looked down you found that this hill was much higher than you had thought: it sank down with shining cliffs, thousands of feet below them and trees in that lower world looked no bigger than grains of green salt. Then she turned inward again and stood with her back to the wall and looked at the garden.

"I see," she said at last, thoughtfully. "I see now. This

garden is like the stable. It is far bigger inside than it was outside."

"Of course, Daughter of Eve," said the Faun. "The further up and the further in you go, the bigger everything gets. The inside is larger than the outside."

Lucy looked hard at the garden and saw that it was not really a garden but a whole world, with its own rivers and woods and sea and mountains. But they were not strange: she knew them all.

"I see," she said. "This is still Narnia, and more real and more beautiful then the Narnia down below, just as *it* was more real and more beautiful than the Narnia outside the stable door! I see ... world within world, Narnia within Narnia ..."

"Yes," said Mr Tumnus, "like an onion: except that as you go in and in, each circle is larger than the last."

And Lucy looked this way and that and soon found that a new and beautiful thing had happened to her. Whatever she looked at, however far away it might be, once she had fixed her eyes steadily on it, became quite clear and close as if she were looking through a telescope. She could see the whole Southern desert and beyond it the great city of Tashbaan: to Eastward she could see Cair Paravel on the edge of the sea and the very window of the room that had once been her own. And far out to sea she could discover the islands, islands after islands to the end of the world, and, beyond the end, the huge mountain which they had called Aslan's country. But now she saw that it was part of a great chain of mountains which ringed round the whole world. In front of her it seemed to come quite close. Then she looked to her left and saw what she took to be a great bank of brightly-coloured cloud, cut off from them by a gap. But she looked harder and saw that it was not a cloud at all but a real land. And when she had fixed her eyes on one particular spot of it, she at once cried out, "Peter! Edmund! Come and look! Come quickly." And they came and looked, for their eyes also had become like hers.

"Why!" exclaimed Peter. "It's England. And that's the house itself – Professor Kirk's old home in the country where all our adventures began!"

"I thought that house had been destroyed," said Edmund.

"So it was," said the Faun. "But you are now looking at the England within England, the real England just as this is the real Narnia. And in that inner England no good thing is destroyed."

Suddenly they shifted their eyes to another spot, and then Peter and Edmund and Lucy gasped with amazement and shouted out and began waving: for there they saw their own father and mother, waving back at them across the great, deep valley. It was like when you see people waving at you from the deck of a big ship when you are waiting on the quay to meet them.

"How can we get at them?" said Lucy.

"That is easy," said Mr Tumnus. "That country and this country – all the *real* countries – are only spurs jutting out from the great mountains of Aslan. We have only to walk along the ridge, upward and inward, till it joins on. And listen! There is King Frank's horn: we must all go up."

And soon they found themselves all walking together – and a great, bright procession it was – up towards mountains higher than you could see in this world even if they were there to be seen. But there was no snow on those mountains: there were forests and green slopes and sweet orchards and flashing waterfalls, one above the other, going up forever. And the land they were walking on grew narrower all the time, with a deep valley on each side: and across that valley the land which was the real England grew nearer and nearer.

The light ahead was growing stronger. Lucy saw that a great series of many-coloured cliffs led up in front of them like a giant's staircase. And then she forgot everything else, because Aslan himself was coming, leaping down from cliff to cliff like a living cataract of power and beauty.

And the very first person whom Aslan called to him was Puzzle the Donkey. You never saw a donkey look feebler and sillier than Puzzle did as he walked up to Aslan, and he looked, beside Aslan, as small as a kitten looks beside a St Bernard. The Lion bowed down his head and whispered something to Puzzle at which his long ears went down, but then he said something else at which the ears perked up again. The humans couldn't hear what he had said either time. Then Aslan turned to them and said:

"You do not yet look so happy as I mean you to be."

Lucy said, "We're so afraid of being sent away, Aslan. And you have sent us back into our own world so often."

"No fear of that," said Aslan. "Have you not guessed?"

Their hearts leaped and a wild hope rose within them.

"There *was* a real railway accident," said Aslan softly. "Your father and mother and all of you are – as you used to call it in the Shadowlands – dead. The term is over: the holidays have begun. The dream is ended: this is the morning."

And as He spoke He no longer looked to them like a lion; but the things that began to happen after that were so great and beautiful that I cannot write them. And for us this is the end of all the stories, and we can most truly say that they all lived happily ever after. But for them it was only the beginning of the real story. All their life in this world and all their adventures in Narnia had only been the cover and the title page: now at last they were beginning Chapter One of the Great Story which no one on earth has read: which goes on forever: in which every chapter is better than the one before.